THE LAKE PAVILION

ANN BENNETT

Andaman Press

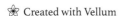

For Ollie, Will and Jamie

PROLOGUE
AMELIA

Darjeeling, India, April 1935

The little train up to Darjeeling took all afternoon, weaving its way through the mountains, stopping at tiny village stations along the route to take on passengers. It was dark when it finally puffed into the station on the edge of the town. As Amelia got out of the carriage and took a breath of the crisp mountain air, she noticed that it was so much cooler and fresher up here than it had been lower down in the valley.

From the station platform, Amelia could see the lights of the little town spilling down the steep surrounding hills. She had visited Darjeeling with her parents for short breaks during the hot weather, but they hadn't had time to go there for at least three years. She asked a rickshaw-wallah to take her to the Planter's Club. It was where she'd stayed with her parents and where her father used to lodge when he came up on Mission business. It was the only place she knew in the town.

The Planter's Club wasn't too far from the station, a sprawling white-painted building with balconies overlooking the mountains. Amelia felt a prickle of nerves as she stepped into the entrance hall alone, with its stuffed leopard and tiger heads displayed on panelled walls. There was a musty, damp smell about the place, that mingled with the odours of smoke and alcohol. She could hear the hum of voices and the chink of glasses from the nearby bar.

The old man on the desk peered at her from behind thick glasses and confirmed that there were rooms available. She was shown along the gloomy passages by a bearer who carried her trunk on his head and a holdall in each hand. On the way, they passed the open door of the billiard room, where a group of men were standing around the table in a haze of cigar smoke. The room she was given on the first floor was sparse but comfortable with an old-fashioned bathroom next door. It felt like pure luxury compared to the family bungalow down in the village that she'd left behind. And not too expensive either.

She sank down onto the strange, saggy bed, suddenly over-whelmed by her loss, and the fact that she was now completely alone in the world. As well as this all-consuming grief, a new panic set in. She needed to do something quickly to provide a living and a home for herself. Her parents had never earned much, and what money they did have they'd contributed to the poor or to the church. They'd left her next to nothing. She had a few scant savings, but she knew they wouldn't last long. She resolved that the next day she would go to the local hospitals and see if there were any vacancies for carers. She lay down on the bed, exhausted. She'd barely eaten that day, but she couldn't face going down to the dining room alone. Eventually, she closed her eyes and fell into a fitful sleep.

1

KATE

Warren End, Buckinghamshire
April, 1970

I t was starting to rain as Kate turned the car off the main road and headed down the hill between the lines of towering chestnut trees. Mist descended on the gently sloping fields and she switched on the wipers, her spirits sagging. It had been raining the day she left, twenty-five years ago, but over the decades she'd envisaged her homecoming so differently. Each time she'd imagined going back there, she thought of the place bathed in sunlight; the sun sparkling on the village pond, the honey-coloured, thatched cottages basking in the warmth of a summer afternoon.

She crossed the brook in the dip and accelerated up the last hill, passing the sign for "Warren End". Her heart beat a little faster in anticipation and she gripped the steering wheel. The car crested the hill and there it was, laid out before her; the village, just as she remembered it. She drove slowly down the hill, past the modern houses and rows of Victorian workers' cottages on the outskirts and turned right at the crossroads.

The whole place seemed eerily empty. There were no children playing hopscotch in the middle of the road, no dogs lounging in the sun or women sitting on front walls gossiping. The buildings on the High Street were the same as the ones in her memory, though. Stone cottages, some of them thatched, some with slate roofs, but looking closely, she saw that there were subtle differences. Both the Methodist Chapel and the blacksmith's forge had been converted into houses, with bottle glass windows and colourful window boxes. In fact, each and every house looked as though it had undergone a facelift since Kate's childhood. Nothing was shabby and workaday now. There was no peeling paint anymore, no rickety outhouses or corrugated tin roofs. Neat porches had been built, houses tastefully extended, thatch renewed. Hanging baskets now hung from eaves, front gardens had been turned to gravel and outside each house, instead of the workers' vans of her memory, smart cars were parked up.

Kate had never considered it before, but Warren End must now be a commuter village, within easy reach of Bletchley and the fast trains to London. It was strange. She'd expected to see the same familiar faces she'd grown up with. In her mind's eye they wouldn't have aged and they'd still be dressed exactly the same. How hadn't she realised that, like her, they would all have moved on?

She crossed the top of the narrow lane where the smallest cottages were and glanced tentatively down it. It had been where the poorest estate workers had lived in her day. A shudder went through her as an unbidden memory surfaced. Did Joan still live there? What was she like now? Had she married and had a family? All these thoughts crowded Kate's mind and she tried to banish them as she turned back to focus on the road.

She drove on past another row of gentrified cottages and

rounded a sharp bend. There it was, the imposing gateway to Oakwood Grange. Stone pillars topped with concrete balls, large white gates that stood open. She pulled the car off the road and in through the entrance, tyres scrunching on gravel. She bit her lip. It was hard to believe that this was all hers now. She drove on through the oak trees on the perimeter and the house came into view. It was still beautiful, if, unlike the rest of the village, a little shabby now. The house was what an estate agent would describe as a "Victorian gentleman's residence". Large and square with beautiful nineteenth century lines. Built of pale stone with a pillared porch at the entrance and an octagonal tower on one corner, looking out over the fields and woodland that dipped away to the west.

Kate got out of the car and stared across at the house, the rain beginning to soak through her sweater. She was half afraid to approach the building, such was the power of the past. As she stood watching, the front door opened, and a short woman with grey hair, dressed in a blue overall came out onto the step.

'Is that you, Miss Hamilton?' the woman called, and from somewhere in the depths of her memory, Kate recognised the voice.

'Yes! One moment. I'll get my things.' She grabbed her bag from the back seat and hurried through the rain to the shelter of the front porch.

The woman opened the door wider for her to pass. Kate stood in the front hall, taking in the sweeping staircase, the oak panelling, the tall grandfather clock. The memories came flooding back.

'The solicitor asked me to come and open up for you today, make sure the place is clean.' The woman closed the front door. Her eyes flitted to Kate's and away again and Kate realised that she was nervous.

'Thank you,' said Kate. 'That was very thoughtful.'

'I don't suppose you remember me,' the woman smiled. 'But I remember you from when you were young. I'm Janet Andrews. I live in one of the cottages down Clerks' Lane.'

'Oh yes! Of course. I do remember you,' and the image of a young, careworn housewife surfaced, hanging out washing in her back garden with a baby balanced on one hip, a cigarette drooping from the side of her mouth, curlers in her hair. Janet would only be ten years or so older than Kate herself.

'You used to be as thick as thieves with that young Joan Bartram, didn't you?

Kate ventured an uncertain smile, wondering fleetingly just how much Janet knew of the truth of what happened that last summer.

'Poor Joan still lives down that lane,' Janet went on, and a wave of surprise went through Kate at the confirmation of something that she'd half expected. She wondered why Janet had referred to her as "Poor Joan".

'She lives in one of the estate cottages, a few doors along from me.'

'Oh,' Kate said, not knowing how to respond. 'Joan and I lost touch, I'm afraid.'

Janet paused for a moment, then said, 'Well, look at me! Standing here gossiping, when you're wet through and catching your death. Come on through to the kitchen. The Aga's on and it's warm as toast in there.'

Kate followed Janet along the flagstone passage and into the cavernous kitchen, with its high ceilings and big sash windows that looked out over the wet lawn. She automatically went over to the Aga and stood with her back to it. As the heat began to warm her through, she remembered how her great-aunt Amelia used to do exactly the same. A pang of guilt shot through Kate. She shouldn't be here.

It had been a shock to get the solicitor's letter the previous week, telling her that Oakwood Grange had been bequeathed to her in Amelia's will. Her immediate feeling was that Amelia shouldn't have left her the house. After all, she hadn't exactly been a dutiful great-niece. The last time they'd seen each other was at Kate's mother's funeral three years or so before. They'd exchanged Christmas cards of course, but Kate was acutely aware that she should have done more. She should have visited Amelia, offered her help and company. She'd suspected that Amelia had become eccentric and reclusive as she got older, and probably far too fond of the whisky. Nobody had actually told Kate, but she was sure that was what had shortened Amelia's life.

'She died peacefully, your auntie,' said Janet, filling the kettle at the Butler sink. 'You mustn't worry about her last years. She had plenty of help, here in the village. I was here every day to clean, the district nurse used to drop in, the vicar. She had lots of friends and neighbours.'

Kate stared down at a dip in the worn flagstones, where generations of housemaids must have stood in front of the scrubbed table to chop vegetables and roll pastry. Was Janet referring to the fact that Kate and Amelia had become strangers, or was she just trying to set her mind at rest? Did she know that it wasn't through neglect that Kate hadn't come back? It was simply that she couldn't face up to the past.

'The solicitor said that you're an architect now. Is that right?'

'Yes,' said Kate, brightening at the change of subject. 'I work in London. Big projects mainly now.'

Janet crossed to the Aga and put the kettle on the hot plate.

'Do you have a family?'

'No... no, sadly not.'

'It was dreadful about your brother,' Janet went on with a sympathetic look.

'Roy? Yes. He died in France a few months after the D-Day landings. Poor Mum and Dad never got over it. It's why we moved away from the village, in fact.'

Janet shook her head. 'Terrible business. I expect they wanted a new start.'

'That's right. They did.'

But the new start hadn't really helped them. They'd grieved for their only son for the rest of their lives. Her father had suffered a breakdown and never fully recovered. He'd died, a broken man, in 1950. Her mother had battled on but had never got over her loss. They'd moved to East Anglia shortly after Roy's death, where Kate's mother had relatives, but even in their new home, they couldn't move on. They'd set up a bedroom for Roy there, a replica of his room in their house in Warren End. It had become a sort of shrine, where his framed photographs stood on the table, his school prizes were displayed on the walls, his football boots, still muddy from his last match, were lined up with the rest of his shoes in the bottom of the wardrobe. Kate had tried to hide it from her parents, but she began to resent Roy after a time. He'd always been her parents' golden boy as the pair grew up. He was always put first, Kate's needs and wants came secondary to his as a matter of course. And even in death he came first in their affections. His achievements overshadowed her own, even when she won a place at university to study architecture and later won prizes and awards for her designs.

Janet filled the teapot and put it with a mug and a jug of milk on the table. 'I'd best be getting on,' she said. 'I've made up the guestroom at the top of the stairs for you. I'll see you at the funeral tomorrow.'

'Thank you. And of course, I'll see you there.'

'The Women's Institute has organised a get together in the village hall afterwards. We thought you wouldn't want the bother of having people in the house.'

'Oh, I wouldn't have minded at all, but that's very generous of them.'

Janet crossed the room and lingered in the doorway.

'I was wondering... would you like me to carry on here? Cleaning, that is? As I said, I used to come in for your auntie every day, but I could carry on once a week if you like?'

Kate didn't intend to be in the house any longer than strictly necessary. Just long enough to clear the place and get it on the market, but she didn't want to offend Janet, and in any case, it would be good to have it clean for potential purchasers to view.

'That would be great. How about Wednesday mornings?'

Janet smiled. 'All right. I'll be here at nine sharp. But I'll see you tomorrow anyway.'

Her footsteps echoed across the hall, the front door slammed, and Kate was alone in the house.

SHE SAT at the kitchen table for a long time, sipping her tea and letting the atmosphere of the old place seep through her; the wind in the eaves, the rainwater in the drainpipes, the creaks of the old timbers. She'd never been alone in this house before. It had always been somewhere she'd been in awe of when she was young. And all these years later, she still felt nervous about exploring it by herself. But, she'd finished her tea and there were no excuses. Gathering her courage, she got up from the table, left the kitchen and crossed the hall to the large living room with the octagonal bay window. It was just as she remembered, with a pale blue Chinese carpet on the floor and prints of landscapes and hunting scenes on the walls. It was still furnished with the same chintzy sofas and chairs that Kate recalled from the 1940s.

On the mantelpiece above the marble fireplace stood several photographs of Amelia and James. One of them in lace and morning suit on their wedding day in 1940, a couple more of them both on horseback with the local hunt, and various other portraits of them together as they grew older. In all the pictures Amelia was smiling, and it hit Kate afresh how beautiful she had been with her slightly exotic looks. No wonder Great-Uncle James had fallen for her when he met her working as a chambermaid in a London hotel, and had given up his status as a confirmed bachelor to marry her in his late middle-age. Peering at these fading portraits of Amelia and Great-Uncle James now, they appeared to be the very image of a devoted couple. Kate sighed heavily. How deceptive appearances could be.

There was one picture that surprised Kate though, and she picked it up and stared at it closely. She could have sworn that it hadn't been here when she used to come to Oakwood Grange as a child. It was of a young Amelia, possibly fifteen or sixteen, between an earnest looking man and a rather dowdy woman. They were standing under some lush greenery, in front of a backdrop of snow-capped mountains. These must be Amelia's parents, the missionaries. Suddenly Kate remembered. They had taken Amelia out to India to live in a remote village in the foothills of the Himalayas when she was in her early teens. She'd not returned to England until her mid-twenties. It was odd that Amelia had virtually never referred to her time in India; she had no Indian memorabilia in the house and it simply never came up in conversation. Kate frowned, wondering. It had never struck her before how strange that was. And it felt a little odd too, that this photograph hadn't been here before. She set it back down and continued on her tour of the downstairs, lingering at the door of the large dining room, with its polished oak floor and gracious furniture. James would always invite Kate's family round for Christmas dinner and she would feel out of place in these intimidating surroundings, like the poor relation that she was. She used to wish that they could spend Christmas alone as a family, at home in the comfortable schoolhouse that went with her father's job as headmaster of the village school.

She closed the door on the memories, and moved on to the next room, which used to be Uncle James' study and which Amelia must have taken over after his death. The oak desk with its tooled leather top was covered in papers and there were files and notebooks piled up on it. There was a cut glass decanter, almost empty, on the desk too. Kate sat down in the leather chair, remembering how James used to sit in here puffing on a pipe as he scanned the Financial Times for the latest share prices. She could almost smell the tobacco he used to favour; spices, fruit and vanilla combined. The room couldn't have been decorated since his death shortly after Kate's father's and the ceiling was yellowed with age and years of smoke.

Kate glanced at the papers on the desk. The solicitor had told her she needed to sort through Amelia's bills and find out what needed to be paid. The chaotic look of the paperwork made her heart sink. She thought wistfully of her office in Lincoln's Inn Fields, a picture of calm and order, white walls with pale oak furniture and thick white carpet, everything in its place. The rain was still pouring down outside and there was nothing else to do, so she sat down and started to sort the bills and letters into piles. Gas bills, electricity bills, water, rates, letters from the bank. Before long she was making some sort of order out of the chaos.

The sky was darkening outside by the time she'd finished. She found a pile of cardboard folders on top of a bookshelf and filed the letters according to subject matter, promising herself that she would return to the task after the funeral. She wondered about putting them away rather than leaving them out on the desk. She pulled open the desk drawers one by one. In the top one, a jumble of old pens, paperclips, drawing pins, and bottles of dried up ink. In the second, a pile of unused writing paper, and in the bottom one nothing at all, but the drawer wouldn't pull out. Curious, Kate knelt down and peered inside. A card-backed envelope was sticking in the mechanism, stopping the drawer from opening properly. With a little effort she pulled the envelope out and stared at it. She recognised Amelia's writing on the front; "Amelia Hamilton – Personal".

Feeling a little like a snooper, Kate fished inside the envelope. There was only one sheet of thick cream coloured paper inside. She pulled it out and scanned it quickly. She read it three times before the meaning of the words sunk in.

"*I, Amelia Alice Holden, of the Russell Hotel, Bloomsbury, London WC1, hereby renounce and relinquish the name of Holden and will henceforth adopt for all purposes and be known by my maiden name of Collins. Signed as a deed this 1ˢᵗ day of February 1938, before William Smith, Solicitor and Commissioner for Oaths, Bedford Square, Bloomsbury.*"

Kate stared at the words, frowning. She'd never known Amelia going by the name of Holden. She'd always been Amelia Collins, and after she'd married Uncle James, Amelia Hamilton. Kate went through the possibilities, but there was only one that seemed remotely plausible to her; Amelia had been married before and had renounced her former married name. But it didn't seem possible. Why would Amelia have hidden that fact? Had she been involved in some sort of scandal and wanted to put it behind her? Amelia had always had an air of mystery about her. It had hardly been credible to Kate that she had been the child of missionaries. But there was the picture on the mantelpiece to prove it. And after all, Amelia was no stranger to scandals. Kate's hands began to tremble as she remembered back to that last summer in Warren End. She'd tried so hard to forget the terrible events of those days and her part in what had happened. After all, it was why she'd stayed away ever since. She'd known it would be difficult to come back, but she'd not realised quite how quickly the old memories would resurface, and alongside them that deep feeling of guilt that burned through her soul.

2

KATE

Warren End, Summer, 1944

Kate could never keep up with Joan as they pedalled through the sun-dappled country lanes around Warren End that summer. Joan's bike was far inferior to Kate's. It was one she'd inherited from her older brother and was heavy, lumbering and far too big, but that didn't daunt her. Even though Joan was skinny, she was strong and fit, always out playing in the fields, climbing trees, building camps, fighting with other children. Just watching her powering along ahead made Kate feel lumbering and cossetted. Sweat would pour from her brow and she would pant up the hills behind her friend. Sometimes Joan even had to stop and get off and wait for her. She would always be laughing as Kate caught up.

'Come on, slow coach!' she would call, and not giving Kate any time to catch her breath, would jump back on her bike and pedal off again, her cries of triumphant laughter carrying on the breeze.

They'd been out on their bikes every day since the beginning of the summer holidays. Their friendship had only been rekindled recently, and they were making the most of the long, hot summer days to get to know each other again. They'd been best friends at the village school until age eleven when they were both sent to the local grammar. Joan had won a bursary, funded by Kate's great-uncle for the education of local children. That was over two years ago. Kate was put into the top set and Joan in the middle and they'd formed new friendships and drifted apart. But at the beginning of the holidays in 1944, Kate had been walking to the village shop with her mother's ration book when a group of boys surrounded her and started taunting her. "Snob", they called her, "Stuck up" "Teacher's pet" as well as the most humiliating of all, which made her cheeks burn; "Fatty Arbuckle". She'd put up with teasing from the village boys for years. It was one of the things that went with being the village headmaster's daughter, but as she grew older the insults stung her more. She put her head down and tried to push past them, all the time tears welling in her eyes. One of the bigger boys, David Pope, moved in front of her, barring her way.

'Where do you think you're going, sissy? Why don't you talk to us?'

'Leave her alone you cowards,' came Joan's voice, sharp and clear as she appeared at Kate's shoulder.

Kate turned to her in relief.

'You'll have my brother Sam to answer to if you don't hop it now,' she said to the boys, tucking her arm into Kate's. 'Now shove off!'

'You going to the shop, Kate?' she asked and Kate nodded, struck dumb by Joan's kindness and the feeling that if she tried to speak at that moment she would probably start to cry. They'd walked to the shop arm in arm, Kate muttering her thanks under her breath. Joan had suggested they cycle out together that afternoon.

They didn't have a particular plan, they just followed the

lanes that took them deep into the undulating countryside, through farms and hamlets, past manor houses and cottages, fields of ripening crops, golden in the sunshine, and dark, ever-green forests. It had been an adventure, and Kate had welcomed the company. Most of her friends from school lived away from the village and now that her brother, Roy, had signed up for the army and been posted to France, life at home seemed very quiet.

After that first day they'd met up every morning and cycled for miles. Kate always brought sandwiches in a tin but Joan never did. Kate was happy to share her food with Joan. She knew her home life wasn't easy. Joan was the second of six children and her mother looked constantly harassed and exhausted. She almost always had a bruise somewhere on her face. Joan's father, Frank Bartram, worked as a gamekeeper up at the Prendergast estate, and it was well known that he was a heavy drinker. It was also known that he wasn't above poaching from his employer, George Prendergast, to put food on his own table.

Kate's mother gave a short, disapproving sniff when she discovered that Kate was spending time with Joan.

'She's wild that one,' she warned over breakfast when Kate announced she and Joan were going on a bike ride again on the second morning. Kate's father looked up from his paper.

'Joan's got spirit, that's all, Freda,' he said in his mild-mannered way. 'It's nice for Kate to have friends in the village.'

'You always see the good in people, Kenneth,' Kate's mother sighed, taking another bite of toast. 'She's from a family of rum 'uns. Look at that brother of hers, Sam. Always in trouble, that boy.'

'It's hardly surprising. You just need to look at the father.'

Kate's parents exchanged knowing glances, then her mother got up from the table.

'I've got to get going or I'll be late for my first appointment,' she huffed, putting her plate beside the sink. 'I expect to see the washing up done, young lady, when I get back, and the spuds peeled for supper. Oh, and you can make yourself some sandwiches for your trip out. There's some cheese in the larder.'

Freda pulled on a cardigan over her blue district nurse's uniform, popped on her blue cap, and was gone through the back door. From the window, Kate watched her wheel her bike down the garden path and set off along the road.

'Don't mind Mum, Kate,' said her father. 'She only wants what's best for you.'

'I don't know why everyone's so anti-Joan,' Kate protested. 'She can't help her family.'

Her father laughed. 'You're quite right. None of us can, I suppose,' he said getting up from the table. 'Well, have a good day. I've got another air raid practice this morning, but I'll be back before supper.'

That day, Kate and Joan cycled in another direction, towards the sluggish river that snaked its way through marshland in a deserted valley a few miles away. Kate had never ventured out that way before; it involved cycling over a big hill and taking a short cut along a track through an abandoned farmstead that Kate had always found eerie. She would never have gone there alone. As they went through the farm gate and entered the track she said to Joan, 'Are you sure it's alright to ride along here?'

'Of course. Why wouldn't it be?' Joan laughed looking at Kate with mocking eyes.

'Well, it said "Private" back there. I just thought, if someone sees us...'

'It belongs to the Prendergasts. Dad works for them. It's fine to go through here. Do it all the time.'

With that she tore off down the track towards the old farmhouse without a backward glance and Kate was forced to follow. Kate didn't like the look of the house. It was covered in ivy, its roof was caved in with timbers sticking up at odd angles and its door and windows were boarded up. She wondered who had lived there and why it had been abandoned like that. She didn't want to be left behind, so she pedalled extra hard to catch up with Joan and they passed the house together.

'It looks spooky, doesn't it?' asked Joan. Kate nodded, not wanting to look at the boarded-up windows. Fear crept through her veins as they cycled on.

Beyond the house were some deserted farm buildings, roofs creaking and doors flapping in the breeze. They pedalled on, but as they passed the stable block a man emerged from one of the empty stables.

'Hey!' he yelled. 'You there. Get off my land!'

Kate's heart began to hammer against her ribs. Joan didn't stop or even turn round, so neither did Kate.

'I'm talking to you! It's private. I've told you before, you little minx.'

'Come on, Kate, quick!' Joan shouted, pedalling on past the final barn and starting down the hill. Kate's heart was in her mouth. It was George Prendergast, she was sure of it. She'd only seen him at church and opening village fetes, but she recognised his face with its elaborate moustache and bushy whiskers. She pedalled after Joan as fast as she could, but as they neared the bottom of the hill, a couple of shots rang out from behind them.

'Come *on!*' They were in a dip and there was another hill rising in front of them. Kate's breath was coming in gulps. She couldn't believe what was happening.

'He's shooting at us,' she screamed as another two shots rang out.

'It's only pellets. He's doing it to frighten us.'

'What if he comes after us?'

They'd reached the top of the hill and Joan stopped and waited for Kate to catch up, her feet astride the bike.

'He won't. He's on foot. He'll never catch us.'

'You said it would be alright. Why did you say that?'

Joan shrugged. 'I didn't know he'd be there. I've never seen him there before.'

'But he said he'd told you before.'

'That was somewhere else. Look, he doesn't like people on his land, OK? He's a bastard. He treats everyone who works for him like dirt. Me dad hates him.'

'So, it would have been better not to come through here, wouldn't it?'

Joan eyed her coldly. Was that contempt in her look? Despite her defiance, Kate noticed that there were spots of high colour in Joan's cheeks and that she was breathing heavily.

'Look, I'm sorry,' Joan relented after a pause. 'I took a chance. It's a long way round on the lanes. You cut off five miles going this way.'

Kate was silent and they started to walk on, pushing their bikes side by side. Kate didn't want to upset Joan, and she didn't want Joan to think she was a coward, so she decided not to say anything. At the top of the hill they got back on their bikes and freewheeled down the track side-by-side.

'So, what happened before, then?' Kate asked, unable to drop the subject for long.

'I was riding up the drive towards the stables near his house. I was looking for Dad. He hadn't come home and Mum was worried. Prendergast came out of the house and yelled at me. He's supposed to be a toff, but you should have heard the language!'

'How awful.'

Joan was gripping the handlebars so tight that her knuckles were white. 'Like I said, he's a bastard. He doesn't pay his workers properly and he'll never pay for the repairs on our house.'

'Does he own your house?'

Joan nodded. 'It goes with me dad's job. It's falling apart. Damp downstairs and the roof leaks and all. Anyway, let's forget about him. It's downhill all the way to the lane, then it's not far to the river. I'll race you!'

When they got to the lane at the bottom, they had to push their bikes across some marshland, through clumps of bull-rushes, teasles and reedy grass to get to the river that meandered between lines of willow trees. When they reached the boggy grass banks, a family of mallard ducks rose squawking from the smooth surface of water, the sun lighting up their brilliant plumage, grey and green with flashes of purple. The girls laid their bikes down and sat on the bank under a weeping willow to eat Kate's sandwiches and drink from the bottle of squash she'd brought in her duffle bag. Then they lay back on the soft grass, under the shade of the trees. The sun was high in the sky, burning Kate's eyelids red when the breeze shifted the leaves, and she found herself drifting off into a half sleep. She'd calmed down now, after the incident with George Prendergast, and it seemed like the perfect way to spend a long, hot afternoon.

But Joan didn't let her rest for long. Soon she was being shaken awake.

'Let's go for a swim, shall we?'

'We haven't got costumes,' replied Kate, frowning, and Joan let out a snort of derisive laughter.

'Listen to you! Who do you think's going to see you here?'

'I don't know. But I'm not going in with nothing on.'

'I didn't say that, silly. Leave your knickers and vest on. They'll soon dry out in this heat,' and Joan whipped off her worn cotton dress to display equally worn and greying knickers and vest. Self-consciously, Kate did the same and followed her friend into the water. She gasped as she felt the sting of the cold water on her skin. Goosebumps broke out all over her body.

'Get your shoulders under, quick, then you won't be cold,'

shouted Joan, swimming away with the current. Kate waded after her, hating the feel of the squidgy mud between her toes and the slimy waterweed that wrapped itself around her legs. She kicked off and started to swim after Joan. The water was flowing more quickly than she'd realised, and soon they were being swept along at an alarming rate. Kate was a strong swimmer, though. She flipped over on her back and stared up at the blinding blue sky as she travelled downstream. She watched from upside down as she was carried along by the current, sometimes exposed to the sunlight, sometimes in the shade of the branches of trees and bushes. She was fascinated with the view from this angle, the flocks of small birds, the odd moorhen, disturbed by their approach, the occasional kite or buzzard hanging on the breeze at a great height on outstretched wings.

After a few minutes the current slowed and the water grew colder as the river ran through a spinney. Kate saw that it had widened out here and was surrounded by tall trees. She looked around for Joan. For a moment, she couldn't see her and was about to panic, when she caught sight of her dark head bobbing towards the other side of the pool. And then Kate saw where Joan was heading. There was an abandoned building at the far end of the stretch of quiet water. It was almost as shabby as the derelict farmhouse they'd passed earlier. It was built of crumbling red brick, three or four stories high, with broken windows and, half submerged in the river, an enormous, rotting millwheel.

'Wait!' Kate shouted and Joan waited for her to catch up. Joan's eyes were shining with excitement.

'I've heard people talk about this place but I've never seen it before. Let's go inside,' she said.

'What's it called?'

'It must be Willow Mill. People say it's haunted.'

Kate shuddered. 'We'd better not go in there then.'

'Oh, come on. It can't really be. There's no such thing as ghosts. Let's see what's in there.'

Joan swam to the bank and hauled herself out. Kate did the same, her heart thumping, wondering why she was blindly following Joan into the most hazardous situations when her better nature was screaming at her not to. She realised then that it was her pride. She wasn't going to let Joan see how timid she was, how her knees were quaking and her mouth suddenly so dry that she could barely swallow.

She followed Joan round the base of the building, wincing as she stepped on twigs and sharp stones and shivering in her wet underwear, even though it wasn't at all cold. At the back of the building they found a door that was sagging on its hinges, the boards along the bottom rotting away. Joan put her hand on the latch, lifted it and pushed it open.

'Come on then,' she said stepping into the gloomy building and Kate followed her, feeling the sudden chill of the dank interior wrap itself around her.

As her eyes got accustomed to the lack of light, Kate could see that the floor was covered in bird droppings and there were a couple of skeletons of dead birds in the corner. The place smelt of moss and mould and wet earth. The room was low ceilinged and appeared to be the basement. Beside the wall next to the river were the remnants of the working parts of the mill; a series of massive, rusted cogwheels fixed to a metal pole that disappeared up through the ceiling. Apart from a few other bits of ancient machinery stacked beside one wall, the place was empty. They stood still in the middle of the room and stared at each other. There was a strange noise coming from outside; an uneven click followed by a thud that repeated itself every few seconds.

'What's that?' whispered Joan and for the first time Kate saw alarm in her eyes.

'It's just the millwheel,' she said and Joan relaxed a little.

'Let's go upstairs,' Joan headed for a rickety-looking staircase in the corner.

A few of the stairs had rotted away, but the two girls were soon on the next floor, which was lit by four broken, dusty windows, one in each wall. In the middle of the floor sat two giant concrete wheels, one on top of the other, covered in dust. Another pole rose out of the centre of them, stretching up through the ceiling, like the one on the floor below.

'This is great,' said Joan. 'We can hide out here whenever we want to. No one will ever know we're here. We can bring sandwiches and just mess around all day.'

Kate wasn't convinced. The place was too dirty to be that inviting, but not wanting to dent Joan's enthusiasm, she agreed.

'Let's come here tomorrow, then,' said Joan. 'And every day if we feel like it.'

So that's what they did. Every morning, they met up straight after breakfast and cycled the five miles round the lanes to avoid having to cross George Prendergast's land. They would spend the day hanging about around the mill, swimming in the pool, sitting on the millstones upstairs chatting, lazing around on the banks of the river in the odd patches of sunlight between the trees.

They made a rough broom from twigs they gathered in the spinney, and swept the boards on the first floor, getting rid of the dust and dried leaves that had built up over the years. They began to smuggle things from home. Blankets to lie on, an old saucepan and some mugs, some plates, cutlery, and an old towel for drying up. They built a small fire within a circle of bricks away from the trees and boiled up the saucepan for tea and hardboiled eggs.

For Kate, those morning cycle rides to the old mill felt like heading into another world. A world where there wasn't

constant talk of the war, of ration books, news of air raids, dominated by an undercurrent of anxiety about Roy. At the mill, she
could forget that the world was in turmoil and that the happiness of her parents depended on news from the front line in
France. Although she never asked, she suspected it was also a
relief for Joan to get away from the chaos and noise of home, the
constant clamouring of her younger siblings and the arguments
of her parents. More than once she'd seen red marks and bruises
on Joan's arms and legs and although Joan was always fiercely
defensive of her father, Kate was sure that it was him who had
put them there.

They'd been coming to the mill for about ten days, when
something happened that would change everything. It had
started to rain and the two girls had gone inside for shelter and
were sitting upstairs on the millstones, finishing their lunch and
chatting about nothing in particular. Suddenly, the unfamiliar
sound of voices came from outside and they heard the door
opening and being pulled aside on the ground floor. They froze
and stared at each other.

The door slammed and then came the sound of raised
voices; a man and a woman arguing. They couldn't hear particular words, just the tone of what was being said. The man's voice
sounded angry; the woman's alternated between pleading and
anger too.

'What if they come up here?' Kate mouthed and Joan shook
her head, frowning dismissively. The two girls continued to sit
stock still as the argument went on for ten minutes or so, the
words drowned out by the sound of the river and the rain and
the click and rattle of the millwheel outside.

When the rain had abated, the couple left the building,
slamming the door behind them. The two girls rushed to the
window and stared down, trying to see who it was. Both wore
raincoats and wellington boots and the woman had a gaberdine

hat pulled down over her head, but there was something in the way she moved that seemed familiar to Kate.

'I bet they're having an affair,' smiled Joan, her eyes glinting with mischief.

'But they were arguing,' said Kate.

'Lovers' quarrel. Perhaps one of them wants to break it off... perhaps they've been discovered, or something like that. Why don't we follow them and see who it is?'

'OK, but what if they spot us?'

'We'll have to be careful.'

They hurried down the stairs, left the mill and ran through the trees after the couple. A grassy track led away from the mill and towards a quiet lane. Keeping under the cover of the trees, the girls followed the couple up the track. Before they'd reached the gate though, they heard car doors slamming and engines starting up. They waited in the cover of the trees, and once the cars had moved away, they climbed over the gate and peered up the lane.

Two cars were heading back towards the village. The one in the rear was easily visible. It was a grey Bentley, recognisable to everyone in Warren End as belonging to the estate.

'George Prendergast!' breathed Joan.

They couldn't see the car in front properly, but as it turned right at the crossroads at the top of the hill, they caught a brief glimpse of some claret red bodywork. Joan frowned.

'Who's that?' she murmured. Kate fell silent, shock washing through her. She was almost sure she'd seen that car before. It was rarely used and was usually covered by a tarpaulin, stored away in one of the garages at Oakwood Grange. It hit her why the woman shrouded in the raincoat had seemed familiar. It was none other than her great-aunt Amelia.

3

KATE

Warren End, Summer, 1944

As they cycled back to the village that day, Joan was uncharacteristically quiet. Normally she kept up a constant chatter on the way home, going over the events of the day, speculating about the next one, gossiping about school friends and people in the village. This silence worried Kate. When Joan was quiet for long periods, it generally meant she was planning something. And the things she planned nearly always made Kate anxious. So, Kate tried to interrupt Joan's thoughts by cycling beside her and trying to engage her in conversation, but each attempt was met with one-word answers. Finally, they reached the village and the top of Joan's lane and both stood astride their bikes to say goodbye.

'Shall we meet up tomorrow ?' Kate asked. Joan met her gaze blankly.

'Of course. We always do, don't we?' Then a glint of mischief crept into her eyes. 'Maybe they'll come back again.'

'Who?'

'Prendergast and his fancy woman, of course.'

Kate's spirits plummeted. She hoped fervently that they wouldn't come back. She didn't want Joan to find out that the woman was her aunt Amelia, someone she revered and admired and often gently bragged about in conversation.

'I've been thinking...' Joan said.

'Oh?' asked Kate, meeting Joan's steady gaze.

'We should do something about it.'

'*Do* something?' repeated Kate, aghast. 'What do you mean?'

'I'm not sure yet. We can't let him get away with this. I know that much.'

'Who? Get away with what?'

'Him. George Prendergast, of course. He's such a bastard to everyone. Think about how he shot at us the other week, how he yells at me dad when he can't pay the rent. And now he's cheating on his wife. We should do something about it.'

'No, Joan. We shouldn't. It's none of our business. And how do you know he's cheating anyway?'

'Oh, come on! What else could it be? A secret meeting, miles from anywhere?'

'But they didn't *do* anything did they?' said Kate. 'They were just arguing.'

'As I said, a lovers' tiff.'

'Well, I bet they don't come back,' said Kate, with no way of knowing whether they would or not, she just wanted Joan to drop the subject. And if they didn't come back, Joan might never discover that the woman in the raincoat was Aunt Amelia.

Several days passed. The two girls went to the old mill each morning as usual and spent their time as they had before. But things had changed. It didn't feel quite the same anymore. It had lost that delicious feeling of being their secret hideaway. The fact that George Prendergast could turn up without warning, and that he probably even owned the place, hovered over them like the dark clouds that gathered over the river on a rainy day. It

tainted their enjoyment of the place. As they cooked over their
fire, scouted for sticks in the spinney, or sat upstairs out of the
rain on the old millstones, they always had half an ear on the
door, listening out for George Prendergast. Neither had any
desire for him to find them there. And they knew that if he did
discover them, he would make quite sure they didn't come back.
He'd probably complain to their parents.

On Sunday, Great-Uncle James invited Kate and her mother
and father for pre-lunch drinks after church. Kate spotted him
ambling up between the pews to speak to her father. She knew
what it meant and she didn't want to go. She had no desire to
speak to Aunt Amelia. How could she hide the fact that she
knew her secret; that her aunt was seeing George Prendergast in
private. She felt betrayed. She'd always loved her great-aunt,
who she'd looked upon secretly as a big sister. After all, Amelia
was far younger than Kate's mother. She was only in her mid-
thirties. It seemed ridiculous to even think of her as a great aunt
with all the connotations that the label brought with it.

Amelia would often take Kate up to her room during family
visits and show her some new clothes, or how to style her hair or
apply makeup. Kate knew her mother took a dim view of this, by
the look on her face when they returned. Amelia would look at
Kate conspiratorially and smile innocently at Freda as if bliss-
fully unaware of the disapproval.

Until the day she'd seen her with George Prendergast at
Willow Mill, Kate had believed she could tell Amelia anything
and that her confidence would be respected. She'd even told
Amelia her innermost secret. She'd described how she had a
crush on Gordon Anderson, a boy in her class, with tousled,
golden hair and blue eyes, and how she thought about him night
and day and blushed scarlet every time he spoke to her. Amelia
had gripped her hand and said, 'How thrilling' and reassured her

that her reactions were quite normal. But now Kate felt as though she'd been let down. That Amelia had secrets of her own that she'd kept from Kate and that they weren't the true friends she'd formerly thought. She was shocked that Amelia could even consider being unfaithful to Uncle James, who was the kindest, mildest man alive, and who so obviously doted on his young wife. Kate was beginning to think that she'd made a grave mistake in trusting Amelia. Perhaps her mother was right about her after all.

'I don't feel well, Mum,' she said as they left the church. 'I think I'll just go home.'

Her mother peered at her suspiciously. 'You look perfectly fine to me, young lady! You're out and about on your bike all hours without getting ill. Half an hour at your uncle's is not going to hurt you. You normally enjoy going up there. You've been spending far too much time out of the house recently. You should spend some time with the family for once.'

So, Kate was forced to walk between her parents up to Oakwood Grange and sit stiffly in the drawing room while the aged butler served drinks. Her mother and father, unused to alcohol, always asked timidly for a sweet sherry, whilst James and Amelia drunk whisky and soda with panache. Kate had no desire to speak to her aunt, so was careful to sit on the opposite side of the room from Amelia, on a chair that was set slightly back from the others. She was hoping that Amelia wouldn't suggest they go up to her room, or out for a walk around the garden as she often did.

Kate kept silent as the others talked of the war, of the news from the front line and of the recent bombing raids in London and on the South East of England, some on small towns and villages.

'You aren't safe anywhere, nowadays,' said Kate's mother with a shudder.

'Too true!' replied James, examining his whisky. 'Any news from young Roy?' he asked after a pause.

There was an awkward silence. Then Kate's father said,

'We haven't heard anything. Which is good news in itself, I suppose. We know he landed in France on D-Day and that his regiment is pushing on down to Paris. We hear more from newspapers than from him, to be honest.'

'It must be so worrying for you,' said James.

Kate stole a glance at Amelia, who was sitting beside her husband on the sofa next to the fireplace. She'd not spoken once since they'd arrived at the house, apart from thanking the butler for her drink. At that moment she was staring down into her lap, twisting her hands over and over each other, and when she did lift her head, Kate saw that her face was pale and her skin looked dull. Her eyes too were downcast and lacked their usual sparkle. Perhaps Joan was right. Perhaps Amelia was having an affair with George Prendergast, and they'd had a lovers' tiff that was making her unhappy. Kate had never seen her aunt look so subdued before and it was a shock to see her like that.

Amelia hardly uttered a word the whole time they were there, apart from to say 'goodbye' absently as they left. As they headed back down the drive, Kate's mother, stomping along stiffly, said, 'Well, honestly! I've never been so insulted. By family as well...'

'What do you mean, dear?' asked Kate's father, mildly.

'Amelia. She didn't speak once. Made me feel most unwelcome. Talk about giving herself airs and graces!'

'I really didn't notice, dear. I'm sure she didn't mean any harm.'

'Oh, are you? She's nothing but a jumped-up chambermaid after all. I don't know why she thinks she can play Lady Muck with us.'

'Please don't talk like that, Freda. Perhaps Amelia was feeling unwell. She's usually so charming.'

'Yes, isn't she just! I've always thought there was something rum about that girl. Somehow, she just doesn't stack up. Why would someone like her be working as a chambermaid in a London hotel unless they had something to hide, I ask you?'

Kate walked a little behind her parents, listening intently as her mother went on and on, over and over the same theme. Kate had always thought that her mother was unfair to Amelia. It was obvious to Kate that it was through jealousy; Amelia was young, rich, and beautiful, where Freda was careworn, in her mid-forties and had to work hard for her meagre living. Freda had always resented the fact that Great-Uncle James, in contrast to Kenneth's father, his older brother, had been successful in business. James had started out as an apprentice engineer at an early age and progressed to owning several profitable factories in Lancashire, before retiring to Oakwood Grange and taking up politics. Kenneth's father had been a humble bookkeeper with no flair for business. Kate knew too that Freda resented the way Kate and Amelia had struck up a friendship and were close in the way that Freda and Kate could never be. But now Kate listened to the rise and fall of her mother's outraged voice and wondered; was there 'something rum' about Aunt Amelia after all?

The following day Kate and Joan resumed their trips to the old mill, trying to revive their early enthusiasm. It began to feel as if they were overcoming the taint that George Prendergast had put on the place. On the Wednesday, they were lying on the riverbank, drying out after a swim. Joan turned on her back and stared up at the leaves.

'It's really good to be away from home,' she said. Kate turned to look at her, surprised. Joan was voicing something Kate long suspected but had never dared to raise with her friend.

'Oh?' she asked tentatively.

'Yeah. Mum and Dad've been arguing. Don't know what it's about, but last night they were really going for it. I heard some cups smashing or something. Then the front door slammed. Shook the whole house. This morning, Mum had a black eye.'

'That's terrible, Joan,' Kate said, propping herself up on her elbow and looking into her friend's eyes.

Joan bit her lip. Was she fighting back tears? She was normally so tough.

'He wasn't around this morning. And Mum says he's left home.'

Kate's heart went out to her friend, but she didn't know what to say. She didn't know anyone whose parents had sepa-rated. Her own parents bickered sometimes, but things usually blew over quickly and her mother normally got her way in the end.

Joan sat up and hugged her knees. 'I don't care if he's gone,' she said fiercely. 'He's a bastard. He hits all of us. Especially Mum and me. Good riddance to him.'

Kate nodded but remained silent. She knew that if she said anything against Frank Bartram, Joan would turn on her, despite what she'd just said, and even though he was a violent, drunken father who didn't deserve her loyalty, Kate wanted to tell Joan that she felt for her, that she was her best friend and that she would help her through this difficult time. She was struggling to find the right words when the sound of voices floated up from the track.

'It's them again!' whispered Joan, her bitterness gone in an instant, her eyes suddenly wide with excitement. 'Let's go and listen through the door once they've gone in.'

'No!' said Kate, terrified that Joan would discover the identity of the mystery woman. 'We can't do that. They'll hear us, then we'll be for it.'

Joan stood up and stretched, droplets of river water covering her tanned skin.

'Well, if you won't go, I will. I know how to keep quiet. They'll never spot me. You can stay round here out of sight and I'll tell you if I hear anything.'

She was gone, and Kate sat up, listening, her heart thumping. She heard the door to the mill slam and then everything went quiet. The only sounds she could hear were the click and rattle of the water wheel, the ripple of the river and the chatter of birdsong in the trees. She felt sick with dread. What if Joan saw that the woman was Aunt Amelia? It wasn't raining today, so Amelia wouldn't be wearing a raincoat. Everyone in the village would recognise her dark hair, her exotic good looks.

It seemed an age before Joan reappeared round the corner of the building. She was brimming with excitement. She sat down beside Kate.

'Well?'

'They're obviously lovers. I didn't hear much, they were talking quietly and the door was shut, but she was pleading with him. *Pleading*. I heard her say, "For God's sake George, have some mercy". Perhaps he wants to end it and she can't bear it.'

'Did you see who she was?' Kate asked, her eyes on the ground.

'I couldn't see. She was wearing a headscarf, and I had to scarper when they came out. It's got to be someone from round here. She sounded like a toff.'

Kate allowed herself to breathe again.

'Well, if it's over, perhaps they won't come back again.'

'Perhaps...' said Joan, throwing a pebble into the pool and watching the ripples spread and multiply. 'We've got to do *something* about it, though. He can't be allowed to get away with this. Think about his poor missus.'

Kate tried to remember Ivy Prendergast. A pale, insignificant slip of a woman, who kept herself to herself. She had mousy, fair hair and a thin face. Kate could never remember having seen her smile. She wasn't like most of the landowners' wives in the area. People described her as a "townie". She didn't seem to like hunting or country pursuits and instead sped round the lanes in a sleek looking silver convertible.

'There's nothing we can do about it,' Kate said. 'Like I said before, it's not our business. We should just drop it, Joan.'

Joan went silent then and Kate felt a little guilty for disagreeing with her, especially in the light of her family troubles. They went home early that day and, as before when George Prendergast had cast a shadow over their day, they hardly spoke on the way home. At the top of the lane, Joan said a quick goodbye and pedalled off towards her cottage. Kate stared after her, watching her square her shoulders and draw herself up tall. Anguished that they'd parted on bad terms, Kate wondered guiltily what sort of atmosphere would greet Joan at home.

She went back to her own house and tried not to think about Joan as she peeled the vegetables and set the table for supper.

'Are you feeling alright?' her mother asked as they ate their meal of stringy stew, dumplings and boiled potatoes. 'You look a bit peaky. Perhaps you'd better have an early night and stay at home tomorrow.'

Kate shrugged and went straight up to her room after she'd helped Freda wash up. She lay on her bed, trying to read a book, her mind going over and over the events of the past few days. She was desperate to remain friends with Joan, but equally concerned to protect her aunt. Whatever Joan had in mind for George Prendergast was probably not going to end well for Amelia either.

She heard her mother and father going up to bed and slid between the sheets herself. It was a stifling hot night so she opened her bedroom window wide. The village was quiet apart from the hoot of the resident barn owl, but Kate found herself unable to sleep. No matter how much she tried to calm her mind, her thoughts kept sliding back to Aunt Amelia and George Prendergast. Whatever did Amelia see in him? He was a deeply unpleasant man, unpopular in the village and amongst the workers on the estate. There was something forbidding about his looks too, with his Victorian whiskers and mean eyes and she'd witnessed his bad temper first-hand. Even Kate's father, who normally saw the best in everyone, didn't have a good word to say about Prendergast. She recalled overhearing some gossip in the village shop about him once. Two women were speaking about him in hushed tones. One of them was the housekeeper at the Prendergast estate. Hovering near them, pretending to be choosing sweets, she'd gleaned that George Prendergast was fond of both alcohol and gambling. If that were true, how on earth could Amelia have fallen for such a person? Kate had thought her aunt had better judgement.

These thoughts still going round and round in her head, she eventually drifted off briefly, but was awoken by an unfamiliar sound. She sat bolt upright, listening. It was a low drone that vibrated the windows and the roof timbers of the house. It was getting louder by the second. Alarmed, she put her head out of the window. The drone was coming from the sky. It was a sound she'd never heard before, but she quickly realised it was an aircraft approaching from the north. The sound became deafening, and as she watched, dumbfounded, a plane burst into her line of sight over the roof of the house opposite and passed low over Kate's house. The moon was bright and she'd caught sight of two propellors on the front of the wings, the dull grey of the fuselage and the black cross painted on the underside of each wing.

Her heart beating quickly, and not knowing what to do, she

pulled on her dressing gown and rushed out onto the landing. Her mother and father were emerging from their own bedroom, ashen faced. Her father was already dressed in his Air Raid Warden's uniform and was pulling on his helmet.

'I've got to go out and raise the alarm,' he said and hurried downstairs. The door slammed and his footsteps pounded away from the house.

'Let's go downstairs. Under the table,' said Freda. They had prepared for this. Even though Warren End was buried deep in the heart of the countryside, they'd been drilled in case any bombers ever came their way, perhaps returning from raids on the big manufacturing cities of the midlands. The hum of the aircraft was already receding as the two of them hurried downstairs and crouched under the dining room table, but within seconds came the terrifying boom of an explosion, followed by three other lesser bangs and the crash of falling masonry.

They exchanged horrified looks as the siren began its mournful wail from the direction of the church tower.

Kate and Freda crouched under the table for half an hour, until they were almost sure the bomber wasn't coming back. As they emerged and stretched their limbs, stiff from crouching in one position, the siren changed tone and the sound of the all-clear came blaring out across the village. As she got to her feet, Kate noticed that grey light was creeping into the sky. It was almost dawn.

'I'm going to get dressed and go along and see if there's anything I can do to help,' Freda said.

'Can I come with you?' asked Kate.

'No. You'd be safer here. Go on back to bed and catch up on some sleep,' and Freda disappeared upstairs to change.

Kate went up to her room, feeling exhaustion descend upon her. She heard her mother leave on her bicycle, then she lay down on her bed and closed her eyes, hoping that sleep would come. But her nerves were so taut and her mind was racing wildly after the shock of the air raid. She couldn't keep still, let alone get off to sleep. She heard voices and footsteps out in the road and she looked out of the window. There were groups of people walking past in the direction that the bomber had hit. It was as if the whole village was on the march.

Kate pulled on some trousers and a pullover and her plim-solls and ran outside to join the crowd. She walked along between a family with a small girl and a couple of boys a little older than her. She recognised them as the ones who had made her life a misery at the beginning of summer, but that morning they were subdued and didn't even look her way. The all-clear signal was still wailing from the church tower. It seemed that sound, together with shock, had robbed everyone of the power of speech.

People were walking silently in the direction of the Prender-gast estate. It was behind some high gates and up a long drive, a little way out of the village. Normally, no one ventured up the drive for fear of incurring the wrath of Prendergast himself, but at that moment no one cared. They wanted to find out where the bomb had fallen, if anyone was hurt, and if there was anything they could do to help.

As Kate walked up the drive, she peered towards the build-ings at the end; George Prendergast's imposing gothic mansion, Warren Hall, the stable blocks behind it and the ancient barns beyond them. As she got closer, it was obvious that the house was intact, and the stables looked to have been spared too. But the big tithe barn where hay and straw was stored and animals housed in the winter had been devastated. The roof was blown in, with splintered beams jutting up at right angles. One wall was completely blasted away, the others had partially collapsed. Smoke and dust billowed from the devastated building and several small fires had broken out in the ruins. As Kate got closer she could see men already at work, sifting through the wreckage, shifting beams and stones, searching for anyone who might have been in there. George Prendergast and his wife, both in dressing gowns, stood helplessly beside the wrecked building.

Behind them was a small crowd of onlookers, but Kate didn't want to stand there gawping. She caught sight of her mother, talking to one of the men and pushed her way through the people towards her.

'What are you doing here? I told you to stay at home,' said Freda as Kate approached.

'I had to come. Can I help at all?'

'Not really, Kate.'

'What's happening? Is anyone hurt?'

'They think there's a man in there somewhere. That's why they're trying to move the beams.'

From the end of the drive came the sound of bells, ringing urgently and the roar of an engine.

'Thank God!' breathed Freda. 'The fire brigade at last.'

The engine pulled up beside the collapsed barn and six men jumped off it and ran towards the building. Two others ran to the hoses, pulled them free and started dousing the fires. Within seconds the six were inside the building, moving beams, searching through rubble, peering under sections of the collapsed roof. Kate watched them, fearing the worst, dread in her pounding heart.

Before long, a shout went up. One fireman held a hand up and others rushed to where he stood pointing under some broken beams. Kate watched as they fixed ropes to the heavy beams and hauled them out of the rubble one by one. Then the men were bending down and straining. Four of them were lifting something from the wreckage with gentle care. With horror, Kate realised it was the body of a man.

'Dear God,' breathed Freda. 'You stay right here, Katherine,' she said, rushing forward to where the firemen were carrying the body. At Freda's direction, the men heaved the body well away from the building and laid it down gently on the grass. Then Freda knelt down and got to work, giving the kiss of life, pressing on the man's chest. Kate watched, tears of shock in her eyes.

Without realising what she was doing, she edged closer. There was something about the man that was familiar. She'd seen that long dark coat that flapped from his body before. She had to find out. She wandered towards him, watching her mother's desperate attempts to resuscitate the man. Something was compelling her to move nearer still and soon she was close enough to see the man's face. His forehead was covered in blood and his face drained of colour, but his eyes were staring out blankly, glazed and expressionless. Kate's hand flew to her mouth. She knew that face. The forehead was normally pulled into a frown, the mouth scowling or uttering expletives, eyes blazing with anger. It was the face of Frank Bartram, Joan's father.

4

KATE

Warren End, Buckinghamshire
April, 1970

The church was half full by the time Amelia's coffin was borne up the aisle on the shoulders of the men from the funeral parlour, to the sound of mournful organ music. Kate, sitting on the front pew alone, glanced round surreptitiously now and again to see if there were any familiar faces amongst the mourners. Janet was there, of course, sitting stiffly beside a red-faced man who looked uncomfortable in a suit a little too tight for him. There were several old ladies too, with permed grey hair, some of whom Kate recognised from her childhood. They'd been friends of her mother's; stalwarts of the Women's Institute and the church, but although the faces were familiar, she was finding it difficult to put any names to them.

The coffin was lowered onto a plinth before the altar, the organ music faded away and the vicar addressed the congregation. He wasn't someone Kate remembered. Old Reverend Lewis had been vicar here when she was a child. He'd been a kindly presence, with his slightly buck teeth and avuncular manner.

This young man looked every inch a modern vicar and she wondered whether he'd known Amelia very well, as he spoke of her good deeds for the community and her pious nature. Perhaps she'd changed in her later years, Kate wondered, but she didn't think so, judging by the whisky decanter on the desk and the paperwork in disarray.

The congregation stood to sing hymns; *All Things Bright and Beautiful* and *Jerusalem*, and knelt to say prayers. The service was mercifully short and as Kate filed out of the church behind the coffin, she got a better look at the congregation. She quickly scanned the pews, half looking for Joan, but she knew she was unlikely to be there. Joan had hardly known Amelia when they were growing up, and Kate wasn't even sure she would recognise her old friend after all these years.

There was one old lady, though, sitting near the back, who Kate couldn't place at first. There was something about her that looked familiar. She was a tiny scrap of a woman, seated next to a young woman in a blue uniform who looked like a carer. The old lady had a white stick propped beside her and wore dark glasses. With a jolt, Kate remembered. She'd been one of two sisters who'd lived together in a rundown house behind the high hedges on the edge of the village. One of the sisters was partially blind and the other completely so, but even so they lived alone without help. The village children had been terrified of them because the blind sister was thought to be psychic. She would walk along the street on her sister's arm, staring ahead of her out of white eyes. Kate recalled that Amelia had befriended the sisters and used to visit them in their ramshackle house occasionally. It had seemed odd to Kate at the time and she used to wonder what they had in common. Perhaps, she reflected now, Amelia was doing it out of charity, acting on the ingrained instincts of a missionary's daughter.

There was someone else in the final pew. Squashed up in the

corner against the stone wall, his head bowed, almost as if he was embarrassed to be there. He had straggly grey hair and a long, unkempt beard, and from his crumpled and ill-fitting clothes, Kate assumed that he was a tramp. What was he doing here? Had he known Amelia? There was no time to speculate, so Kate walked on, following the coffin out through the porch and into the weak April sunshine.

In the chilly churchyard, under the spreading cedars, the congregation stood around the freshly dug grave in silence, some with tears in their eyes, some with their faces cast down, others dabbing with handkerchiefs and sniffing. Not for the first time that morning, Kate felt like a fraud. She hadn't been close to Amelia for her last years and it didn't feel right for her to be here amongst those who were Amelia's true friends.

Amelia's grave had been dug right beside a plot with a large white headstone where Great-Uncle James had been laid to rest all those years before. The coffin was lowered sedately into the grave and the vicar began to intone the burial service, to the sound of subdued sobbing.

Feeling awkward, Kate glanced beyond the bowed heads, to the mossy gravestones beyond, taking in the path that led under the trees to the rear entrance of the church. To her surprise the shabby old man she'd seen sitting in the corner of the church was now walking along the path towards the gate. He walked slowly and painfully with a stick, his head bowed and his back bent. She wondered why he hadn't come to stand beside the grave. Perhaps, after all, he had nothing to do with Amelia, and had just been sheltering inside the church from the chilly April weather. She turned back to the burial ceremony and tried to put him out of her mind.

Later, she sipped stewed tea from an urn in the village hall and made small talk with the ladies from the W.I. and others who had known Amelia. She heard stories of how kind Amelia had been over the years, how she'd given up her free time for numerous local causes, had delivered meals on wheels until her last few weeks and had often hosted charitable events at home. Kate kept nodding and listening, thinking how Amelia must have changed since her early married days, and soon her jaw ached from smiling for so long.

'She was much loved, your auntie,' said Janet, hovering nearby with a cup of tea.

'Oh yes, I can see that,' Kate smiled. 'It's a wonderful send off for her.'

'So many people cared for her.' Janet was looking around the hall with misty eyes.

'I was wondering...' Kate lowered her voice. 'There was an old man in the church. He looked a bit like a tramp. Sitting on the back row next to the wall. I wondered if you knew who he was?'

'Yes, I know him. Everyone does. He looks a bit eccentric now, but he's getting old.'

'Who is it? Would I know him?'

'Oh yes, I'm sure you would. He was definitely living in the village when you were little. He lived at the big house. Warren Hall. It's old Mr Prendergast.'

'What, George Prendergast?' Kate's mouth dropped open.

'Yes. That's him.'

'So, does he still live up at the big house?' she asked when she'd recovered her composure.

'Oh no, dear. No. He fell on hard times. I'm not quite sure of the details. But he's been living in one of the little bungalows at the bottom of Clerks' Lane for a very long time now.'

Kate was speechless. She thought back to those last few fateful weeks that summer of '44, when things had happened that had changed lives forever. But when she'd left Warren End towards the end of that year, George Prendergast had still been living in gothic splendour up at the hall. Had the terrible events of that summer brought his downfall? Kate suddenly felt the guilt all over again.

The throng of mourners was beginning to thin out. Kate was relieved that it was almost over. She was itching to get back to Oakwood Grange and make a start on Aunt Amelia's paperwork. Once that was done she would make arrangements for the furniture to be sold and the house to be put on the market. She'd taken a month off work. She was between projects, so her partners were happy to agree, but she didn't want to be away for any longer than that. As the only female partner in the firm, she had to fight to maintain her position against those jostling to replace her.

Many people came up to give Kate their condolences before they left. They shook her hand, looked into her eyes and said how much Amelia would be missed. One of the last to leave was the old lady she'd seen at the back of the church. She walked slowly, leaning on the arm of the young woman accompanying her. She took Kate's hand in hers and lifted her face to look up at Kate. Kate couldn't see through the old lady's dark glasses and found that a little disconcerting.

'I'm Edna Robinson,' the old lady said, her voice tremulous. 'I don't know if you remember me, but I remember you.'

'Do you really?' Kate was surprised. She didn't recall ever having spoken to Edna or her sister.

'Oh yes. Your aunt used to talk about you a lot. Especially when you were young.'

Kate smiled. Again, she felt at a disadvantage not being able to see the old lady's eyes; it felt as if she was being scrutinised carefully from behind the dark glasses. 'We were very close back then,' she said.

The old woman's bony grip tightened around Kate's hands and she pulled her close.

'Your aunt was a very troubled girl in those days,' she said in a hoarse whisper. 'She had been through so much, you know.'

'Oh?' Kate had no idea how to respond. *Had* Amelia been through a lot? Kate frowned, trying to work out what the old woman meant. The fallout from the events that summer must have affected Amelia badly, but surely she wouldn't have divulged anything about that to Edna Robinson.

The old woman didn't release her hold on Kate's hand, in fact she grasped it even tighter. Kate could feel her trembling beneath her iron grip.

'Come on, Miss Robinson,' said the young woman gently, 'We really should be going now. You don't want to tire yourself out.'

'Come and see me one day, my dear,' the old lady said to Kate, releasing her hand. 'I live in The Meadows now. Anytime. We can talk about your aunt.'

'Of course,' said Kate, puzzled. What was the old lady trying to tell her about Amelia? Did she know her secrets? Kate had no desire to revisit the events of the summer of '44. Hadn't she spent the past twenty-five years trying to put them behind her? There was nothing the old woman could tell her that would change what happened, or change what Kate felt about it.

She watched as Miss Robinson crossed the hall towards the door with the help of her young carer. Perhaps it wasn't about that summer after all. Perhaps she was just missing Amelia's company and wanted an excuse to talk about her again. Kate sighed. She'd no real desire to take time off to visit the old lady in her care home, but there was something a little intriguing in what she'd said, and she'd looked so lost and lonely. Perhaps Kate would be able to find the time once she'd broken the back of the packing.

The only people left in the hall now were the ladies who'd organised the get-together. Kate thanked each of them in turn,

said her goodbyes, then set off to walk the half mile or so
through the village, back to Oakwood Grange. As she walked,
Edna Robinson's words kept going round in her mind. What did
she mean, Amelia had been through so much? Wasn't she happy
with Uncle James? Kate reminded herself that Amelia *had* been
unfaithful to him, so something must have driven her to act that
way. But would she have told the Robinson sisters about that?
Kate doubted that very much. She thought about the deed she'd
found the day before, revealing that Amelia had changed her
name. It was all so puzzling. Amelia had clearly harboured
many secrets over the years. Yes, there was still an air of mystery
about her, there always had been, and that mystery had even
survived Amelia herself.

Back at the house, Kate made a sandwich, took it through to
the study and made a start on the paperwork. The job was long
and tedious, working out what bills needed to be paid, writing
out cheques, drafting letters to inform utilities and tradesmen of
Amelia's death. It was dark outside by the time she'd finished,
and it was raining. As she got up from the desk she realised how
cold she'd got sitting still in the chilly room. She went through
to the kitchen to warm herself beside the Aga, but when she
touched the surface it was barely warm.

Damn! She'd just paid an overdue bill for oil, so perhaps it
had run out. The antiquated radiators were stone cold too and
she'd no idea if there was any fuel to make a fire. Perhaps there
was an electric fire somewhere to take the chill off until she
could sort something more permanent. She sighed, missing her
comfortable flat in Islington, with its central heating and instant
hot water. There was no sign of an electric heater in the pantry,
in the broom cupboard or scullery. She went through to the hall
and looked in the coat cupboard under the stairs; nothing there.

It occurred to Kate that Amelia might have had a fire or a fan
heater in her bedroom. She hadn't ventured into that room

since she arrived. There was something stopping her; some respect for Amelia's privacy perhaps, but now she hurried up the wide staircase, crossed the landing and opened the door to the master bedroom at the top of the stairs. Switching on the light, she was struck by how little the room had changed since the 1940s. There was Amelia's glass-topped dressing table in the same position in front of the window, with its pink velvet buttoned stool. She'd sat there many times while her aunt brushed her hair or helped her put on lipstick. There was the giant oak wardrobe from which Amelia would produce the latest item of clothing she'd bought on a trip to London, and the trunk at the end of the bed where Amelia used to sit while they chatted. Kate sat down on it heavily. For the first time that day, her eyes welled with tears and guilt and grief threatened to overwhelm her.

'I'm sorry, Amelia,' she said aloud. 'I'm so sorry.'

As she wiped away her tears, she remembered what she'd come up here for. There was a fireplace in the bedroom, which in the winter in the forties had always been lit to warm the room, but although it had been boarded up, there was nothing in its place.

She left the room and wandered through the other bedrooms, finding nothing, then up the narrow, winding stair-case to the servants' quarters. This was where the housekeeper, the scullery maid and the old butler had their rooms in the old days. Kate opened the door to each room, but they were empty now, just bare boards, bedsteads and little furniture. At the end of the passage was a smaller door. She opened it and flicked on the light. It was a huge storage cupboard, full of clutter. Broken chairs, hat boxes, old pictures stacked against one wall. And there it was, an old-fashioned, curved, two-bar electric fire. She picked it up, wound the flex around to carry it and tucked it under her arm. As she turned to leave, she noticed a leather trunk stowed in one corner, half hidden by an old mattress with its stuffing protruding, and an empty bookcase.

She put down the fire, pulled the mattress and bookcase aside and stared at the trunk. A faded, dusty label was stuck on the side; "Miss Amelia Collins, Russell Hotel, London".

This was too inviting to resist, particularly as her curiosity had been piqued by the events of the day. She unfastened the buckles and lifted the lid. On top lay several pieces of material; lengths of beautifully woven silks in startlingly bright colours; green, purple, red, some shot through with gold. Underneath them were two cotton dresses, one pale blue with tiny white flowers, the other salmon pink with lace insets. Kate held them up to the light. They were in the style of the 1930s, low waisted, scoop necked, and were made for a very slim woman. A pair of white summer shoes and a straw hat were under the dresses and, at the very bottom, a pile of letters and a few photographs.

Kate picked up the letters and scanned through the envelopes. The pile was in date order; all had Indian postmarks and the early ones were addressed to Miss A Collins, c/o the Russell Hotel, Russell Square, London WC1. After 1940, they were addressed to Mrs A Hamilton at Oakwood Grange. Wedged between the envelopes and the photographs was a small piece of card. Looking at it closely, Kate saw it was a dog-eared luggage label. "P&O S.S Strathmore, Bombay to Southampton, January 5th 1937" was stamped on one side in faded print, and underneath that in flowing handwriting, was written the name, "Miss A Collins."

Puzzled, she looked through the photographs. There was a copy of the one on the mantlepiece downstairs of Amelia standing between her parents. "With Mummy and Daddy, Darjeeling, 1928", was scrawled on the back in childish writing. And a further one of Amelia, who looked to be in her mid-twenties by then, standing between another couple who looked a little older than her. They were dressed casually, arm in arm and all were smiling broadly at the camera. On the back was written; "Remember that day, September '36, Ganpur? With love, Mabel and Giles".

There was one last photograph that Kate almost missed. It was a small, oval portrait of a young, dark-haired woman. At first, she thought it was Amelia herself, with her high cheekbones and almond-shaped eyes, but on closer inspection she realised that it wasn't Amelia, but someone who looked remarkably like her. A sister, perhaps? No, Amelia had been an only child. A cousin maybe? She turned it over to look at the back and a name was written in pencil: *Ava*. Kate stared at it, puzzled.

'Who are you?' she murmured.

Laying down the photographs, Kate turned the envelopes over in her hands, bursting to rip the first one open and discover something of Amelia's hidden past, but there was one more package in the bottom of the trunk that was demanding her attention. It was an official-looking, brown envelope with a stamp on the front that read; "Ganpur Office of Births, Marriages and Deaths". She fished inside and pulled out a document that having been folded for so many years, threatened to come apart when she opened it out. She was stunned at what she read.

"Official extract of the Marriage Register of Ganpur; On this 10th day of May 1935, marriage of Miss Amelia Collins, spinster, to Mr Reginald Holden, District Officer of this district." Kate leaned back against the lumpy mattress, amazed. So, Amelia *had* been married out in India. To a District Officer no less. Whatever had happened to Mr Reginald Holden, and why had Amelia never mentioned her first marriage to anyone?

5
———

AMELIA

Pankhabari, Darjeeling District, India
April, 1935

The missionary who had been appointed by the Baptist Mission in Calcutta to take over from Amelia's parents was due to arrive at midday. Amelia already had her bags packed so she could leave as soon as she'd given him the keys. Her trunk and two holdalls were waiting, stacked beside the front door as she walked around the sparsely furnished bungalow for the last time. It tore her heart to say goodbye to the place that had been her home for so many happy years. She went into each empty room, stared out of the windows at the magnificent views of the snow-capped mountains that stretched as far as the eye could see and melted into the milky sky on the horizon.

She'd always loved that view, and she'd loved the bungalow too, for all its lack of creature comforts. It had been home since the family had arrived in the Himalayan village of Pankhabari, fresh from rural Surrey, and it was where Amelia had learned everything she knew about India, the local people and their language. It was where she and her parents had been at their happiest, and where she had lost the two people she loved most in the world in the space of a few days.

Her parents had come out to India to establish a small field hospital to serve the people who lived in the remote villages of the Himalayan foothills south of Darjeeling. They were both medical missionaries – her father a qualified doctor and her mother a nurse. They had both trained in London but had met while working in a Calcutta Mission hospital, their strong Christian faith bringing them together. They had married and raised Amelia, returning to live in England for her early years. However, they'd always felt their true calling was in India, and when Amelia was fifteen an opportunity had come up to join the Christian Mission in Bengal. It was the chance they'd been waiting for for years, so they jumped at it. Her father arranged for Amelia to attend a boarding school in England so she wouldn't miss out on her education. But she'd been so homesick during the first term that her parents had bought her a passage on the next boat from Southampton to Calcutta to join them.

She didn't feel her education had suffered greatly; her father taught her in the evenings after a long day caring for patients at the hospital, and during the daytimes she read and studied on her own. Of course it meant that she couldn't take any exams, but that didn't trouble her; she wanted to become a nurse like her mother and when she was eighteen, began by helping out in the field hospital where it wasn't necessary to have qualifications.

She learned the skills of an auxiliary nurse; how to care for patients, to make them comfortable, administer medicines and injections, take blood pressures and temperatures. Her father would go weekly to outlying villages to hold clinics. He would travel there by pony and when she was old enough, Amelia accompanied him to assist him with the patients. She looked forward to those trips and enjoyed every moment of them; riding into the hills on remote trails, through pine forests and over rough grassland, past tiny farmsteads, and all the way the mighty peaks of the Himalayas dominated the horizon. She felt very close to her father on those occasions; they would talk about anything and everything; art, literature, philosophy, religion. She was a little surprised when he confided to her that he was less concerned with forcing Christianity on the locals than ensuring they had access to healthcare. He confessed that he himself was drawn to the Buddhist teachings, finding that they struck many chords with him, so he had no real wish to displace them in the hearts of the faithful.

'Obviously, keep that to yourself, Amelia,' he said. 'It wouldn't go down well if anyone at the Mission got to find out.'

On another occasion, he told her something that shocked her to the core.

'There's something I need to tell you, Amelia,' he began. They'd been travelling some time that morning, and she'd noticed that her father had been uncharacteristically quiet until that point. 'I'm afraid that I... we've kept it from you until now, but I think the time has come, and that you're old enough to know.'

'Really, Father?' she asked, surprised. They were riding side-by-side on a wide stretch of track, but unusually her father was not looking at her. He was sitting up ramrod straight and staring ahead, between his pony's ears.

'Old enough to know what?'

'Look, it's really difficult to tell you this. You know that both your mother and I love you more than anything in the world, don't you?'

She nodded, becoming alarmed, where was this going?

'Well, it doesn't matter a jot to us, but the fact is... you are not *actually* our birth daughter. When I say that, I mean that you are *my* birth daughter, but... but not Mother's...'

Waves of shock washed through her. She pulled her pony to a standstill.

'What do you mean, Father? I don't understand.'

He stopped beside her. 'Perhaps we had better get down and sit on those rocks.'

Once they were seated, the ponies chomping the short grass on the track, he began to speak, his eyes on the ground, his voice choked with embarrassment.

'You know, I went through something of a wild period during my early years. When I first came out to India, I fell in love with an Anglo-Indian girl, and... well, she became pregnant. She died when you were born, sadly, but I took you in and looked after you in my house in Calcutta. I employed an ayah to care for you and carried on working at the hospital. Then I met Mother. We hit it off straight away, and I knew I wanted to marry her, but I was worried she would feel differently about me if she knew about my circumstances. But on the contrary, she loved you from the moment she saw you and willingly took you on as her own.'

There was a long silence as the meaning of his words sunk in. It felt as if everything had changed. As if the foundations of Amelia's world had been removed and she was hovering on thin air.

'Why didn't you tell me before?' she asked at last, bewildered.

'I don't know, really. It was too hard to explain to a small child, and everything was so wonderful in our little family. I didn't want to upset that.'

'But you're upsetting it now. Why did you lie to me? How can I trust you now?'

'I'm so sorry, Amelia.'

He looked down at the ground, shamefaced. But it was all beginning to make sense. She'd often stared into the mirror and wondered how she'd got her glossy black hair and creamy skin when her father was mousy and her mother blonde with a pale complexion. Amelia's looks and colouring bore no relation to her mother's; her mother was tall and angular where she was petite and compact.

'What was she called? My... my mother?' she asked suddenly.

'She was called Ava. She was a teacher at one of the mission schools in Calcutta. She was a kind, generous, loving person. She used to bring the children into the hospital if they were sick. That's how we met.'

'Do you have a photograph of her?' she asked.

He nodded. 'Just one. She was very beautiful. You can have it if you like. Look, I'm so sorry, Amelia... I know it's hard to bear, but Mother loves you as if you were her own daughter. You know that, don't you?'

She didn't reply, just stared at the ground for a long time, listening to the chomp-chomp of the horses, the babble of a nearby stream. Without realising it, she was uprooting clumps of grass from the bank beside her and soon there was a patch of bare earth next to the rock where she sat, and her hands were covered in soil.

He was right, she supposed. What difference did it make? Her mother loved her, and she loved her mother in return. Her mother had cared for her ever since she could remember. She knew that nothing could alter the fact that she loved both her parents fiercely. Although their silence had hurt her, she tried to understand why they had kept her in the dark and how they must feel now about telling her the truth.

She hated to see her father looking so downcast. He'd only done what he thought best, after all. She got up from the bank and turned to him. 'I'm sure I'll get used to it, Pa,' she said, trying to alleviate his guilt, 'Just give me a bit of time.'

When they got home that evening, she rushed straight to her mother and flung her arms around her. 'Pa has told me about my real mother. But I want you to know that I'll always love you and that nothing will ever change that for me,' she said.

Later that evening her father brought her a small, framed portrait of a young woman with lustrous dark hair, dressed in a simple white cotton dress. It was like looking at a slightly older, more glamorous version of herself. There were her high cheekbones, her tip-tilted eyes, her full lips. She slipped the photograph into her drawer and vowed to keep it with her always.

That had been only a few months ago, and the three of them had never mentioned it again, but it had hovered in the air between them unspoken and unresolved. Although she'd protested that nothing had changed, it had caused her to reflect on their relationships. She'd never been quite as close to her mother as she had to her father and she wondered then if that was because they were not blood relatives. She began to think about the little arguments and differences of opinion they'd had over the years and these thoughts caused her to withdraw from her mother, to put some distance between them emotionally.

She'd carried on accompanying her father on his rounds as she had been doing by then for a few years. One day though, she couldn't ride because she'd sprained her ankle, so she stayed behind while her mother took her place. It was that day that her mother and father visited a village where the inhabitants had been struck down by an outbreak of cholera. When they returned, they sent a messenger to Amelia at the bungalow to stay at home; they were going to remain isolated in the hospital until they were sure they hadn't contracted the disease.

Amelia kept away from the hospital as they'd requested, but lived for two days in terror of losing them, realising with horror that it should have been her on that ill-fated trip, if not for a silly sprained ankle. It felt as if she'd sent her mother to her certain death. On the third day, the same messenger came shuffling to the door. He handed her a note from the local doctor who worked alongside her parents.

Devastated to report that your mother and father both passed away peacefully in the night. My sincere condolences to you, they were truly noble human beings and will be mourned by everyone in this community and beyond. Doctor S. Tamang.

The blow of losing them both so suddenly was too much to bear. How she regretted the way she'd distanced herself from her mother during those last months. She stopped eating, could not sleep and became severely depressed in the space of just a few days.

Her parents were cremated on a pyre beside the river in the bottom of the valley. She'd wanted to bury them beside her father's little Baptist church, but Doctor Tamang shook his head sadly. 'With cholera we cannot bury, my child.'

He conducted the service himself. Amelia attended like a sleepwalker, alongside other workers from the hospital, and many villagers her parents had helped over the years. She could barely think coherently, let alone speak. Everyone stood forlornly beside the funeral pyre while the doctor read from the Bible, his words almost drowned out by the sound of the river in full flow, rushing over rocks down in the valley. None of it seemed real and she couldn't rid herself of the pressure that weighed down on her chest constantly, stopping her from breathing, filling her throat with pain that was more than physical.

The next day a letter arrived for her from the Mission in Calcutta.

Please accept our heartfelt condolences for the death of your parents, much loved members of our community. We have now appointed another medical missionary to replace them. Dr Joshua Williams will arrive on 15th April and will take over the residence.

She knew at once what those words meant. She had to leave there straight away. The 15th was less than a week away. She had no clear idea of what to do, but she knew she couldn't stay in Pankhabari. She knew that Doctor Tamang would ask her to, and that many of the villagers would happily give her a room, but she didn't want to stay in a place that held so many memories. She especially didn't want to stay where someone else would be occupying her home and taking over her father's role.

She packed her trunk, throwing in the beautiful silks she had collected from local bazaars, a few treasured pictures, including the one of Ava, and her mother's jewellery. On the morning of 15th April, she arranged for a pony cart to take her to Kurseong where toy trains on the Darjeeling railway ran through twice a day. She would go up to Darjeeling and make a new start.

The new medical missionary arrived earlier than she'd anticipated. He looked very young, with fresh pink cheeks straight from the English countryside and eyes full of religious fervour. He held her hand and gave her his condolences, then she handed him the keys, introduced him to the cook and the bearer and prepared to leave.

'You'd be more than welcome to stay on,' he said, hovering in the doorway. 'I've heard that a great deal of work needs to be done here to bring things up to scratch on the preaching side. It would be good to have some help.'

She shook her head, smarting at this slight to her father, thanked him curtly, and hurried down the path to her waiting tonga.

6

AMELIA

Darjeeling, India, 1935

For a few fleeting, panicky moments when she awoke, she wondered where she was. Then it all came back to her in a rush; the grief for her parents, the home where they'd been so happy for so long, and the fact that she was now completely alone in the world. And here she was, waking up in that saggy bed in the Planter's Club in Darjeeling. She sat up and forced herself out of bed, remembering her resolve of the night before. There was no time to waste if she was to find a position before she ran out of money.

There were three hospitals in Darjeeling. Amelia decided to start with the most imposing; the Eden Sanatorium was a beautiful two-storey building with verandas running the whole length of both floors, dominating a hilltop a little way out of town. She decided against paying for a tonga, acutely aware that her savings wouldn't last long unless she made some sacrifices. Instead, she walked. The route was breathtaking; along a walkway that wound around the edge of the mountain, with views out over the rooftops below and across the valley to the mountains beyond. Many British families were out for their morning walk, dressed in their best clothes, their ayahs walking behind with the children at a respectful distance. Amelia couldn't help noticing how the women in particular stared at her with ill-concealed disdain. She knew that her clothes were simple and worn, and she began to worry that she didn't look smart enough to enquire after a job.

At the hospital, she asked at the reception desk to see the matron. She waited on a hard, wooden chair in an echoing corridor until a large Englishwoman dressed in a starched nurse's uniform appeared. Amelia stood up, told the woman that she'd been working at the mission hospital in Pankhabari, that her parents, who were in the medical profession, had both died recently, and that she was looking for work. The matron looked her up and down with a caustic eye.

'Do you have qualifications?' she asked. Amelia shook her head.

'No... just experience. I worked in the hospital for several years. I'm willing to learn though, and to study,' she said quickly.

'I'm sorry, Miss Collins,' said the woman, tilting her head back and looking down her nose at Amelia, 'but we have no vacancies for unqualified staff at present. You might want to try the Indian hospital in Chowrastra. It might be more suitable for someone like you.'

Then the woman turned on her heel and strode away. Amelia watched her go, puzzled by her words. What did she mean, 'Someone like you?' But she quickly told herself that she had two more places to try, and not to give up at the first hurdle. She set off to walk the mile or so back to Chowrastra, the big, open square in the town centre. As she walked it was hard not to think about what had just happened, or feel wounded by the way the matron had treated her, especially as her grief was so raw that tears would often come unbidden anyway. But she bit her lip and walked on, determined not to be daunted.

The Indian hospital, in a narrow side street off the main square, was hot and chaotic, people crowded into a tiny waiting room, squatting on haunches in groups or lying stretched out on the bare floor. She picked her way through them to the harassed receptionist and asked if there were any vacancies for helpers. The woman turned and shouted to a colleague and in a few moments an Indian nurse appeared, her apron streaked with blood, tucking a grey hair behind her ear.

'You are more than welcome to help us out on a voluntary basis, miss, but I'm afraid we have no money to pay you,' she said.

Amelia's face fell. She would have loved to help them out, she could see that this place was crying out for people with experience like herself, but she would never survive like that. She needed paid employment.

The last hospital was a small nursing home on the road out of town towards Ghoom. It was a converted house with big windows overlooking the valley, covered in neat tea plantations and the layers of mountains beyond. But the woman on the desk shook her head quickly and told Amelia, without looking her in the eye, that there were no vacancies. Then she went back to her paperwork and left Amelia to show herself out. She walked slowly back to the Planter's Club fighting back the tears, wondering what to do.

Back at the club, it took all her courage to go into the bar. But she was thirsty after her long walk and needed a drink. It was just before lunch and all the tables were full. People stopped talking and stared openly as Amelia walked between the tables to the bar. The old Indian barman gave her a scathing look and at first was reluctant to serve her, even with a soda water.

Unable to bear the hostile looks in the bar, she took her drink out into the lobby. There was a seat in the corner beside the front entrance, and she crossed the room towards it, but then a noticeboard on the wall caught her eye. She scanned the items pinned there; rooms for rent, shared passage to England wanted, guns for sale. But there were two others that she read over and over again. One was:

"Wanted; Educated young English lady as governess to our two young children; Clarissa aged 6 and Samuel aged 8. Please apply Mrs Dunstone, Craigmore, Gleneary Road", and a second;

"Young native Englishwoman needed for the position of live-in companion to an elderly lady. Light caring duties may also be required. Apply to Lady Avery, Mountain View, Eden Hill."

Amelia scribbled down the details in her notebook and breathed a little more easily. She could do either of those jobs easily. Perhaps she would find something after all.

Her stomach was taut with hunger, but not wanting to face the hostile treatment in the bar, she went out to a food stall on the street to eat some fried noodles. In the afternoon she went up to her room and on the club writing paper wrote letters to both Mrs Dunstone and Lady Avery, careful to emphasise her background as the daughter of Baptist missionaries and her experience in the mission hospital. Feeling a little more optimistic about the future, she went out to deliver the letters by hand to ensure they would arrive straight away.

On her return to the Planter's Club, there was a commotion at the entrance; a tonga was drawn up in front of the steps and bearers were scurrying about unloading luggage. She waited patiently until they had carried it all inside, then went into the lobby and up to the desk to ask for her room key.

'Wait one moment, madam, while I register this guest,' said the old man on reception. A tall Englishman was signing the register. Amelia waited beside him and took a surreptitious look at him. She couldn't help noticing the chiselled cheekbones and the fine, distinguished lines of his face. The newcomer was tall, good looking and well-built, if a little intimidating, with black hair swept off his face and a military moustache.

'Thank you, Rajish, I shall take my normal suite,' he said, turning away from the desk, his eyes alighting on Amelia for the first time.

'Well, good afternoon!' he said, raising his eyebrows in appreciation. Amelia felt blood rushing to her cheeks.

'Good afternoon,' she said, unable to lift her eyes to his. He held out his hand.

'I don't think we've met before. I'm Reginald Holden, District Officer of Ganpur district.'

She took his hand, suddenly aware that her own was moist and clammy.

'Amelia Collins,' she said softly.

'Let's meet up in the bar later. I'll buy you a drink.'

Even in her state of embarrassed confusion, Amelia noted that it sounded more like an order than a request. She didn't have the front to refuse him. Besides, perhaps if she was with this eminent guest, the other occupants of the bar wouldn't stare at her quite so rudely as before.

'Six o' clock alright? I'll see you later,' he said, and with a slight incline of his head swept away in the direction of the stairs.

Feeling nervous, Amelia arrived a little early in the bar that evening. She'd put on her best dress, the one she'd reserved for rare special occasions at Pankhabari. It was royal blue with a scoop neck and full skirt and just putting it on boosted her confidence. Once again, the established Europeans, particularly the women, looked at her with undisguised hostility as she entered. She wondered if perhaps they were reluctant to welcome a young single woman with no family or connections in Darjeeling into their midst. Perhaps the wives felt a little resentful of her presence? Either way, she shrugged it off and maintained a serene smile as she navigated her way between the tables and found one beside the window.

As Reginald Holden entered, a hush fell over the company. He went straight up to the bar and ordered two gimlets, then joined Amelia at the table. She was amused to see eyes popping as he sat down opposite her.

'So, how did such a beautiful bloom end up in a backwater like this?' he asked crossing his elegant legs and lighting a cigar.

'Oh, I don't think Darjeeling is a backwater,' she replied. 'On the contrary, there is a lot more going on here than where I've come from.'

'Really? Hard to imagine anywhere duller. Where was that?'

'Pankhabari. A village in the hills to the south of here. My parents were medical missionaries. They established a church and a small field hospital there.'

Reginald's eyebrows shot up. 'You don't look like the daughter of missionaries,' he said. 'Far too interesting, if I may say so... but you haven't said what brings you here.'

The bearer brought the drinks to the table and Amelia took a sip. She wasn't used to alcohol; her parents had been abstemious, if not complete teetotallers, and she'd rarely tasted it. But there was something about the atmosphere of the place, and the feeling of tension she was experiencing, that made her think that a drink would relax her. And it did, even after the first sip she felt it steal through her veins, dispelling her nerves, relaxing her muscles.

She knew she had to face telling people about losing her parents and now was as good a time as any to begin. She took another sip and plunged in. She told him all about them; about the quirk of fate that had meant her mother took her place on the trip to the ill-fated village, about the cholera, about the agonising days while her mother and father were in hospital and finally about losing them.

'What a very, very sad tale,' said Reginald, shaking his head slowly. 'It's so dreadful losing your nearest and dearest. I know what you must be going through. My dear wife died around a year ago now.'

'Oh! I'm so sorry to hear that,' she said, shocked. Holden could not have been more than forty-five, so his wife must have died relatively young.

'She was taken tragically early,' he said, as if reading her thoughts. 'It's been hard to move on. Especially for our son.'

'Of course. It must have been. How old is he?'

'He's almost ten. And he's taken it very badly. She doted on the boy,' he said, then added, after a pause, 'As do I.'

They were both silent for a few moments. Amelia reflected on her surprise that she'd found an immediate source of closeness in such an unlikely candidate.

Reginald raised his glass. 'To absent friends,' he said and Amelia raised her own glass and chinked it against his.

When she went down to breakfast the next morning two letters were waiting for her on a silver platter on her table; one from Mrs Dunstone and the other from Lady Avery. Both invited her to appointments that very day. She finished her food quickly and rushed upstairs to change.

The first appointment was with Mrs Dunstone at Gleneary Road. Amelia retraced her steps from the day before, along the ridge past the zoological gardens and along a narrow road behind some beautiful colonial villas with the best views in the town. Craigmore was the last house in the road. She rang the bell with trepidation.

The bearer showed her into a drawing room with polished furniture, sofas with flowered loose covers and watercolours on the wall. It could have been anywhere in the English home counties, if it wasn't for the stunning views out over the tea plantations and rolling mountains towards the mighty peaks of Kanchenjunga.

Mrs Dunstone was middle-aged, with an angular face, a long thin nose and startlingly blonde hair. She shook Amelia's hand and as she looked into her face, her eyes widened in shock and she drew her hand away. The interview was perfunctory.

'What experience do you have of teaching children?' she asked.

'I used to teach at the Sunday school in Pankhabari,' said Amelia, trying to smile, although the sour looks from Mrs Dunstone were making her want to get up and run away.

'I mean *English* children, my dear,' Mrs Dunstone said, pointedly. 'Teaching natives is one thing. Quite another thing altogether to teach English children.'

Amelia looked down at her hands and racked her brains.

'Oh, I also used to help out at our Sunday school in Surrey too,' she remembered.

Mrs Dunstone looked down and smoothed her skirt. 'Yes, my dear, but I expect that was a very long time ago, wasn't it?'

There were a few more questions, but Amelia could tell that whatever she said in response wasn't going to please Mrs. Dunstone and that the woman was just going through the motions. When it was clear there was nothing more to ask, Mrs Dunstone said,

'Thank you. The bearer will show you out. I have other candidates to interview and I will write to you with my decision in a day or so.'

She did not get up from her chair or even look Amelia in the eye as she left. Amelia hurried away from the house, smarting with indignation. Who did the woman think she was to treat her like that? Even if she offered her the job, which she was sure wouldn't happen, Amelia wouldn't even think of taking it.

Lady Avery lived in a rambling, near derelict bungalow on the other side of town. The elderly bearer took Amelia through cluttered rooms stuffed with antique furniture, enormous pot plants and memorabilia of the Raj, to a crumbling conservatory. There, an ancient, white-haired woman sat in a wicker bath chair staring out over the mountains.

'Good morning, Lady Avery,' she said, and the old lady looked up at her and held out a bony hand.

Amelia sat down in a cane chair next to the old woman, who turned towards her, and put on a pair of pinces nez. Without speaking, she leaned forward and examined Amelia full in the face for several seconds. Finally, and with a great sigh, she said,

'I don't think you're quite right for the job, I'm afraid, my dear. I won't waste your time further.' She rang a bell on the table beside her and within seconds the old man shuffled through and waited until Amelia rose from her chair to show her out.

She let the tears fall unchecked as she walked back to the Planter's Club, devastated at the treatment she'd received and terrified that she would never find a position here with that attitude to contend with. She walked on and, oblivious to the magnificent surroundings, began to worry seriously about money. She did some convoluted calculations in her head, trying to work out how long she could last on her savings and meagre inheritance. She even considered putting her pride aside and returning to the village to work with Joshua Williams, but she knew that it was the last thing she would do; that her loyalty to her father would prevent her.

As she walked across Chowrastra, she remembered that Reginald Holden had asked her to dinner with him that evening and a feeling of warmth crept over her, dispelling for a moment all the disappointment and worry. At least there was someone who, even on one evening's acquaintance, made her feel safe and protected. She felt sure that he was a valuable ally to have and that if she confided her difficulties to him, he would go out of his way to help her.

She bought a Darjeeling Times from a newsstand and returned to her room to scan the classified columns. There were several other advertisements for companions and governesses. Perhaps one of those might be suitable. She spent a couple of hours making lists and drafting applications for jobs that looked even vaguely possible.

When she looked out of the window it was almost dark outside. It was quarter to six. She washed and changed hurriedly, applying face powder and lipstick, the only concessions to vanity she had available. She examined herself in the mirror. She was wearing her only suitable dress, the same royal blue one she'd worn the previous evening, but it couldn't be helped. Apart from that she was pleased with her appearance. Her skin glowed, despite her grief and the tribulations of the past few days, and her glossy hair still bounced around her face and shoulders.

Down in the lobby, a British man approached her.

'Ah.. Miss Collins. We haven't met. I'm John Prentice, the manager here. I've been away for a couple of days. Could you come to the desk please for a discreet word?'

She followed him, bewildered, looking around for Reginald. She didn't want to be late for their appointment.

'Now, Miss Collins, this is very awkward, I'm afraid,' said Prentice, colour rising in his cheeks. 'As I said, I've been away for a couple of days and you booked in during that time. Rajish on the desk is a trifle... shall we say, short-sighted?'

She looked at him enquiringly and he cleared his throat and glanced down at his shoes.

'Well, the fact is, I've received a couple of complaints about your presence here. As you're probably aware, the Planter's Club is a European-only establishment... so strictly you do not qualify as a resident.'

The shock drained the colour from her face and made her mouth drop open. So that was it! That was what was behind the vicious stares, the rejections, the snide comments and insinuations.

'But... but,' she stammered, 'I *am* European. I am British. My parents were both English missionaries... and – and, we've stayed here before!'

'Well, that must have been a while ago, and you must have been with your parents. Of course, there could have been no question of excluding you then and you would have been a minor at the time. Look, I'm most terribly sorry, Miss Collins. I'm going to have to ask you to leave. There are several decent Indian establishments in the town that I could recommend.'

At that moment Amelia felt something brush her shoulder, and looking round she saw that Reginald Holden was standing beside her.

'What's all this, Prentice?' he demanded. Prentice visibly shrank backwards at his words.

'Did I hear you ask her to leave?' Reginald continued without waiting for an answer. 'Now, you don't know what you're talking about, my man. Miss Collins here is as British as you and me. And what's more, she is here as my personal guest. Let's have no more discussion about this. If you force her to leave, I will leave too, and let's see what that does for your precious reputation!'

7

KATE

Warren End, April, 1970

Kate stood in the gloomy attic room, staring down at the faded marriage certificate for a long time. The wind was getting up, stirring the oak trees in the garden and whipping and howling around the eves. It was chilly in the attic, but Kate was paralysed with shock. She read the words over and over again.

"Official extract of the Marriage Register of Ganpur; On this 10th day of May 1935, marriage of Miss Amelia Collins, spinster, to Mr Reginald Holden, District Officer of this district."

That made two intriguing facts Kate had discovered about her great aunt in the space of twenty- four hours. Amelia had changed her name by deed poll when she'd returned to England, and she'd also been married to a district officer in British India 1935. How very strange that she'd never mentioned her first marriage, when she'd always seemed to be such an open person. Kate's curiosity was piqued. What other secrets had her aunt harboured for a lifetime?

Kate could still recall Amelia as she'd been when she first

met her in 1940. A fresh-faced, vibrant young woman, impossibly full of life and seemingly frank and straightforward. Uncle James had brought her to Oakwood Grange from London and Kate, her brother and their parents had been invited to dinner on that first evening to introduce her. When Amelia entered the room, Kate had immediately been struck by her unusual beauty and her obvious charm. Dressed in a tight black dress, she was petite and slim, but fashionably curvy at the same time. She'd been smiling broadly when she walked in on Uncle James' arm, her beautiful brown eyes lit up with happiness, an exquisite diamond ring on her finger. She'd greeted everyone warmly, speaking to each member of the family in turn, giving her whole attention to that person, as if she was genuinely interested in what they had to say.

When she'd been introduced to Kate she'd taken her hand and said, 'My, you look grown-up for an eleven-year-old. I can see you're going to be breaking hearts in a few years' time.'

Kate had felt her cheeks growing pink with embarrassment and pleasure and, unusually for her, had been lost for words. Her mother was looking down at her with disapproving eyes which increased her shyness. Kate's father and her brother Roy had both been star-struck too, her father going pink and muttering some welcoming words and Roy's puppy-dog eyes following Amelia round the room wherever she went.

Amelia and Uncle James were married within a few months of that first meeting. It was a quiet, family affair presided over by Reverend Lewis, the Warren End vicar, with tea for a select few at Oakwood Grange afterwards. Amelia hadn't wanted anything extravagant, given that it was wartime, which had surprised Kate a little at the time. A few months afterwards Uncle James was elected to Parliament at a by-election as the member for Buckinghamshire North. After the wedding, he whisked Amelia off for a weekend in Brighton after which he rented a flat in Westminster where the two of them would stay during the week while Parliament was sitting.

'She wanted a quiet wedding, but she'll be hard-pushed to avoid the limelight now, that one,' remarked Freda unkindly, but Kate noticed that Amelia rarely, if ever, appeared in newspaper pictures beside Uncle James, never gave interviews herself and always took a back seat when her husband opened village fetes or gave speeches. Kate had often wondered about that. It seemed odd and out of character; Amelia was naturally charming and outgoing, so what was behind her reticence to appear in the public eye?

'She's not straightforward, like I said,' Freda would say darkly, and now, twenty-five years on, Kate was beginning to think there was some truth in her mother's words. But what had Amelia been hiding?

Now Kate's mind wandered back to the last time she'd seen Amelia. It was at Freda's funeral three years ago in Saxmundham in Suffolk. Kate had been distracted and feeling very low herself, but she'd been shocked at the change in her great aunt. Amelia had aged dramatically. Her skin that had once bloomed with health was lined and saggy. Her hair was steel grey and her eyes had lost their sparkle. Although she would have only been in her late fifties, she had the appearance of a much older woman and already walked with a stoop. She'd seemed vague and distant when Kate had tried to open up a conversation with her. It was as if she could barely remember anything about Kate and how they'd been so close when she'd first come to Warren End. Kate couldn't help noticing that Amelia's breath reeked of alcohol that day, even though the funeral was held in the morning.

Now Kate wondered why Amelia had aged so quickly and had died so young. Had the secrets she'd been harbouring for years finally destroyed her?

Shivering in the draughty attic room, she closed the trunk carefully. Then she gathered up the letters and photographs, tucked the electric fire under her arm, and took them all down the two flights of stairs to the drawing room. There, she plugged in the fire and, sitting down on the armchair nearest to it, pulled a rug over her knees and settled down to read the letters.

The first one was dated March 1937.

My Dearest Amelia,

I'm so glad to hear that your journey went well and that you have found a good position at the Russell Hotel in London. Giles and I have been praying for your safe arrival in England since the day you left so you can imagine how relieved we were to receive your letter. Of course, I have destroyed it as you suggested, in case it should get into the wrong hands. Please have no fear on that score. Your secret is completely safe with the two of us as you know.

Since you left Ganpur, we have had very little contact with R, and we will keep it that way if possible. There was a memorial service at the cantonment church yesterday, and although we attended, we remained at the back of the church and did not go to the reception afterwards.

Giles has been kept very busy tending to the sick in and around the station. Malaria has been running rife this rainy season as has diphtheria. He has tried to save as many souls as he can, but as you know the conditions here make it a losing battle particularly in the outlying villages where people are so poor and conditions so basic.

Do you remember that day Ali took a photograph of us after tiffin on our porch at Ganpur? It seems so long ago and so much has happened since then. I thought you'd like the photograph as a reminder of one happy day amongst all the sadness, so I'm enclosing it for you to keep.

The arrests and independence demonstrations are going on much as before, but I won't trouble you with the details as I know how distressing you find it all.

Do write back and tell me how life is treating you in Blighty and I'm hoping that one day we will meet up again, God willing.

With love

Mabel.

Kate read the letter a couple of times before slipping it back into its envelope. Then, ensuring she was looking at them in order, she took each letter out of its envelope and began to read them through. There were a lot of letters from Mabel. At least one per month for several years. But after the first few, Kate began to tire of reading them. The first was by far the most interesting; the others were about cantonment life, gossip about British people in Ganpur; who'd had had a baby, who had got married and who had died. There were long descriptions of the outbreaks of disease and illnesses that Giles was battling against, and a few references to the independence movement. None of the names Mabel wrote about meant anything to Kate, and there was little allusion to Amelia's circumstances, what had caused her to leave Ganpur, or to the mysterious "R" again. Kate had read ten by the time her eyes were drooping and she was ready to give up and go to bed. She realised that this source of information, however promising it had appeared at the outset, wasn't going to yield up the key to Amelia's secrets. She packed up the letters, resolving to continue reading them the next day, and went upstairs to bed.

In the morning, she awoke with a headache. Perhaps it was the tension of the funeral or having sat up late into the night to read Mabel Harris' letters. Realising she had no painkillers, she put on her raincoat and boots and set off on foot towards the village shop. It was a blustery day and she walked quickly, hunched against the cold and the sporadic rain. She'd almost forgotten

what Warren End was like in cold weather; in her mind's eye it
was always sunny there, just like during that long, hot summer
of 1944, every day of which was seared indelibly into her
memory.

To get to the shop she had to walk past the house where she
was born and had lived until the autumn of 1944. It was stone-
built, Victorian, in the same style as the school itself that stood
behind it, set back from the village street. She sensed that the
headmaster of the village school no longer lived here, and that
the house had been sold off, like so many in the village, to
commuters. Children were being dropped off by their parents at
the school gates, many of them arriving in cars and pulling up
on the pavement.

Kate put her head down against the rain and was about to
hurry on. Out of the corner of her eye she saw someone she was
almost sure she recognised and her heart missed a beat. It was a
woman, about her own age, pushing a toddler in a pushchair,
bending down to kiss a young boy before he ran gleefully up the
drive and into the school with a group of other children. The
woman was still short but no longer skinny; on the contrary, she
was stout, her calves were wide, her ankles overflowing the tops
of her shoes, the hem of her too-short dress stretched around
her thighs. She still had short, dark hair, but now it was back-
combed in a style that had gone out a few years before. Kate was
standing just across the road, watching her as she bent to speak
to the child, her heart thumping, her mouth dry. Should she
cross the road and say 'hello'? Could she just do that as casually
as if they'd seen each other the day before? And as if they didn't
share that terrible, guilty secret that had driven them apart and
meant they'd not spoken since Kate had left the village.

The woman suddenly looked up, glanced at Kate momentarily, frowned slightly, then turned and pushed the pushchair back
in the direction of Clerks' Lane without looking back. Had Joan

recognised her? Kate knew that she herself had aged well. She'd kept her figure trim and her fair hair was cut in the latest style. Someone who had known her when she was in her mid-teens would probably still recognise her now. So why hadn't Joan come over to speak to her? Probably for the same reasons she hadn't crossed the road to say hello to Joan; guilt and regret and not wanting to confront the memory of a painful experience.

Kate walked on towards the shop, her eyes on the road, trying not to think back to that summer, trying not to wonder why Joan had got so dumpy and looked so downtrodden. The shop was now a shiny new Co-op with wide, self-service aisles. It had been expanded and updated and was a far cry from the shop Kate remembered from the 1940s where customers queued behind a counter and point to the goods they wanted. She bought some aspirins and swallowed them straight away. They stuck in her throat and tasted bitter without water.

She hovered outside the shop for a few moments, wondering which way to return to Oakwood Grange. She knew the most sensible route was to go back the way she had come, but the pull of the past was calling her in the other direction. Struggling with conflicting emotions, she set off to walk back by the other route, which took in Clerks' Lane. Curiosity was compelling her to go that way.

She walked along the street past a row of cottages which had changed little since the forties, except, like the rest of the houses in the village, they appeared to be better maintained now. They looked out over a big, open stretch of common land which sloped downwards towards a small valley through which a brook ran. This field had always been known as the Warren, and from it, the village had taken its name. At the top of the hill on the far side of the Warren, stood the church, and beside that a large red-brick house where the Robinson sisters had lived. In the old days it had been a shabby, forbidding sight, covered in rambling ivy, with holes in the roof and some of the windows boarded up. But, even from this distance it was clear that it had been restored to its original glory; the roof and the windows had been renewed and the ivy removed. Looking at it reminded her of old Edna Robinson, and the strange things she'd said about Amelia at the funeral. With a shudder, Kate remembered the rasp of her voice and the urgently whispered words, *'Your aunt was a very troubled girl in those days...She had been through so much, you know.'* Those words, alongside the discoveries Kate had made about her aunt only added to her mystery, and to the growing urge to get to the bottom of Amelia's secrets.

She walked on and soon reached the bottom of Clerks' Lane. Slowly and tentatively, she began to walk up it, between the high hedges, but as soon as she'd rounded the first bend she realised that it had changed a good deal since she'd left. A row of modern council bungalows had been built at this end of the lane where before there had been a field and some scrubby farm buildings. They had neat front gardens with concrete paths and had the appearance of sheltered housing. Was this where George Prendergast lived now? A net curtain in one of the windows twitched. She hurried on not wanting him to spot her staring. Even after all this time, she'd no desire to speak to him.

The long row of estate cottages where Joan's family had lived in the forties was still there at the top of the lane. Unlike most other cottages in the village these hadn't been gentrified. The front gardens were bare and unkempt; in one a rusting Ford Anglia stood on bricks, in another an upturned fridge lay abandoned in an overgrown flowerbed. Ragged curtains hung in the windows, some cracked, others patched up with cardboard. Outside one front door with peeling paint, a pushchair had been left out in the rain. With a start Kate recognised it as the one she'd seen Joan pushing outside the school. She stood in the lane outside the broken front gate for a couple of seconds, thinking about Joan, wondering what her life was like now.

The front door opened and Joan emerged, a cigarette drooping from one side of her mouth. She bent down to get something out of the pushchair and as she straightened up, and noticed Kate standing there, she gave a start and her expression hardened.

'I saw you staring at me outside the school,' she said, walking towards the gate, arms folded defensively, eyes flashing. 'What do you want?'

Then she stopped a couple of yards in front of Kate. 'Good God!'

'It's me. Kate Hamilton. Didn't you recognise me before?'

Joan shook her head and took a long drag on her cigarette. 'I thought there was something familiar about you, but I didn't clock. It's been a long time.'

'Yes... a very long time.'

They locked eyes for a long moment, and Kate was instantly transported back to that summer of '44, to the friendship they'd enjoyed, the confidences and the laughs they'd shared, the highs and the lows, and the final, devastating blow that had torn them apart. The look in Joan's eyes told her that she was back there too, but Kate noticed something disturbing. There was a livid red mark on Joan's cheekbone and a bruise under her fringe, both partially hidden with foundation. Kate dropped her gaze.

'Why don't you come in for a coffee?' asked Joan. 'We could catch up. You'll catch your death out here.'

'Alright.'

Kate pushed open the gate which caught and scraped on the concrete path and followed Joan towards the house. As she went, Joan bent down and retrieved a muddy teddy bear from the scrubby lawn.

'Come on in. You'll have to excuse the mess. Kids!'

The house held that smell that reminded Kate powerfully of Joan's own childhood home, only a few cottages along from this one. Old cooking oil, woodsmoke and dirty drains. She followed Joan into the kitchen, a small, chilly room with quarry tiles on the floor. A yellow Formica table stood in the middle, and around the edge, a couple of tall kitchen cabinets and a large sink with a wooden draining board. Every surface was stacked with dirty dishes. On the table were open boxes of breakfast cereal, used bowls with spilt milk around them and an over-flowing ashtray. Joan began to clear the table, shoving the dishes into the sink and wiping the surface carelessly with an old grey dishcloth.

'Sit down,' she indicated, lighting another cigarette. 'Do you smoke?'

'I gave up a couple of years back.'

Kate pulled out a chair and sat down at the table. This felt surreal. How many times over the years had she imagined meeting Joan again? But in her mind's eye, it had never been in surroundings like these.

'I'll put the kettle on. I've only got instant I'm afraid,' said Joan, lighting an old-fashioned gas stove in the corner.

'Instant's just fine.'

Joan sat down opposite her and drew on her cigarette, eyeing Kate with a level gaze. It was unnerving and Kate looked away, but it was the first indication that the old Joan was still there; the old, clever, perceptive Joan, inside that body that had grown out of all proportion and that pudgy face that looked beaten and exhausted.

'I suppose you came back for your aunt's funeral?' asked Joan, blowing smoke into the air.

'That's right. I'm going to clear out her house. Get it on the market.' Kate stopped short of telling Joan that Amelia had left her the house.

'Big old place that. A lot of work, I bet.'

Kate smiled. 'Yes. I've taken a month off work, though, so I'll be around for a while.'

Joan frowned, blowing smoke out through her nostrils. 'So, what is it you do exactly? Accountant or something, I heard.'

'Architect.'

Joan raised her eyebrows. 'You always did have talent. You could have done anything you wanted.'

'So could you,' Kate replied and Joan let out a short, sardonic laugh.

'But I didn't, did I?' She leaned forward, still smiling, but there was a bitter edge to her voice. 'Ended up just like me mum. No qualifications. Burdened with a load of kids and nothing to show for anything.'

'Oh, but surely...' Kate began to protest.

'Did you have any yourself?' Joan cut in and Kate shook her head.

'No. I... I left it too late,' she muttered, not meeting Joan's eye. But that wasn't quite the truth. She could have done things differently. She could have settled down, got married and had children, but for some reason she could never let anyone get close enough for that to happen. She'd sabotaged relationship after relationship through wilful neglect, focusing too much on her career, on forging ahead. It had been far easier to concentrate on something that was predictable and rewarding, that enabled her to be completely self-sufficient, than to let anyone else in or admit to needing them.

'The opposite to me, then,' said Joan. 'I've got six of the so and sos.'

'Six! How old are they?'

'Two daughters aged twenty-two and twenty. The eldest one's married herself now, then another girl of eighteen, then three boys – fifteen, nine and three.'

'Goodness,' Kate didn't know what to say. The gulf that had opened up between them all those years ago seemed only to have widened over time.

The kettle began to whistle, starting softly and building to a piercing crescendo. Joan leapt up, stubbed her cigarette out and rushed over to take it off the cooker.

'God! It'll wake little Anthony,' she said. 'He's having his nap.'

Joan made the coffee on the counter, heaping granules into two mugs, slopping the water as she poured it. 'Milk and sugar?' she asked.

'Just milk, please.'

'Well!' Joan handed Kate a mug and sat down opposite her. 'It's been so long, it's difficult to know where to start.'

'It is,' agreed Kate, thinking back. Should she mention that last summer? She had no desire to, but she had the feeling that they would never be able to talk properly unless they did at least acknowledge it. It was like a huge black cloud that hovered over them. From the expression in Joan's eyes, she could tell that Joan was thinking the same thing. But when she spoke, Joan neatly side-stepped the issue.

'So, where was it you moved to? You and your mum and dad?'

'East Anglia. Near a little town called Saxmundham. We liked it there, actually. We lived in a village. A bit like this one, to tell you the truth.'

'Only *not* quite like this one,' Joan countered, her steady eyes on Kate's again, that unnerving, knowing look that made Kate feel like a butterfly under a pin.

'Not quite, no,' Kate admitted quietly, looking down into her coffee where black granules circled on the surface.

'So, have you seen anyone you know since you've been back?'

Kate took a sip of the bitter brew.

'A few people at my aunt's funeral. Ladies from the W.I., I don't remember all their names. Old Miss Robinson, and Janet of course. Janet Andrews.'

'Oh, lovely lady, Janet,' smiled Joan. 'She sometimes helps me out with the kids.'

Kate couldn't help her eyes wandering to the marks on Joan's face. It was hard to believe that the Joan she had known, with all her spirit and verve, could have become a victim like her own mother; a battered wife.

'What about your husband?' Kate blurted out without thinking. There was an immediate transformation in Joan's expression. The vague smile she'd worn when speaking of Janet vanished and she frowned.

'What about him?' she asked in an aggressive tone.

'I...I don't know. I just wondered who he was, that's all... If I knew him at all.'

'Oh. You might remember him, yes. He's a bit older than us. Used to hang around the village with the other lads. Dave Pope. That's his name.'

Kate was silent for a moment, trying to remember. And then it came to her. He was one of those boys who used to jostle her and taunt her in the street for being the headmaster's daughter. In fact, he might have been one of those Joan herself stood up to that first day the two of them had renewed their friendship. Tall and dark-haired, good looking in a rough sort of way, with an angular face and sly eyes.

'I do remember him, yes. Of course I do. So... what does Dave do now?'

'Works in the meat factory. In the abattoir to be precise.'

Kate shuddered. There was nothing good she could think of to say about that. No pleasantry she could conjure to fit the image.

'Drinks too much, like me dad,' Joan went on, lifting her

chin and meeting Kate's eyes with that arrow-straight look again. It was like a challenge. As if Joan was willing her to say something about the marks on her face.

Kate returned Joan's stare, wondering what she should say. Then she decided to be brave. She opened her mouth, but before the words were out, a wailing sound came from upstairs.

'That's Anthony,' Joan said, getting up hastily and going to the bottom of the stairs. Turning to Kate, she said,

'Look, I'm sorry, but he's shy of strangers, especially when he's just woken up...'

Kate got to her feet. 'Of course. I'll go then. It was lovely to see you, and thanks for the coffee. Look...'

Joan was hovering in the doorway, 'Yes?' she snapped. The crying from upstairs grew louder.

'If there's anything I can do to help...' she knew as soon as the words were out of her mouth that it was the wrong thing to say.

'Help?' asked Joan sharply. 'Whyever should I need *your* help?'

'I meant... if you ever want to talk,' Kate stammered.

'Talking isn't going to change what happened back then,' Joan snapped. It was out in the open, the spell had been broken.

'I know that,' said Kate, desperately searching for the right words. 'But I meant talk about anything. Anything at all. Not just about the past.'

The screaming upstairs had increased to fever pitch. 'Mum, Mum!'

'I think you'd better go now. You can let yourself out,' Joan said coldly, turning away and running up the stairs.

8

KATE

Warren End, Summer, 1944

Kate awoke with a start. The sun was bright in the gaps in the blackout curtains and she scrambled out of bed to pull them open. It was a beautiful day. Just like all the other glorious days that summer. Above the thatched roofs opposite, the cloudless sky was a startling blue and the cottages were drenched in sunlight, their stone walls glowing a rich golden colour.

She had that delicious feeling of anticipation that she always had before a day out in the countryside with Joan. But in the back of her mind there was a niggling concern that she couldn't immediately pin down. Something was telling her that she couldn't relax and be happy that day. Then she noticed the clothes she'd pulled on to run out after her mother the night before, thrown on the floor, her plimsolls covered in mud. It came back to her then, the wrecked barns at Warren Hall and the frantic search for survivors, her shock when the body had been pulled out of the devastated building, the deathly pale face covered in blood and the blank, staring eyes.

Kate's mother had gone with him in the ambulance, but Kate was almost certain there was little hope he would survive.

'Poor, poor Joan,' she muttered as the memories surfaced, a great lump forming in her throat. She wanted to cry for her friend, but no tears would come.

Downstairs, her mother and father sat in shocked silence over breakfast.

'What happened to Joan's dad?' she asked, sitting down and eyeing the meagre fare. White bread toast, margarine and home-made jam. She didn't feel hungry.

Her father put his hand over hers and looked into her eyes.

'He died, Katie, love. He was killed outright by the falling beams.'

'Why did they take him to hospital, then?' she protested. 'I thought there might at least be a chance...'

'It's normal procedure,' said her mother.

'What about Joan and the family?' asked Kate.

'I went round there to break the news to Mrs Bartram earlier,' said her father. 'The vicar is driving her over to the hospital this morning.'

'How *awful*,' said Kate, unable to understand what it might feel like to lose your father like that.

'I need to go and see Joan,' she said, getting up. She had to do something. She couldn't just sit there, eating toast and jam as if nothing had happened.

'There's nothing you can do, love. Why don't you eat your breakfast and go round later on, maybe?' said her mother.

'I don't want any breakfast,' said Kate, getting up from the table and rushing from the room.

She cycled the few yards round to Joan's cottage in Clerks' Lane and propped her bike up against the front fence next to Joan's. The house was unnaturally silent and there were butterflies in Kate's stomach as she knocked on the door. What would she say? Would they even want to see her? People in her class at school had lost their fathers in the war; three at Dunkirk, two more at D-Day. The girls had come to school pale and red-eyed, and everyone had given them sympathetic looks at first, but had gradually started to avoid them, not knowing what to say. Kate had been just the same and she felt guilty now, but she hadn't been close to those girls like she was to Joan.

At last the door was opened by Joan's older brother, Sam. His eyes were red raw and his nose was running.

He peered at her as if confused by her presence. Kate asked if Joan was in and he opened the door wider. She stepped into the hallway. Through the open door to the living room, she could see Mrs Lewis, the vicar's wife, cradling two of the younger Bartram children on her lap.

'She's up in her room,' Sam said, jerking his head in the direction of the stairs.

Kate went up the bare wooden stairs which were cluttered with toys and piles of laundry. Joan's room was at the front of the house. She shared it with her two little sisters. Kate knocked on the door. There was silence for a moment, then Joan said,

'Who is it?'

'It's me, Kate.'

There was another pause, then Joan said, 'Come in.'

She was sitting on the edge of the bed, in a faded, pink cotton nightie. Her face was so white it appeared almost translucent. Her eyes were rimmed with red, but she wasn't crying. She looked up at Kate, her face expressionless.

'I'm sorry about your dad,' said Kate, sitting down beside Joan and putting an arm around her. Joan stiffened and didn't yield to Kate's touch.

'You must be feeling awful,' said Kate, aware that there was nothing she could say to make things better.

'I'm not,' Joan snapped. 'I'm not feeling anything.'

Kate wasn't prepared for this. She fell silent, not knowing how to respond.

'The truth is, I won't miss him,' said Joan. 'I won't miss him one jot. In fact I'm *glad* he's gone.'

Kate took her arm away, shocked. 'Oh, you can't mean that.'

'I do! I know I should be upset, but I'm not,' Joan said. 'He was a bastard. I've told you before. He used to hit mum and me, and the others too, except Sam, who's too big.'

'I know,' said Kate gently. She wanted to say *but he was still your dad*, but resisted. It made it sound as if she didn't understand how Joan felt, that she was judging her.

Joan carried on talking. She spoke quickly, in a low voice, as if she needed to get the words out, 'He'd got such a temper on him. He'd fly off the handle at the slightest thing. Especially when he'd been down the pub. He hit me once just for looking at him wrong, once for forgetting to buy something on the shopping list, once for doing my homework late and having the light on. Anything would set him off. It was like living with a volcano, living with that sod.'

It all came out in a rush; how he'd beaten Joan's mother many times while the children cowered in the corner, how he'd smashed a doll Joan had got for Christmas when she was tiny because she'd wet her knickers. Kate sat mute, shock preventing her from saying anything. It was so distressing, part of her wished Joan would stop, but she sensed it was helping Joan to talk like this.

In the end Joan fell silent. Kate put her arm around her again, squeezing her tight. This time Joan didn't stiffen up, she leaned against Kate and put her head on her shoulder, and they sat there together on the edge of Joan's bed in the same position for what seemed like an age. The sound of Joan's younger siblings grizzling and whining, and Mrs Lewis' voice as she tried to soothe them floated up the stairs.

Finally, Joan lifted her head and rubbed at her face.

'Let's go out,' she said standing up. 'I can't stand it in here anymore.'

'Don't you want to be here when your mum gets back from the hospital?' asked Kate.

'Sam will be here. He's her favourite. Anyway, who knows when she'll be back.'

'Alright...' Kate wasn't sure about it, but she normally let Joan have her way, and that day, even more than before, she was willing to give in to her.

'Go on out then,' Joan said, hands on her hips impatiently, 'While I get changed.'

Kate stood on the landing outside Joan's room while she waited, noticing the torn wallpaper on the wall opposite, the jagged hole that had been kicked in a door, the mess of blankets, dirty clothes and broken toys in the back bedroom.

Joan emerged wearing trousers and a short-sleeved blouse and Kate followed her downstairs. As Joan opened the front door, Sam's voice came from the kitchen.

'Where the 'ell do you think you're going?'

'Out,' said Joan.

'Oh no you ain't,' he said. 'Not with me dad lying stone dead in the hospital.'

'Try stopping me,' she said defiantly. Sam came out of the kitchen and went to grab Joan, but she ducked under his arm and was down the garden path in a flash. Kate, feeling awkward, ran after her.

'Quick!'

They grabbed their bikes and started off down the lane with Sam shouting after them, but Kate didn't look back.

'Let's go to Willow Mill,' said Joan as they reached the edge of the village.

'It's a long way... are you sure?'

'Yes. It's nice there. It feels miles away from... from all this,' Joan said, waving her arm back in the direction of the village. Kate knew exactly what she meant. Going to the mill was like stepping into another world and leaving everything behind, the village, their families and all their problems, and the war. They could make believe there, that nothing bad or violent or upsetting was happening anywhere.

This time they took a risk and cut through on the private road, past the abandoned farmhouse and the barns and stables where George Prendergast had yelled at them the day they'd discovered the mill. The gamble paid off. The place was empty, the stables and barn were closed up and the old house appeared as forlorn and deserted as ever.

'He'll be too busy clearing up after the bombing to be out and about today,' Joan said as they freewheeled down the hill towards the river. Kate didn't reply. The image of Frank Bartram being pulled from the rubble came back to her again, his staring eyes, the blood on his forehead. How could Joan speak about the air raid so casually? But she knew Joan was just putting on a front, pretending, perhaps even to herself, that she didn't care.

They reached the bottom of the hill and turned right along the valley towards the mill. They normally hid their bikes behind a hedge at the start of the overgrown track that led from the road through the wood towards the mill. They opened the gate and wheeled them through. There were tyre tracks on the ground and two cars were parked just inside the gate, tucked away out of sight of the lane, partially hidden by branches. The girls stood stock still, staring at them. George Prendergast's silver-grey Bentley and beside it Amelia's claret coloured Austin. There was no doubting it now.

'It's Prendergast and that woman again,' whispered Joan. 'Let's hide here and wait for them to come back.'

Kate's heart started to beat faster, anxiety mounting inside.

'What if they see us?' she protested weakly.

Joan shrugged. 'They won't. We can hide our bikes over there and wait behind this bush.'

She wheeled her bike a little way along the hedge, round a huge thicket of brambles where the hedge was overgrown, and leaned it up against it on the other side. 'Come on! They could come back any time.'

Miserably, and not knowing how to stop Joan, especially on this day of all days, Kate followed her. She leaned her bike up against Joan's and pushed them both back into the bush so that they were hidden by the brambles.

'I don't think this is a good idea, Joan,' she began, her heart in her mouth now. But Joan ignored her and went to crouch behind a bush from where there was a view of the two parked cars.

Kate crouched down beside her and they waited, silently. Their faces were so close that Kate breathed in the sour smell of Joan's breath, the smell of sweat on her clothes. Kate was dreading the moment when her aunt would appear through the woods with Prendergast. Would they link arms as they walked? Would she kiss him goodbye? A shudder went through her at the prospect.

They didn't have to wait long. The sound of voices came to them through the trees. A man's and a woman's. Joan gripped Kate's arm. 'Here they come,' she said, her eyes shining. Kate hung her head, held her breath and waited.

The two figures approached and as they came closer it was immediately clear that the woman was Aunt Amelia. She was wearing a headscarf again so her hair was hidden, but her features were unmistakeable. The colour drained from Joan's face and she turned to Kate.

'It's your auntie!' she breathed.

At least they weren't holding hands, but as Amelia passed

the bush where the girls were crouching, it was clear that her cheeks were wet with tears. Her face was a picture of misery, her brows knitted into a frown. She went towards her car without a word, got inside and slammed the door. Prendergast pulled the gate back and Amelia started the engine and accelerated through the narrow gap and out onto the lane. The engine strained as she roared away.

George Prendergast leaned against his own car and lit a cigarette. He had a smug smile on his face and as he stood there smoking, he took something out of his pocket, the smile broadening. It was a small leather bag. He unzipped it and peered inside. Then he started laughing out loud.

Joan stared at Kate wide-eyed.

'She's given him something. A keepsake,' she whispered.

'But... but she was crying...' protested Kate.

'Perhaps she was trying to tempt him back with a present. Who knows?'

Prendergast put the bag into the back of the car and finished his cigarette. Then he got in and with much manoeuvring swung the big vehicle out through the gate. He stopped in the lane and returned to shut the gate. The girls held their breath until he was back in the car. It was only when the sound of the Bentley's engine had died away did the two girls get up and stretch their limbs, dust the twigs and grass from their knees.

'I didn't know it was your auntie!' said Joan, outrage in her voice still. Kate hung her head.

'I thought it might be. I had a feeling before that it was her,' she admitted.

'Well, why didn't you say something?'

'I didn't want it to be her. I was hoping it wasn't. My uncle is a lovely man. I can't believe she would do something like that.'

They began to walk towards the mill, but as before when

Prendergast and Amelia had been there, the joy had gone out of the day.

'You've got to face it, though. It's obvious. They've been having a lovers' tiff, otherwise she wouldn't look so upset. She's given him a present in that zip-up bag. He's using her and he's pretty pleased with himself too.'

Although Kate was desperate for it not to be true, she could think of no other explanation for Amelia meeting George Prendergast down here at the abandoned mill at least three times over the past few weeks, and perhaps many more. The tears on her face, the way she'd driven off, it all added up to the same thing.

They reached the mill, went inside and up to the top floor where Joan pulled their blankets out from their storage place in the old chimney.

'Let's go and sit by the river,' Joan said, and Kate followed her out to their favourite bank.

They sat down side-by-side on a blanket under the hot sun. The river looked inviting, but Kate didn't feel like swimming.

'We need to do something about it,' said Joan, returning to the subject that Kate wanted to drop.

'What do you suggest we do about it?' she asked quietly, dreading the answer.

'We need to tell them about it. His wife and her husband. They need to know.'

Kate sat upright, shock coursing through her. 'They do *not* need to know,' she said. 'It's none of our business, Joan. My uncle would be devastated if he found out. He's not that young, you know.'

'It's only right that they know,' Joan said, lifting her chin, 'And now that we know, it's up to us to tell them.'

Kate rounded on Joan then, she grabbed her by both arms and shook her hard, staring into her eyes.

'Don't you dare tell them. Why do you want to make people unhappy? It's not fair...' she was shouting at Joan now, losing control. To her surprise, Joan's eyes filled with tears, her face crumpled and she started crying. Great, gulping, hysterical sobs. Her nose was streaming and her face was soon wet with tears.

'Don't shout at me. Don't do that to me!' she said, 'Me dad used to do that. Shake me. He used to shake me until I thought me neck would snap. And now he's gone and he won't ever do it to me again...'

She flung herself down on the blanket and lay there sobbing, her shoulders heaving, her throat rasping every time she took a breath. Kate had never heard her cry before. She put a hand on Joan's shoulder and rubbed her back gently, trying to soothe her.

'I'm so sorry,' she said. 'I didn't mean to upset you,' but nothing she could say would make Joan stop, so Kate let her carry on until she'd cried herself out. Finally, Joan sat up and rubbed her eyes.

'Let's go home,' she said. 'I don't want to be here anymore.'

They folded the blanket and Kate took it upstairs to its hiding place. Then, they walked back to their bikes in silence and set off towards the village. Kate tried mumbling apologies a few times as they rode, but Joan said nothing in response. This time they didn't risk the short-cut through the abandoned farm, but instead went round the long way. By the time they arrived at Joan's house, Kate was hot and thirsty.

'You can come in for a drink if you like,' said Joan. 'I don't mind.'

It seemed to be her way of telling Kate that she'd forgiven her and that things were back to normal between them. Kate had no desire to see Mrs Bartram or any of the others, but she followed Joan inside anyway, sensing that it was important to Joan for her to go in.

Mrs Bartram was sitting on the torn settee in the sparse

living room, a tiny child on her lap, Joan's small brothers and sisters playing around her feet. Her face was white and her eyes bloodshot. In her hand she held an official-looking letter.

'What's that, Mum?' asked Joan. Kate stood awkwardly beside her in the doorway.

'Eviction notice,' muttered Mrs Bartram. 'Prendergast just delivered it. Now Frank's gone we can't live here no more. The cottage is tied to his job and they'll need it for the new gamekeeper.'

'Oh, Mum! Where can we go?' Joan rushed over to her mother, sat down beside her and put her arms around her.

'Search me. I just don't know at the moment.' Great tears spilled from Mrs Bartram's eyes and ran down her careworn cheeks. She didn't bother to brush them away.

Joan took the letter from her mother's hands and scanned it quickly.

'Prendergast's a bloody bastard,' she said, looking straight at Kate. 'He deserves to pay for this now. He doesn't deserve no mercy.'

9

AMELIA

Darjeeling, 1935

Amelia couldn't work out how she felt about Reginald Holden stepping in and standing up for her when John Prentice, the manager of the Planter's Club asked her to leave. Part of her was as humiliated by Reginald's behaviour as she was by Mr Prentice's. Why did Reginald feel the need to lie by saying that she was here as his guest? What assumption was he making when he said that? Didn't that compromise her and humiliate her in a different, more subtle way than Mr Prentice's own implication that she was of mixed race and therefore not welcome as a guest in the club?

She stood in the lobby, staring from one man to the other. Reginald was taller, larger framed, more imposing and of course far more important than John Prentice.

'Well, of course, Mr Holden,' said Prentice, 'If Miss Collins is here with *you*, there can be no question of her having to leave. I'm *so* sorry. There must have been a dreadful mistake somewhere along the line.'

The man was fawning now, holding his hands together as if

in prayer, almost bowing to Reginald, his face red and flustered. 'If you'd like to go straight through to the bar, Mr Holden, please allow me to offer you drinks on the house this evening.'

'Alright, Prentice,' said Reginald, 'Let's hear no more of that ridiculous talk. And we'll take you up on that offer of drinks.'

With that, he took Amelia's arm and propelled her towards the bar. Amelia allowed him to guide her, still in a state of shock, not knowing whether to be grateful or annoyed by Reginald's intervention. They entered the bar and as she walked on his arm between the tables, people looked up and when their eyes lit on her they frowned indignantly, but on noticing Reginald beside her, their faces took on that ingratiating, obsequious look that Amelia had seen in Prentice's eyes a moment before.

When they were seated at the table beside the window and waiting for their first cocktails to arrive, Amelia finally found her voice.

'Why did you say that to the manager?' she asked. 'Why did you say that I'm your guest?'

Reginald leaned back in his chair and lit a cigar. 'Why?' he asked, his eyes playful. 'Would you rather have had to leave?'

She looked down, resenting his amusement.

'Of course not. But... the fact is. We hardly know each other. It makes it look...' she felt a flush rising in her cheeks.

'Compromising?'

She dropped her gaze, too embarrassed to answer.

'Oh, don't be so old fashioned,' he said. 'It doesn't look anything of the sort. After all, I'm practically old enough to be your father.'

Now, embarrassment was replaced with pain. The thought of the loss of her beloved parents, on top of all the indignities she'd suffered over the past couple of days, brought an immediate lump to her throat.

'I'm so sorry,' said Reginald, slipping his hand over hers on the table. 'That was tactless of me. I didn't mean any harm by that remark. I was merely pointing out that there is a large age difference between us and it is unlikely that people will jump to the conclusions you're worrying about.'

Amelia blinked hard and swallowed her tears. The bearer bustled up with two gimlets. She took a large gulp of hers to settle her nerves. The alcohol rushed through her veins, making her limbs feel heavy, calming her mind. Perhaps, after all, Reginald was only being kind when he'd said what he'd said to Prentice. She watched him as he sipped his drink. Was it better to take the snubs and prejudice she'd experienced that day in her stride and accept his protection, or to go upstairs and pack and take herself straight off to an Indian hotel?

It had never entered her mind previously that British India could be so intolerant. She'd never been the subject of discrimination before, not down in Pankhabari, where the villagers were naturally welcoming and tolerant, and not back in England either, where everyone had just accepted her as one of them without question. She was beginning to realise that these bigoted members of the old guard had their antennae finely tuned to detect anyone of mixed blood, no matter how dilute that connection was. Their refusal to accept anyone even remotely Indian must be because they felt their own world slipping away.

'You don't need to worry, Miss Collins,' Reginald said, breaking into her thoughts. 'Your secret is safe with me.'

'Secret?' she asked, alarm surging through her.

He closed his eyes momentarily and toyed with his glass before going on.

'I've done a bit of digging over the past day or so, with contacts I have in the Baptist Mission in Calcutta.'

'Oh?'

He leaned forward. 'You mustn't be alarmed by this. It's just that... in my position, and at this particular time, I need to be very careful who I associate with.'

'Whatever do you mean?'

His eyes scanned the room quickly and he leaned closer. 'I've been the subject of death-threats you see, back in Ganpur. The Independence movement. They're very active there and indeed here too. We've had to make a number of arrests.'

'Oh, I see.' She'd read about the movement in the newspapers, the marches and the protests, the violence and the arrests.

'Yes. Gandhi visited not so long ago, and the Congress Party held a rally in Ganpur only last year. It is a hotbed of sedition there, I'm afraid. We've traced some of the protagonists back to Darjeeling, which is why I'm here. I'm having meetings with the Governor.'

'So, what does that have to do with me?'

'Well, naturally, I have to be very careful who I mix with. It stands to reason. Anyone could be a Congress plant, trying to get close to me. I wouldn't be the first British official to be attacked.'

Amelia laughed. 'So, you thought I was a member of the Indian Independence movement?' she asked, incredulous.

'I didn't think that, no, I just have to be very careful. So, I'm afraid I had my assistants check you out.'

For the second time that evening, Amelia was astounded. Holden's arrogance seemed to know no bounds.

'You will know what we found out, of course. My assistants discovered that Mrs Collins, the missionary nurse, was not your mother. Your mother was...'

'Yes *I know*,' she said fiercely. 'You don't need to repeat it. So, what difference does that make?'

'Well, as you will have gathered, it can make a *lot* of difference in a place like this. It is probably why you are having difficulty finding a position. But with my protection, you don't need to worry anymore.'

'Your *protection*?'

'Yes, haven't you noticed? No one dares to question your presence while you're with me.'

'Yes, I had noticed,' she whispered. Another drink arrived so she took a large gulp. This was all so hard to cope with.

'So, as I said, your secret's safe with me. And I will make sure you're not challenged while you're here.'

'But why? Why would you do that?'

'Because, my dear Miss Collins,' he said, leaning forward and looking into her eyes earnestly for the first time that evening. 'You have made a great impression on me. I enjoy your company. You are beautiful. And not only that, you are like a breath of fresh air amongst all these old harridans of the empire, and since I met you, for the first time, since the death of my wife, I've begun to feel whole again.'

OVER THE NEXT FEW DAYS, Amelia sent off applications for several jobs that had been advertised in the classified section of the Darjeeling Mail. She decided to wait a while before asking Reginald for his help in finding a position. She didn't want to be any more in his debt than she already was and she was now wary of him and the attention he was paying her. Besides, she wanted to test out the theory that her mixed blood was a bar to her being employed. It was always the same, though. She'd be invited for an interview, but when she arrived, it quickly became clear that there was something about her appearance that was stopping people from engaging her. They almost always suggested awkwardly that she wasn't quite right for them, and that perhaps she should apply for something a little more menial.

In the evenings, she would sit with Reginald in the bar and

he would ask her about her day. She was loath to tell him about her failure to find employment, but there was no hiding it from him. After cocktails, they would go through to the dining room and eat together from the buffet. She felt awkward about spending so much time with him, but it was the only way to stave off the looks and the comments from the other guests, and besides she was lonely for the first time in her life. And although she felt ambivalent about Reginald, and didn't want to encourage his advances, she found his company reasonably congenial and welcomed the protection it gave her. Nothing in her upbringing or education had taught her how to deal with the situation she was in. Her mother had never discussed men or relationships with her. No one in the village had ever paid her this sort of attention and she had no one to turn to for advice.

During those evenings, Reginald never spoke of his own day or of the work he was doing in Darjeeling. She accepted that it was off limits and never asked. And after that first time, he didn't pay her compliments or allude to the fact that he found her attractive, although she could sense it in his eyes when he looked at her across the table. On the fourth evening, Amelia arrived in the bar feeling more dispirited than ever. She'd been to see two British families that day and had been rejected none too subtly from both. She'd decided that the next day, she would go to the Indian school and see if they needed helpers there, although she knew that *they* would probably prefer to employ an Indian person, and that even if she did secure something, the pay would be insufficient to live on.

Reginald was already seated when she made her way to their usual table.

'I've got you a gin fizz,' he said. 'And I can see from your expression that you probably need it.'

'Thank you,' she said, sitting down with a deep sigh and taking a sip gratefully.

'Bad day again?' he asked, lighting a cigarette.

'Same old story,' she said. 'But I'm not giving up. I'm going along to the Indian school tomorrow.'

'It'll be the same there, I fear,' he said, blowing smoke in the air. 'But I admire your spirit.'

Amelia felt a prickle of concern that he had immediately found the obvious flaw in her plan. Perhaps the time had come to ask him for his help. She sipped her gin and tried to think of the right way of putting it. But before she could formulate her request, Reginald spoke himself.

'There's something I need to tell you,' he said draining his glass and clicking his fingers for the bearer to come with fresh cocktails.

'Oh?'

'I need to cut my visit to Darjeeling short, I'm afraid. There's been some trouble down in Ganpur that I need to attend to. So, I'm afraid I will have to leave here tomorrow.'

Amelia felt a wave of panic. How would she cope here alone? Who would help her navigate the social etiquette of this place and stop her from being turned out on her ear?

'I've been thinking about you, though. I don't want to leave you here alone at the mercy of all these old dinosaurs. So, I was thinking... why don't you come with me to Ganpur? It could be a mutually beneficial arrangement.'

Amelia stared at him, her mouth open. Ganpur? She knew it was down in the plains and there was a large British presence there, so why would it be any different to Darjeeling. And what did he mean, a mutually beneficial arrangement?

'To Ganpur? But what would I do there?' she asked.

At that moment, the bearer arrived with a bottle in an ice bucket, which he set up on a stand next to the table. She watched him, confused. They'd never had champagne before. Reginald leaned forward and grasped her hand.

'Well, you could help me look after my son. That would be such a weight off my mind. It was a big blow to him to lose his mother.'

Amelia softened, her heart filling with pity for the boy. She knew exactly what he must be experiencing, and he was so young too...

'In other words, you'd be my wife,' he said. 'I'm asking you to marry me, Amelia,' he said, leaning forward and fixing her with his most beseeching look.

'Oh!' she felt the colour rush to her face and suddenly she felt trapped. What had she been doing, encouraging this powerful, self-centred man, who seemed to command servility in everyone around him and was used to getting his own way in everything he did?

'I... I'm not sure,' she stammered.

'It has probably come as a shock to you, my dear, but I have hinted at my admiration over the past few evenings. I had to move swiftly, because, as I said, I have to leave for Ganpur tomorrow and it seems that your position here might be difficult without me.'

She looked down at the table, not able to meet his eyes. It was all so confusing. How she wished that she had someone to talk to. Was this the normal progress of a courtship? She had no idea how a woman should feel about her prospective husband, but she was sure she should experience some element of desire. She was grateful to Reginald for the way he had taken her under his wing over the past few days, and when she'd been able to relax in his company she'd found him entertaining and amusing, but her overwhelming feeling about him was that he was intimidating and a little overpowering.

He released her hand and fished in his breast-pocket. He took out a small square box and opened it on the table. Inside was a silver ring set with a delicate, shimmering white stone.

'I'd like you to have this,' he said. 'It's a moonstone by the way.'

Amelia was transfixed by the ring. Nobody had ever bought her a piece of jewellery before. Her mother had never worn anything other than a plain wedding band and eschewed adornment of any kind. The moonstone shone delicately in the light from the chandeliers and seemed to beckon to her.

'You know,' he said quietly, his hand on hers again, still looking earnestly into her eyes, 'Even if you haven't been thinking that way about me, why don't you think of it as... well, like I said... as a beneficial arrangement? You'd be looked after and cared for. There would be no need to worry anymore about not getting a position. As my wife you could do whatever you liked in Ganpur. No door would be closed to you. Of course, if you didn't want to do anything, you could simply do what most memsahibs do and live a life of unashamed luxury whilst providing some congenial company for me and my young son.'

She didn't take her eyes off the moonstone as her mind raced through her options. Perhaps what he said made a lot of sense. After the blows and humiliations she'd suffered trying to get a job, she felt weakened, her confidence shot. It was as if everything was stacked against her and she would never succeed. And she only had money for a further week at the Planter's Club. Would she find a position in that short space of time?

Her mind quickly ran over the alternatives; she could go back to Pankhabari, admitting defeat, and offer her services to Dr Joshua Williams, but how could she do that after he'd been so scathing about her father's efforts at the Mission, and what would it be like working there now, without her parents, but with small reminders of them everywhere she looked. Their loss would be even harder to bear back in the village. She had thought about returning to England, but now she no longer had enough funds for a passage, and who could she turn to there?

Like her, her parents had both been only children so there were no surviving relatives, and she'd long ago lost touch with the girls she'd known at school. Perhaps the arrangement that Reginald was suggesting was a more inviting alternative. She didn't want to think too deeply about what else might be involved in being his wife. She knew so little about that side of things. All she knew was that Reginald was a well-built, attractive man, so whatever was involved might not be so bad after all.

'So?' Reginald asked. 'Can I ask the bearer to pour the champagne? Is it a "yes"?'

'It is,' she whispered, still unable to lift her eyes to his, and then came the click of his fingers as he beckoned the hovering bearer forward.

10

AMELIA

Ganpur, India, 1935

They were to be married in Ganpur Baptist Church by special licence three days later. Reginald couldn't delay his trip back to Ganpur, so they'd set off on the Darjeeling Railway the morning after his proposal. They caught the night mail to Ganpur at Siliguri once they were down on the plains, occupying separate compartments in the first-class sleeper car. As the train rattled across the parched plains under cover of darkness, Amelia lay down on her bunk and allowed herself to relax for the first time since her parents had died. She lay awake, listening to the clack-clack of the wheels on the track and, through the open window, breathed in the heavenly scent of India at night; woodsmoke mixed with dung, spices and the smell of mist rising from the parched earth. She was glad to leave Darjeeling and the Planter's Club far behind her. It was a pretty town in a majestic setting, but to Amelia, her stay there represented failure, anguish and loneliness. Although, as word had got around that evening that she and Reginald were to marry, many of the old retainers who'd previously scorned her, came up to congratulate her and shower her with compliments. She'd smiled politely but wasn't taken in by their superficial words. Whatever the future may hold, she felt sure that as Reginald's wife, she would never feel such an outcast ever again.

Reginald had been the model of care and consideration since she'd accepted his proposal. As she lay on her bunk, rocked by the rhythm of the train, staring up at the ever-shifting pattern of the moonlight on the ceiling, she realised that as well as gratitude and admiration, she was beginning to feel affection for this man who was whisking her away from shame and humiliation to a new life.

Protocol demanded, of course, that Amelia couldn't stay with Reginald at his residence until they were married, so when the train pulled into Ganpur Junction in the morning, he took her straight to the Ganpur Gymkhana Club. This place was worlds apart from the Planter's Club in Darjeeling. It was housed in a gracious, sprawling, two-storey building, with white walls, red roofs and deep verandas that ran the length of the ground floor. Here, down on the plains, the climate was tropical, and the building was surrounded by palm trees. There were stewards in gold and white livery on the door and the lobby was cool and echoing, with marbled floors and high ceilings. Where the Planter's Club had been dog-eared and musty, this place oozed charm and luxury.

Reginald personally checked Amelia in and, to her embarrassment, insisted on showing her round the palatial building and introducing her to everyone who happened to be sipping drinks in the bar or lounging in a planter's chair on the shady veranda at the time. As they each shook her hand, she noticed the flash of surprise in their eyes, which was always quickly concealed. But these people were more relaxed and welcoming than their hill-station counterparts, and she was being introduced as the District Officer's fiancée, which must in their

minds, surely, cancel out any hint of unsuitability. She understood straight away why he was making such a point of doing
this. He was laying down a marker, advertising to the entire
community that Amelia was here under his protection and that
there was no question that she was as welcome here as any other
member of the British community.

As soon as he'd settled her into her suite on the first floor, he
was off again.

'Like I said, darling, duty calls,' he said, hovering by the door.
'Arrests have been made and I need to go straight along to the
police station and do my bit, overseeing the police interviews of
the suspects.'

'What are they suspected *of*, Reginald?' she asked. Before
they'd arrived in Ganpur, she'd not given much thought to why
he was returning home early, but now she was here the whole
thing seemed very real.

'Civil disobedience, of course. Various crimes of non-co-
operation. You don't need to trouble yourself about it, my dear.
It's a most unpleasant business. I will be back later on this afternoon and I'll take you to show you the house and to meet young
Arthur.'

'Oh, that will be lovely!' she said, brightening momentarily,
but when he'd gone, she wandered over to the window and
leaned on the sill, wondering about his words. The garden
immediately beneath was lush and green, with pink and white
roses in full bloom in beds around the edge. A small army of
uniformed gardeners were watering the lawn. Beyond the palm
trees at the edge of the immaculate compound, the land was
parched and dusty and the plain shimmered in the heat of the
day. Despite the exotic beauty of the surroundings, she couldn't
help her mind wandering back to life in Pankhabari and how
her father used to express sympathy for the leaders of Congress
and the Independence movement. He had a deep admiration for

Gandhiji as he called him, his egalitarian ideas and peaceful protests. If all they were doing in Ganpur was protesting peacefully, why should these people be arrested and questioned by the police?

She sat back on a chair deep in thought, a feeling of unease creeping through her now. What would Father make of a man who made it his business to apprehend and interrogate peaceful protesters? She pictured Father now, seated in his cane chair on the simple wooden porch at the front of the bungalow, lighting his evening pipe and talking about history and politics. Although he was here in India as a member of the ruling class, he never behaved that way and had never embraced the idea of empire.

'Britain has no right to be ruling here, you know, Amelia. Don't you ever forget that,' he would often say. And when news of arrests appeared in the newspaper, he would shake his head sadly. 'Why do we persist in persecuting them? They will get their independence one day, whatever we do to try to stop it.'

For the first time since Reginald had made his proposal, which after all was less than forty-eight hours before, she felt anxiety gnawing in the pit of her stomach. She couldn't let go of the question: what would Mother and Father have made of Reginald? She couldn't imagine anyone less like them than him. But that wouldn't have necessarily bothered them. They were loving and tolerant people. Surely they would have seen that Reginald was kind and loving, that he had Amelia's best interests at heart and that he was willing to care for her and protect her, when everyone else was shunning her? Of course they would have approved of her decision. The fact that his job required him to enforce the law against independence protesters surely wouldn't have altered that.

Despite having been introduced to everyone in the club, Amelia didn't have the courage to go downstairs alone for lunch.

Instead, exhausted from the journey, she called down and got her meal sent up to the room. It was late afternoon when Reginald arrived to take her to his residence. She was leaning out of the window at the time, her elbows on the sill, drinking in the beauty of the surroundings, when a large black motor car drew up and the syce hopped out to open the rear door. Reginald emerged from the back seat and spoke briefly to the syce, before turning and walking up the path towards the front entrance. He walked quickly and purposefully, with the confidence and assurance she'd come to know, striking an imposing figure in his well-cut linen suit. The sight of him sent a multitude of emotions swirling round inside her and she sat down suddenly in the chair, her face in her hands, wondering whether she'd done the right thing.

He was with her in seconds, opening the door, striding over to kiss her, his elegant face wreathed in smiles. She looked up at him and smiled back, hoping passionately that she'd made the right decision and that it was all going to work out.

The Residence was twenty minutes' drive away on the edge of the bustling town. Reginald sat beside Amelia on the back seat while the syce drove them slowly through the busy streets of downtown Ganpur. How different this was from Darjeeling which was quiet and sleepy in comparison. These streets were teeming with traffic of every conceivable description; rickshaws pulled by men in loin cloths walking barefoot on the stony surface, pony carts, bullock carts, bicycles and the odd motor car. On the roadside, beggars jostled with stallholders and food sellers and their customers, while men and women wove through the crowds carrying loads on their heads. White Brahmin cows wandered freely amongst the traffic and pariah dogs rootled in the rubbish strewn drains. Dust clouds rose from the dry road and blew in through the open window.

'We'll soon be there,' said Reginald as Amelia rubbed dust

from her eyes. 'It's very different from the hills, I know, but you'll get used to it in no time.'

'Don't worry, I'm used to India,' she reassured him. 'I *was* born here, after all, as you know.' They exchanged a smile at this reminder of the predicament that had brought them together.

The car turned off the road and out through the straggly outskirts, through a crumbling stone archway that Reginald told her marked the limits of the old town and the beginning of the British quarter. From then the roads were smoother and the buildings grander, set in landscaped grounds behind well-clipped hedges. After a few minutes, they turned in through some majestic gates. The drive wound through a patch of shrubbery and emerging from it, the Residence was there in front of them – a sprawling white stucco house with a grand portico in front.

'This is amazing,' Amelia said, admiring the beauty all around, but experiencing at the same time a twist of homesickness for the simple hill bungalow in Pankhabari that for all its sparseness was homely and comfortable.

The car swept beneath the portico and they came to a halt outside the front door. The syce came round to open the door for Amelia. Reginald guided her up the steps and she smiled and put her hands together to greet two men in turbans on the door who bowed as they entered. In the high, marble hallway, Reginald stopped and turned to one of the servants who had followed them inside at a respectful distance.

'Where is Master Arthur, Ravi?'

'He is sick sahib. Ayah is with him in his room.'

'Oh, not again!' sighed Reginald and Amelia glanced at him, wondering at his reaction. 'Fetch ayah, Ravi,' he went on, 'I need to speak to her about this.'

The man hurried away, disappearing into one of the corridors that opened off the palatial hallway.

'I'm so sorry about this, my dear,' Reginald said. 'Would you like a drink? Whisky? A gimlet maybe?'

Amelia shook her head. 'Later, perhaps,' she replied, not wanting the boy to smell alcohol on her breath the first time she met him.

A small, elderly woman in a blue saree appeared with the servant, her plump face a picture of concern. She stood in front of Reginald and bowed her head respectfully.

'What's the meaning of this, ayah?' asked Reginald. 'Master Arthur sick again? It's not long since he recovered from the last bout of fever.'

'I'm so sorry, Holden sahib, he is not a strong boy.'

'Not strong? Don't be ridiculous, ayah. He's *my* son. Has he been eating the right food? Getting enough exercise?'

'I do my best, sahib, but he often refuses his food,' said the woman, her brows knitted together in an anxious frown.

'Well then you should insist. Be tougher on him, ayah.'

'So sorry, Holden sahib,' said the woman, her gaze sliding towards Amelia and back again, 'But young sahib misses the memsahib. He hasn't been well since....'

'It has been over a year now, ayah... I understand his sadness, of course I do, but this situation really cannot go on. I'm looking to you to ensure he recovers quickly and doesn't fall ill again. Understood?'

'Of course, sahib,' said the woman, bowing her head.

'Now, let's go along and see him. I have an important guest to introduce him to. Is he awake?'

The woman nodded reluctantly and led them along the echoing corridor to a room at the far end. She opened the door slowly and beckoned them both inside. The room was hot and airless, although electric fans whirred on the ceiling. It had that unmistakeable sickroom smell, stale and cloying. Reginald went pale, pulled out a handkerchief and held it to his nose, but it didn't trouble Amelia; she was used to sickness.

The narrow bed in the corner was shrouded in a mosquito net suspended from the ceiling. Through the folds of the net, Amelia could just make out a slight figure, covered in blankets, propped up on several pillows. Reginald moved forward and pulled the mosquito net aside. The boy flinched and looked up, a fearful look in his eyes. His face was pallid, his lips cracked and dry and there were dark circles beneath his eyes. His dark hair was plastered to his head.

'Good afternoon, Father,' he said in a thin voice.

'Good day to you, Arthur. I'm sorry to see you're sick again. I've brought someone to meet you... this is Miss Collins. Miss Amelia Collins.'

The boy stared at Amelia. 'Good afternoon, Miss Collins,' he said obediently.

'Good afternoon, Arthur, it's lovely to meet you,' she said, her heart filling with compassion for this sad, weak-looking boy.

'Miss Collins and I are to be married, Arthur. The day after tomorrow. I am hoping you'll be well enough to attend our celebrations.'

'Married?' the boy murmured. He looked bewildered and his sunken eyes instantly became moist.

'Indeed. You'll get used to the idea very quickly, and I'm hoping that you and Miss Collins will soon become the best of friends.'

The boy turned his head away to face the wall, his shoulders beginning to shake. The ayah stepped forward and took the boy's hand, began stroking his brow, making gentle, soothing sounds. A feeling of helplessness washed through Amelia. Why had Reginald delivered the news in such an abrupt and insensitive way? Perhaps he thought it was best to be straight, or hadn't realised how painful such news could be for the child. She was sure he didn't mean to hurt Arthur, but what could she do or say to ease the boy's shock and grief?

'Come now,' said Reginald taking her arm. 'I'll show you the rest of the house. We can look in on Arthur again later.'

'We should stay and comfort him, surely?'

The boy turned his head back to look at Amelia, and her eyes met his. Pity washed through her as she saw in his gaze a look of deep despair and anguish. But there was something else too. It was almost as if he was making a plea to her through that look to help him. She could feel the pressure of Reginald's hand on her elbow and she tore her eyes away from Arthur's.

'That's what ayah is for,' said Reginald firmly, steering her out of the room and shutting the door.

As he propelled her along the corridor she said, 'You know, that room is far too hot and airless for someone with fever. You should ask ayah to open the windows, let the air in.'

'Alright. I'll speak to her later. She is doing her best, but she doesn't have medical training I'm afraid.'

'You know I've worked in a hospital, Reginald. I know a lot about fever patients. His temperature needs to come down. Bathing him with a cold flannel will help. And he shouldn't be covered up with blankets like he is.'

'Well, thank you, my dear. As I said, I will talk to ayah... it's such a worry to me. The boy is weak, I'm afraid. His mother insisted on spoiling him and it made him soft, prone to sickness... now, here is the drawing room...' he pushed open double doors to a palatial room with a high, raftered ceiling, with floor to ceiling windows opening onto a shady veranda.

'It's beautiful,' she murmured. Her eyes scanned the room with its tasteful pale sofas and low tables, its watercolours and silk curtains, but all the time she was thinking of that unhappy, sick child and the pleading look he'd given her. Reginald clearly had trouble relating to the child and in her own grief, Amelia's heart went out to that young, motherless boy. If she didn't have a good reason for marrying Reginald before, she certainly had one now. In that moment, she made up her mind to answer Arthur's pleading look and to do what she could to comfort and care for him.

ARTHUR WAS JUST ABOUT WELL ENOUGH to attend the simple wedding service at the Ganpur Baptist Church. He came holding hands with his ayah, looking pale and weak, and sat near the back of the church, his head bowed. In the intervening two days, Amelia had been on her own to visit him whenever she got the opportunity. She would make sure the windows were open, the fans were on full, and dab his brow with a cold flannel. Then she'd sit by his bed and try to gain his trust by talking to him about her own childhood and telling him stories about her days in the hills. He would smile at her anecdotes and ask her questions.

When she thought it safe to do so, she told him that she'd recently lost both her parents. The boy's eyes had instantly filled with tears, but he turned his head away and didn't volunteer anything about his mother. Amelia squeezed his hand and moved quickly on to talk about something else. Gradually, he had begun to speak to her, about the books he liked to read, about his pony that he loved to ride, who lived in the stables behind the house, about friends he liked to play with; some from British families, others the children of servants. They built a rapport in those two days, and his fever had come down too. When Amelia walked up the aisle, she felt she'd done what she could to ensure that Arthur would be able to accept the marriage.

There was only a smattering of other people at the service; the

Baptist minister, a few others Reginald had introduced Amelia to at the club, including a dashing young couple, Eileen and James Blackburn. James was Reginald's assistant district officer and in the intervening days, Eileen had taken it upon herself to take Amelia under her wing and prepare her for the wedding. She'd personally escorted her to a tailor's shop and ensured she was fitted out with an elegant but simple silk dress for the wedding; she'd arranged a bouquet of pink orchids from the club florist, flowers for the church and a discreet reception at the Gymkhana Club. Amelia was grateful to Eileen, but found her a little intimidating. Eileen was in her thirties, several years older than Amelia herself, and seemed to Amelia to be impossibly sophisticated and worldly wise.

The ceremony was short and simple, and Amelia was almost overcome with nerves beforehand. What was she doing marrying this man more than twenty years her senior less than a month after losing both her parents? Was it the right thing to do? Would they have approved and given her their blessing? She felt rudderless; everything was so unfamiliar now, so removed from her previous reality, that she wasn't sure what her parents would have thought at all. All she knew was that she couldn't have survived on her own and that Reginald had been there at exactly the right moment to help her. She was glad of the familiar surroundings of a Baptist church as she took her vows. The prayers and the soothing but simple words of the ceremony felt like her only anchor to the past.

Afterwards, at the club, where Eileen had arranged a buffet for fifty or so guests, she was introduced to more unfamiliar faces and she smiled and shook hands and made small talk until she felt she would drop with exhaustion. At one point, when Reginald was talking to another group of people, the minister took her arm and said gently,

'I'd like to introduce you to two special friends...'

In the corner of the room sat a young couple, a little apart from the main crowd. They looked to be a few years older than Amelia herself. The young man had an open, smiling face, fair hair with a floppy fringe and the woman was pale and a little mousy. She was dressed in a plain blue dress; far more simply than most of the other women at the reception.

'Allow me to introduce Mabel and Giles Harris. *Dr* Giles Harris I should say. Dr and Mrs Harris, this is Mrs Amelia Holden.'

Both got up from their seats and shook her hand warmly, their faces filled with genuine pleasure.

'I knew your father slightly,' said Giles. 'I'm a medical missionary myself, here in Ganpur. I heard about his death and that of your mother. I'm so sorry for your loss. He was a wonderful man. They were wonderful people.'

Amelia shook both their hands, glad to have found some connection with her parents and with her own past at last. She sat down beside them. The minister melted away and before long the three of them were chatting together as if they were old friends. The Harrises told her all about their work in the area and Amelia was glad to be able to talk about her life in Pankhabari to someone who would understand.

'I'm doing some work with women in outlying villages,' said Mabel when Amelia asked her how she filled her days. 'There's a terrible problem here with female infanticide.'

Amelia frowned, she'd heard of it, but wasn't quite sure what it meant.

'Really, Mabel, I'm sure Mrs Holden doesn't want to think about such issues on her wedding day,' said Giles quickly. Mabel went pink.

'Oh, I'm so sorry. I forgot myself,' she said.

'Not at all,' said Amelia, 'I'd be so interested to hear more about it,' she glanced around the room to check Reginald wasn't looking for her. 'Please, do go on.'

'Well,' said Mabel, hesitantly, glancing quickly at Giles. 'Very sadly, girl babies aren't sought after by families in poor villages in this district. It's expensive to have a baby girl. The dowry her family is expected to pay when she marries is crippling for many. So, often they take it into their own hands when a girl baby is born.'

'What do they do?' asked Amelia, dreading the answer.

'Sometimes they take their newborn baby and drown her in a nearby lake.'

Amelia's hand flew to her mouth. 'Oh. How dreadful.'

'We're doing our best to work with them to stop that happening... but it's not easy. There's a lot of suspicion here towards missionaries. And many of our volunteers become discouraged and give up.'

'Well, I could help you,' said Amelia quickly. 'I helped my parents in the hospital for years. I'd love to be of some use here.'

Mabel and Giles exchanged looks. 'Are you sure that your husband would be happy with that arrangement?' asked Giles.

'I'll speak to him,' she said wondering what he meant by that question. 'I don't know why he would mind. I expect he's very busy with his work. I'll be spending time with Arthur of course, but I'm sure I'll be able to spare time to help out.'

At that moment, Eileen appeared behind her.

'I'm sorry to drag you away, Amelia, but the photographer's outside. He'd like to start with some photos of the bride.'

Amelia hardly had time to say goodbye to Mabel and Giles before Eileen was ushering her through the guests towards the veranda.

'Is Arthur still here?' Amelia asked as they walked. 'I haven't seen him since the church.'

'No, sadly he felt unwell and his ayah took him home. I'm afraid you've got your work cut out with that boy.'

'He seems a lovely child,' murmured Amelia, 'It's so sad for him, losing his mother so young.'

'And so suddenly too!' Eileen guided Amelia out through glass doors to the veranda.

Amelia cleared her throat. 'To tell you the truth, I don't know anything about how his mother died. Reginald avoids the subject and I don't want to press him. But it might help me when I'm with Arthur if I do know.'

Eileen looked uncomfortable. She cast her eyes down and the colour had drained from her face, leaving two high spots of rouge on her cheeks. 'So, you don't know?'

'I'd assumed she died of malaria or some other type of fever. Didn't she?'

Eileen stared at her. 'Well... no. I suppose you do need to know, though, for the boy's sake. She died in a shooting accident, out on a shikar with Reginald. They were pursuing a tiger and she fell into the path of the animal... it was really very shocking indeed.'

Amelia fell silent, horrified, imagining the terror of coming face to face with a tiger, seeing the glint of the kill in its eyes, the strength of its tensed muscles and the sharpness of its teeth and claws before it pounced.

'How awful,' was all she could say sinking heavily into one of the planter's chairs on the veranda, feeling the blood draining from her face. How could Reginald have let that happen to someone he'd promised to love and protect? She pictured poor little Arthur, so lost and vulnerable without his mother's love. Her heart swelled with pity for the boy again. She renewed her resolve to love him and care for him as a mother would. For a few moments, until she'd recovered from the shock of Eileen's words, all the joy went out of the day.

11

KATE

Warren End, April 1970

Walking back to Oakwood Grange from Joan's house that day, Kate found it hard to keep the tears at bay. Her encounter with Joan had made such an impression on her that she barely noticed the rain that was still pelting down. Was it pity for Joan that she was feeling, or for herself at the way she'd been summarily dismissed from Joan's house? Perhaps it was tactless to have mentioned that she was there if Joan ever wanted to talk. She'd been wrong not to take more notice of the look in Joan's eyes, that look that seemed to be challenging her to say something about the marks on Joan's face. She should have recognised the signs from years ago that Joan was looking for a reason to be annoyed with her.

She reached the gates to the house and walked quickly up the drive under the oak trees, her head bowed against the rain. There was something deeply distressing about the scene she'd just witnessed and she couldn't get it out of her mind. Joan, overweight and downtrodden, still living in exactly the same unhappy circumstances as she had as a child. She'd grown up in an atmosphere of abuse, drunkenness and violence and had had so many reasons to break free from that cycle. She'd had everything going for her. She was a bright, pretty, feisty girl. So why had she ended up as she had, living in poverty with an abusive husband, tied to her situation by her lack of qualifications and the fact that all the drive and confidence had been beaten out of her? It was a vicious downward spiral. Kate wished she'd been able to get through to Joan, but she also knew that it was partly guilt that was making her feel such pity for her old friend. Guilt at her own part in Joan's plight. She couldn't help thinking that the events of that last summer must have had a lot to do with the path that Joan's life had taken.

The house was icy cold as she let herself in. She went through to the kitchen, rummaged in the cupboards until she found an electric kettle and made herself some coffee. Sitting down at the table to drink it, her thoughts turned away from Joan to herself and her own life. She sighed. She was all too ready to condemn and pity Joan, but who was she to cast stones in that way? Her own life represented a different sort of failure, didn't it? She knew she'd never been able to let her guard down enough to let anyone close. Joan, on the other hand, had taken the plunge. She'd got into a relationship that seemed to have ended up miserably, but at least she'd dared. Kate herself had never even got as far as trying. Whose was the worse failure?

Finishing her coffee, she went through to the study. She needed to order some oil to get the Aga going again, and some coal and logs for the fires. She sat down at the desk and reached for the phone and the telephone directory. While she was at it, she might as well call an estate agent to come to the house and give her a valuation. The morning's encounter and the memories it had stirred up made her want to get the house on the market as quickly as she could. She found a list of estate agents

in the Yellow Pages and called up the first on the list; Andersons
in Midchester.

'Mr Anderson can come to see you this afternoon at about
five o'clock,' said the receptionist. 'It's on his way home, actually,
and he'll be happy to fit you in, I'm sure.'

Kate put the phone down, relieved to have taken the first
step towards severing her connections with Oakwood Grange
and the village. Then her eyes strayed to an envelope she'd left
on the desk when she'd sorted through the papers the other day.
It was the one marked *Amelia Hamilton, personal*; the one with
Amelia's deed poll inside. The sight of it reminded her that she
must find out as much as she could about her aunt's past before
she left Warren End for good. The letters in the attic, the shock
of discovering her marriage certificate and the photographs, and
the encounter with old Miss Robinson, so loaded with meaning:
*Your aunt was a very troubled girl in those days... She had been
through so much, you know*.

An image of Amelia's distraught face swam into Kate's mind,
as Amelia had walked beside George Prendergast at the old mill;
Amelia's car accelerating away from the encounter, her preoccupied expression during family visits, as if she was a million miles
away. Did this all somehow relate back to India and the secrets
she was carrying from her time there? Or was it all about Amelia
and George Prendergast? Kate felt a compulsion to know. Some
instinct told her that unlocking these secrets might throw fresh
light on the events of that fateful summer. It might allow her to
move on from the guilt she bore and, if she could manage to get
through to Joan somehow, perhaps it could help her as well. But
she was running out of time.

She quickly telephoned round to arrange deliveries of logs
and fuel, then continued for an hour or so to sort Amelia's
paperwork, hoping to uncover more clues into her aunt's mysterious past. But she was disappointed. There was nothing in the

office but overdue bills, receipts, bank statements and general household paperwork. Frustrated, Kate flicked through the Yellow Pages again, scanning the entries for old people's homes. Her finger stopped at the Ms. There it was "The Meadows", where Miss Robinson had told her she now lived. From the address Kate realised that it was only a few miles from Warren End. She scribbled the number down on the pad and dialled it quickly, before she could change her mind.

'Are you family?' asked the woman on the phone, when Kate asked to make an appointment to see Miss Robinson, a hint of suspicion in her voice.

'Not exactly. I met her at my great-aunt's funeral in Warren End a few days ago, and she invited me to come and see her.'

'Ah. You must be Miss Hamilton. Miss Robinson has been asking if you've called yet. She even came round to reception about an hour ago to ask. We've been expecting you.'

A shudder went through Kate. She hadn't made any firm promises to Miss Robinson, but the old woman had known she would call. Miss Edna Robinson clearly shared something of her late sister's psychic powers.

Kate arranged to visit The Meadows at eleven the next morning and put the phone down with the feeling that someone had walked over her grave.

There were a few hours left before the estate agent was due to arrive. Kate wandered back up to the bedroom where she had left the letters Mabel Harris had written to Amelia. She flicked back through them to check she hadn't missed anything, and realised, from scanning the addresses at the top of the letters, that in early 1940, something changed. The word "Ganpur" was no longer written at the top of the letters. After that, for a few years, Mabel had been writing from Benares, and after that, Simla. In 1948 the letters stopped altogether. That would have coincided with Indian independence. She quickly scanned the last letter Mabel had written. There were the usual few paragraphs wishing Amelia well, and news of Giles' medical work, but in the final paragraph, Mabel wrote,

I have mixed feelings about returning, Amelia. We've been out in India for so long that it has become home to us. As you know, the last few years have been difficult here and going home is the right thing to do. We British have no rightful place here anymore, even those of us who had nothing to do with government or the armed forces. One of the good things about it though, is that we will be able to meet up again. I'm so looking forward to seeing you in person after all this time. I realise that you probably wouldn't want us to visit Warren End, quite naturally, but perhaps we could meet up in London sometime? Giles is hoping to find work in the suburbs somewhere, but we haven't anything fixed up quite yet. I will write again when I know more.

In the meantime, do take good care of yourself and send me your news,

With love, Mabel.

Kate put the letter back into the envelope, puzzled. Why wouldn't Amelia want Mabel to come to Warren End? Perhaps she didn't want too many reminders of her time in India, or to draw attention to it? Perhaps she had secrets from Uncle James. Perhaps she'd never told him about her first marriage and Mabel didn't want to risk giving something away. It was all entirely possible. But what the letter *had* told her was that Mabel and Giles had almost certainly returned to England in 1948. Had Amelia kept in touch with them after that? If she had, why hadn't she kept the letters? Had they met up in London? She recalled that Amelia had made regular trips up to London to go to Harrods, and Dickens and Jones for clothes. Perhaps that was when she met up with her friend?

Sighing at the number of unanswered questions the letters raised, she put them away in the drawer beside her bed. The carriage clock on her bedside table said three o'clock. She had two hours to kill before Mr Anderson was due to arrive. Kate glanced out of the window. The rain had stopped and the sky was clear. It was one of those bright, early spring days, when you can sense the changing seasons by the quality of the light and the air. Why not take another walk around the village? There was little to do in the house, Mrs Andrews had cleaned it thoroughly only the day before. She could sit and read through Mabel's letters again, but that seemed to be more of a job for an evening in front of the fire. Besides, she was hoping that old Miss Robinson would be able to solve some of the mysteries surrounding Amelia's time in India.

Something was drawing her back to Clerks' Lane, although she wouldn't admit it to herself. She was aware that it was approaching the end of the school day, and that mothers would soon be collecting their children from school. If she were to happen to bump into Joan while she was out walking, she might have a chance to apologise for the clumsy things she'd said earlier. She might be able to tell her that she was looking into her aunt's past as a way of breaking the ice between them; as a way back to discussing the events of that summer.

Kate went downstairs and pulled on her coat and boots. She let herself out of the front door and strode down the drive with a new sense of purpose, noticing the drifts of snowdrops under the oak trees at the perimeter of the garden. Once through the gates, she set off in the direction of Clerks' Lane, retracing her steps from the morning. This time, though, she wasn't having to bow her head against the rain. She looked around her, admiring the pretty stone cottages and the gardens full of spring flowers. She turned into Clerks' lane and began to walk down towards Joan's house. Before she'd gone very far, she saw someone coming in the opposite direction pushing a child in a pushchair. For a second, she wondered if it could be Joan, but as she drew closer she saw who it was behind the pushchair. Her heart plummeted. It wasn't Joan, but a tall man dressed in a maroon tracksuit with untidy black hair. She wanted to turn round and walk the other way, but he was too close by then and it would have looked too obvious. Instead, she carried on walking, her eyes on the road, hoping he wouldn't recognise her. As they drew level, he stopped.

'Hey, don't I know you?' he said, his tone aggressive. His voice took her straight back to her teenage years, when he and his cowardly friends had made her life a misery.

'I don't think so,' she said, stopping and lifting her head to meet his eye. It was unmistakeably Dave Pope, with his mop of dark hair now streaked with grey, pale skin prone to flushing, his high cheekbones and narrow, dark eyes that never stayed still. He was taller now and more muscular than she remembered. But he looked unkempt too; his tracksuit was stained and grubby and his trainers were falling apart. His top was open a few inches and a gold medallion nestled amongst wiry chest hair. A cigarette was burning down between the fingers of his right hand.

'I think you do recognise me,' he said. 'It's Kate Hamilton, isn't it? I'd know you anywhere.'

'Yes,' she said, aware that colour was creeping into her cheeks, but refusing to show that he still had the power to intimidate her.

'I never thought you'd come back 'ere,' he said.

'No,' she said, remaining vague, her heart thumping. Did he know what she and Joan had done? Had Joan told him?

'And you're not welcome, neither,' he drew on his cigarette and blew a stream of smoke directly at her. She didn't flinch or turn away.

'I don't have anything to say to you,' she said as calmly as she could. 'I've got to get on now.' She started to walk away, concentrating hard on every step.

'Don't you come near my Joan again,' he shouted. 'She don't want nothing to do with you. D'you hear me?'

Kate walked faster, not turning back, not looking round.

'And don't you come to the 'ouse again. We don't need the likes of you meddling.'

She carried on walking down the lane, not looking round, until she drew level with Joan's house. Without turning her head, she stole a glance at the windows. It was difficult to see for sure, the front garden was quite long, but she thought she could see Joan at the kitchen sink. She paused, wondering whether to go to the door and knock, to reassure Joan that she wouldn't be put off by Dave's threats if Joan wanted to speak to her. But glancing behind her, she saw that Dave was still walking towards the top of the lane. Perhaps now was not the time to approach Joan. She carried on, thwarted, resolving to come back another day.

KATE WAS in the study sorting through yet more of Amelia's old paperwork when she heard the scrunch of car tyres on the drive. Glancing out of the window she saw a large yellow Rover parking up beside her own car. A man got out and collected a briefcase from the back seat. He was tall and slim, with thinning blond hair and smartly dressed in a well-cut navy suit. Instead of going straight to the door, he strode about on the front drive for a while, walking to and fro, leaning back to look up at the roof, peering closely at the front of the house. It irked her slightly that he was surveying the house in that proprietorial way before she'd even engaged his services. It smacked of arrogance. She raised her eyebrows but told herself she mustn't let it rattle her.

She'd dealt with enough agents and developers in her job to know how they operated.

She put down her papers and went through to the hall. By the time she'd reached the front door, the doorbell was ringing.

'Mr Anderson?' She smiled politely as she opened the door.

'Miss Hamilton,' he said, holding out his hand. She shook it, noticing that he was looking into her eyes and smiling back at her with a surprisingly genuine look.

'Come on in,' she said, standing aside for him to enter.

'Don't you recognise me?' he asked when he was inside the hall. He was smiling broadly now, a teasing sort of smile, a twinkle in his blue eyes.

She looked again. Of course. Gordon Anderson! It had been years since he'd even crossed her mind, but now it all came flooding back. The golden boy of her school year. She'd admired him from afar, just as all the other girls had. She'd thought he would never even notice her, but towards the end of the second year, he'd started to try to open up conversations if they saw each other in the corridor. Every time this happened, she would feel herself blushing and stammer something quickly in response. Afterwards she would go over and over the exchange in her mind, berating herself for not being able to think of anything even vaguely intelligent to say.

'I knew who you were as soon as the receptionist told me your name and address,' he said. 'We were in the same year at Midchester Grammar school.'

'Yes, of course I remember you. How wonderful to see you again,' she said feeling a little heat creeping into her cheeks despite the fact that more than twenty-five years had passed since she'd experienced the fluttering in her chest every time she caught sight of him. Now they were both over forty and schooldays just were a distant memory.

'So,' he said, glancing around him at the panelled entrance

hall. 'I was sorry to hear that your great-aunt had died. I take it you're looking to sell the place?'

'Yes, I think so. I work in London now, so wouldn't be able to get here very much if I kept it.'

'There are excellent train services from Bletchley, you know. Lots of people do it nowadays.'

'Yes, I know. Warren End does have the feel of a commuter village now, sadly. I wouldn't want to do that myself. Besides, what would I want with a huge place like this?'

'You don't have any family?' he enquired casually.

'No, it's just me.'

'Your great-aunt lived alone here for many years I believe,' he said, an earnest expression on his face.

'You *do* want to handle this sale, don't you?' she asked, laughing, and he laughed too.

'Of course. I don't want to do myself out of the business. But I was just thinking of you. People often rush to sell after the death of a loved one. I sometimes think that if they stopped to consider it for a moment, they might think again.'

'There is the small question of money,' said Kate. 'Most people need to sell for that reason, don't they?'

'True, but if it's just a question of money, perhaps you might consider keeping the place for a while and renovating it before putting it on the market? I haven't looked round properly yet, but I can see from the outside that it needs a bit of work, and I expect the inside could do with some updating.'

Kate couldn't keep her face from dropping at the idea of staying in Warren End any longer than necessary. 'I don't think so. I wouldn't have the appetite for such a big project.'

'But you're an architect, aren't you? I thought you might want to put your own stamp on the place.'

'However do you know *that*?' she asked, surprised.

'Oh, I bump into old Gerald Chapman in the pub sometimes. Do you remember him? He was the headmaster at the grammar school. He keeps tabs on all his old pupils. It was Mr Chapman who told me.'

'That's extraordinary,' said Kate. 'Especially as I left the school at the end of the second year, before the end of the war even.'

'Yes, I remember that...' He looked as though he might be about to say something else, but left the subject hanging.

'Well,' Kate went on briskly, not wanting him to dwell on the events of that time or the reasons for her leaving the village. 'I tend to work on new-builds, offices, apartment blocks, not old houses.'

'Interesting. So, why don't you show me round and I can tell you what I think it might fetch.'

They started in the drawing room and moved gradually round the ground floor. Gordon made appreciative noises as she showed him into each of the large, beautiful rooms, and as they walked, they began to recall the people in their year at school. Gordon was able to fill Kate in with news of many of them. At least the ones who'd remained in the area. Kate found herself recalling people she hadn't thought about for years and remembering one name brought back memories of others. They were soon exchanging anecdotes about classmates and teachers alike. Kate found herself laughing out loud at the memories, relaxing for virtually the first time since she'd come back to the village.

When they'd completed the tour, they went back into the kitchen and Kate made a pot of tea. Gordon scribbled some notes in a file. She put a cup of tea in front of him and waited for him to finish. In the end he looked up and smiled.

'This is a beautiful, historic house. As I said, it needs some updating, but houses like this don't come onto the market very often. It would fetch a far better price if you were to do the renovations yourself as I said, but if you want a quick sale, I think you'd probably be able to achieve around £25,000.'

'That's a very good price indeed,' she replied, after a pause to let it sink in. 'I hadn't expected it to be worth that much.'

Kate had no immediate need for the money; her partnership was doing very well and she'd already paid for her flat in London. She had no desire to give up work. After all, what else would she do with her time?

'Let me think about it for a day or so,' she said, sipping her tea. 'I'll give you a call.'

SHE WATCHED from the window as he got back into his car and drove away. As his taillights disappeared around the bend in the drive, Kate imagined him driving through the lanes to the village where he lived, getting out of the car outside a large family home, two children rushing out to greet him, clamouring for his attention, wrapping themselves around his legs, a woman standing in the doorway waiting for his embrace. Kate felt an unaccustomed pang of regret, of disappointment that she was so alone in the world. She didn't often feel that way, but speaking to Gordon about her schooldays had stirred something deep inside. She hadn't laughed like that for a long time, enjoying unreservedly the company of another human being. It struck her that she'd been able to speak about her schooldays without regret. It was the first time she'd even thought about that time without guilt and shame weighing her down.

In the morning, she was up early to take delivery of a lorry load of logs and coal, and supervise the man who came with the tanker to fill the oil tank. She got the Aga started and managed to light the ancient boiler housed in an outhouse behind the scullery. When she went back inside, the place was already warming up and the comforting gurgle of water was coming from the cast-iron radiators.

She went into each room to check they were working, turning off those in empty rooms where she didn't need to spend time. Upstairs, she stood at the threshold of Amelia's bedroom, gazing at the elegant furniture, the tall windows, memories of her aunt flooding back.

The valve of the rusting radiator had seized up and was too stiff to turn off. Kate glanced around the room to see if there was an old cloth she could use to help her to grip it. The room was tidy. Mrs Andrews had cleaned it thoroughly since Amelia's death so there was nothing obvious lying about. Kate went over to the bed and opened the drawer to Amelia's bedside table. Inside was a collection of old pens, some scratched spectacles and an old floral headscarf. That would do. Kate took it out.

Underneath the scarf, in the bottom of the drawer, was a small photograph mounted on card. Puzzled, Kate picked it up and looked at it closely. It was very old like the pictures she'd found in the trunk upstairs and, like them, black and white fading into sepia. Amelia smiled out at her, looking very young, wearing a white summer dress, squinting in the sunlight. She was sitting on a bench beside a young boy and had her arm around him. The boy looked sickly, pale and thin with dark hair. He wore a timid smile, but his eyes were cast downwards. The two of them were seated on a cane bench, with potted palms behind them. It must have been taken in India. But who was the boy? One of her father's patients perhaps? He must have meant a lot to Amelia for her to have kept the photograph all these years. He looked about eight or nine, so he would probably now be in his forties. Roughly the same age as Kate herself. Where was he now?

Glancing at her watch, Kate realised it was time to set off to the Meadows to see Miss Robinson. Perhaps the old lady would be able to tell her about the boy? Had Amelia told the Robinson sisters everything about her past? Kate hoped so. There were so many secrets to uncover. She wasn't ready to sever her ties with Oakwood Grange and Warren End completely until she knew the truth.

12

AMELIA

Ganpur District, India, 1935

A melia pulled her headscarf tighter around her face and shielded her eyes from the sun. The land shimmered in the heat as far as she could see, as the car sped towards the low brown hills on the horizon, raising dust clouds all around. Through the heat haze she spotted an occasional village where wooden houses clustered together under trees, where lean livestock wandered, and the occasional farmer worked bravely under the bleached sky.

'That's where we're headed,' said Mabel, turning to her from the driving seat. 'Those little hills up ahead. The lake I told you about is behind that first group of hills, and the villages where we've been working are just beyond that.'

'It's terribly barren,' said Amelia, thinking wistfully again of the greenery of the Himalayas, the pine forests, the lush rhododendrons, the tumbling waterfalls.

'Yes. It's very hard for people here to grow crops. They have to irrigate their land before anything will take, and if the monsoon fails, which it sometimes does, they go hungry.'

'It's unimaginable,' Amelia murmured, as they rattled through a dusty village, where buffalo lazed in a muddy pond-bed and villagers gathered in the shade of a huge, wilting banyan tree out of the heat of the morning sun. It was only a few miles outside Ganpur, but it felt like a different world.

Amelia lapsed into thought. Conversation was difficult above the noise of the engine and the rush of the wind in the open-topped vehicle, which juddered and vibrated over every bump in the road. And anyway, she hardly knew Mabel. She'd been surprised when Mabel had turned up to collect her, actually driving the ancient vehicle herself. Even in the short time Amelia had lived in the Residence, she'd got used to being ferried around in the back of a limousine by Amir, Reginald's syce. Seeing Mabel's smiling, unaffected face reminded Amelia with a pang of her own roots, of her humble parents, and of the ancient jalopy her father had taught her to drive in along the dirt tracks near Pankhabari.

How far from that those beginnings the first few weeks of marriage had taken her. Now, away from the Residence and Reginald's orbit for the first time since she'd promised to love, honour and obey him, she could reflect on her impressions of her new life; her life with him. She skipped over the wedding night, going hot and cold with embarrassment when she thought about it. She'd not been completely unprepared for what might happen. Her mother had never spoken of such things, but Amelia had picked up some information from the whispered conversations of the nurses at the mission hospital and the young mothers who came to her father's clinics with their babies.

Reginald had been caring and patient, but the actual act of lovemaking had taken her by surprise and she'd cried out in terror at the pain and the force of it. He'd held his hand over her mouth to muffle her cries and to stop the servants from hearing.

On subsequent occasions, she'd begun to understand what was required, and even to allow herself to relax and feel the first glimmerings of pleasure at his touch. Afterwards, he would gaze into her eyes and tell her that he loved her, that she was all his, and that he would kill any man who came near her. She tried to laugh it off, but lying awake after he'd drifted off to sleep, she realised that his intensity was beginning to alarm her.

Reginald was always up early in the mornings to ride before breakfast. After they'd eaten, he would kiss her and Arthur goodbye and leave for Government House in one of the cars. Amelia spent those early days getting to know Arthur. Little by little he lost his initial shyness of her and would take her hand as they walked around the garden, or through the streets of the cantonment. The first time this happened, a little thrill went through Amelia at this breakthrough.

They quickly fell into a comfortable routine. After breakfast they would head out to the stables and ride out of the cantonment together, following a track at the edge of the grounds that took them into the countryside through farmland and past little settlements. Arthur would ride his favourite pony and Amelia an old grey mare. She suspected the horse had belonged to Arthur's mother, but she never asked.

They would return to the house and spend the rest of the morning together. Amelia would try to teach Arthur a few basic lessons. The bookcase in his schoolroom was filled with children's books. She would read to him from them and listen to him reading to her. After lunch and an afternoon siesta, when the heat of the day was subsiding, they would spend time outside, playing hide and seek or ball games, or take a walk together through the neat, tree-lined roads of the cantonment to some neglected gardens with a fish-pond. Occasionally one of the Indian children who lived in the compound at the back of the residence would call for Arthur, and they would disappear off together hand-in-hand to play, chattering in Hindi.

Reginald had told Amelia that these days wouldn't last; that the following year he would be engaging a tutor for the boy.

'His schooling has suffered dreadfully,' he said. 'His mother wouldn't hear of employing a tutor for him. She insisted on teaching him herself. Then, of course, after her death, he became very ill for months, and there was no question of schooling for him. Now, he has a lot of catching up to do.'

'He seems to be a very bright boy,' said Amelia, thinking of the way he listened closely when she read to him, picked up on every nuance of a story. And he loved facts and figures. When she'd shown him a book about the kings and queens of England, he'd absorbed the information like blotting paper and recited dates and names back to her.

'Yes, I agree, he is quite bright,' Reginald replied, 'But his mind is undisciplined. He needs proper tutoring, like all men. The tutor I've engaged will get him ready for school. When he's eleven he will go back to England for his education. His name is down for Haileybury.'

'Oh, Reginald. Would you really send him so far away from home?' she asked, dismayed. Reginald stiffened.

'Of course. It's what all British children do out here. It won't be easy, I grant you. He'll have to toughen up, but that's part of the point of it.'

'You know, my parents sent me to boarding school when they first came out to India. I was wretched. Thinking about them so far away from me... It didn't last long.'

'Well, that's different. You're a girl,' he said.

'But I don't see why it should be different...'

'No buts. My mind is made up. I don't want to hear any more about it. I really don't want to go through the same arguments with you that I had with...'

He stopped and checked himself. A strained silence followed. It lengthened and lengthened, and the tension built between them until Amelia felt she had to say something to diffuse it.

'You *can* talk about her to me you know, Reginald,' she said in a small voice.

'I don't want to talk about her,' he said with an air of finality. 'Please don't mention it again.'

They fell into an unhappy silence and Amelia felt guilty for having crossed an invisible line. At the same time, she felt shut out, and until Reginald spoke to her about the loss of his first wife, there would always be a chasm between them which could never be breached. She was also filled with pity about Reginald's plans for Arthur, knowing how sensitive and vulnerable the boy was. How would he ever cope in the hurly burly of the school environment, six thousand miles away from home and everything he knew and loved?

Arthur hardly spoke about his mother, but sometimes he would let drop a little information. Once when they were out riding, they came across a stretch of open land and Arthur asked if they could canter across it and jump a ditch at the far end. After they'd done that and pulled up the ponies, Arthur was laughing, his eyes sparkling and there was colour in his cheeks for the first time since Amelia had arrived.

'Mummy used to love doing that,' he said. And when Amelia once read Snow White to him from a leather-bound book of fairy stories that she found in the bookcase in the drawing room, he said, a wistful look in his eyes; 'That was Mummy's favourite fairytale.'

One day, he surprised Amelia when they were deciding where to walk that afternoon.

'Could we go to Mummy's grave?' he asked, with a pleading look. Amelia was taken aback at his request and for a few minutes, until her heart slowed down, she couldn't look at him, or think of how to reply.

'Have you been there before?' she asked carefully.

'Oh yes. Ayah takes me sometimes. We don't tell Daddy. He wouldn't like it if he knew.'

'Whyever not?' she asked without thinking. Arthur went silent then, twisting and turning a model airplane in his lap until the propellor snapped.

'Of course, we'll go,' she said quickly. 'You'll have to tell me where it is.'

'Amir knows. He will take us,' replied Arthur. 'And he won't tell Daddy either.'

So, they went the next day, in the dead hours of the early afternoon, when most British people were asleep under whirring fans and mosquito nets or dozing the afternoon away in their offices. Amir, the syce, drove them to the Church of England cemetery near the centre of Ganpur. The grave was in a neglected corner of the graveyard, where the grass wasn't mowed. Amelia was terrified there might be snakes as Arthur plunged ahead of her through the luxuriant undergrowth. A simple white headstone stood there alone with the words; *Here lies Elizabeth Holden, beloved wife and mother. Born 20th January 1905, died 5th Feb 1934. May the Lord watch over her.*

Amelia stared at it, chills going through her despite the extreme heat of the afternoon. Until that moment, she hadn't even known her name. Arthur knelt in front of the grave and laid the bunch of roses they'd picked from the Residence garden that morning. When he looked back up at Amelia, his eyes were full of tears.

She'd tried to comfort him, hugging him to her and whispering soothing words. Going back to the Residence in the car, neither of them spoke, but when they got home, and Amelia took him back to his bedroom, he turned to her and said, 'Would you like to see a picture of Mummy?'

'If you'd like to show me,' Amelia replied and watched him as he dived under the bed and pulled out a drawer on castors. She'd wondered why there were no photographs of Arthur's mother anywhere in the house and whether it was out of deference to herself. But now she had her answer. 'I've only got one and it's hidden away under here. Daddy has forbidden us to keep any.'

'Oh?' Amelia answered in alarm.

'He said he didn't want to be reminded.'

'Poor Daddy,' she murmured. Arthur got up from the floor and handed Amelia a small photograph in a silver frame. It was immediately obvious where Arthur got his delicate looks from; his fine-boned face and pale eyes. The photograph was taken in silhouette and the woman's eyes were cast downwards. She had blonde hair, twisted into a bun at the nape of her neck and but for a string of pearls her shoulders were bare. She looked very young and, like Arthur, very vulnerable. Above all, a sense of sadness exuded from the woman in the picture. Amelia found it deeply unsettling.

'She's beautiful, your mother,' she said handing the photograph back. 'I'm sure she'd be very proud of you now.'

Mabel had turned to her now from the driver's seat and was trying to say something. Jolted out of her reverie, Amelia tried to lip-read her words.

'I said, we're turning off in a moment,' Mabel yelled as she swung the car off the main road, 'We're nearly at the lake now.'

The side road to the lake was no more than a rutted track, with the occasional sharp boulder sticking up from the surface that Mabel had to negotiate around. It climbed steadily for a mile or so, switching back on itself, until they were above the plain and could see it stretching away from them for mile upon mile. The buildings of Ganpur, just visible in the heat haze, were the only interruption in the rolling brown landscape. As they went higher, the colours became softer, the grass greener. Soon they were over the top of the rise and laid out in front of them was a huge lake, nestled into the forested hills, reflecting the sky and the hills and glittering in the sunlight.

Mabel drew off the road onto a sandy area and stopped the car. She turned off the engine. Across from the beach, a few yards from the shore stood a little white bathing pavilion with flaking white paint, crenelated domes and arches, lapped at by the waters of the lake.

A group of buffalo dozed in the muddy shallows around it, some standing, others lying down, half submerged in the water, their hides glistening. A flock of white egrets took off from the surface of the lake, disturbed by the approach of the vehicle. Amelia watched them as they rose into the clear sky in perfect formation, soaring high over the lake and on over a forest on the opposite shore, a tingling feeling, like vertigo rushing through her body.

'So, this is it,' said Mabel quietly. 'This is where the mothers from the villages come with their newborns. Usually in the dead of night.'

'What – right here?' asked Amelia, hardly being able to contemplate what this would mean for mother and baby.

'Sometimes here, sometimes over there by the forest. It's less exposed there, but they usually come under the cover of darkness anyway.'

'How terrible,' said Amelia. 'Have you been able to persuade anyone against it?'

'A few, yes, but it's difficult. There's always pressure from families, other villagers...'

'I'm hoping I can be of some help... but it sounds very daunting.'

Mabel smiled. 'It's good that you could come. I'm so grateful. It will be of tremendous benefit to have your support. Was Reginald alright about it, by the way?'

Amelia fell silent, recalling their conversation. It had surprised her that she'd felt awkward about mentioning the trip to him. For some reason, she had the impression that he didn't really approve of the Baptists and Giles and Mabel Harris and that he would have preferred her to spend time with Eileen James and the club set. She mentioned it during the evening after they'd finished supper. The bearers were clearing away the plates by then. She'd intended to talk about it during the meal but Reginald had been preoccupied. When she'd asked him what was wrong, he'd said, 'We're having a lot of trouble with the protesters we have in custody. They've gone on hunger strike now. Gandhi has a hell of a lot to answer for.'

That had troubled Amelia. 'It's been weeks now, hasn't it? Have they been charged with anything?'

'Justice moves slowly in this country, my dear. You need to understand that. We're trying to get information out of them before we can charge them and bring them to trial. And it's not proving easy.'

'Didn't you get any information from Darjeeling?' Amelia asked.

'Yes, a little. Some of the local leaders have gone to ground in the villages up there, so I was able to exchange what I knew with the Governor to help him out. But we need more names. And we need to know what they're planning next.'

'Planning? It's just peaceful protests surely?'

'That's the message they'd like us to believe, but there's a current of violence just under the surface. We need to stamp it out before it threatens to bring down the whole empire.'

Amelia fell silent, then remembered that Mabel had telephoned earlier to ask her to accompany her into the nearby hills the next day and she needed to broach the subject with Reginald. Although she was confident that he could have no valid objection to her doing such valuable work, she already sensed that he may object to it on principle. She found herself paralysed, rehearsing what to say to him over and over again. The table was almost clear and Reginald was just gathering up his cigarettes and whisky to move through to the drawing room when she spoke.

'Reginald,' she said as he was poised to get up. He looked mildly irritated and settled back down in his chair. 'Mabel Harris called today. When I met her at the club she asked if I would help her with some work out in the villages. She asked me if I would go with her tomorrow.'

It had all come out in a rush and her heart was beating fast as she finished speaking. Reginald lit a cigarette and leaned back in his chair.

'What kind of work?' he asked, his eyes steady on her face.

'It... it's working with women in the villages to try to stop them drowning their baby girls,' she replied.

'I thought your missionary days were behind you, Amelia,' he said in a mocking tone. 'You're a District Officer's wife now. You'd do well to remember that.'

'I'm just doing it to help Mabel out. She has trouble getting volunteers for this work,' her voice trailed off as her mouth was suddenly dry.

'Well, there's a good reason for that. It's interfering in the business of the villagers. Sensible Englishwomen don't do that; meddle in local customs.'

'But surely... no one could stand by while innocent children are killed?'

'Your place is here, now, Amelia. With me and with Arthur.'

'It's just one day...' she said, her eyes fixed on the polished surface of the table.

He pushed his chair back and stood up.

'Well, go if you like. But it will be a thankless task, I can tell you that for nothing. You'll get nowhere. And if there are repercussions from this that affect my standing in the community, it'll have to stop.'

With that he strode out of the dining room.

She got up from the table and hurried after him. 'What do you mean, repercussions?' she asked, following him across the hall. Instead of making for the drawing room, he went towards his study at the front of the house.

'I need to catch up on some paperwork. I'll thank you to leave me in peace,' he said, going into the room and slamming the door after him.

'I take it, from your silence, that he was none too happy about it,' said Mabel. Amelia shrugged.

'I don't understand why,' she said. 'He told me before we married that I could do exactly as I pleased in Ganpur.'

'There's always been a bit of tension between the missionaries and the British administration,' said Mabel. 'We don't always toe the line they'd like us to. But you must do what you think best. I don't want to put you in a difficult position with your husband.'

'No, I *want* to help out. And if my parents were still alive, I'm sure they'd want me to do what I could to help people, rather than lounging about at the club drinking my days away.'

'We'll go then, shall we?' said Mabel smiling and starting the engine and moving off the beach.

'What's that place?' asked Amelia, her eyes on the pavilion.

As she stared at the crumbling structure, streaked with rain damage and bird droppings, a lone egret took off from its roof.

'Oh, that used to be a bathing pavilion for the wives of maharajas a couple of centuries ago,'

'How interesting,' said Amelia, turning round to stare at it as they drew away.

'But no-one goes there anymore,' said Mabel. 'Legend has it that one of the wives drowned and the place was abandoned after that. The villagers in the hills are convinced it's haunted.'

'Oh!' a shudder went through Amelia. The chilling story only added to the sense of tragedy that seemed to haunt this beautiful place.

They drove the length of the lake, over the next hill and down into a small village which was no more than a collection of huts at the edge of the forest. Mabel parked up under the shade of a tree and a crowd of curious villagers gathered around the car; women with babies on their hips in brightly coloured sarees, holding their veils over their faces, children staring with huge brown eyes; a few old men, hobbled up from the shade of their huts to survey the interlopers.

'Come with me. Best foot forward,' said Mabel, getting out of the car.

The crowd parted to let them through and Amelia followed Mabel through the hamlet, between the rows of ramshackle dwellings, where stringy chickens pecked and pigs rooted in the dust. The villagers followed them at a safe distance, murmuring in subdued tones. They walked on past a tethered Brahmin cow and a wooden pen crowded with scrawny goats, to a hut on the far edge of the village. It reminded Amelia of the trips into the mountains with her father when villagers had flocked to his clinics. She was suddenly glad she'd come and that she hadn't given in to Reginald's petulance.

'In here,' said Mabel, as she ducked inside the hut through

the low doorway. Amelia followed her into the stifling heat of the interior. Her eyes took a moment to get used to the gloom, but as they did, she saw two women were sitting side by side on a mat in the far corner. The younger one was heavily pregnant. The other woman got to her feet and greeted Mabel and Amelia with wide smiles and her hands held together.

'This is Jamila,' Mabel told Amelia, 'and her daughter-in-law, Parvati.'

'Namaste,' Jamila said, 'You would like tea?'

Amelia sat down beside Mabel on a wooden crate while Jamila went outside to boil the water. She listened while Mabel spoke quietly to the young woman, Parvati, in Hindi. Amelia wasn't fluent in Hindi but she knew a smattering of the language. Her father had spoken several Indian languages, and she'd learned Nepali herself – the language of the hill villages in Darjeeling province. She could tell, though, from Mabel's faltering attempts, that Mabel's Hindi wasn't good and that she spoke it with a heavy English accent. Once or twice, Amelia was even able to step in and help her out.

As Mabel talked to Parvati, who nodded and smiled, sometimes glancing in the direction of the door nervously, Amelia began to understand how the Mission was attempting to persuade the villagers to keep their baby girls. Mabel was explaining, in her halting Hindi, that the mission would help Parvati financially if her baby was a girl. Four payments would be made. One that very day, and she could keep the money whatever the gender of her baby; one instalment when the baby was born, and a further two during her first year of life. The sums were not huge, but they were large enough to be tempting, and would go towards any dowry the family may have to pay upon the girl's marriage.

Jamila returned with chai in earthenware cups and all four

women sat there sipping the sweet liquid, exchanging small talk and smiling at one another.

When they'd finished their chai, Mabel gave Parvati the money in an envelope. She took it with smiles and thanks and tears in her eyes. Then they said goodbye to the two women and returned to the car, with the same group of villagers following them. A bony dog was lying under the running board asleep, and one of the boys shooed it away.

'This is the culmination of several months of persuasion,' Mabel told Amelia as they drove away from the village. 'Even now, I'm not sure it will work. When Parvati's husband and father-in-law come home from the fields, they will probably take the money from her and there is no guarantee that she will keep her baby.'

'Has the Mission tried any other ways of persuading people to keep their baby girls?' Amelia asked looking back through the cloud of dust that rose behind the car at the village boys running after them whooping and shouting.

'There's one other thing that we've tried,' said Mabel. 'We also work with the Catholic Nunnery and Orphanage in Ganpur.'

'Really?' Amelia was surprised. Sometimes Catholic and Baptists in India didn't see eye to eye.

'Yes. The orphanage will take in any girl baby that's put in their porch on Sunday mornings before sunrise. It means that no one has to go through any formalities for the baby to be accepted into the orphanage and possibly found a new home. We at the Mission spread the word amongst the villagers, and if they are determined not to keep their babies, we will take their babies down to the orphanage for them. It's difficult for them to get there themselves and it is preferable to the alternative. However, we've had more success with helping the families financially, lately.'

At the next village, the woman they had visited had already given birth to her baby girl and Mabel was delivering her second payment. Amelia stood by a little shyly as Mabel cooed over the baby. The young mother was proud to show the tiny, wrinkled little girl off and this time other women from the village crowded into the mother's hut to share in the occasion. Amelia was touched by the welcome of the women and their pleasure in the new birth, but as they returned to the car two of the village men shook their fists angrily at them.

'They disapprove of us, I'm afraid,' said Mabel as she got into the driver's seat. 'It's a common reaction.' Amelia was reminded of Reginald's words; *Sensible Englishwomen don't do that; meddle in local customs.*

They visited a further two villages. In the first, Mabel stood beside the car as the village women gathered around. In a loud, clear voice, but still in faltering Hindi, she explained what she was here to do. There were shocked faces in the crowd, and some women heckled her, but she stood firm. Amelia found herself admiring the strength of this diminutive, seemingly unremarkable woman. Mabel reminded her of Mother.

In the last village they went to, there was another pregnant woman to visit who, like Parvati, was accompanied by her mother-in-law, this one more suspicious and less welcoming than Jamila had been. She didn't offer them refreshment and wouldn't allow them inside the hut. So they stood in the baking sun on the doorstep while Mabel explained to the young woman what the Mission would offer if she gave birth to a baby girl.

'She'll come round,' said Mabel as they drove away in the direction they'd come.

On the way back to Ganpur, Mabel asked Amelia if she'd enjoyed the day and whether she'd be prepared to help out on a regular basis.

'I can't always get up to the villages enough,' she said. 'To be effective we need to visit regularly. And I have to put in a lot of time raising funds. As you can imagine, we get through donations pretty quickly.'

'I'd love to, but I'm not sure,' Amelia replied, biting her nail. 'Arthur needs my company, and...' She didn't finish the sentence, but she sensed that Mabel could tell what she was thinking. Could she really face a battle with Reginald each time she wanted to help out?

When they drew up under the portico at the Residence, Amelia asked Mabel if she'd like to come in for tiffin, but Mabel politely declined.

'I've got lots to do at home, but thank you. You should come and visit us for tea one day, though. Giles would love to see you.'

'I'd like that,' said Amelia.

∾

WHEN REGINALD CAME HOME after sunset that evening, he didn't ask Amelia how her day had gone, or anything about her trip to the hills. He went straight through to see Arthur. Amelia could tell he hadn't forgotten about her trip out with Mabel by the pointed way he asked Arthur how he'd felt being on his own all day.

'Oh, I wasn't alone, Daddy. I was with ayah and Amir,' replied Arthur, with an innocent smile.

'Of course,' Reginald replied absently.

Reginald's face was etched with lines of exhaustion and after leaving Arthur's room he went outside and flopped down in one of the cane chairs on the veranda with a whisky.

'Are you alright?' Amelia asked, following him, a little concerned.

'Had a bloody awful day. Trying to get those blighters to talk. Like getting blood out of a stone,' he said.

'Isn't that for the police to do?' she asked.

'It *is* for them, you're right. But I need to be there too. It's a matter of security for the district. Besides, the suspects are far more likely to talk if I'm there,' he added grimly.

'Why's that?' she asked with a prickle of alarm.

'Don't ask,' he said, draining the glass.

'I'll go up and change now.' He got up with a stretch and left Amelia alone on the veranda.

He'd left his linen jacket slung over the back of the chair. Amelia picked it up to take it to him, but as she did so, she noticed something that sent horror and disbelief rushing through her. She held the jacket up to the lamp and looked closely at it, holding her breath. There was no mistaking what she saw; the linen lapels and front panels of the jacket were sprayed all over with tiny flecks of red. It was blood. It had to be. Amelia sank back into the chair, the cloth of the jacket screwed tight in her fists. What could this mean? Whose blood could it possibly be? She didn't want to contemplate the answer and sat there trying to calm her breath and stop herself from screaming.

13

KATE

Warren End, 1970

As Kate drove out of the village that bright April morning, and took the road out towards Buckingham, she thought about Gordon Anderson. She recalled their conversation the day before, the way they'd laughed so naturally and easily together and how much she'd enjoyed chatting with him. It had been refreshing to be with someone who had no expectations of her and who wasn't trying to prove anything. She'd been able to relax and be herself for the first time in as long as she could remember.

She drove on through the lanes, past woodland, fields of sheep or early crops, and tried to understand why that was. At work, she was always so busy maintaining a professional front, needing to prove herself so as not to be trampled underfoot, side-lined or overlooked by her male colleagues, that she rarely let her guard down enough to hold a normal, relaxed conversation with anyone. In her private life too, most people she mixed with in London were acquaintances rather than true friends. They knew little about her background, her childhood or where she came from. She was always wary of giving away too much, of revealing her weak spots, terrified that if anyone got close to her secrets, her carefully constructed façade would collapse and her life would unravel. She gripped the steering wheel accelerating up a hill, not even wanting to think about it; it would mean facing up to the guilt that she'd kept buried down the decades – guilt that had kept gnawing away at her from the inside, corroding her peace of mind.

But now, back in the place where it had all started, she was at least trying to understand how the events of 1944 had affected her life. She knew it was at the root of all her failed relationships.

It had been a couple of years since the last one had finished. It wasn't Kate who had ended it, finally, but it was she who had brought it to its knees. Jonathan had wanted commitment. He was a lawyer working on the sale of one of the buildings she'd designed. They'd got close over drinks after meetings that had run on late into the evenings. He'd never been married and he was a few years younger than Kate. They'd dated for several months, it had even felt like love, and then he'd suggested they move in together. That was when Kate's shutters came down. She told herself that she valued her own space, that she was too set in her ways to share her daily existence with another human being. It was all very well spending time with Jonathan, visiting galleries at weekends, theatre on weekday evenings and wining and dining in tucked away restaurants, holding hands over the table and looking into one another's eyes. But sharing her life with him was something else altogether. She wasn't ready to let him into her heart.

She wondered now what had made her that way. How had she become such a cold, ungiving human being, unwilling to risk closeness even with someone she loved and knew she could trust? What a contrast with her schooldays, when an encounter with Gordon in the school corridor had set her pulse racing, her heart soaring with joy. Now, from the depths of her memory, their last encounter came back to her. She realised that she must have blotted it out for years, because she had completely forgotten it until that moment.

She'd been shopping with her mother in Midchester one Saturday early in the summer of '44. She'd resisted going because she'd promised Joan she would call for her after breakfast and that they would go to the mill that morning, but her mother had insisted.

'There's a lot to carry and your father can't help me today. He's got some sort of air raid business on this morning in the village hall.'

So, she'd gone with Freda on the nine o'clock bus, feeling guilty that she'd be letting Joan down. She knew that Joan would be annoyed with her and if she was honest with herself she was a little afraid of Joan's temper.

The queue for the butcher's stretched a long way down the High Street and was moving at a snail's pace, so Freda had asked Kate to run along to the hardware shop to buy some matches and cakes of washing soap. As soon as she'd entered the gloom of Bendall's shop and closed the door behind her with a jangle of the bell, she saw him there behind the counter. He was serving another customer and didn't see her at first. She felt her face grow hot and was on the point of turning round and rushing out again when he looked up and noticed her.

It was too late then. She felt trapped. She could feel the colour rise to her cheeks, but there was nowhere to hide. Her heart started to pound, but she knew she had to tough it out. She straightened her shoulders and approached the counter.

'Hello!' said Gordon, with a smile, turning his blue eyes towards her. 'What a surprise to see you here.'

The old man he'd been serving gathered up his purchases

and shuffled away, slamming the door behind him. They were alone in the shop. Kate was aware of the smell of paraffin and paint and the sound of someone rummaging about in the back room.

'You too. I didn't realise you worked here,' she said.

'I'm just helping out my uncle during the summer holidays.'

'Oh,' she stared down at the counter, wishing the heat in her flaming cheeks would recede. She was thinking about the last day of school when she'd emerged from the cloakroom with a group of other girls and Gordon was waiting outside, hands in pockets, his eyes fixed on the door. He'd walked away quickly when he'd seen them together, and they'd all speculated on the way to the school bus, whether he was waiting for one of them, and if so, which one. Kate didn't dare to hope it could be her.

'What can I get for you?' he asked, and she remembered abruptly what she was there for. She told him that she wanted soap and matches and he reached up to the wooden shelves that lined the walls behind the counter, got them down and wrapped them in brown paper. All the time, she was watching him, mesmerised by the closeness of him, the way his blond hair flopped over his forehead as he bent forward, by his tanned fingers wrapping the parcel so deftly. He handed it to her with a smile and she put it into her bag.

'Well, goodbye then,' she said, after she'd paid, turning to leave. She walked the length of the shop, aware of his eyes on her back, and she'd just reached the door when he spoke again.

'I was thinking...' he began.

'Yes?' she asked, turning back to look at him, her heart in her mouth.

'I was thinking that, well... maybe we could meet up one day. One day when you're free, that is...'

Kate's mouth dropped open and her mind scrambled. She had no idea what to say.

'If you don't want to, of course, that's fine,' he stammered. 'It's just... it's just that. Well, it would be nice to see you. It seems a long time since we broke up from school.'

As he spoke, she'd been looking down at the scuffed floorboards, but when he'd finished, she ventured a look into his eyes and to her surprise he looked away. She couldn't believe that he could be nervous.

'Alright. That would be nice,' she managed to blurt out, wondering how they could arrange it. Should they make the arrangement now? Would he write to her? That all seemed very formal.

'How about next Saturday?' he asked as if reading her thoughts. 'I'm working all week here, but I've got the Saturday off. We could... we could buy some lunch and walk by the river maybe.'

'Yes. Yes. That would be lovely,' she replied.

'How about twelve o'clock then? On the market square. Outside the town hall maybe?'

'Alright. Yes. I can get the bus in at eleven. I'll see you then.'

She raced out of the shop, her heart hammering with nerves and excitement and virtually ran down the street towards where her mother was still standing in the butcher's queue. But even as she hurried, she was thinking of Joan. What would she say about this surprise development? They'd been so close the whole summer; inseparable in fact. No one had spoiled their togetherness and their unspoken routine. She'd let her down today and she would be letting her down again if she spent next Saturday with Gordon. Joan wouldn't like it, she knew that much.

'What's up with you?' asked Freda as she arrived breathless outside the butcher's shop. 'You're all flushed. You look as if you've just seen Clark Gable.'

Now, thinking back to that day, and the fateful week that had followed, Kate realised that for years she'd blanked out the fact that she'd never made it to Midchester to meet Gordon the following Saturday. Friday was the day *it* had happened, the event that had blown her life apart, and the fact that Gordon would be waiting for her outside the town hall had been a long way from her mind on the Saturday.

She drove down a hill into the river valley, past some dense woodland on her left. She registered that this place looked vaguely familiar, as she wondered whether Gordon himself remembered that she'd not turned up to meet him that day. When they'd returned to school at the start of the autumn term, she'd been a shell of her former self. She'd not wanted to speak to anyone, certainly not Gordon, and they'd both carefully avoided each other. Within a few months she'd left school anyway; her father had found another job in Saxmundham and the three of them had gone to start a new life in a new place.

Now, she was driving along the bottom of the river valley. Nothing had changed here. It was just as it had always looked with acres of boggy marshland between the road and the river. And there it was, the river itself, glinting in the early spring sunshine, like a glass track snaking along between the rows of pollarded willows.

Kate's heartrate sped up as she realised that she would be driving past the ruins of Willow Mill in half a mile or so. There was another route to Buckingham, via the main road, so why had she taken this one? Was it an unconscious desire to revisit old places, to remind herself of the source of all her pain? Or had she just gone this way because it was mapped onto her brain like the migration route of swallows in springtime? She gripped the steering wheel.

'Face up to it, Kate,' she said out loud. 'There's no ducking out of it anymore.'

And in that moment, she vowed that she would do just that.

Just as she was doing her best to get to the bottom of Amelia's secrets, trying to understand why her aunt had kept her past life hidden and whether it had a bearing on the way Amelia had behaved that summer – the way she'd become withdrawn and preoccupied; her betrayal of Uncle James – Kate would, at the same time, face up to her own past. She would confront how what she and Joan had done that summer had forever changed their own lives and the lives of others. After all, what they'd done and Amelia's secrets were inextricably linked.

Kate knew that the route to facing up to it all was by befriending Joan again and getting to the point where they could talk about what had happened that summer. She thought about Joan now, overweight and defeated, harassed and abused. And she thought about Dave too. How he'd threatened her and warned her off. Kate wasn't going to let Dave's bullying stop her; in fact, it was central to the reason she needed to get close to Joan again. She was sure that behind all that defensiveness and bravado, Joan was crying out for her help.

She slowed the car down and negotiated the bend in the road beside the spinney. There it was, its red-tiled roof visible above the treetops with their dusting of early spring leaves. The old mill. It hadn't been restored or converted. It was just as it always had been, only more dilapidated. The roof had caved in in places, and the chimney had partially collapsed, smothered with ivy and with elder bushes sprouting from it.

And there was the gateway where she and Joan let themselves in with their bikes, and where George Prendergast and Amelia had hidden their cars for their secret trysts. It was overgrown now, covered in brambles and knee deep in grass, the wood of the five-barred gate sagging and green with lichen. On an impulse, Kate pulled the car off the road and parked up on the grass. Still gripping the steering wheel, she took several deep breaths to calm herself down. Glancing at her watch, she saw that she still had plenty of time to get to The Meadows; enough time to spend ten minutes here. She got out of the car and leaned against the door for a moment, debating whether or not to go through the gate and visit the mill. The place had an eerie feel about it that sent chills running through her, but the pull of the past was strong.

Despite the brambles and the condition of the gate, it wasn't difficult to open. She pushed it aside and went through into the wood. The muddy track was still visible underfoot, although the trees were taller now, the undergrowth thicker. She began to walk through the wood towards the mill. The quiet was palpable here; the only sounds were birdsong and the faint ripple of the river. Looking up, she saw two crows chasing a blackbird across the sky between the branches. She stopped when the old mill came into view and stared at its shabby walls. It looked just as she remembered, only now the windows were boarded up and a sign with red lettering was fixed on the bricks on the lower floor.

DANGER: DO NOT ENTER

Joan's laughter, her mischief. And the guilt. It all came back so clearly.

The creak of a door broke the air, loud enough to make her start. There was someone else here. Panicking, she stepped off the path, pushed through the brambles and stood behind a tree, her heart thumping. From where she stood she could see the corner of the building and beside it the path that led round from the door of the mill. Whoever it was would come that way. She waited for what seemed like an age. Then a figure emerged round the building. Moving slowly, with exaggerated steps, it was an old man, bundled up in a grey hat and coat despite the warmth of the day. He was walking with a stick. Kate knew instantly who it was. George Prendergast.

She also knew that she didn't want him to see her there. If she moved quickly, she could get back to her car before he saw her. Instead of going back to the track, she pushed her way through the brambles and undergrowth parallel to the track, thorns scratching her legs, snagging her tights, thistles sticking to her coat, until she reached the hedge, from which it was only a few steps back to the gate. She hurried through it and fastened the lock with clumsy fingers. Back in the car, her heart hammering, she started the engine and roared away along the valley, driving as quickly as the narrow lane permitted until she crested the brow of a hill. There she had to slam on the brakes so as not to plough into a herd of cows crossing the road.

She switched off the engine and watched the placid black and white animals as they plodded across the lane from a field on the left to a farm entrance on the right. Some stopped and turned their heads to stare at her with their doe eyes before moving on, others paused to lift their tail and deposit a pat of dung on the road. The sight of those serene animals made Kate smile and reflect on what had just happened. It had taken a lot of courage to open that gate and walk towards the mill, and the sight of George Prendergast had banished that confidence, turned her into a frightened jelly, running for cover. He was the last person she had expected to see at that moment. She wondered why he was visiting the old place alone. There was no car there, so he must have walked. Walking with his stick as he did, it would have taken him all morning to walk from the village, even if he took the shortcut. She wondered why he went there and how often. Was he revisiting the place where he used to meet Amelia? Was he trying to come to terms with the past just as she herself was?

The last cow crossed the road and the farmer emerged from the field, closed the gate and followed them, waving to Kate as he went. She drove on towards the main road, more slowly now she'd recovered from her shock, enjoying the scenery unfolding around her, realising how much she had missed these gentle, wooded hills.

The Meadows was housed in a former stately home built on a hill a few miles north of Buckingham, with sweeping views stretching far and wide. The sign on the gate proclaimed: "Elegant retirement for the discerning senior", and as she drove up the drive between avenues of oak trees, across its well-tended acres, she remembered that although the two Miss Robinsons had lived in a deteriorating mansion and appeared penniless, their father had been a boot and shoe magnate, one of the biggest employers in Northampton, and before his death had sold up to an American company. So Miss Robinson could afford to live in these stately surroundings.

Kate parked up outside the building with its palladium columns and long steps up to the grand entrance, the architect in her awed at such graceful design, perfectly suited to its setting, such perfection of proportion.

Inside the high-ceilinged entrance hall, which resembled a luxury hotel more than a care home, after waiting for a few moments, she was collected by the same young woman who had escorted Miss Robinson to Amelia's funeral.

'I'm Sandra by the way,' said the girl. 'It's very nice to see you again, Miss Hamilton. Miss Robinson has been looking forward to your visit.'

She led Kate along wide, cream-carpeted corridors lined with panelled doors, passing the occasional well-heeled resident walking with a Zimmer frame, staff pushing trolleys laden with silver-domed dishes. At the end she stopped at one of the doors and knocked discreetly before opening it.

The room was palatial, with elaborately corniced ceilings, a large marble fireplace and elegant furniture. Miss Robinson was sitting in a reclining chair beside the fireplace in which artificial gas flames flickered. Her knees were covered in a red tartan rug and she was wrapped up in a shawl.

'Come, my dear,' she said, beckoning Kate forward and motioning her to sit in a chair opposite hers.

Kate sat down and smiled at the old lady. Her eyes were not obscured by sunglasses this time, but they were almost closed, the pupils invisible.

The shiver of a memory went through Kate. The image of Miss Robinson and her blind sister walking through the village arm in arm, the sister staring ahead through blank, occluded eyes. How cruel the village children had been to fear them and mock them for their afflictions. But it wasn't really their blindness that had frightened them, it was the rumours that the younger sister was psychic. She was said to be able to see into the past and predict the future, to know when a disaster or accident would befall someone, when people would die and when they were due a stroke of good fortune.

Now Miss Robinson turned her head in Kate's direction and smiled.

'I knew you would come, my dear. When you started looking through your aunt's belongings. I knew you would find things there that raised questions in your mind. You did, didn't you? You did find such things?'

'Yes. I found a marriage certificate from India. Some photographs and some letters.'

'But the letters didn't answer your questions. They just raised more in your mind, didn't they?'

Kate nodded and her eyes wandered to the flickering fire. It was so hot in the room, her face was already flushing from the heat. And flushing too, from the old lady's words. Edna Robinson seemed to know so much about her, perhaps she knew everything there was to know. Even the things Kate hadn't properly faced up to herself yet. She felt exactly as she'd felt at

Joan's house. Trapped, with nowhere to run to, nowhere to hide.

As if to give voice to her fears, Edna went on, 'And you've got pressing reasons for wanting to find out, haven't you?'

Again, Kate nodded. At that moment, the door opened and Sandra came in with a tea tray. Neither Miss Robinson, nor Kate spoke as Sandra poured the tea and handed them cups that rattled on bone china saucers. Then she left, closing the door noisily behind her.

'You know, just like you, your aunt had things in her own past that she couldn't reveal. Your uncle had given her a home and a new life, and she was happy with him and eternally grateful to him. But still, underneath all that, she was a troubled young woman.'

'But how do you know all this?' Kate managed to ask.

'We befriended poor Amelia, my sister and I. We had seen her in the village and my sister always used to say, "Edna, there's something about that young lady. Darkness clings to her like a shroud. I can see it all around her". She was never wrong about that sort of thing. We went into the church one day and there was your aunt, sobbing her heart out in one of the pews. We sat down either side of her, put our arms around her and comforted her. After that she started to come to our house for tea. And bit by bit she confided in us. She told us everything. Of course my sister was always one step ahead of her, but Amelia filled in the gaps for us.'

'So, will you tell me?' asked Kate in a small voice. 'I... I need to know.'

'Of course. That's why I asked you here, my dear. It's time you were told the truth.'

14

AMELIA

Ganpur, India, 1935-'36

I t took a supreme effort of will for Amelia not to scream out in shock, sitting there on the veranda of the Residence that stifling June evening, the cloth of Reginald's blood-stained jacket screwed up in her fists. She was paralysed with fear and horror. What should she do? What *could* she do? Her instinct was to follow him upstairs to their suite where he'd gone to take a bath, and ask him for an explanation, but she knew that was pointless. She wouldn't get a straight answer and he would then know that she'd noticed the blood and was suspicious.

As she sat there, immobile, listening to the deafening whirr of cicadas in the garden, breathing in the scent of frangipani and bougainvillea, she gradually began to calm down. She started to tell herself that there must be a perfectly good explanation for the flecks of blood on Reginald's jacket; it was possible that he'd witnessed an accident at close quarters on the way home; or maybe he'd walked through the covered market and past a butcher's stall earlier in the day. She'd been inside the stifling Ganpur Central bazaar with Arthur and had had to hold her nose at the pungent, sickly smells emanating from the meat counters, where butchers chopped meat and poultry with huge axes on filthy wooden slabs. It would be all too easy to get sprayed with blood whilst walking past one of those stalls. Yes. That must be it. Any other explanation was unthinkable.

So, as her heartbeat gradually returned to normal, Amelia got to her feet and returned the jacket to the back of Reginald's chair, being careful to ensure it was hanging in the exact position he had left it. She then went inside to the drawing room to pour herself a stiff brandy. After a couple of sips she felt calm enough to go upstairs to face him, and by the time she'd reached the top of the stairs, she'd convinced herself that everything was fine and that she could safely forget all about the jacket. She went through into the bathroom and there was Reginald, soaking in the bath, calmly reading a book, a drink by his side. The sight of him sitting there made her pause in the doorway.

'Everything alright, darling?' he asked, casually, looking up.

'Of course,' she said, taking another sip of her brandy.

'I'll be out in a minute. Do *you* want a bath before dinner?'

'No... it's alright. I had one when I came home,' she said, and his eyes flicked back to his book. She knew, by the way he tilted his chin and his refusal to speak about it, that he was reiterating his disapproval of her trip to the hill villages with Mabel. Deciding not to rise to the bait, she went to the bedroom to change for dinner.

That night when they went to bed, despite her decision to put the blood-spattered jacket out of her mind, she shivered in disgust when Reginald touched her. But she didn't want to arouse his suspicions by drawing away. Experience had already taught her that he would sulk or become angry if she didn't respond to his advances. So, she lay there stiffly, letting him run his hands over her body, move on top of her and tell her how much he loved her, while all the time she was shrinking inside.

Days and weeks passed and as Amelia adapted to her new life at The Residence the incident with the jacket gradually faded from her mind. The next time she saw Reginald wearing it, it had been laundered and pressed, and bore no trace of blood nor even a speck of dirt. She even began to wonder if she'd imagined what she'd seen.

Life fell into a regular routine. She continued to spend most of her days with Arthur. She would teach him basic lessons and read him adventure stories and fairy-tales. They would ride out into the scrubby wasteland that surrounded Ganpur, play ball games in the garden, or walk together along the neat roads of the cantonment. Under her care, Arthur's health returned gradually, and each day, although still delicate and skinny, he appeared a little stronger. He had colour in his cheeks, and when he laughed, which he did often now, Amelia was delighted to see a mischievous sparkle in his blue eyes.

The rapport grew between the two of them and it felt to Amelia as if they were starting to understand and appreciate each other like mother and son. But she was careful to keep Elizabeth in their thoughts and conversations; she didn't want Arthur to think she was trying to replace his mother in his affections. She was all too aware, though, that these days were numbered, and that before long the tutor would arrive and this new-found closeness would change forever.

Once a week, Amir drove them to the Church of England in the centre of town. They would make their way through the graveyard, past the white church with its looming tower, to Elizabeth's grave in the forgotten, overgrown corner. Arthur would kneel before it just as he had on the first occasion, and lay flowers for his mother. Amelia would also bring her own bunch of flowers, and think not only of Elizabeth as she laid them on her grave, but also of her own mother and father whose remains had been scattered in the mountain stream so far away. Although they had no grave, their spirits accompanied her every moment of every day.

Amelia and Arthur would walk back to the car hand in hand, and sometimes Arthur would ask if they could spend some time in the Indian quarter, and not go home straight away. He loved to visit the bazaar and mingle with the noisy crowds marvelling at the stalls overflowing with fruit and vegetables, pungent spices or brightly coloured silks, or to visit one of the many temples in the town to breathe in the exotic aroma of incense and candles, and watch the Hindu faithful making puja. Sometimes they would take a walk down to the wide, brown river that ran through the centre of the ramshackle old town to watch the dhobi-wallahs pounding the dirt out of laundry on the rocks.

Amelia enjoyed going to these places as much as Arthur did, it was such a contrast to the calm sterility of the Residence and the British cantonment, and it brought back memories of her trips into the hills with her father. It surprised her a little that Arthur was so drawn to such places, although he had many Indian friends and he spoke fluent Hindi. One day, as they shouldered their way through a bustling street full of food sellers and street vendors, she asked him tentatively if his mother used to bring him to the Indian quarter.

'Oh yes! She loved it here,' he said. 'She used to bring me here with Deepak sometimes.'

'Deepak?'

'Yes. But he's gone now,' he said sadly, 'He doesn't live in Ganpur anymore.'

'Oh?' she asked, wondering if Deepak had worked in the house or garden, but Arthur had let go of her hand and was slipping through the crowd towards a stall selling sweet lassi.

'Can I have one, Amelia?' he was shouting over his shoulder. 'Please?'

Once or twice a week, Reginald would expect her to accompany him to the Gymkhana Club for a drink in the bar followed by supper in the palatial dining room. As they entered, he would take her arm gallantly and escort her through the lobby, to the bar. As they crossed the room the eyes of the entire British community would be on her; the women's eyes narrowed with envy or displeasure and the men's with admiration in equal measure. It reminded her of the ripple of disapproval that had greeted her in the Planter's Club in Darjeeling before Reginald had taken her under his wing. Experiencing an echo of the gratitude that she'd felt for him back then, she would turn to him, smiling, and see the pride in his eyes that came from the knowledge that the most beautiful woman in the room was on *his* arm. But that feeling was often replaced with confusion and a feeling of dread in the pit of her stomach as the evening wore on, as Reginald's pride was often replaced with jealousy. If she so much as smiled at one of the other men, he would accuse her of making eyes at them, when all she was doing was being polite. She quickly learned to keep her eyes cast down and never to look another man in the eye.

As Reginald drew his invisible boundaries around her ever tighter, she began to see Arthur as an ally in her struggle to maintain some sort of independence and life of her own. She saw how Arthur too struggled with his father's demands and mercurial temper. Reginald clearly despaired of having a sensitive, thoughtful son who, despite the fact he enjoyed being outdoors, playing with his friends and riding out with Amelia, had no desire to partake in the "manly pursuits" Reginald would frequently mention.

'He needs to learn to shoot, to ride out in the jungle after wild boar, that sort of thing,' he would say to Amelia over dinner.

'He's very young, Reginald,' she would protest. 'And perhaps he's never going to enjoy that sort of thing, as you call it. He's a sensitive boy.'

'Yes. That's what worries me. It's quite unnatural for a boy to be indoors with women all the time. The sooner that tutor arrives to lick him into shape, the better.'

'But he's not inside with women all the time. He has lots of friends, as you well know. And he spends time with Amir and with you.'

'But for the vast majority of his time, he's with you and ayah. And I can see already that you're indulging the boy, just like... well, just like his mother did.'

'He's just a little boy,' she said, dropping her eyes to her plate. 'It's what mothers do.'

Reginald began to grow angry then. She could see the colour rising in his face and his eyes narrowing. It was like a storm approaching.

'But you're *not* his mother, Amelia,' he snapped and she jumped at the force of his words, 'I think you sometimes forget that. When I met you, I thought you were different.'

'Different? Whatever do you mean?' she asked, alarmed.

'It doesn't matter. Whatever I mean, it doesn't alter the fact that a boy of his age should be taught to toughen up. Shikar season will be on us soon and I intend to teach him to shoot before that. I shall be taking him with me and the other men from the club on camp. We can shoot game and introduce him to pigsticking at the first opportunity.'

'Reginald, surely not...' Amelia stared at him, open mouthed, the colour draining from her face. Eileen's words came back to her; *She died in a shooting accident, out on a shikar with Reginald.*

They were pursuing a tiger and she fell into the path of the animal... it was really very shocking indeed.

Apart from the obvious dangers involved, how could Reginald even contemplate teaching Arthur to shoot and taking him hunting when it was the way his mother had met her sudden and horrific death? Didn't Reginald realise how insensitive that was? How it would bring it all back to the boy, just when he seemed to be getting over his grief? And leaving aside the death of Arthur's mother, how could he think about forcing the cruellest of blood sports on a boy like Arthur, who was gentle and sweet, who loved animals and wouldn't swat a mosquito because he didn't want to kill another living being.

'Whyever not?' he said. 'It's exactly what he needs, and I'd thank you to stop mollycoddling him.'

Amelia carried on eating her meal in silence. How could she protest when he didn't know that she'd been told that Elizabeth had died that way? If she let slip that Eileen had told her the truth, he would surely accuse her of gossiping about him, of being disloyal. Arthur had never spoken of the details, he'd only said tearfully that Mummy had passed away suddenly. Amelia wondered how much the boy actually knew.

Reginald finished his meal and pushed his plate away.

'I want to hear no more about it. I'll come home early tomorrow and ride with him out into the countryside. We'll take the guns and I'll start teaching him to handle one. I should have some free time in the afternoon. I'm not needed at the police station for the time being.'

'Oh?' she asked in alarm. 'What happened to your suspects?'

He leaned back in his chair and lit a cigarette, concentrating on the match.

'We had to release one of them,' he said, blowing smoke rings into the air. 'His father is a lawyer and kicked up quite a

stink. Another one died, unfortunately. We're letting the
remaining two sweat in the cells for a few days.'

'Oh, Reginald! However did he die?'

'The coward hanged himself in his cell. Now, enough of that
talk,' he said getting up from the table. 'Shall we go through for
a nightcap?

ON TUESDAYS AND THURSDAYS, after Reginald had left for
Government House, Amelia would ask Amir to drive her across
town to the Baptist Mission housed in a shabby colonial building. There, in a stuffy office, with crumbling walls and func-
tional furniture that reminded her faintly of an English church
hall, she would write letters to businesses and benefactors back
in Britain, explaining the work of the mission and requesting
donations for the project.

On the first occasion, she told Reginald that Mabel had
asked her to help out. He greeted the news with eye-rolling and
sighs. After that, she said little to him about these visits, and he
never asked her directly about the Mission. Perhaps he questioned Amir about her movements, or perhaps he asked Arthur.
From Reginald's silence, she realised that he was aware of where
she went on Tuesdays and Thursdays, but he wasn't going to
condone what she was doing by asking her about it. On other
days of the week he virtually cross-examined her about what
she'd been doing all day and with whom.

But what she stopped short of telling him was that often,
after her shift, she would have lunch with Mabel and Giles at
their home. They lived in an unfashionable part of Ganpur, well
away from the Gymkhana Club and the landscaped avenues of
the British cantonment. Their home was a few streets back from

the Baptist Mission in a humble area where British and Indian people lived side by side.

On the first occasion, when Amir dropped her off by the front gate, she paused outside for a moment, taking in the simple clapperboard bungalow with its shady veranda. She opened the gate and stepped into the front garden. The neat gravel path was lined with earthenware pots overflowing with geraniums, marigolds and chrysanthemums. A powerful wave of nostalgia washed over her for the bungalow in the hills and the life she had there with her parents, filled with love and happiness. Mabel came out onto the porch wearing a pinafore over her dress, her arms open to welcome Amelia. Giles was hovering behind his wife, in his shirt sleeves. He held out his hand and shook Amelia's warmly.

'Come on in,' he said. 'Let me show you around our little place.'

'You do that, Giles,' said Mabel, 'I'll just pop into the kitchen and make sure the lunch is ready.' She disappeared into the bungalow and Amelia stared after her, impressed. It was unusual for a European woman to spend any time in the kitchen. Even Amelia's mother, the least imperious person she'd ever known, had employed a khansama, or cook, in India and never cooked herself.

'Well, there's not much to see,' said Giles, smiling amiably. 'But do come in. It's a pretty poor show compared to the Residence, I'm afraid.'

'Oh, not at all. It's beautiful,' said Amelia, stepping over the threshold and looking around in wonder at the cosy living room with a floral sofa and chairs and watercolours of Indian street scenes. There was an upright piano on one wall, and on another a low bookshelf filled with Bibles and prayerbooks. Above that, hung a large painting of St. John the Baptist in a red cloak, baptising Christ. It was the same reproduction that had hung in all the homes she'd lived in since childhood. She was familiar with every brushstroke. A lump formed in her throat at the powerful memories it evoked.

This must be where Mabel and Giles sat in the evenings, reading or talking, cooled by the ceiling fan and lit by a pool of lamplight. It was just how her parents had sat in companionable silence every evening of her life. It was a stark reminder of how she spent her evenings at the Residence; eating at a large, polished table waited upon by servants, making stilted conversation with Reginald, worried she might say something to incur his anger, then drinking a nightcap in the palatial drawing room which felt more like a museum than a family home.

'So, you see, it's pretty basic,' Giles said cheerfully, interrupting her thoughts. He showed her a tiny dining room containing an oval cottage table and chairs. Finally, he opened a door to the only bedroom, with its simple wooden bed, muslin curtains and a plain cross on the wall.

Mabel appeared from the kitchen carrying a tray of dishes, followed by a smiling Indian man who padded through the house barefoot behind her, carrying some bowls.

'We're eating out on the veranda,' she said, beckoning them out onto the front porch where another fan whirred on the ceiling and a cane table was laid for three.

'Do tuck in,' said Mabel as they sat down. 'It's just kedgeree. But help yourself. We don't stand on ceremony here.'

It was refreshing not to be waited on for once, and to be able to relax and chat freely amongst friends. Amelia told Mabel about her morning and Mabel spoke about the new places she'd been visiting, a little further away from Ganpur.

'It will take time,' Mabel said. 'I've often encountered hostility at first, but most of the women come round to the right path in the end. Of course, they don't actually *want* to drown their baby girls.'

'It's poverty that drives them to it,' said Giles, shaking his head. 'We're really very grateful for your help, Amelia. I'm sure your mother and father would be extremely proud of what you're doing.'

'I hope they would be,' she murmured and another bout of yearning for her old life, kindled by the familiar surroundings and the warmth of like-minded friends, threatened to overcome her.

Sometimes Mabel would take her up into the hills to speak to the village women as she had on the first visit, to persuade them to keep their baby girls. The women soon got to know Amelia and would flock excitedly to surround the car when they saw her arrive seated beside Mabel. They would take her arm and invite her into their homes, offer her tea and food. She couldn't help noticing that they responded to her far more warmly than they did to Mabel. Perhaps it was because she spoke their language more fluently, or perhaps it was because she had spent years amongst villagers with her father and understood their needs and concerns instinctively. Or maybe it was because, with her luxuriant black hair and dark features, they saw her as one of them. Mabel would follow in her wake and stand aside while Amelia was encouraged inside homes to drink tea and chat to the women.

Although she already knew Mabel to be a generous and kind-hearted friend, Amelia couldn't help worrying that Mabel might be offended by her popularity. Perhaps Mabel would think that Amelia was trying to upstage her? But one day, on the way back to Ganpur, as they drove alongside the lake, Mabel turned to her and said,

'You know, Amelia, I have to hand it to you; you've exceeded all my expectations. You're such a success with the ladies in the villages. You're a real asset to the project. I'm so glad you're helping us.'

'I'm glad too, Mabel,' she said, relieved. 'I'm really enjoying doing something worthwhile. It's what my parents would have wanted for me.'

Mabel pulled the car onto the same sandy beach opposite the pavilion where they'd parked the first time and turned the engine off. The quiet of the lake enveloped them and the only sounds were the cawing of crows which circled above the forest on the opposite side of the lake and the tick-tick of the chassis as the car cooled down.

'I've stopped because I'd like to ask you something and it's difficult to speak above the noise of the engine. You've so impressed me that I was wondering if you could come up here by yourself sometimes, so that I can start going to villages a little further away? I can see that you don't need me here anymore.'

'I'm flattered you should ask me,' Amelia said, her nerves already on edge at the thought of coming here alone. 'Of course, I'd be happy to come alone, but there's just one thing...'

'Oh?' said Mabel.

Amelia took a deep breath and looked down.

'Is it Reginald? Does he disapprove?' Mabel asked gently.

'To tell you the truth, I haven't actually been able to face telling him that I've been coming up here with you,' Amelia admitted. 'Not after the first time. He knows I help out at the Mission, but I haven't mentioned that we've been visiting the villages.'

'Oh, Amelia,' said Mabel, slipping her hand over hers. 'I had no idea. Look, if it would make it easier for you, forget what I just asked. I don't want to put you in an awkward position with Reginald. I can carry on coming here alone. And I'll try to fit in other villages around my work here. You're not to worry about it.'

'But I do worry about it, Mabel. You need my help. I can see that,' she said, biting a nail, torn between taking the easy route and giving in to Reginald, and doing what all her senses told her was the right thing to do, taking a stand against his control and telling him she was going to keep coming up here to help Mabel and the Mission.

'Well, whatever you think's best,' said Mabel slowly. 'Perhaps you should talk to him about it, but... well... if he *really* doesn't want you to come, I wouldn't want you to do anything to displease him. And you must come and have lunch again next week with Giles and me. He asks about you every day.'

'Oh really?'

'Yes. He's concerned about you. We both are.'

'Oh?' Amelia said, her scalp tingling in alarm at the direction the conversation was taking. 'Why is that?'

Mabel placed both her hands on the steering wheel and took a deep breath. She opened her mouth to say something, then she seemed to check herself.

'Because you're a member of our community, of course,' she said briskly. 'We Baptists all look out for each other. Now, shall we get on? It's getting awfully hot sitting in the sun like this.'

Mabel started the engine and moved the car off the sandy beach and onto the track. Amelia stared out at the lake, wondering what Mabel had been about to say. But her attention was caught by something. The lake was lower than she'd ever seen it before; it hadn't rained for a long time and the water had receded several yards, exposing the cracked earth of the lake bed. Just above the water's edge, something gleamed white in the sun. It looked like a pile of tiny white sticks.

Amelia stared at it as the car pulled away, realising with a start that it wasn't sticks she was looking at, but a pile of fragile bones, bleaching in the sun. Was it the remains of an animal, a large bird perhaps? But then her hand flew to her mouth as she realised. It must be the skeleton of a tiny baby; one of the new-born girls that had been brought here to die. Tears formed in her eyes as the image of a young woman, someone like Parvati, came into her mind. Hardly more than a girl herself, she stumbled along the dirt road from the village in the dead of night with only the moon to light her way, carrying her baby girl in her arms. When she reached the little beach, she knelt down at the place where the water lapped the shore, her shoulders drooping with the magnitude of her task. Pausing briefly to check she was alone, she lowered the baby into the water, holding its struggling, slippery form under the surface, until it struggled no more.

In that moment, Amelia made her decision.

'No, Mabel,' she said, surprising herself with the force of her own voice. Mabel put the brakes on and the car shuddered to a halt.

'Whatever's the matter?' Mabel asked.

'I *will* keep on coming,' said Amelia. 'I will tell Reginald about it, of course. It's just finding the right words. But he doesn't have the right to stop me doing what I want and what I know to be valuable and worthwhile.'

15

AMELIA

Ganpur, India, 1936

A s shikar season approached, Reginald stepped up the intensity of Arthur's shooting lessons. He would arrive home early two or three times a week and appear at the door of Arthur's schoolroom, or on the veranda if Amelia and Arthur were in the garden. He would stand there, unannounced, and beckon Arthur to him with an expectant, raised eyebrow, as if to say; *You know what time of day it is, my boy. You're going to damned well learn to shoot whether you like it or not.* Arthur's face would drop instantly and fear would darken his eyes. Although he never made a fuss, Amelia could tell from the way his shoulders drooped and how he dragged his feet as he went over to join Reginald, how much Arthur loathed these outings, and how difficult he found his father's demands.

Amelia watched anxiously from the veranda as the two of them walked towards the stables, her heart aching with concern for the little boy. She would wait there, gripping the handrail, until she spotted them riding out of the back gate and onto the plain, Arthur on his Shetland pony and Reginald on his great black stallion. One of the syces would follow on a third pony at a respectful distance, spears and gun cases slung over his shoulder. Reginald's horse was skittish. He champed at the bit, shying at the slightest sound and at every bush or animal he encountered along the route. Reginald took pride in the fact that he was the only person who could control him.

While they were out, Amelia would be unable to settle to any task. She would sit in one of the cane chairs on the veranda and try to read, but every few seconds her eyes would stray to the gates, tormented by thoughts of what might be happening out on the plain. She would imagine all sorts of things that could happen to Arthur; a nasty fall from the pony, an accident with a spear or one of the guns. But her most recurrent worry was that Arthur would fail to hit the target again and again, and that Reginald would lose his temper and yell at the boy, calling him weak and soft and a disappointment, while Arthur flinched at the words, trying not to let his father see his tears.

Usually, they would return just before dusk, as the sun was sinking rapidly into the shimmering haze on the horizon, and the smell of woodsmoke from a thousand village fires filled the air. Reginald would arrive first, with Arthur and the syce several minutes behind him. He would rush back to the house, tight-lipped, radiating anger, and go up to the bedroom taking the stairs two at a time, while Arthur, his cheeks streaked with tears, would dash past Amelia and run along the passage to his room. Amelia sometimes followed him and stood outside, about to enter the room, when she would hear his sobs and ayah's soothing voice through the door.

'Never mind, Master Arthur. You're not to worry. You will get better at it with time. And then Sahib Reginald won't need to shout. You'll see.'

As shikar season got ever closer, Arthur grew increasingly nervous and withdrawn. He lost his appetite, stopped taking pleasure in his lessons and was far less ready to laugh. Amelia was afraid that the fragile bond between them that she'd worked so hard to cultivate was slipping away. But even though she tried to get him to speak about what was troubling him, he refused to be drawn. He seemed unwilling to share with Amelia what he could speak freely about with ayah.

After about a month of Reginald's afternoon humiliations, when Amelia took Arthur to lay flowers on Elizabeth's grave, the boy broke down in tears, flung himself onto his mother's grave, hugging the headstone. Fighting back her own tears, Amelia prised his fingers gently from the stone and, wrapping him tightly in her arms, held him until he stopped crying. Then, taking him by the hand, she led him slowly back to the car, which Amir had parked up beside the gate.

Amir frowned and shook his head sadly as Amelia and Arthur slid onto the back seat.

'Straight home, memsahib?' he asked and when she nodded, he turned the car round in the road, holding up the traffic. Two rickshaw-wallahs and a man driving a bullock cart shook their fists at the car and yelled insults at Amir.

'What's the matter with them?' asked Amelia.

Amir shook his head. 'Very bad feeling in the town right now, memsahib. I'm sorry to say, many, many people are angry with British.'

A sense of dread and foreboding went through Amelia at those words. Reginald was punishing people for protesting peacefully against British rule. She thought of the man who'd hanged himself in the police cells and those Reginald was holding there without charge. Did this have something to do with that?

But Arthur was still sobbing beside her. She put her arm around him and pulled him close, trying to put the protesters out of her mind.

'I'm so sorry you're feeling this way,' she said quietly to Arthur, kissing his soft hair, 'Why don't you tell me all about it?'

He didn't reply, but carried on crying, his little shoulders heaving against her chest. She fished in her pocket and handed him a handkerchief. He blew his nose, took some shuddering breaths and gradually the sobbing subsided. At first, she thought he was going to keep his silence, perhaps out of loyalty to Reginald, but in a minute or two, as the car moved slowly towards the old town, he started to speak.

'I know I should try to be strong and brave, like Daddy,' he sobbed, 'But I'm just not. I can't be. And he's so angry with me. He always shouts at me when I don't shoot straight, or if I don't dare jump a ditch or if I'm scared. I *hate* going out with him.'

'I'm sure he doesn't mean to upset you,' Amelia said, searching for the right words to comfort him. 'Daddy only wants what's best for you.' But even as she said it, she knew how weak and unconvincing those words sounded.

'He doesn't care about me. He wants me to be like him. But I'm *not* like him,' Arthur said, his voice cracking with emotion. 'I'm never going to be angry and proud and brave like him. I'm just not like that.'

'I know. I know,' she said, cuddling him to her.

'And I don't understand why anyone wants to kill wild animals. I don't *want* to learn to shoot. Mummy understood,' he said. 'She hated people shooting and killing things too.'

'Oh?' asked Amelia, wondering how Elizabeth had come to meet her death on a tiger hunt if she felt that way.

'*She* wouldn't let Daddy take me shooting.'

Amelia said nothing. She suddenly felt inadequate and overcome with guilt. Perhaps she'd let Arthur down? Perhaps she hadn't been firm enough with Reginald? Perhaps, if she'd been more forceful, she could have stopped him from taking Arthur out shooting.

As all these troubling thoughts swirled around in her mind, her attention was taken by what was going on outside the car. It was stationary now; trapped in a narrow street in the Indian quarter. The way ahead was blocked with traffic; jammed with rickshaws, bullock carts, horse drawn tongas, bicycles and motorcycles. Pedestrians were crowding either side of the street and swarming between the vehicles, pushing past the car, some stopping to stare inside. There were families with children and babies in the crowd, but it consisted mainly of groups of young men. As they peered in through the open window Amelia shivered as she caught sight of the naked hostility in their eyes. There was an odd atmosphere too; a mixture of excitement and rage such as she'd never experienced before and the sound of angry voices. Amelia was afraid now. She felt trapped.

But Arthur seemed oblivious to what was happening around them.

'I wish Daddy was more like Deepak,' he blurted out suddenly. '*He* didn't like guns and shooting. *He* was gentle and kind. *He* never shouted at me. Not once.'

Amelia turned to him confused. She was about to ask him who Deepak was when the sound of chanting broke out all around and someone banged on the roof of the car.

'We have to get out of here, memsahib,' said Amir. 'I will try to get to that turning up ahead.'

'Do you think you can?' she asked, holding Arthur even closer, wanting to shield him from the angry, hostile eyes peering into the car. 'There's so much traffic.'

'I will try. There are only rickshaws between us and the turning. They can move aside. Please do shut the window, memsahib.'

She leaned forward to wind the window up but the handle was stiff and as she struggled to release it, one of the protesters leaned in and spat on her head. She felt the glob of phlegm seep through her hair and trickle down her scalp. She carried on winding furiously until the window was shut.

Amir manoeuvred the car forward, gesturing to the rickshaw-wallahs in front to move aside. They did so slowly with reluctant shrugs and scowls. All the time protesters were surging past, peering in, banging on the roof and windows. As the car inched forward towards the turning, Amelia peered through the windscreen and spotted a sea of banners up ahead blocking the traffic, some proclaimed "British go home", but others said; "D.O. Holden Out"; "Evil Holden"; "Holden must quit". She felt sick with fear. Did they know that Reginald's wife and son were in the car? She shrunk down in the seat, trying to hide her face, not wanting to look into the eyes of any of the men who stared in at her as they pushed their way past. Arthur had stopped crying now and as he clung to her, she realised she was trembling as much as he was.

She closed her eyes, not wanting to look any more. Still the banging and the shouting went on. She felt the car bank and tip as Amir mounted the narrow pavement to pull round the glut of rickshaws, then she felt it turn the corner. The banging moved to the boot now as the car started moving down the side street and, as it picked up speed, the banging ceased and the roar of the crowd receded.

She held Arthur tightly to her as the car surged forward, swerving around obstacles, braking at junctions. When Amelia sensed that they were speeding along a wide, straight road, she opened her eyes. They were in the cantonment, screaming along Wellesley Drive, the main thoroughfare. She leaned forward and touched Amir on the shoulder.

'You can slow down now, Amir,' she said and lurched forward as he applied the brakes.

'Sorry, memsahib,' he said, looking over his shoulder. His face was running with sweat.

'Don't be sorry. Thank you for getting us out of there,' she said, sinking back against the leather of the seat and putting her arm around Arthur again. As he cuddled up close to her, and the shock of the past few minutes faded, she remembered what he'd been saying about Deepak being gentle. But they were at the gates of the Residence by then and Amir turned the car into the entrance and started up the drive. The house came into view round the bend in the drive and there was ayah waiting anxiously on the steps. Amelia realised that her questions would have to wait until another time.

AMELIA WAS READING on the veranda when Reginald came home that afternoon. She saw straight away that he was simmering with anger.

'Where's the boy?' he asked without sitting down. 'You knew I wanted to take him out shooting.'

Amelia put down her book. 'He's having a nap, Reginald. We had a bit of a shock today. Perhaps you could give the lesson a miss this afternoon?'

'Bit of a shock?'

Amelia realised too late that telling Reginald about getting caught up in the demonstration could involve explaining where they'd been. She was unsure why Amir, ayah and Arthur had never told Reginald about visiting Elizabeth's grave, but her heart started to pound with panic imagining his reaction to the fact that they'd all been colluding in deceiving him.

'Yes...' she said weakly, desperately trying to think of what to tell him about their outing.

'Bit of a shock? Well, let me tell you, *I've* had a bit of a shock myself today. Those bloody insurgents have been stirring up trouble again and there was an ugly demonstration in town this morning.'

'Oh?' she asked, not meeting his eye, waiting for him to go on.

'Of course, we had to make a number of arrests, but several policemen were injured in the process.'

'Injured?'

'Yes. Hit by stones, that sort of thing. Of course, our men were armed with truncheons and gave as good as they got. Better in fact.'

'What about the demonstrators?' she asked, her scalp prickling in alarm. 'Were any of them hurt?'

'Nothing they didn't deserve. Of course, in a situation like that, there are going to be casualties. A few broken bones, bloody noses. But they're safely in the cells now. Being looked after by the police doctor.'

Amelia fell silent, imagining the conditions at the police station; dozens of men crowded into caged cells in sweltering conditions, some lying on the bare floor, covered in blood, groaning in pain.

'So, what happened to you?' he asked.

She cleared her throat and looked him straight in the eye. 'As a matter of fact, we were caught up on the edge of it in the car ourselves,' she said. 'It shook Arthur, and myself.'

'Oh?' the now familiar look of suspicion clouded his eyes. 'Where were you going?'

'Just going for a drive...' she said, her heart pounding again, trying to keep her gaze fixed on his.

He frowned. 'Are you in the habit of just going for a drive?' he asked. 'The motor car costs money to run, you know. I'd thank you to let me know beforehand if you need to go out.'

She opened her mouth to protest, but to her astonishment

he reached for her hand, lifted it to his lips and smothered it in kisses.

'I couldn't bear anything to happen to you, you see?' he said in a pleading voice, 'I need to know where you are and what you're doing. I've had one tragic loss. I couldn't bear another one. I love you so much, Amelia.'

He'd caught her off guard and she was at a loss as to how to reply. He'd never alluded to Elizabeth's death so directly before. She swallowed and smiled nervously at him.

'So,' he said, letting go of her hand. 'Go and get the boy up, my dear. I'm not going to let this trouble with the natives stop me from teaching my son to shoot and use a spear like a true son of the Raj.'

'He was really very shaken, Reginald,' she said gently. 'Wouldn't it be better to leave it for today?'

'No! I've told you not to mollycoddle him. He's got to toughen up, and letting him lie in bed like a baby isn't going to help him one jot.'

She got up from the chair. 'Please, Reginald, if you have to take him out shooting, could you just go a little easy on him today? That's all I ask.'

'Do stop worrying and go and fetch him. Otherwise the light will have gone before we've even got out there.'

THE NEXT DAY WAS THURSDAY; Amelia's day to travel up to the hill villages beyond the lake for the Mission. She'd been going alone for several weeks by then and had established a routine and a strong rapport with all the women she'd met. Parvati had given birth to a baby girl and Amelia was due to deliver Parvati's second payment instalment from the Mission. Because she had no car of her own, Amir always took her up there in the Residence car. She'd not needed to tell him not to mention those trips to Reginald; it was an unspoken agreement between them, just as their weekly trips to Elizabeth's grave had become. On their return to the Residence in the early afternoons, Amir would drive straight round to the stables and wash the dust from the hills off the car before Reginald returned from his office.

That morning, as they drove out of the town on the trunk road towards the hills, Amelia stared out at the rolling brown plain and thought about Arthur. He'd gone out with Reginald for his shooting lesson the previous afternoon at Reginald's insistence and by the time they'd returned, it was after sunset. Instead of running straight to his room that time, Arthur went up to Amelia who was sitting on the veranda, put his arms around her neck and rested his face against hers. His skin seemed to burn against her cheek and she felt his forehead anxiously. Was he hot from the exertions of the ride, or was it something more serious? She wanted to pull him onto her lap and cuddle him, but she knew that Reginald would be coming from the stables shortly.

'Would you like a story before bed?' she asked, getting up and taking his hand.

In Arthur's room, she sponged the boy's forehead with a cold flannel, as she'd done so many times before, hoping he wasn't going to get sick again. He dropped off to sleep as she read to him, so she'd kissed his brow, made sure the mosquito net was fastened around him, and tiptoed from the room. To her relief, in the morning he appeared a little better and he'd eaten his breakfast without complaint. She'd checked in on him again before setting off and had asked ayah to make sure he didn't tire himself or go out in the sun while she was out.

Now, as Amir turned the car off the road and started up the bumpy track towards the lake, she remembered what Arthur had said about someone he called Deepak. Because of his fever, she hadn't had an opportunity to ask him about it again.

'Amir?' she asked now, leaning forward on the back seat, having to shout above the sound of the engine. 'How long have you worked for my husband?'

'Oh, a few years, memsahib,' he said, glancing over his shoulder with a smile. 'Since he became District Officer. When he moved into the Residence. I already worked there for the previous D.O. as syce. Perhaps fifteen years?'

'So, you know all the servants who've worked in the house since my husband took over?'

'Oh yes, memsahib,' he said. 'I know them all. Some have left, though. If they displeased the sahib...' he trailed off, leaving Amelia to imagine what he might mean.

'And was Deepak one of those who left?'

Amir's shoulders stiffened immediately, and he redirected his gaze straight ahead. They were travelling along beside the lake now, the car pitching and rolling on the bumpy track. Amelia allowed her eyes to wander to the water. To her relief, there was no sign of any tiny skeletons that morning. It must have rained since they'd last travelled this road. The lake was tranquil, shimmering in the sunlight, reflecting the surrounding hills and forests and the cloudless sky. Despite its beauty, Amelia couldn't look at it without a shudder, knowing the dreadful, desperate acts that took place there.

'Amir?' she asked. Perhaps he hadn't heard her question. 'Did you know a servant called Deepak? Arthur talks about him sometimes.'

Again, there was a long silence. By the time Amir finally replied, they had passed the old pavilion, reached the end of the lake and were beginning the final bumpy section of the journey through the forest to the first village. His voice sounded different when he spoke, subdued and a little embarrassed.

'The Indian gentleman you speak of did not work at the Residence, memsahib.'

Amelia paused herself then. It wasn't the answer she'd expected.

'So, if he didn't work at the house,' she asked slowly, 'how did Arthur get to know him?' Her curiosity compelled her to persist, even though she was aware her questions were making Amir uncomfortable.

'He was... he was an acquaintance of memsahib Elizabeth. I know no more... Please do not ask, I beg you, memsahib. I know no more.'

They rounded the bend and the village came into view. Amir pulled the car off the dirt road and parked up under the banyan tree. The village women, seeing them arrive, hurried towards them, greeting Amelia with warm smiles. And for the rest of the morning, while she visited Parvati to give her the payment and to admire her beautiful baby girl and drank tea and talked to pregnant women in several other homes, she put Amir's strange reaction to her questions about Deepak out of her mind.

As they drove back to Ganpur in the scorching heat of the early afternoon, the issue resurfaced. Who was this man whom Arthur seemed to trust and admire? She wondered whether to probe Arthur himself, but was aware of how fragile he was, both emotionally and physically. She didn't want to cause him any more pain than he was already suffering. Perhaps she should just forget all about it. Why was it troubling her anyway? So, as the car moved steadily towards Ganpur, she tried to think of a way of letting Reginald know, without incurring his wrath, that his shooting lessons were slowly destroying his son.

THE FOLLOWING DAY, Amelia went to have lunch with Mabel and Giles again. As usual, she took comfort in the simple surroundings of their bungalow, and the chance to relax and enjoy the company of friends, eating on the veranda overlooking the comings and goings in the vibrant quarter.

After they'd discussed the recent trips she and Mabel had made to the villages, she asked Giles about his work in the hospital. As he spoke about his patients, his eyes lit up and his passion for the work shone through. He talked about how fulfilling it was to help people who otherwise would have no access to medical care.

'My father found exactly the same,' said Amelia warmly. 'Up in the villages he would treat anyone and everyone. British people as well.'

Giles smiled. 'Well, here in Ganpur, the British are spoiled for choice. There are several excellent hospitals to choose from; the Military hospital, and the St Theresa's Catholic hospital.'

'So, you don't get to treat British people?' she asked.

'Only those who don't want to go to their own doctors for one reason or another,' he said and Amelia caught a quick, meaningful look exchanged between him and Mabel. There followed an embarrassed pause until Mabel cleared her throat and changed the subject.

'And how are you getting along with little Arthur?' she asked.

'Oh, very well. It was difficult at first, but he seems to be getting used to me now.'

'How is his health nowadays?' asked Giles.

'It did improve for a while, but the last couple of weeks he's become a little weaker. The day before yesterday, I thought he was coming down with another fever. But he was much better this morning.'

'Well, do watch him carefully. He's never been very strong, I'm afraid.'

'I can tell. Reginald is... well, I'm afraid to say that he's very tough on Arthur,' she lowered her eyes.

'It must be such a worry for you,' said Giles. 'You know, I don't think it's a secret, but I did come to the Residence to treat the boy a while back. It wasn't long after his mother's death. His ayah came to the hospital to tell me to say she was worried about him. I went over to the house on two occasions...'

'Oh? No, I didn't know about that.'

'Well, on the first occasion, Reginald wasn't at home. Ayah took me along to see the boy and I was able to examine him and give him some medication.'

'And what happened the second time?'

'Well... It was a little odd, actually. Reginald was at home when I arrived. He seemed very reluctant to let me see the boy. But in the end, he took me along to his room. Arthur seemed a lot better on that occasion. His temperature had come down and he was far more alert than he'd been the previous day. Reginald hovered over me all the while I was with the boy, then he ushered me out as quickly as he could. At the door he told me that I didn't need to come back. He said that the next time Arthur was sick, he would call a doctor from the Military Hospital.'

'Why would he have been so hostile towards you, I wonder?' asked Amelia, puzzled, but not surprised at Reginald's odd behaviour.

'I got the feeling that he thought the boy should get over the illness by himself. He seemed to imply that seeking medical help showed some sort of weakness...'

'That *does* sound like Reginald,' said Amelia. 'He is determined that Arthur shouldn't be "mollycoddled" as he calls it. That he should grow up and become a man. He's teaching him to shoot,' she admitted in a quiet voice, 'And poor Arthur loathes every moment of it. It tears my heart out to see him go, but I can't intervene ...'

'Oh dear,' said Mabel, 'I do feel for you. It's such a difficult situation...'

'Yes... it is. But I wonder why he didn't want you to treat Arthur?' she asked turning to Giles. 'I was even thinking of calling you the other day when he was sickening again. Reginald has never mentioned that he's been treated by you or by any other doctor.'

Again, Mabel and Giles exchanged a look. Then, Mabel spoke.

'He might be reluctant to consult Giles for another reason. And I'm so sorry to bring this up with you, Amelia.' Mabel put her hand on Amelia's arm as if to comfort her. 'But you see, his first wife, Elizabeth, came to see Giles at the Mission hospital a few days before she died.'

'Oh, really?' asked Amelia, a wave of shock going through her. Mabel had never mentioned Elizabeth to her before. She'd carefully avoided the subject, so it felt strange that she should do so now, and in this very odd way.

'Yes,' said Mabel. 'It's part of the reason we've been looking out for you.'

'Looking out for me?' she asked weakly, remembering the conversation in the car the first time she and Mabel had driven up to the lake. Mabel had hinted that she and Giles were concerned about her and she'd asked why. *Because you're a member of our community, of course ... we Baptists all look out for each other.* She'd sensed at the time that this wasn't the full answer.

'I thought... I *had* thought,' she said, looking from Mabel to Giles and back again, 'that we were friends.'

'Oh, we *are* friends, Amelia,' said Mabel, squeezing her arm again and looking into her eyes earnestly. 'Of course we are. But

Giles and I feel we have a duty... we owe it to you and to the memory of your parents, to...to *warn* you.'

Amelia felt her whole body go weak. 'Warn me? Warn me of what?' she asked, her mouth dry.

It was Giles' turn to speak. He leaned forward, looking into Amelia's eyes.

'Elizabeth came to see me because she thought she might be expecting another child,' he said gently. 'She seemed distressed. Thin, and very tearful. And when I examined her, I'm afraid to say I noticed several bruises on her arms and back. I asked her what they were, but she wouldn't be drawn. I could tell she was very afraid.'

16

AMELIA

Ganpur, 1936

Amelia stared out of the car window at the shabby
streets of the quarter as Amir navigated his way
through the various obstacles in their path; Brahmin
cattle sleeping in the road, porters carrying loads on their heads,
bicycles wobbling around in front of the vehicle. The rioting was
over now, the whole town appeared peaceful again, but there
was still a restless atmosphere in the air. People were going
about their business quietly, almost furtively. The riots had been
quelled, the ringleaders were in the cells, but from the hostile
way people stared at Amelia as the car crawled through the
narrow streets, squeezing past rickshaws and Amir tooting the
horn at pedestrians to step off the road, she could tell that it
wouldn't take much for the whole unstable tinder box to flare up
again.

People stared at her, resentful of her presence, but it seemed
to Amelia that although she was inside the car and they were
out there sweating on the streets, there were parallels between
their respective situations. The Indians who lived here in

Ganpur and she herself were all subject to Reginald's iron control. In fact, although she lived a cossetted, privileged life in comparison to theirs, hers could possibly be the more perilous.

Despite the heat, Amelia shuddered as she thought back over the conversation with Mabel and Giles. The clear implication was that it was Reginald who'd given Elizabeth those bruises, although neither Mabel nor Giles had said as much. And the news of Elizabeth's pregnancy had come as a shock too. Reginald had never hinted at that, but had he even known about it?

'We've told you this because we think you should know. So that you're forewarned,' Mabel had said, spots of colour in her cheeks, obviously uncomfortable about imparting such sensitive and shocking news, 'Giles and I have talked this through a great deal. We've had misgivings about telling you, of course.'

'It is a breach of patient confidence,' said Giles, 'and even though the patient is sadly no longer with us, I was very reluctant to do that. But in the end, we both agreed it was necessary.'

'At first, I thought you were coping well with life at the Residence, and that there was no cause for concern,' Mabel chimed in, 'but in recent months, I'm sorry to say, you've looked increasingly unhappy.'

Amelia's eyes had filled with tears at those words. It was true, and she hadn't done much to hide it.

'Of course, Elizabeth could well have fallen down and got those bruises that way, but ... there was so much fear in her eyes,' said Giles, shaking his head. 'She was obviously terrified that someone would find out she'd been to see me.'

Amelia had been stunned into silence for a long time, digesting their words, shocking images spinning through her mind, but finally she found her voice.

'I don't understand,' she said, her mouth dry. 'If Reginald suspected that Elizabeth had come to you for medical treatment and he had something to hide, why would he have invited you to our wedding?'

'Oh, that wasn't Reginald,' said Giles. 'The Minister knew that your father had been in Calcutta as a medical missionary at the same time as me. It was he who asked Eileen to invite me and Mabel. Reginald didn't speak to us once. At one point, he saw us there in the corner speaking to you. He blanked us and walked away.'

The warm feelings Amelia had experienced when she arrived at the bungalow had quickly evaporated. The conversation dried up, the curry had grown warm on the plates, and all the joy had gone out of the occasion. Amelia was relieved when Amir arrived in the car to collect her.

As she left, Mabel took both Amelia's hands in hers and looked into her eyes earnestly.

'I know what we've told you must have been a shock to you, Amelia, and I'm so, so sorry. I hope you'll keep on coming to visit, though. And I want you to know, both Giles and I are here for you at any time of the day or night. You only have to come and find us, telephone the Mission hospital, or send us a message and we will help you.'

'Thank you,' said Amelia.

'And I hope this won't mean you'll stop coming along to the Mission and doing your valuable work in the villages.'

'Of course not,' she said. 'It means everything to me. Nothing would stop me.'

Now, as the car left the old town behind and swept beneath the crumbling, stone archway and on into the British cantonment, Amelia's mind focused on Arthur. The little boy had been in the middle of all this fear and misery. Did he know of his mother's distress, of her secret trip to the Mission hospital during her last days? Her heart went out to the child afresh,

wondering how much he'd witnessed and how much pain he
was suppressing even now.

WHEN AMIR DROPPED her off at the front door of the Residence,
Amelia rushed straight inside and along the passage to Arthur's
room. To her relief he was out of bed, kneeling quietly on the
floor, his head bent over a jigsaw. He looked up and smiled at
her and his face no longer wore that feverish glow that had so
worried her. She knelt down beside him and hugged him tight.

'Are you alright, Amelia?' he asked.

'Yes,' she breathed, kissing his head. 'I'm so glad you're
better, that's all.'

'Can we go for a walk?' he asked.

'Of course. We haven't for a few days. Let's go straight out
now, shall we?'

They took their usual route along Wellesley Drive, past the
mansions and palatial bungalows of the wealthiest in the British
community; those in the highest echelons of the Indian Civil
Service, the successful businessmen, some of the higher-ranking
army officers, who chose not to live in army accommodation.
Like the Residence, all the houses were set well back from the
road behind well-tended grounds. Arthur seemed happy to be
out, and as they walked along, he kept up a stream of chatter
about any and everything they encountered.

None of the British people who lived in these houses were
ever to be seen at this time of day; they would be resting
indoors out of the sun or dozing on their verandas, but the
gardeners were very much in evidence, pruning and raking,
weeding and watering. Every one of these households
employed an army of them to fight the never-ending battle
against the encroachment of wilderness. The gardeners all

knew Arthur by sight; many of them waved and shouted a greeting as they walked past.

That afternoon, in the grounds of a large, white house a few hundred yards along from the Residence, the vast lawn was being mowed by a lawnmower being pulled along like a cart by a pair of white bullocks; one gardener was perched on top of the mower controlling the bullocks with reins and a stick, while the other walked behind, balancing and guiding the machine.

Arthur got very excited at the sight of the lawnmower, jumping up and down, tugging at Amelia's hand. They paused to watch it make its laborious progress back and forth across the lawn. When it came close to the fence, Arthur waved to the gardeners, asking them in Hindi if he could have a ride on the machine. They joked and laughed with him but shook their heads, telling him it wasn't safe for him to ride on the back.

As they waved goodbye and walked on, Amelia remarked on how good Arthur's Hindi was. He shrugged.

'I've always been able to speak it. I learned it before I could speak English, and I've got lots of Indian friends,' he said. 'So, it's easy for me.'

'It's more of a struggle for me,' admitted Amelia. 'I lived in England for a long time, so when I came back to India, I had to learn the language all over again. And in the hills near Darjeeling where I lived with my parents, the people spoke a different language altogether.'

'You're a bit like Mummy, then,' he said, looking up at her with a big smile, his eyes squinting in the sunlight.

'A bit like Mummy?' she asked carefully, her scalp prickling, wondering what he meant.

'Well, Mummy told me that *she* couldn't speak any Hindi when she came to India. And she had a lot of trouble with it. She wanted to learn, so Deepak taught her. He was her teacher.'

Amelia's heartbeat sped up at the mention of the man about

whom Amir had reacted so strangely. They had turned off the main drag of Wellesley Drive now, onto a shadier, narrower road.

'Oh yes. You mentioned Deepak before,' she replied again very carefully. 'Did he teach you too?'

Arthur laughed. 'No, of *course* not. He was just Mummy's teacher. But we used to go to the bazaar with him sometimes. And other places too...'

He trailed off and Amelia wondered whether to ask him more about Deepak, but decided, now Arthur had brought up the subject of his mother, to find a way of asking him the questions that had been burning in her mind since lunchtime.

They hurried past the Military graveyard, where British officers and their families had been buried since the time of the Indian Mutiny, and reached the public gardens in the corner of the cantonment. There was a pond full of koi carp in these gardens in front of an old stone summerhouse covered in moss and creepers. They normally sat inside, out of the sun for a while before returning home via a different route.

Amelia opened the metal gate, pushing it aside to let Arthur through. Then she took a deep breath.

'I was wondering,' she began. 'Do you know if your mummy ever had a fall? I mean, did she ever injure herself or anything like that?'

Even as she said the words, she realised how strange they must sound.

Arthur frowned and shook his head. 'What a funny question. I don't think so. Why?'

'I... I just wondered,' she said, as they walked across the gardens, 'You said your mummy was like me, I just wondered if she was... she was a bit clumsy like I am sometimes...'

Arthur looked up at her frowning and she couldn't meet his

eye. In truth, she was very rarely clumsy herself, so it was no wonder he was suspicious.

But how could she find the right way to ask a nine-year-old boy whether he had ever seen his father beat his mother? What words could she use, so as not to upset him? If he *had* seen such a thing, he might well have buried the memory. It could be such a shock to have to confront it, it might even make him sick again.

They reached the shade of the summerhouse and Amelia sunk down gratefully on the cool, stone bench. Arthur dashed to his usual position on the little wall on the edge of the pond, so he could marvel at the huge, sinister-looking fish that lurked beneath the surface.

'I'm sure this fat orange one's grown even more since we last came,' he said, his voice full of laughter. 'Come and look!'

She went to sit beside him on the wall, to watch the koi carp as they jostled and wove around in the murky depths of the pond, occasionally surfacing for flies, their giant mouths breaking the surface of the water. Arthur was completely absorbed now, just as he always was here at the pond. Amelia realised that she couldn't ask him the questions she wanted to ask. Not at that moment, and not without making him anxious and possibly setting him back several steps.

When Arthur had tired of watching the fish, they walked back through the gardens, out onto the road, and started back through the cantonment towards home. They walked in companionable silence through the shady side-roads, past the houses and bungalows that belonged to lower ranking, less wealthy members of the British community.

As they emerged onto the wide drag of Wellesley Drive, Amelia's heart stood still as a figure appeared around a sweep in the road. It was Reginald on his black stallion, which snorted and strained at the reins as it trotted at a fast clip towards them.

'Oh! There's Daddy,' Amelia said, her voice falsely bright.

Arthur's shoulders drooped as the stallion drew up in front of them, prancing and pawing the ground.

'Where the hell have you been?' said Reginald, frowning, his face an angry shade of red.

'We just went for our usual walk,' said Amelia.

'The servants told me you'd gone out. You know it's past four o'clock, don't you? It's time for Arthur's shooting lesson.'

'I hadn't realised the time,' said Amelia weakly, not able to meet his eye, an image of wheals and bruises on pale skin flashing through her mind.

Reginald clicked his fingers. 'Come on up, young man. It'll be quicker if you come back with me on the horse,' then, turning to Amelia, 'You don't mind walking home, do you, dear? Help him up, would you?'

She approached the restless horse. Then, she put her hands under Arthur's armpits and with an effort lifted him high enough for Reginald to grab him and haul him into the saddle.

Once Arthur was seated in front of him, Reginald turned back to her.

'I don't know why you feel the need to walk out of the Residence grounds. There's really no need. It could be dangerous. Especially at the moment.'

'Oh Reginald, surely not? The cantonment is very safe.'

'Nevertheless, I'd prefer it if you didn't take these strolls from now on,' he said sharply.

Then he wheeled the horse around, Arthur clinging to the pommel for dear life.

'Oh, and by the way,' Reginald yelled over his shoulder as the horse began to trot away. 'Make sure you're changed and ready to go out when I get back. We're going to the club this evening.'

'Oh?' she asked, her spirits sinking.

'Yes. I've arranged a meeting with the other fellows who're

coming on the shikar with us. If I can get things under control here in Ganpur, I'm planning to leave within the next ten days or so.'

She stood in the road and watched them trot off in a cloud of dust, anxiety mounting inside her, both for Arthur and for herself.

Back at the house, she went straight upstairs to wash the heat and dust of the day from her body. She ran a bath, and throwing off her sticky clothes, slid into the warm, deep water. Getting as far under as she could, she leaned back and closed her eyes. The house was silent at that hour, the only sound the twilight cawing of the jungle crows that gathered in the trees behind the house. She took deep breaths and tried to relax and unwind, but it was impossible. Her mind was alive with restive thoughts about Elizabeth and the shocking revelations she'd heard that day; her bruises and her secrecy; the fact that she was painfully thin and obviously terrified of something or someone.

Amelia sat up suddenly. She'd had an unsettling thought, one that sent shivers right through her. Elizabeth must have lain here in this very bath many, many times, just as Amelia was doing now, trying to relax, anxieties coursing through her mind. Suddenly the bath wasn't such an attractive place to be anymore. She got out quickly, wrapped herself in a towel and let the water out.

It had occurred to her before, but she'd never really examined the thought closely, how very odd it was that the only evidence at all of Elizabeth in the house was the photograph Arthur kept under his bed, out of sight of his father. She padded through to the bedroom and sat on the edge of the bed, her head in her hands. What had happened to Elizabeth's clothes, her belongings, her books and photographs, all the trappings and paraphernalia of a woman's life? Had Reginald got rid of absolutely everything? She imagined him, in his grief, lighting a bonfire in the scrub behind the stables, ordering the servants to carry everything out to throw onto it. She recalled the passionate way he'd taken her face in his hands and his words; *I've had one tragic loss. I couldn't bear another one.*

She pulled on her dressing gown and started throwing open cupboards and pulling out drawers, searching for some evidence of her predecessor. She knelt down on the floor and peered under the bed, she even rifled through the clothes in Reginald's wardrobe and through his bedside drawers, her heart telling her that what she was doing was wrong, but her thirst for the truth urging her on. But there was nothing. Not even a scarf or a purse or comb or a piece of jewellery to be found.

As she searched, the daylight faded quickly. She put the lamp on to enable her to continue, and realised, with a shock, that Reginald and Arthur had been out for almost two hours and would soon be back. She grabbed a pale blue silk dress from her wardrobe and pulled it on, quickly ran a comb through her hair, and was applying lipstick in the dressing table mirror when she heard Reginald's footfalls along the passage outside and the click of the bedroom door as he entered the room.

In the mirror, she watched him cross the room towards her. He put his hands on her shoulders. She shrunk from his touch, but he bent over and kissed her neck. Then he straightened up.

'Aren't you ready yet? Whatever have you been doing?' his eyes scanned the room and widened as he noticed that his wardrobe door stood ajar. He strode over to it and pushed it shut, then turned back to face her. Amelia dropped her gaze to the glass surface of the dressing table, her hands trembling.

'The boy was a lot better today,' Reginald said. 'I'll make a marksman of him yet.'

Amelia got to her feet. 'I'll go and say goodnight to him, then,' she said, her throat catching on the words. She was desperate to get out of the room.

'You do that. I'll join you downstairs as soon as I've changed.'

THE ATMOSPHERE in the Gymkhana Club bar felt different as Amelia entered the smoke-filled room on Reginald's arm that evening. People were gathering for cocktails before supper and there was an unusual energy and buzz about the place.

Eileen was sitting over by the windows with four or five other women, their heads close together in gossip. When she saw Amelia, she jumped up and made her way over between the tables.

'How are you, darling?' she asked kissing her on the cheek. 'You haven't been here for afternoon tea with the girls in an age.'

Amelia glanced at Reginald, but he'd already moved away to speak to a group of men standing at the bar.

'Come and talk to the others,' Eileen said, taking Amelia's arm.

Amelia followed reluctantly and took the chair that Eileen pulled out for her beside her own. The women were all people Amelia knew slightly; most had been guests at her wedding or were people she'd chanced upon on the occasions she had been to the club. The conversation stopped abruptly as she sat down and although these women all smiled and greeted her politely, she experienced an echo of the feelings she'd had in Darjeeling. These people weren't openly hostile, but she knew that if it weren't for her position as Reginald's wife, they would probably snub her openly.

'You must come and play rummy with us all after dinner,' said Eileen lighting a cigarette.

'Oh, I expect Reginald will want to go home,' she said as the bearer placed a gin fizz on the table in front of her.

'Didn't he tell you?' Eileen said, 'After dinner, all the men are having a little meeting in the smoking room to plan that damned shikar of theirs. So, we'll be left to our own devices. We'll set up a little gambling circle. It'll be fun.'

'I'm not sure,' said Amelia, taking a sip of the drink. It was strong and she felt herself beginning to relax as it coursed through her.

'Whyever not?' asked Eileen, laughing.

'I can't gamble,' she replied quietly.

It was Eileen's turn to frown, puzzled, then her face cleared.

'Oh, of course. I always forget about your missionary roots. Well, don't worry about it. The other girls can play cards and you and I can have a nice chat at another table.'

'Why are there so many people here this evening?' Amelia asked.

Eileen drew on her cigarette and scanned the room.

'As I said, everyone's here to plan the shoot. Some people have brought guests along.' Then she leaned closer to Amelia and said conspiratorially, 'There are one or two quite dishy men here, I don't know if you've noticed? There's one in particular that none of us can take our eyes off.'

Amelia was lost for words, reminded of why each time she came along to the club, she regretted it. The idle gossip and trivial interests of Eileen and her friends left her cold.

'He's over there in the corner, look,' said Eileen, waving her cigarette in the direction of a group of men. The stranger was on the edge of the group with his back to the room, so it was impossible to see his face. 'It's Willy Prendergast's brother, George. He's over from Blighty for the shooting season. He's so damned handsome, we've all been going weak at the knees just looking at him.'

There was a gale of laughter from the other women at Eileen's words, and the subject of their interest turned round to see what the commotion was. When he saw all the women looking his way, he raised his glass, smiled gallantly and turned back towards his friends again, but as he did so, his eyes lingered for a moment on Amelia. She instantly looked away, humiliated that he might think her part of the charade.

Later, after the meal, at which Amelia sat stiffly beside Reginald whilst he talked to the man on the other side of him about the rioting and the frustrations he was having with the leaders of the protests, as Eileen had indicated, the men all melted away to the smoking room to plan their shooting expedition. Amelia followed the other women back into the bar. Most of them sat down at the tables to play cards.

'Come on,' said Eileen, taking Amelia's arm. 'Let's go and find a quiet spot. We haven't had a proper talk in ages.'

Once they were seated in a pair of planter's chairs in an alcove, Eileen clicked her fingers for the bearer to bring drinks and said,

'Now you can tell me, darling. Whatever's the matter? You look very pale. I can tell something's wrong. You've hardly spoken all evening.'

Amelia felt her heart swell with emotion. She swallowed hard. She couldn't cry. Not here in the club bar in front of everyone.

'What's happened?' said Eileen, putting her hand on Amelia's.

Amelia screwed up her eyes in an effort to keep the tears at bay, but they began to spill over and roll down her cheeks. She shook her head.

'Nothing,' she whispered. How could she confide in Eileen? Her husband, James, worked closely with Reginald, and Amelia wasn't sure whether she could trust her not to speak to him about it.

'Oh, come on,' Eileen's voice was gentle. 'If it was nothing,

you wouldn't have anything to cry about, would you? It's something to do with Reginald, isn't it?'

'It's just that... well, he's quite tough on Arthur,' Amelia
began. 'I worry about it.'

'And he's tough on you too, isn't he?' said Eileen, her eyes full
of sympathy. 'He's an arrogant man. He's used to getting his own
way, and it can't be easy to live with that.'

Amelia nodded, trying to work out how she could broach
the subject of Elizabeth, when Eileen murmured, 'I think his
first wife probably used to find that too.'

'Did you know her?' Amelia asked.

'Not very well. James and I only moved here from Delhi a
few months before her death, but I've heard quite a bit about
her from the other wives.'

Shivers ran through Amelia. Was that why they all looked at
her so strangely – they were all comparing her to Elizabeth,
gossiping about her in their malicious way?

Eileen leaned forward and looked around her.

'You know there were a lot of rumours about Elizabeth
Holden. Not all of them kind.'

'What sort of rumours?'

'That she kept herself to herself. That, a little bit like you, she
didn't really want to mix with the club set... well, that sort of
thing. And...'

Eileen took another drag of her cigarette.

'And?' Amelia's tears had dried up now, she'd almost stopped
breathing too.

'Well... and this really is just speculation... and I'm only
mentioning it to explain why I said I thought she must have
found marriage to Reginald difficult...'

'Please tell me, Eileen. I need to know about her. There's so
much Reginald won't talk about.'

'Well, the word on the street is that Elizabeth Holden was a little bit too close to her Indian tutor. I'm sure I don't need to spell it out to you, my dear. But it's only a rumour, of course, and probably a malicious one at that, so I wouldn't take it too seriously if I were you.'

Amelia stared at Eileen, stunned. She remembered all the times Arthur had mentioned Deepak, how fondly he spoke of his mother's tutor. Surely these rumours were just the result of idle women indulging in vindictive gossip.

17

KATE

Warren End, 1970

It was almost lunchtime when Kate left Edna Robinson's room in the Meadows on that beautiful spring morning. She didn't want to leave; Edna hadn't finished telling her Amelia's story, but the old lady had started dozing off between sentences. Miss Robinson's carer, Sandra, was gently insistent,

'You can come another day, Miss Hamilton,' she said, ushering Kate out of the room. 'I'm sure Miss Robinson would appreciate another visit from you but talking for a long time tires her out, I'm afraid. She needs a rest and something to eat.'

'Of course,' said Kate, picking up her bag. Then, looking back at Edna who was snoring gently in her chair, her chin slumped onto her chest, she asked, 'She's all right, isn't she?'

Sandra smiled. 'Yes, she's all right at the moment, but she has good days and bad days and she's a lot frailer than she looks, I'm afraid.'

At the reception desk, Kate made an appointment to see Edna at the same time the following day, then left the building.

Driving home, she thought over what Edna had told her about Amelia's life in India; the strange circumstances surrounding her birth, the tragic loss of both her parents, rushing in haste into marriage to a powerful, controlling and much older man who'd whisked her away from poverty and humiliation. As her great-aunt's story unfolded through Edna's words, Kate had found herself filled with pity and sympathy for Amelia's plight. But none of this explained why Amelia had hardly spoken of her time in India, and why she'd kept her marriage to Reginald a complete secret from the family. Had Uncle James known? What had become of Reginald, and what had become of little Arthur? Kate knew now that the young boy sitting on the cane bench in the photograph that she'd found in Amelia's bedside drawer must be Arthur. Had Amelia left both Reginald and Arthur behind when she'd returned to England in 1937 under her maiden name? It had been a shock to discover that George Prendergast had been to Ganpur and had seen Amelia in the club. Had they started their affair then and carried on until 1944? Surely not, because in the intervening years, Amelia had come back to England and met Uncle James. None of it added up, and Kate couldn't wait to get back to the Meadows the next day to hear more from Edna.

She could have carried on towards Midchester and Warren End on the main road, but the junction with the back road was up ahead. She turned off and started along the country lanes towards Willow Mill. The old building was drawing her back, but she wasn't sure why. Maybe this time she would be able to walk right round it, sit in the clearing beside the river where she and Joan used to bathe, and think back to those summer days in 1944. Perhaps, sitting there alone would help her find the courage to face up to the past?

She passed the farm where the cattle had crossed the road earlier, tyres bumping through the cowpats, and reached the top of the hill. There was the roof of the old mill, nestling in the trees beside the river with their dusting of spring leaves. Her heart beat a little faster as she drove down towards it, but as she rounded the final bend, she noticed an open-backed truck parked up in the gateway. Two men in boiler suits were unloading materials from the back. Kate slowed down and peered as she drove past. The men were carrying planks of wood and steel bars; it looked like scaffolding. The old mill was going to be repaired, or rebuilt perhaps? Kate felt a twinge of sadness. Perhaps she'd never be able to go there again.

She drove quickly back to the village and, as she turned into the drive of Oakwood Grange, there was the yellow Rover parked up on the front drive. Gordon Anderson was sitting in the driver's seat, his head bent over some papers. She parked beside it, her heart beating a little faster, regretting the fact that she hadn't even the time to check her makeup in the mirror when she saw him approaching. He opened the door for her.

'What a surprise,' she said, getting out.

'I popped in on the off chance,' he said. 'I didn't realise you wouldn't be in. I should have called before turning up.'

'It's fine,' she said. 'Have you been waiting long?' He didn't ask her where she'd been and she didn't offer an explanation.

'Only a few minutes. I've got a first draft of the house particulars. I'm on my way to show some people round a farmhouse a couple of miles from here, so I thought I'd drop in with them.'

'Would you like a cup of tea while you're here? Have you had lunch?' Kate asked as they walked across the gravel to the front door. 'I could always make a sandwich.'

'Well, as a matter of fact I haven't. Busy morning. That would be great. If it's not too much trouble.'

'Of course not,' she said unlocking the front door and stepping inside. 'Come on in. I can't promise anything special, I'm afraid.'

Gordon followed her down the flagstone passage to the kitchen. He sat down at the table as Kate put the kettle on the Aga and scouted around for bread, butter and cheese.

'Which farm are you going to see?' she asked.

'Park Farm. Between Warren End and the river. You might not remember it.'

'Oh, I remember it,' she said, pausing to think about the old house that everyone had thought was haunted. 'When we were kids, we used to cycle through there as a short cut to get to the river. It was derelict then... quite spooky,' she trailed off, remembering the anger in George Prendergast's voice as he shouted after her and Joan.

'Oh, it's been done up for years,' said Gordon. 'Prendergast sold it just after the war, alongside a large swathe of other property. A family bought the house and restored it. No expense spared.'

'So, it's probably not haunted any more then,' she said, smiling briskly, making light of the memory.

'Only with designer ghosts,' said Gordon.

She put the plates of sandwiches and mugs of tea on the table and sat down opposite him.

'Do you know anything about Willow Mill?' she asked. 'I happened to pass it today and there were some builders outside.'

'Willow Mill? Yes, I do,' said Gordon, taking a sip of tea. 'That property is being done up too. Converted into a house. Beautiful spot, that, down by the river. Fishing rights thrown in too. It will fetch a bomb when it's finished.'

'How sad,' Kate reflected. 'All these old places, just vanishing away.'

'Sad in one way,' said Gordon with a twinkle in his eye. 'But it will make a great home for someone. Surely, as an architect, you can appreciate that?'

'Well yes, in normal circumstances. But when it comes to Warren End, I seem to be losing my professional judgment.'

She fell silent, wondering whether to mention that she'd also stopped at the mill much earlier on and had seen George Prendergast there. Did Prendergast still own the mill? Was that one of the properties he'd kept when he'd sold up after the war? She doubted it. Janet Andrews had told her that he'd fallen on hard times. It was unlikely that he would be living in that tiny bungalow in Clerks' Lane alone if he had any wealth left at all. Gordon would be able to tell her for sure, but she held back from asking him. Until she'd got to the bottom of Amelia's past and her connection with Prendergast, she didn't want to discuss the events of the summer of '44 with Gordon. It might lead to difficult questions and she wasn't ready to answer those yet.

'Shall I look at the house particulars now?' she asked instead. 'As you brought them over specially.'

'Oh, I was just passing, as I said,' he replied and she looked up and met his eyes. It was clear from the way he held her gaze that that wasn't true. She looked away again, momentarily confused and he slid the envelope across the table.

'You could look through them quickly now,' he said. 'I've got a few minutes before I need to get off, or you could give me a call tomorrow once you've had a chance to read them through properly. The sooner they're finalised, the sooner the house will be on the market.'

'Of course,' Kate replied, 'But we don't want to rush things and make mistakes. I'll look over them this evening and call you tomorrow.'

'You're not having second thoughts, are you?' he asked with a teasing smile.

'Of course not! I told you yesterday that I need to sell it.'

'It's just that for a moment there, when you came up the drive in your car, you looked as if you fitted the place perfectly. As if you had actually lived here for years. You didn't look like someone desperate to sell up at all.'

'You know, Gordon,' she said, smiling back into his eyes. 'I've never met an estate agent like you before. I *am* keen to sell, and I'll call you tomorrow once I've had a look over your drafts.'

'I shall look forward to it,' he said, then glancing at his watch and getting up from the table. 'I'll have to push on now. Thank you so much for the tea and sandwich.'

She showed him to the front door and as he went out, he turned back momentarily as if he was about to say something else, but he simply said, 'Goodbye, Kate. I'll wait to hear from you tomorrow.'

What had he been about to say? Kate shrugged and put it out of her mind, too preoccupied with Amelia's story to wonder too long about Gordon.

As soon as she'd closed the door, Kate went straight up to Amelia's room. She sat down on the bed and took the faded photograph out of the bedside drawer.

'Arthur,' she murmured, noticing again how Amelia was holding him close and how they were both smiling, squinting into the sun. How frail Arthur looked; how vulnerable. Amelia had loved the little boy, it was clear from what Edna had told her. As she looked at the photo now, knowing their connection, Kate could see the sadness and desperation in both their faces. Lost souls, bound together by shared grief.

Taking the photograph, she went back up to the top floor, opened up Amelia's trunk and retrieved Mabel Harris's letters, the photographs, Amelia's luggage label from Bombay to Southampton. Then she carried everything back down to the study and laid them out on the desk alongside Amelia's marriage certificate to Reginald Holden. What Edna Robinson

had told her that morning had fuelled Kate's desire to understand Amelia's mysterious past, but the most intriguing revela-
tion of them all was the fact that George Prendergast had been
in Ganpur when Amelia was living there. Coming only a couple
of hours after Kate had seen the same George Prendergast, now
old and feeble at Willow Mill. The very place where he and
Amelia used to meet; the place where all the trouble had started.
She was convinced now that this connection between them lay
at the root of everything.

What would Joan make of this new information about
Amelia? She'd surely have some ideas about it, with her quick
brain and wild imagination. It was time they spoke about it,
cleared the air and faced up to what had happened together.
Glancing at her watch, Kate saw there were a couple of hours
left before the end of the school day. She really needed to speak
to Joan again, despite Dave's bullying threats. Kate frowned to
herself, thinking about Dave. What if he had a day off work and
was at home again? Guilt pricked her as she recalled how she'd
walked past the house after Dave had warned her off, she'd
sensed rather than seen Joan's silhouette at the kitchen window.
She'd walked straight on past without even waving at her old
friend. She drew herself up. So what if he *was* there? What right
had *he* to tell Kate not to go round?

Before she could change her mind, Kate gathered up
Amelia's papers and photographs, shoved them into one of
Amelia's shopping bags that hung on the back of the study door
and pulled on her coat.

She walked the few hundred yards to Clerks' Lane as quickly
as she could, her head down. This time she didn't glance at the
cottages or linger to admire the spring flowers in the gardens. By
the time she'd reached the top of the lane though, her courage
was beginning to wane. Despite the passage of time, inside

lurked that teenager whose knees quaked as she walked to the village shop for fear of running into Dave Pope and his cronies.

Joan's voice was in her head now, sharp and clear. *Leave her alone, you cowards.* Joan had been there for *her* then. She mustn't let her fear of the same bullies stop her going to Joan now. Taking a deep breath, she turned down the lane and walked the few yards to Joan's front gate. The pushchair was outside the front door. Her pulse was racing as she walked up the front path and knocked on the door. She could hear muffled voices, a child crying inside, then footsteps on the stairs. Joan spoke from the other side of the door.

'Who is it?'

'It's me, Kate.'

There was a pause, then Joan's voice again. 'Why've you come? Dave told you not to come round, didn't he?'

'He did, but what's it got to do with him? I need to speak to you, Joan.'

'You can't come in. You'll have to go away.' Joan spoke urgently, fear in her voice.

'Look, it's time we talked about what happened that summer, Joan,' she said. 'Please. Let me come in. You want to talk about it as much as I do, don't you?'

'I'm not well. I can't talk today.'

'What's wrong with you? You don't sound ill.'

'Well, I am. I've kept the kids off school so I don't have to go out. They're upstairs. I've got my hands full.'

'Is Dave at work?' asked Kate.

'Look. I can't let you in and that's that.'

'You shouldn't let him bully you, Joan. Look, I've found out some things about my Aunt Amelia. I've got some of her papers with me. I wanted to show them to you, to ask you what you think.'

There was a long pause, then the sound of a key in the lock and the door opened a crack.

'He'll kill me if he knows you've been here,' Joan said, drawing the door back. 'We'd better be quick.'

As Kate stepped inside she saw the reason why Joan didn't want to leave the house. Her right eye was red and almost closed-up with swelling, the beginnings of purple and yellow bruising blooming around the edges.

'It's an eye infection,' Joan said quickly. 'You'd better keep away, or you'll catch it.'

'Eye infection! He hit you, didn't he?' said Kate, aghast.

'I don't know what you're talking about. You'd better come and sit down in the kitchen. We'll have to be quick. Dave's on the early shift today. He could be back any time after four. Cup of tea?'

Kate nodded and sat down at the kitchen table. This time the room was tidy, spotless in fact. No dirty dishes stacked up in the sink, no milk spilled on the table.

'You should leave him, Joan,' Kate said quietly as Joan filled the kettle at the sink. She had her back to Kate, but at those words her shoulders stiffened.

'It's none of your business,' she muttered after a pause, putting the kettle on the stove, her eyes averted from Kate's. 'Now if you've got something to tell me about your aunt, like I said, you'd better be quick.'

Joan sat down heavily at the table and watched silently from her one good eye as Kate took the papers out of the shopping bag and laid them one by one on the table. The certificate, the letters, the luggage label, the photographs.

'What are all these?' Joan asked, frowning.

'I've been clearing up the house and I found them all in various places,' began Kate, looking straight at Joan. 'You know, I was scared of coming back here after all this time because of what happened.'

Joan huffed. 'You were lucky you could go in the first place,' she said. 'Look at me. Stuck here. *I* never got away.'

'I know. And I'm sorry we lost touch. I just wanted to put it all behind me. I didn't want to think about it. I suppose I just assumed that you would have got away yourself. Gone off to... well, to college or something.'

'I should have. It just never happened. After... well, after that summer, I wasn't interested in school anymore. I just stopped studying. It wasn't easy anyway, living with my gran after we were evicted from the cottage by Prendergast. But I didn't care anyway. I got into a bad crowd and in the end I was expelled from the grammar school.'

'Oh, Joan. I'm so sorry.'

'Don't be sorry! I don't want your pity. I made my own decisions. Bad ones, granted, but they were my decisions.'

They stared at each other across the table. The years that had passed since they were close suddenly seemed to Kate like an unbridgeable divide, so much had happened in that time. The sound of Joan's children playing floated down the stairs; laughter and chatter, the occasional raised voice. Had the two of them really changed so much, deep inside? Had they changed so much that they could never face the past together? Had they left it to fester for too long? The kettle began to whistle, and Joan got up to take it off the gas. She put two mugs, a bowl of sugar and a bottle of milk on the table.

'You know, I saw George Prendergast today,' said Kate, taking the plunge. 'Down at Willow Mill. There was no car there. He must have walked all the way from the village, even though he walks with a stick.'

'What were *you* doing there?' asked Joan with a flash of her old sharpness.

'Isn't it obvious? It's where it all started, isn't it? Everything bad that happened then. You know, Joan, I've carried it with me my whole life. I'm sure you have too. That burden of guilt. And it all started there. That's why I went. I'm trying to face up to it after all these years.'

'I've never been back there,' said Joan with a shiver. She poured milk and tea into the mugs and pushed one across the table to Kate. 'Sugar?' Kate shook her head and Joan spooned two heaped spoonsful into her own mug and stirred it vigorously.

'But you have thought about it, haven't you?'

'Of course, I have. I think about it all the time. It's why... oh, I don't know. I suppose it's why I did nothing at school. It's why I can't get out of me rut.'

Kate took a sip of the tea and put the mug down again.

'So that's why I brought these papers round. We both need to face up to it all. But as part of that, I need your help. Aunt Amelia had a lot of secrets. I had no idea, but apparently she was married in India when she was very young, but she never told anyone in my family about it. Her marriage certificate is here.'

Joan picked it up and peered at it with her good eye. Then put it down again.

'So?'

'But she came back to England at the beginning of 1937 using her maiden name. Here's a luggage label showing she took the SS Strathmore from Bombay to Southampton. It looks as though she might have left her husband. He was pretty domineering from all accounts.'

Joan shrugged. 'Why does any of this make a difference to what we did? Nothing about her past is going to change that, is it?'

The words hit Kate like a hammer blow. It was true. Joan had cut straight to the heart of the matter. No amount of digging into Amelia's past would alter or justify what the two of them had done, the events they had put into motion that stifling Friday afternoon in the August of '44.

'I think they might have known each other in India, though,' she said weakly. 'Amelia and George Prendergast. He was out there for a hunting trip one season. They probably met then.'

'So what if they did,' Joan's voice was firm. 'It makes no difference, Kate. We did what we did. He's a broken man. You saw him this morning, didn't you?'

Kate nodded. He was indeed a broken man. Feeble, old and desperately poor. Once a proud, arrogant landowner, the two of them had brought him to his knees. All they'd intended to do was to give him a shock, a comeuppance, but events had spiralled out of their control. And they'd been living with the guilt of that ever since that day.

18

AMELIA

Ganpur, 1936

Amelia sat beside Reginald on the back seat of the limousine as Amir drove them home from the club through the dark streets of old Ganpur. Flashes of light from pavement fires and open doors lit up the interior of the car every few seconds. She felt exposed in those brief moments, registering Reginald's linen-clad thigh pressing against her blue silk dress, his hand with its manicured fingers resting lightly on her knee. The usual hostile faces stared in at them through the windows. Amelia shrunk back from them, aware that she was being driven through these narrow streets beside the most hated man in Ganpur. What if these angry people recognised him and started beating the car, blocking the route as they had before?

But she held her fear in check, not wanting Reginald to sense weakness in her; admitting to herself that she was probably less afraid of the crowd than she was of him. Her emotions were reeling from everything she'd discovered that day about

Elizabeth. Eileen's confidential tone as she'd imparted the words; *Elizabeth Holden was a little bit too close to her Indian tutor. I'm sure I don't need to spell it out to you, my dear.*

Amelia had pressed Eileen for details, 'Who was he, exactly?'

'Oh, he was a pretty sophisticated fellow. Good looking too. He was a lecturer at Ganpur University on a visiting fellowship from Benares, or so I'm told. Offered Hindi language tutoring to boost his salary. Well, Elizabeth must have got it into her head that she wanted to learn the language.'

'Arthur mentioned a teacher,' said Amelia. 'Someone called Deepak, I think. How did she get to know him?'

'Someone at the club put her in touch with him, I believe. But as I said, malicious rumours. Probably quite innocent, but Reginald took against him, or so I understand.'

'I can well believe it,' muttered Amelia. 'Has he left Ganpur?'

'Of course. Rumour has it that Reginald made sure his fellowship was terminated early. He was sent packing. Probably back to Benares. That was just a couple of months before Elizabeth died. Such a tragic story...' said Eileen, blowing smoke rings in the air and looking at Amelia sideways.

'I saw him looking at you this evening,' Reginald said suddenly, his voice broke into her thoughts. She swallowed, knowing what was to come.

'Who?' she asked.

'Willy Prendergast's brother. You know who I mean. All the women were flocking round him like bitches on heat. But he couldn't keep his eyes off *you*. I notice that sort of thing, my dear. You should know that by now.'

She was silent, glad of the cloak of darkness now they were clear of the bazaar.

'Haven't you got anything to say?' Reginald asked.

'Oh, Reginald. I'm sure he wasn't looking at me. I certainly didn't notice,' she replied but he ignored her protestations.

'You *know* I can't stand it. I don't know why you torture me like that.'

'I didn't do anything, Reginald.'

'I love you so much Amelia. I couldn't bear to lose you.'

He squeezed her knee hard and she held her breath in an effort not to flinch. They passed under the old arch and swept on along Wellesley Drive towards the Residence. Her mind was racing, searching for something to say, desperate to deflect from his jealousy.

'How did the meeting go?' she blurted, grasping a new subject gratefully.

'Meeting?' he loosened his grip on her knee. 'Oh, you mean about the shikar. Yes, very well. Very well indeed. Things are in motion now. We're engaging fifty beaters and twenty shikaris. Bearers, cooks, elephants to carry everything, and horses of course. James Blackburn has all that underway.'

'It sounds quite a big operation,' she said, able to breathe again.

'Oh yes. It's a fairly big camp this season...by the way, you're not put out about it, are you?'

'Put out? Why on earth would I be?'

'Well, I wondered if you might be feeling excluded. It's just men. No wives this season, I'm afraid. It will be so good for Arthur, though, to be away from womenfolk.'

She opened her mouth to say, 'poor Arthur' but checked herself. That would be like a red rag to a bull. Instead, she said, 'Don't worry about me, Reginald. I wasn't expecting to come. I'm not sure I would enjoy it anyway.'

'Nonsense,' he said, 'You'd love it. You're so at home in the saddle. Next year, eh?'

The gates of the Residence loomed in the headlights and the car swept through them, the chowkidar bowing as they passed. How impressed she'd been the first time she'd been driven through those gates. How her eyes had widened at the beauty and scale and sheer luxury of the place. Now her heart just yearned for that wooden bungalow in the mountains, her unheated room with its narrow bed and wooden cross on the wall. She would have done anything to turn the clock back.

THE DATE WAS SET for the shooting expedition. It was exactly a fortnight after the evening of the meeting at the club. Amelia counted down the days with mixed emotions. Reginald would be away for several weeks; it would give her time to think, to plan, to find out as much about Elizabeth as she could and to work out what she needed to do for herself. His absence would also mean that she would be free to go up to the villages in the hills as often as she wanted. On the other hand, every day closer to the expedition meant a day closer to parting with Arthur. She was dreading seeing him setting off on his pony, riding beside Reginald, knowing how much the boy loathed the idea of cruelty to animals and how terrified he was of his father.

The afternoon shooting lessons were now far less frequent. Reginald seemed satisfied with Arthur's progress, but he was also working longer hours. He was either at Government House or Police HQ, often missing dinner and arriving home late in the evening for a swift but large nightcap before bed. On those occasions he seemed preoccupied and uncommunicative, his brow furrowed with the burden of his responsibilities. The riots had been stamped out for now, but the unrest simmered under the surface and he was having to maintain a heavy police presence on the streets. There were still many men in custody, too. He was clearly nervous that things could blow up again in his absence.

Amelia carried on going to the Baptist Mission to help out in the office. It was all she could do during those days. There were police roadblocks on every road out of Ganpur and Amir was reluctant to drive her out of town.

'Police will stop us, memsahib. And they will tell sahib Reginald where we go,' he said shaking his head gravely.

'You're right, I suppose,' she said, thinking about all the young women she was failing by not travelling up there, all the babies who might perish because she hadn't returned with the promised instalments or been able to speak to the women again to drive her message home. Her own weakness angered and frustrated her. She should have been firmer with Reginald; if she'd had the courage to stand up to him at the outset, to come clean about her trips into the hills, he would have accepted it by now and she wouldn't have to fear the police on the roadblocks informing on her.

So instead, Amir drove her across town to the Mission building, through the quiet streets patrolled by policemen carrying brutal looking weapons; long, whip-like lathi sticks, ugly truncheons, even rifles. Amir would wait patiently on a bench in the entrance to the building, gossiping with the chowkidar while Amelia wrote her letters, counted donations, or made entries into the accounts. When she'd finished, he would drive her deeper into the old town to visit Mabel, if Mabel wasn't up in the hills herself. Mabel and Amelia would have tiffin on the porch while Amir would eat with the servant in the kitchen.

Sometimes Giles would be there, on his lunch break from the hospital. The two of them would question Amelia anxiously about how she was feeling, how she was coping, how Arthur was faring in the build-up to the shooting expedition. Amelia was relieved that everything was out in the open between them. She took comfort from their friendship and the familiar surroundings of their home, glad to have this kind, caring couple to speak to about her innermost fears and her suspicions about Reginald; to know that they were there for her should she truly need to turn to them.

'Why don't you take this opportunity to leave, my dear? When Reginald is away on the shikar?' Mabel suggested one day, her eyes full of concern, after Amelia described how Reginald had treated her at the club.

'I couldn't do that,' Amelia replied, nerves rushing through her at the very prospect. 'I have nowhere to go. No money of my own and besides, if I tried, he would track me down and bring me back.'

'We could help you,' said Mabel, 'We could give you some money. Think about it carefully.'

Amelia shook her head. 'I couldn't do it. I could never leave Arthur.'

It was true. She often felt as if it hadn't been an accident that she'd met Reginald in the Planter's Club in Darjeeling. It was as if this were her destiny; to step into Elizabeth's shoes and run the dangerous gauntlet of marriage to Reginald purely for that little boy's sake.

AT LONG LAST THE morning of the shikar arrived. The hunters, their Indian shikaris, their servants, their mahouts with elephants to carry all the tents, cooking equipment and voluminous baggage were due to assemble at dawn on the rough scrubland behind the mansions of Wellesley Drive. Amelia barely slept the night before. She lay beside Reginald's snoring form, her mind plagued with anxieties about how Arthur would cope in the coming days. When she finally drifted off, her dreams exhausted her even more. She dreamed about a tiger lurking in the bush behind the house. When the bearer knocked at the door, bringing morning tea, it felt as if she'd had no sleep at all.

While Reginald was taking his morning bath, she dressed quickly and rushed downstairs to say goodbye to Arthur. The little boy was already awake, sitting up in bed and drinking the tea that ayah had brought him.

'Are you alright?' she asked. He glanced up at her and her heart twisted with pity at the look of brave determination in his eyes.

'Of course. I'll be fine. And I'm sure Daddy will be proud of me.'

Amelia exchanged a look with ayah.

'I'm *sure* he will,' she said, kneeling beside the bed and hugging Arthur close, knowing she wouldn't be able to do that when they said goodbye after breakfast in Reginald's presence.

'Now you take good care of yourself at the camp,' she said, holding him at arm's length and smiling into his eyes, 'You'll be back in no time, you'll see.'

Half an hour later, shivering in the chill before sunrise, she stood with Arthur and Reginald in the stable yard as the syces brought the horses out of the stables and saddled them up. She held the stirrup as Arthur mounted his pony.

The syce holding Reginald's black stallion was having difficulty controlling him.

'Hold him fast, my man,' said Reginald sternly, then turning to Amelia he kissed her on the lips, 'Goodbye, my darling. Make sure you behave while I'm gone.'

Then, with an athletic leap, he was up on the horse's back, cracking his thin whip against the stallion's flank. The animal wheeled round towards the open gate.

'Come on, Arthur, let's go. Try to keep up, now,' said Reginald setting off at a fast trot.

Amelia stood beside the gate with a lump in her throat as they trotted side by side across the plain to join the crowd of pack elephants, horses and their assorted riders, all gathering in the morning mist. Then she turned back towards the house and with a strange mixture of anxiety for Arthur and elation at her temporary freedom from Reginald, she crossed the lawn and went inside.

Most of the servants were already up and about. She went through the hall and down the front steps expecting Amir to be there, but he wasn't in his usual place near the front door. Puzzled, she wandered along the drive that wound back towards the stables and found him polishing the limousine under the shade of a frangipani tree.

'I need to go up to the villages today, Amir, to visit the young mothers,' she said. 'Now that Holden sahib has left for the shikar, I'm hoping there shouldn't be a problem leaving the city.'

He lifted his head slowly, his brow furrowed. Without meeting her eyes he shook his head.

'So sorry, memsahib, but sahib gave strict instructions for me not to drive you out of Ganpur.'

She paused, watching him buff the already shining black metal with a vigorous, circular motion. She was momentarily lost for words.

'But Amir, we have an understanding, you and I, don't we?' she said finally. 'Sahib doesn't have to know exactly where we've been each day…'

'No, memsahib. Not normally, memsahib. But he came to me yesterday evening and told me that the police at the roadblocks have a note of the number plate of the limousine. They have been told to report directly to him if we leave the city.'

Fresh anger at Reginald built up in her chest. How dare he?

'Well why don't we go anyway,' she said, 'He hasn't got the right to restrict my movements like that.'

But Amir shook his head again, 'I'm so sorry. He gave strict instructions, memsahib,' he said, glancing up at her. As he did so, Amelia saw that he was on the point of saying something else.

'Well, if you won't take me,' she said more gently, trying to coax him, 'do you have any suggestions as to how I might get there?'

He stopped polishing, but his eyes were still fixed on the shining surface.

'There is another car, memsahib,' he muttered without looking up.

'Another car?' she asked in surprise. 'What do you mean? Where is it?'

He straightened up.

'It is kept in a lockup, near the city gate,' he said.

Amelia stared at him, puzzled. Why on earth would Reginald keep a spare car locked up in a garage over a mile from the house. There were many empty stables and garages in the yard within the perimeter of the Residence itself. She opened her mouth to ask, when Amir cut her short.

'Sahib Reginald does not know about the car, memsahib.'

'What?'

'The car belong to memsahib Elizabeth.'

Her mouth fell open as the impact of his words hit home.

'So,' she said slowly, 'Elizabeth kept a car in a lockup. And Reginald knew nothing about it?'

'That is correct, memsahib.'

'Does anyone else know about it apart from you?'

He shook his head gravely. 'Only ayah. Ayah and myself.'

'What about Arthur?'

He shook his head again, his eyes fixed on hers now. 'Master Arthur does not know about the car.'

The sun had moved round while Amelia had been standing there and she was dimly aware of how hot and sticky she felt, how her arms were beginning to burn, but she couldn't move. She was rooted to the spot, her mouth was dry.

'Do you know *why* she had the car?' she asked at last.

Amir shook his head and then the familiar shutters came down over his eyes.

'I know nothing about that, memsahib,' he replied. She knew immediately there was no point probing him further.

'But does it still work? Do you think it would be alright for me to use it?' she asked instead.

'I keep the key locked away in my quarters, memsahib,' he said. 'On my days off, I sometimes go there to clean and polish it and make sure it is shipshape. Nobody owns it now. If you need it to go to see the mothers in the hills, I believe Memsahib Elizabeth would understand.'

The words echoed in her mind *Memsahib Elizabeth would understand*. Of course she would. She would understand exactly what it was like to be a virtual prisoner in the Residence, to have one's freedom curtailed each and every day, for policemen to be spying on you, asked to report if you so much as went outside the city. Amir understood what it was like, and ayah too. They had both understood Elizabeth and they understood her. And now they were trying to help her.

'Thank you, Amir,' she said. 'Do you think you could take me there?'

'Of course,' he said. 'I will take you there now if you are ready, but memsahib, just one thing... although the policemen don't know the car, you could still get stopped at the roadblock.'

'I'll run that risk, Amir,' she said, 'I just need to get my bag from upstairs, then we can go. Thank you so much.'

AN HOUR LATER, Amelia was driving along the dusty trunk road that led across the shimmering plain towards the purple smudge on the horizon, where the hills rose from the flat land. Her hair was tied in a bright red headscarf and sunglasses covered her eyes. At the police checkpoint on the edge of the city, she'd been waved through by deferential policemen; just another memsahib from the cantonment on her way out of town.

The car was a dark green French cabriolet, low slung and powerful, unsuited to Indian roads. She wondered how it would fare once she turned off the trunk road, but for the time being her heart soared with the unfamiliar and delicious sense of freedom. Here she was, completely alone for the first time in an age, heading for the hills under a vast blue sky. As the miles slipped easily by, she thought of Elizabeth. How extraordinary that she'd somehow purchased the car without Reginald's knowledge and kept it hidden as she had. Somebody must have helped her arrange it, surely. Amelia was impressed by her predecessor's resourcefulness and courage. The lockup was in a narrow, muddy side road, in a row of shambolic single-storey workshops and sheds, where men in filthy loincloths sweated away repairing rickshaws, bicycles and broken-down vehicles. Amir had parked at the end of the road, and they'd picked their way between the vehicle parts and puddles of oil and across a running sewer to the garage. Amir had unlocked the padlock, his face brimming with pride.

'Here it is, memsahib' he said pushing the wooden doors aside. The vehicle was in perfect condition, shining subtly in the gloom of the garage, looking out of place in the oil and dirt of the street.

'It works well,' Amir said. 'I have made sure of that.'

Had *she* driven out this way towards the hills sometimes, perhaps with Deepak by her side? An image of them looking into each other's eyes and laughing as the wind buffeted their hair flashed through Amelia's mind. Had they been in love, or just friends? How much of what Eileen had told her that evening at the club was the speculation of idle, malicious minds and how much fact? And Eileen hadn't even known what Giles and Mabel had told Amelia that very same day. Elizabeth had been carrying a child when she died. *Had Elizabeth's unborn child been Deepak's?* This question had plagued Amelia's thoughts and dreams ever since. *And if it* was *Deepak's baby, had Reginald found out?* Amelia flinched, imagining him yelling at Elizabeth, slamming her against the bedroom wall, his face full of thunder, shaking her by the shoulders, striking her with the full force he was more than capable of.

Suddenly she wanted to put distance between herself and Ganpur. She put her foot down on the accelerator and the car surged forward, dust and grit spraying from the tyres. Gripping the steering wheel, she clenched her teeth against the vibrations and drove as fast as the car would go. It felt as if she'd been possessed by some kind of madness, as if by driving this way she could leave her fears behind. The little car rattled over the bumps and stones in the road, the engine juddered so hard that it was difficult to control the steering wheel. Sooner than she'd anticipated, the junction with the little road that led into the mountains came into view. She slammed on the brakes just in time and skidded onto the side road, her heart beating fit to burst.

The car fared better on the uneven and twisting side road than she'd imagined. It was more powerful than Mabel's ramshackle vehicle, and more manoeuvrable than the Residence limousine. Soon, she'd completed all the twists and turns of the ascent into the hills and was driving alongside the lake. When she reached the sandy beach, she pulled off the road, turned off the engine and took deep breaths to calm her shattered nerves.

The water level was low again that day and she scanned the exposed lakebed for new bones with dread in her heart, but could see nothing. Ahead of her, a few yards from the shore was the little white pavilion. Her eyes were drawn to it as before, and this time three crows took off from one of the openings, soaring into the blinding sky. Mabel's words came back to her; *No one goes in there anymore. It used to be a bathing pavilion for the wives of maharajas a couple of centuries ago, but legend has it that one of them drowned and it was abandoned. The villagers are convinced it's haunted.*

It was the first time Amelia had been here alone. There was something movingly forlorn about the little pavilion that must once have been the scene of so much colour, laughter and happiness. Now, it stood sentinel over this still, beautiful lake, bearing silent witness to the saddest and most desperate act a young mother could perform. With a shudder, she turned the engine on and started along the road again, anxious to leave this place behind and reach the first village.

As usual the women and children came out and surrounded the car, greeting her warmly with huge smiles, opening the door for her, ushering her out, excited at the fact that she was alone this time and that she was driving herself. She left the car under the banyan tree, in the charge of a group of small boys, and allowed herself to be swept along by the crowd of women. They were taking her to a shabby wooden hut on the edge of the village, a little apart from the rest.

'Be careful,' said one old woman as they neared the hut, 'They don't like strangers, but the young girl is near her time. We will wait here.'

As Amelia approached the hut, she jumped as two dogs with mangy fur rushed at her, their teeth bared. Reaching the limits of their chains, they stood on their hind legs, straining, barking and growling. Amelia edged her way around them and made it to the doorway of the hut.

'Namaste,' she said tentatively into the stifling gloom.

After waiting a few moments and getting no reply, she stepped inside. As her eyes adjusted to the darkness, she realised that there was a young girl in the corner. She was sitting cross-legged on a pile of matting, fanning the flies from her face with a bundle of twigs. Her eyes were darkened with kohl, and there was a red tikka mark on her forehead, but she had the face of a child. Amelia recalled having seen her on the edge of a group of women she'd spoken to a few months back. The girl looked far too young and fragile to be a mother, but her distended belly told another story. When Amelia moved towards her, she shrunk back against the wall, looking up at her with wide, terrified eyes.

'Don't be afraid. I'm here to help you,' Amelia said gently. 'What's your name?'

Amelia crouched down in front of her, waiting for a response.

'Kiara,' whispered the girl eventually.

'Where is your husband?' Amelia asked. Kiara shrugged, her eyes widening still further but when Amelia asked if he was out working, Kiara nodded slowly.

'What about his family? Your mother-in-law?' Amelia asked.

'Lakshmi? Working too,' ventured the girl.

'Can I talk to you about your baby? You were there once, weren't you? When I explained to the other women what I'm here to do?'

Kiara nodded tentatively, and Amelia moved round and sat beside her on the matting. She told her gently and slowly all about the project and how the Baptist Church would pay her in instalments if she gave birth to a baby girl. Kiara listened in silence while Amelia was talking, but when she'd stopped, she said, 'They won't let me keep a baby if it's a girl.'

'I know it's difficult, but you can explain to them that there's another way,' Amelia said.

'A girl would cost too much,' Kiara replied miserably. 'The dowry. When she grows older. The family only want boys.'

'I know that's what they say,' said Amelia, 'but this is how we can help. By giving you enough money so you can afford to keep the baby. You can tell them all about it when they come back from the fields.'

'No. I can't talk to them about it. They will only get angry.'

'Shall I wait with you and talk to them myself?' Amelia asked, but Kiara shook her head vehemently, and in the girl's terrified eyes, Amelia caught a reflection of herself, of her own fears.

'When is the baby due?' she asked after a pause.

Kiara shrugged. 'I don't know.'

'In the next couple of weeks, maybe?' Amelia ventured and the girl suddenly reached out and gripped her hand.

'I'm so afraid,' she said, tears welling in her eyes and spilling down her cheeks, leaving tracks of smudged kohl in their wake.

Amelia stayed with her for a long time, trying to comfort her, trying to reassure her that the village midwife would help her and that she was young and strong and her baby would be healthy. All the time she was speaking she could hear the voices of the other women growing restive outside and the dogs snarling and rattling at their chains. She was with Kiara for longer than she'd ever been in any of the homes before. By the time she left and went out into the startling sunlight, Kiara had calmed down and had agreed to speak to her husband's family, but as Amelia re-joined the rest of the women outside, she realised that her conversation had shaken her in more ways than she wanted to admit.

After that, she drove from village to village in the area, retracing the route she'd taken with Mabel and Amir on previous occasions. In each place she was greeted by the women like an old friend. Two babies had been born since she'd last been: a boy in one village and a girl in another. Amelia gave the girl's mother the promised instalment and admired the beautiful little girl with her beady black eyes, suckling at the mother's breast.

The scorching heat had gone out of the sun as she returned to the car in the final village. As usual, she'd left it in the care of a few of the village boys. They rushed up and surrounded her as she neared the vehicle, all talking at once.

'We cleaned it for you, madam,' they said, their eyes sparkling.

'Oh, how kind,' she said, reaching in her purse for some annas to give them.

'Inside and out,' said the ringleader, holding up a cloth, brush and bucket as proof.

'Well, I didn't expect that,' she said laughing, finding some coins and handing them out to the outstretched hands.

'We found this, madam,' said another of the boys, fishing in his pocket and handing her a small square of carboard. 'A picture.'

She took it from his outstretched hand. As she stared down at it she froze, and everything around her became a blur; the faces of the boys looking up at her, the colourful sarees of the village women, the smoke rising from the cooking fires. Even the sound of their voices became distorted. She held in her hands a miniature photograph of a young Indian man; dressed smartly in a suit and high collar, he was astonishingly good looking, with high cheek bones and liquid, intelligent eyes which looked straight at the camera. She turned it over and on the back was written,

To darling Lizzie, with all the love in my heart, and hope for our future happiness together: Deepak.

'Where did you find that?'

'Here – I show you!' the boy said eagerly, taking her hand and tugging her towards the car. He opened the door and scrambled inside.

'In here, madam!' he said, pointing to a space between the seat moorings. Amir must have missed it when he cleaned the car, or perhaps he'd left it there, not wanting to disturb anything of Elizabeth's.

She drove back through the hills, along the lakeside road and, as she passed the pavilion there was a pink tinge in the sky, reflected perfectly in the still surface of the water. It was late afternoon, she'd spent longer in the villages than she'd expected to. Kiara's family would be back from the fields by now; would she have the courage to tell them about Amelia's visit? A twinge of guilt crept through her. She should have gone back and faced them herself, but Kiara had been more terrified by that prospect than ever, and Amelia had promised Amir she would meet him back at the lockup by six o' clock.

Arthur had not been far from her thoughts all day. They would have set up camp by now, beside the river on the edge of the forest where they'd planned to shoot, the bearers and servants and shikars on one side where the elephants and horses were tethered, Reginald and his group on the other. What was Arthur doing now? Would the ride have exhausted him? Would Reginald make sure he was properly fed and looked after during the evening, or would he just sit round the campfire, drinking and talking with the other men, while the boy was left to wander alone?

How little he knew, that innocent child, of everything that had been happening around him. 'Deepak had to go away,' he'd said. And now she knew without a doubt that Deepak and Elizabeth had been in love and that they had probably been planning a life together away from Reginald.

19
———

AMELIA

Ganpur, November 1936

For the next three days, Amelia made the most of her unaccustomed freedom, riding out onto the plain alone to watch the mist burn off the parched land as the sun rose, lazing on the veranda with a book, walking alone around the streets of the cantonment in the afternoons. One morning she went to the Mission to write letters and collect money for her next visit to the hills. As Amir drove her through the streets, groups of policemen were still patrolling with their batons and lathis.

'There are a lot of them around today,' she remarked to Amir.

'Sahib's orders,' he said. 'People are very angry about the men he keeps in the cells. He cannot keep them down like this for ever. And he is off hunting, shooting game.'

There was a new bitterness in his voice. Amelia was surprised. She'd never heard him speak like that against Reginald directly.

'Are *you* angry, Amir?' she asked. He drove on, not turning his head.

'Of course,' he said at last, and she could see that his knuckles on the steering wheel were white, he was gripping it so hard. 'We are all angry.'

'Why do you carry on working for Reginald?' It had puzzled her since she'd first found out that Amir and ayah, out of all the servants, had formed a secret alliance against their employer.

'I stay for Master Arthur,' he said quietly, 'and before that, I stay for his mother. And now I stay for you too, memsahib.'

A lump formed in her throat at such kindness and she was unable to reply.

'And anyway, I am old,' he went on. 'I cannot do other work. I have no sons to support me and my family are in a village a long way from here.'

She leaned forward, sensing her opportunity to press him for information.

'Amir, you *must* tell me about what happened to memsahib Elizabeth,' she said urgently. 'I need to know. I need to know if my husband... well, if he had anything to do with her death.'

There, she had said it. She'd said the words out loud for the first time. She waited breathlessly for his reply, but he just carried on driving, slowly and carefully, as if he hadn't heard her. He navigated his way around a pair of white Brahmin cows lying together in the middle of the road. He took so long to reply, that by the time he did, they had arrived in front of the Mission building. He took his time to park the limousine between a stationary bullock cart and a group of rickshaw-wallahs smoking cheroots on the kerbside. Then he spoke.

'That, I do not know for sure, memsahib,' he said gravely. 'Nobody knows, except perhaps...'

He turned round to look at her, frowning, his eyes suddenly

faraway, as if he'd stumbled across something he was turning over in his mind.

'Except? Except who, Amir? Who would know what really happened on the shikar?'

But he shook his head and turned away from her again to face the windscreen.

'Nobody, memsahib. They were alone,' he said quietly. 'Sahib Reginald came back alone on his stallion, leading her horse. Poor memsahib Elizabeth, her body was tied onto the saddle. She was covered in blood. Her back was ripped to shreds.'

He faltered, tears standing in his eyes. 'I will never forget that day.'

'That's truly terrible,' Amelia whispered, horror and revulsion creeping through her at the vivid picture evoked by his words, and her heart went out to Amir, who in his quiet way had been a pillar of strength and courage for Elizabeth, Arthur and herself for so many years.

ON THE THIRD day of Reginald's absence, she took Elizabeth's car from the lockup and drove up into the hills again, carrying the money from the Mission in a leather bag on the passenger seat. She was keen to follow up on the conversations she'd had two days before; it was important that the village women saw her keep her promises, especially as she'd had to stay away for so many weeks before that. Out of all the people she'd spoken to, Kiara was the one she was desperate to see. The image of the girl's sad, terrified eyes had haunted Amelia since she'd stepped inside that gloomy hut on the edge of the village. Had Kiara managed to speak to the family about Amelia's proposal? Had they beaten her for even mentioning it?

This time, the girl was not alone. Her mother-in-law stood in the doorway as Amelia approached, the mangy dogs setting up a racket, just as they had before. She was a strong-looking woman, her skin weather-beaten and lined from working in the fields, her black eyes flinty and cold. She watched Amelia as she approached and made no attempt to call off the dogs, who barked and strained at their chains.

'What do you want?' the woman shouted, above the noise of the dogs. 'Stop there, lady. You and your kind are not welcome here.'

Amelia stopped walking. 'I've come to see Kiara,' she said boldly. 'Did she tell you I came the other day?'

The woman's expression didn't soften but she nodded curtly. 'She told me alright. As I said, you're not welcome. We don't need the likes of you to tell us what to do.'

Amelia paused, taken aback by the aggression in the woman's voice. 'I'm not trying to tell you what to do, but...'

'Oh yes, you are,' the woman cut in. 'And you've no right.'

'Look, we can help you,' Amelia said, 'Did Kiara tell you about our scheme? We can pay you... pay you so that if the baby is a girl...' the words came out in a rush. How nervous she must sound.

'Yes. She told me all of that. You think that because we are poor, you can buy us like that?'

'It's not that,' said Amelia. She swallowed, her mouth dry, her resolve beginning to waver. Wouldn't it be easier just to run back to the car and drive on to the next village? But again she thought of Kiara, inside the house, crouching in her corner, overwhelmed by fear.

'It would just be to help you along,' she called, 'You know, you can keep the first instalment of money even if the baby is a boy?'

The woman frowned and peered back at Amelia, but now a glint of greed entered her eyes.

'What's that you say?' she asked, coming forward a few steps, then, turning on the dogs, she snapped, 'Be quiet, you filthy hounds.'

They stopped barking and dropped to the ground whimpering.

Amelia dipped her hand into her bag and brought out a bundle of soft rupee notes. She held it out, her hand trembling.

'I said, you can keep this,' she said, 'even if the baby is a boy. It's a gift either way. If it is a girl, I will bring more money for you.'

The woman walked forward and snatched the notes, all the time eyeing Amelia as coldly as she had from the start of the exchange.

'Can I see Kiara please?' Amelia asked, as the woman turned back to the hut.

'I don't want strangers inside the house. You shouldn't have come in before.'

'Please...' her voice caught in her throat; she was panicking now. She'd parted with the money, but how could she make sure that Kiara was safe in there? Was she even in there still?

'I said no!' the woman turned back suddenly and the dogs started barking again.

'I will come back,' shouted Amelia. 'In a few days when the baby is born. I will bring more money. Please let me see her.'

She rushed after the woman as she entered the hut. The woman turned and pushed her away roughly with both hands. Amelia stumbled backwards and narrowly managed to avoid falling over in the mud, but in those seconds she'd seen what she wanted to see. Kiara was there in the corner of the hut, cowering this time, wide eyes staring out from the gloom.

Amelia's visits to the other two villages were uneventful that day; she distributed the money she'd promised amongst expectant and new mothers and exchanged news and gossip with some of the older women. Then she drove home past the lake and the abandoned pavilion, down the twisting mountain road and along the long, dusty trunk road back to Ganpur. She drove towards the setting sun, a giant red globe slipping down behind the horizon, streaking the rose-coloured sky with splashes of purple and gold.

It was dark by the time she reached the lockup in the backstreet and, as she turned onto the end of the road, Amir was already there waiting for her in front of the doors. As she drew up, she could tell from the hunched way he was standing, the way he was twisting his hands together, that something had happened.

'What is it, Amir?' she asked, stopping the car and cutting the engine. 'What's happened?'

He leaned towards her, his eyes full of pain. 'It's Master Arthur, memsahib. The syces have brought him back home from camp. He is very sick.'

A wave of shock washed through her. 'What's wrong with him?'

Amir shook his head. 'Fever, memsahib. Same fever as before. Only worse. Very, very bad this time.'

'And Reginald? Has he come back too?'

Amir shook his head again, dismay and shame in his eyes. 'Sahib Reginald stay at shikar, memsahib. He send the boy back with the syces alone.'

Together, they locked Elizabeth's car away as quickly as they could, then hurried to the limousine, parked at the end of the road. Amelia was desperate to get to Arthur's bedside and her mind was in turmoil. How could Reginald have sent him back and stayed on in the camp himself? How could he have done that? This callous act was a fresh blow. There was terror and helplessness in her heart now. She had tied herself to this man for life. How could she carry on living under his control and in his power, knowing he had done this to his only son, that he had a heart of stone?

When they drew up at the Residence, Amelia dashed up the front steps, across the marbled hallway and along the passage to Arthur's room. Ayah was kneeling beside the bed, mopping Arthur's brow. She looked up as Amelia entered, tears in her eyes. Amelia knelt beside her. The boy's face was drained of colour and his eyes flickered in delirium. Sweat plastered his hair to his head and trickled down his face. He was moving about restlessly, moaning in pain.

'Ayah, please go with Amir and ask Doctor Harris to come,' Amelia said, seeing how serious it was. 'You know him, don't you? He'll either be at the Mission Hospital or at home in his bungalow,' she said. 'Tell him to come here straight away. I will stay with Arthur.' She fished in her bag and handed ayah the card Mabel had given her.

It was a desperately long wait for Giles to arrive. Amelia tried not to let her thoughts spin out of control. Instead, she busied herself, remembering the skills she'd learned from her father and mother. She made Arthur as comfortable as she could, sponging his face and body with cold water, turning the fans on full blast. She tried to get the boy to take some sips of water through his parched and blistered lips. And all the time, she talked to him softly, gently, willing him to open his eyes or to say something to her. Sometimes he let out a moan or muttered something she couldn't understand. She couldn't tell if he was aware of her presence.

It seemed like an age before she heard footsteps in the passage and Giles strode in the doorway carrying a battered leather bag, followed by ayah.

'I'm glad you asked me to come,' he said.

Amelia stepped aside as he went straight to the bed, opened up his bag of instruments and started to examine Arthur. She stood there silently, watching the skilled hands of the doctor as he felt Arthur all over, his joints, his stomach. He took his temperature and tried to look into his eyes with a tiny torch, but the pupils just flickered up into Arthur's eyelids.

'Where's his father?' asked Giles, turning towards Amelia, his brows furrowed.

'He's still at the hunt,' admitted Amelia, bowing her head.

'How far away is it?'

Amir stepped forward from the doorway. 'It is a day's ride, doctor sahib. You cannot get there by road.'

'Then please send someone to fetch him right away. He needs to be here. The boy is very ill indeed.' Amelia's scalp prickled in alarm.

'Very well, sahib,' said Amir, turning to go. 'I will tell one of the syces to go back on the quickest horse.'

'Why? Giles, tell me why?' asked Amelia.

'I'm going to administer quinine right now, but it could be too late. His temperature is dangerously high.'

She watched helplessly as he produced a vial and syringe from his bag. He held it up to the light as he pulled the plunger back, then turning back to Arthur, he slipped the needle skilfully into Arthur's thin arm.

'I'll need to admit him to hospital,' Giles said as he straightened up. 'I know Reginald won't like it.'

'Don't worry about Reginald,' Amelia replied, her voice shaking. 'He sent Arthur back from the shoot and didn't even bother to come home with him. He's got no right to object.'

Suddenly, overwhelmed with anxiety and sadness, she sat down heavily on Arthur's little schoolroom chair and burst into tears. 'I can't believe he did that, Giles,' she sobbed.

'Amelia,' Giles said, putting a soothing hand on her shoulder,

'You need to be strong now. Don't upset yourself. Perhaps the fever wasn't so bad when Arthur set off from the camp? It could well have escalated on the journey. Perhaps Reginald just wasn't thinking straight.'

'Perhaps,' she said, taking a shuddering breath, trying to pull herself together.

'Now, I need to call for an ambulance. Is there a telephone somewhere?'

'Of course, ayah will show you,' said Amelia. 'I'll stay here with Arthur.'

She went with Arthur and Giles in the ambulance to the Mission hospital, sitting opposite Giles on a pull-down seat beside the boy's stretcher, gripping his hot, lifeless hand as the vehicle rattled through the cantonment. She was so consumed by anxiety that she hardly noticed the journey, but she did register when they passed under the old arch out of the cantonment and the vehicle slowed down as the road surface became rutted and potholed. As they drove deeper into the old town, she became dimly aware of angry voices on the road, growing louder by the second, gradually building to a roar. Fists hammered on the side of the ambulance. She tore her eyes away from Arthur and exchanged an anxious look with Giles.

'The riots have started up again,' he said. 'It was simmering when Amir drove me through an hour ago.'

'Reginald shouldn't have gone away,' Amelia muttered. 'Putting all those police into the old town was bound to make things worse.' Her eyes were fixed on the back doors of the ambulance. She was terrified that the mob would break them down and burst inside.

'We're nearly at the hospital now,' said Giles. 'The rioters won't stop this ambulance. The Mission hospital is where the poorest Indians come for help.'

The vehicle gradually edged forward through the crowd. It

was probably only another ten minutes, but it seemed like an age before the angry voices subsided and they were clear of the rioting crowds. The ambulance came to a stop in front of the hospital gates, the driver exchanged brief words with the gate-keeper and they were through and speeding towards the entrance.

Amelia rushed alongside as two turbaned porters carried Arthur's stretcher into the building. along the echoing, tiled corridors and through a narrow doorway into a high-ceilinged room at the far end.

The room was sparsely furnished, with only a narrow iron bed, a hard chair and a small cupboard. There was a wooden cross on the wall, just as there had been in her father's hospitals. She stood aside as Arthur was eased onto the bed and Giles and a nurse made him comfortable.

'It will be touch and go for the next few hours, I'm afraid,' Giles said gently when they'd finished.

'Can I stay with him?'

'Of course. But there's nowhere to sleep, I'm afraid.'

'I don't mind that,' she said, 'I'm used to caring for malaria patients.'

'I remember,' he said, his face relaxing into a smile. 'If you need anything, or if his condition worsens, Nurse Gupta here will be out on the main ward. I need to do my rounds of the other patients now, but I'll be back here as soon as I can.'

As he left, he paused and turned back in the doorway. 'Shall I ask Mabel to come?'

'Don't disturb her now,' Amelia said. 'Perhaps tomorrow... and Giles, I can't thank you enough for what you've done today.'

When Giles and Nurse Gupta had gone, Amelia pulled the chair up close to the bed, so she could watch Arthur; observe every minute change in his condition. His face was still pallid and sweaty, his eyes closed, his breathing shallow. Although he was worryingly still for long periods, every so often he would jerk one of his limbs suddenly or cry out in his delirium. Sometimes he would thrash around wildly. When that happened, Amelia would lean over him and put her arms right round his body and hold him tight to stop him falling from the bed. When he was still, she bathed his face and body with a damp cloth from the bowl the nurse had left by the bed. It reminded her poignantly of the first time she'd done that for him, so many months ago now. But he hadn't been as sick then; he'd been conscious, able to look up at her every so often with a grateful smile that had melted her heart. It had brought them close, during those early weeks, it had forged the bond between them that couldn't ever be broken.

The hours passed. Nurse Gupta came and went, checking Arthur's temperature, bringing a syringe to top him up with quinine. Each time, the nurse shook her head, looking gravely at Amelia with sympathetic eyes. Amelia lost track of time as she sat there, her body stiffening in the hard chair. From the slatted opening, high up in the wall, she could hear shouts and yells from the rioting crowds, the sound of crackers going off, and loud bangs that shredded her brittle nerves. Were they explosions?

She sat there nursing Arthur, all through the long, dark, terrible night, until the grey light of dawn appeared between the slats. Mabel came at first light. She went straight over to Amelia and put her arms around her.

'I'm so sorry,' Mabel said, tears in her eyes. 'You look exhausted. I'll sit with him while you stretch your legs. There's a kitchen along the corridor. They'll give you some tea and breakfast if you ask.'

With a heavy heart, Amelia tore herself away from the bedside and took Mabel's advice. One of the kitchen staff handed her a bowl of porridge and a steaming cup of chai, and pointed her in the direction of a wooden table and chairs in the corridor. She took a few sips of the sweet, cloying chai, but found she couldn't eat any porridge. Her mouth flooded with nausea each time she tried.

She and Mabel took it in turns to sponge Arthur down throughout that endless day. Time slipped by and was only marked by regular visits from Nurse Gupta and Giles. Amelia and Mabel barely spoke as they sat there. Amelia didn't want to talk about Reginald, her anger was so raw, and she didn't want to talk about Arthur either, not wanting to put her fears into words. He was slipping away and there was nothing they could do. His fever still raged and he was still delirious. The quinine was too late. Amelia's worst fears *were* coming true right before her eyes.

As the day drew on and the shadows lengthened, the sound of violence out on the streets returned. Glass smashing, shouting, the crack of explosions. But in that room it was as if everything outside was happening in another dimension.

The light had gone from the sky when Arthur's little body gave up the struggle and succumbed to the ravages of the disease. Amelia held his body tightly to her and wept for a long time, weeping for the waste of this young life, for the loss of her young soulmate and for the loss of her own life too. She held him and wept until she felt a hand on her shoulder and looked up. But it wasn't Mabel or Giles standing behind her. It was Reginald. He'd entered the room without her noticing, his face ravaged with grief and unmistakeable guilt.

20

KATE

Warren End, 1970

Kate put the phone down with a heavy heart. Sandra from the nursing home had called to tell her that Edna Robinson had been taken into hospital. The old lady had collapsed the previous evening and was under observation in the intensive care unit.

'I'm so sorry, Sandra,' said Kate, shocked. 'Poor Miss Robinson! You must be so worried.'

'It *is* very worrying for all of us. Everyone at the Meadows is praying for Edna, she's such a well-loved resident here. Sadly, the poor lady is unconscious at the moment. The doctors aren't sure whether it was a stroke or some sort of brain haemorrhage.'

'That sounds very serious,' said Kate. 'How awful for you all.'

'I'm calling because I know you had another appointment to see her soon. Just to let you know that it won't be possible now.'

'Of course not. How thoughtful of you, to remember that at such a difficult time,' said Kate, pricked with guilt as she thought back over her conversation with Edna the day before. 'She did seem very tired yesterday towards the end of our conversation. I really hope that wasn't the cause of her illness.'

'Please don't blame yourself, Miss Hamilton,' Sandra replied. 'Edna's been up and down for a long time now. She was so pleased that you visited her and that she had a chance to talk to you about your great aunt. She was so fond of Amelia. Nothing would have made her happier than helping you with your family research. She often talks about the wonderful friendship she and her sister had with Amelia.'

After she'd put the phone down, she thought back over her visit to Edna the day before. It had been a chilling experience in lots of ways. The old lady had seemed able to see directly into Kate's soul, into her own secret past, to know exactly why she was there asking about her great aunt. Kate recalled the heart-stopping words of Edna's sister about Amelia: *there's something about that young lady. Darkness clings to her like a shroud. I can see it all around her.*

The conversation had revealed so much to Kate about the pain of Amelia's marriage to Reginald Holden, about her love for his vulnerable young son Arthur, about the mysteries surrounding Reginald's first wife. Edna's revelations had brought Kate tantalisingly close to understanding Amelia's story, but not quite close enough. And now poor Edna was lying unconscious in the hospital. Despite Sandra's reassurance, had the trauma of reliving Amelia's story brought on her collapse?

Her eyes strayed to the house particulars Gordon had left with her the previous afternoon that were on the desk. She'd promised to call him that morning. It was time to make a decision, she knew that, but as she flicked through the glossy photographs, and the lavish descriptions, showing Oakwood Grange at its gracious best, the past tugged at her heart strings again. Was she really ready to say goodbye to this old house that held so many secrets and so many memories?

She put down Gordon's papers with a heavy sigh. She needed to find out what had happened to Amelia in Ganpur; why she had left that life behind and kept it completely secret for decades, locked away in a chest in the attic. There *was* a connection between Amelia's secret past and what had happened in 1944, Kate was convinced of it. Now she knew that George Prendergast had been in Ganpur when Amelia was, that they had met at the club. An image of a diminished and aged Prendergast entered her mind, struggling with his stick to get to the place where he and Amelia used to meet. He must have been going there for one last look before the builders moved in to gut the old place. Guilt pierced her heart. She and Joan had brought him to this. They were responsible.

She would decide about Oakwood Grange later; she couldn't focus on it at that moment; Amelia's story was calling her back. She reached for the bag in which she'd stuffed Amelia's photographs, letters and certificates when she'd rushed them round to Joan's house the afternoon before. Now she took them out, one by one, spreading them out on the desk, just as she'd done when she'd first discovered them. And as she did so, her mind ran over the conversation with Joan over tea in her little kitchen, Joan sitting opposite her, trying to pretend her swollen eye was nothing out of the ordinary.

Kate had really thought she was getting somewhere with Joan that time. At least they'd begun the first faltering steps towards being frank with one another. The news that Joan had stopped working at school and from that point had entered a downward spiral of failure pricked Kate's conscience. If only she'd not walked away completely that summer, if only she'd just written to Joan now and then, things might have gone so differently for her friend. She was determined to make up for that now. At least yesterday they'd both acknowledged that they needed to talk about what they'd done that summer of '44; the actions that had had such a devastating effect on so many lives. But just when Kate thought they were getting somewhere, mayhem had suddenly broke out in the room above them.

'They're fighting again. I'll 'ave to go up and sort it out,' said Joan heaving herself up from the table and going to the bottom of the stairs. 'Oi. Stop it you lot,' she yelled. 'I'm coming up.'

Kate waited, awkwardly, sipping her tea, while Joan stomped up the stairs to sort out the fray. She couldn't hear the words, but there were bangs on the floorboards and a lot of shouting and crying. When Joan returned, her face was red and flustered.

'Bloody kids,' she muttered, her hand on the doorframe.

Kate knew there was no chance of returning to the point in the conversation they'd reached before they'd been interrupted.

'You'll have to go now,' said Joan, her eyes on the clock on the kitchen wall. 'Dave will be back soon.'

Kate gathered up her papers from the table. It was only quarter past three, but it wasn't worth arguing. The moment had passed. She felt Joan's impatient eyes on her as she picked up her bag, then Joan ushered her out of the kitchen and to the front door. She pulled it open and peeped out quickly, looking up and down Clerks' Lane in either direction.

'It's alright. He's not coming yet,' Joan said breathlessly. 'If you go now, it'll be OK.'

'Joan,' said Kate firmly as she stepped out of the door. 'I really don't mind if I do run into Dave. And if I do happen to, I'll give him a piece of my mind.'

Joan's face fell. 'No. Don't do that. Don't ever do that.'

Kate looked straight into Joan's eyes. 'I know he did that to you,' she said. 'You owe it to yourself to face up to what he's doing and stop putting up with it. He's still a bully and a coward, just like he always was when we were teenagers.'

Joan stared at her, stunned into silence.

'I know I haven't been a friend to you for years and I'm very sorry for that,' Kate went on. 'But now I'm back, I want to make it up to you. I'll help you in any way I can.'

There was a pause as they held each other's gaze. There was turmoil behind Joan's eyes for a second, but then the shutters came down again.

'I can manage. I don't need your help,' Joan said lifting her chin. 'And anyway. You're *not* back, are you? You said you're here to put the big house on the market. You'll be back in London soon, living the high life and you'll forget all about Warren End again. Just like you did before.'

Kate opened her mouth to answer, but she had no reply. It was true. She *had* told Joan she was just back to sell up, and that's what she was doing, wasn't she? Gordon's particulars were lying on Amelia's desk in the study at Oakwood Grange, just waiting for her approval.

'Go on then,' said Joan, urgently. 'Off you go. I need to shut the door.'

'I meant what I said,' called Kate as the door slammed. 'I will help you if you'll let me.'

Then she walked away, full of regret that the encounter had ended that way.

There was a new urgency to get to the bottom of Amelia's story. Until she'd done it, she couldn't possibly make a decision about the house. She thought about poor Edna, unconscious in the hospital. It was an awful thought, but perhaps Edna wouldn't be able to tell her any more about Amelia, even if she *were* to gain consciousness.

Now, Kate picked up one of the letters from Mabel to Amelia and read it again. It was the one on the top of the pile; the last one Amelia had kept, but possibly not the last one Mabel had ever written. It was certainly the last one from India in which Mabel had written about leaving India on Independence and how she was looking forward to seeing Amelia again. *I realise*

that you probably wouldn't want us to visit Warren End, quite natu-
rally, but perhaps we could meet up in London sometimes? Giles is
hoping to find work in the suburbs somewhere...

Kate was sure that they would have met up in London, that
Mabel would have been a source of support to Amelia as long as
she was alive. But was she still alive? Surely not. Otherwise she
would have come to the funeral. It struck Kate that if Mabel was
still alive, she would be the obvious person to fill in the blanks
about Amelia's life.

'Why didn't I think of that before?' she muttered. It shouldn't
be difficult to track Mabel Harris down through the Baptist
Church somehow? She reached for a tattered old edition of the
Yellow Pages in Amelia's bookcase, found the telephone number
for a Baptist Fellowship in Midchester, and started making calls.

An hour and a half and several conversations later, she had
scribbled down the address and telephone number of Mrs
Mabel Harris, widow of Dr Giles Harris, former missionary
doctor to the Baptist Mission in India. Mabel was still alive,
living in Mile End in London, where, according to the minister
she'd spoken to, she played an active part in the community and
in the life of the local Baptist church. Kate stared down at the
address for a long time before she had the courage to pick up
the phone to call.

It only rang twice before it was answered. The voice of an
elderly woman, sprightly and efficient answered.

'Mrs Harris? Mrs Mabel Harris?' Kate asked.

'It is indeed. Who's calling please?'

Kate took a deep breath and cleared her throat. 'Well, we
don't know each other, but I think you knew my great-aunt in
India before the war.'

There was a short silence, then Mabel said, 'You mean
Amelia, of course. Amelia Hamilton. Is that Kate?'

'Yes it is,' Kate replied, taken aback.

'I thought you might call sooner or later.'

Kate's mouth dropped open in surprise. Edna had had exactly the same reaction when she'd arrived at the Meadows. This was the second time someone she'd approached about Amelia's past already knew she would be in touch. It was uncanny.

'You do know that Aunt Amelia... well, you do know that she's passed away, don't you?' Kate asked, gently.

'Yes, I do,' said Mabel. 'It's so tragic. So sad that her life was cut short like that. But I was half expecting it, I'm afraid. She was quite ill and dangerously thin the last time we met up in London. I wasn't entirely surprised when I heard the news.'

'I'm so sorry,' said Kate. 'I didn't know that you and she were friends until I started to go through her papers. Otherwise, I would have made sure that you were asked to the funeral.'

'Oh... well actually I *was* at the funeral,' said Mabel. 'I didn't stay long, just long enough to say a prayer for poor Amelia. I'd never been to Warren End before. As you may have already gathered, she wanted to keep her Indian past as private as she could.'

'Yes, well, it's about her time in India that I'm calling you,' said Kate. 'There's a lot about that time that I had no idea about at all and I was wondering if you could help me. Do you have time? I could always call back another time.'

'I'm happy to talk about Amelia, Kate. I have a few minutes now. I assumed that once you'd started looking through her old papers and things, you might have a few questions. I don't know everything myself, of course, but my husband and I supported Amelia through some very difficult times back then. We exchanged letters until Giles and I came back from India in '48. By then Amelia had been married to your uncle for several years. He made her very happy, but I'm sure you know that.

After Giles and I moved to London, I used to meet up with Amelia sometimes.'

'But what I don't understand, Mrs Harris, is why Amelia kept her first marriage a secret from everyone in the family... it just doesn't seem to make sense.'

'Well, there were lots of reasons why she wanted to leave India firmly behind her. You know she was terrified of people finding out about her first marriage. Especially when your Uncle James became a Member of Parliament. That was why she kept herself so much in the background during his election campaigns. I believe your Uncle James was rather surprised about that. Amelia was so stunning looking and so accomplished, she would have been a great asset to him if she'd wanted the limelight, but he loved her so much, he just accepted her wishes without question.'

'Yes, he did love her. They seemed so happy together,' Kate said, thinking about how her bachelor Uncle's life had been transformed when he'd brought Amelia home from London, that day in 1940. How everyone, except Kate's mother, had been captivated by her. But then if Uncle James had made her so happy, why was she having clandestine meetings with George Prendergast down at Willow Mill within a few years of her marriage?

'I'm sure I don't know everything about your great aunt,' Mabel went on, her voice less strident now. 'She still had her secrets, even from me. You know, I could tell there was something troubling Amelia that she never wrote to me about or told me about when we used to meet up. There was something wrong, I knew it, just reading between the lines of her letters. Something happened towards the end of the war that was a blight on her new-found happiness. I could tell that there was something eating away at her. But she would never say what it was, not even to me.'

Kate's heart started beating faster, the guilt surfacing now that the conversation was getting to the heart of the issue. She had to know, she had to find out the truth. She took a deep breath.

'Did she ever mention a George Prendergast to you?' she asked, her voice a little higher than before. She'd said it now. There was no going back.

'George Prendergast?' Mabel mused, and there was a short pause before she spoke again. 'I don't think so, but the name does ring a bell. Come to think of it, I do remember there was a Prendergast in Ganpur when we were there. A Willy Prendergast, I think. I didn't know him. He was in the Gymkhana Club set. Didn't mix with us missionaries. Could they be related?'

'Well, an old lady from the village who knew Amelia well, told me that George Prendergast had been out to Ganpur for a hunting expedition while Amelia was there. The same George Prendergast lives in Warren End.'

'How extraordinary... I vaguely remember that Willy had a brother to stay. But Amelia never mentioned to me she'd met him afterwards in Warren End. I would certainly have remembered that. How very strange.'

'Perhaps she had something to hide?' said Kate. 'You know, back in 1944, when I was young, my friend and I saw the two of them out together several times.' Kate's voice faltered. She'd never told anyone about it before. Only she and Joan knew the full extent of what had happened. Her heart was beating sickeningly in her chest but she forced the words out. 'Amelia and George Prendergast... they were having an affair.'

There, she'd finally said it. She waited for Mabel's reaction, the seconds beating away in her ears.

'No! I can't believe that of Amelia,' there was outrage in Mabel's voice when the words finally came. 'She was a Christian.

She lived by the Ten Commandments. And she loved your Uncle James.'

'I know it sounds incredible. But we were convinced of it,' said Kate. 'My friend and I. We saw them meet secretly several times. It was obvious to us. They often had lovers' tiffs.'

'Well, I have to say I'm speechless... but, as I said, she did seem to have something to hide from the end of the war onwards. It was when she started withdrawing into herself. Drinking too much. I'm afraid that just got worse and worse when your great uncle died. I always thought it was about the other thing, but she always clammed up if I ever tried to ask about it.'

'The other thing?' asked Kate. Whatever did Mabel mean by that?

'Yes. Her coming back to England as she did. Look, it's rather a difficult matter to speak about on the phone. And I'm due down at the church hall in half an hour. I need to go and get ready now I'm afraid.'

'Could I call another time, perhaps?'

'Perhaps it would be better if you came to see me one day. Could you do that?'

'Of course. I could come anytime. Whenever is convenient for you.'

'I have plenty of time tomorrow. Why don't you come in the morning at around eleven-thirty? You have my address, don't you? I'll make us some tiffin.'

Kate put the phone down, her stomach churning with a mixture of nerves and excitement. She sat there at Amelia's desk, surrounded by her letters and photographs, motionless for a long time. She needed to let the conversation with Mabel Harris settle in her mind and adjust to the fact that she could be within twenty-four hours of finally finding out the truth about Amelia.

21

KATE

London, May 1970

The rush hour traffic was heavy as Kate joined the motorway and headed south towards London. The slow lane was nose-to-tail with convoys of vans and lorries, so she quickly moved out to join the fastest moving vehicles in the outside lane and put her foot down. It would take her an hour to reach the North Circular, but then she would have to navigate through north and east London to Mile End and she wasn't quite sure of the way. The heavy, repetitive chords of Spirit in the Sky was blasting out of the car radio. It didn't match her mood so she switched it off. She needed to concentrate at this speed, and there was a lot playing through her mind.

She'd put off calling Gordon Anderson all afternoon after she'd spoken to Mabel Harris, but in the end he'd called her just before he left the office.

'Are you happy with the drafts?' he'd asked. She tried to stall but he'd seen through her excuses straight away.

'Just say if you need more time. I understand,' he said, and she caught a note of amusement in his tone again. For some reason the laughter in his voice irritated her.

'And why would you find that funny, Gordon?' she asked.

'It's not funny at all,' he said, serious again. 'I didn't mean to annoy you. I know you're in two minds about selling up, but I really don't mind waiting for you to decide. It's a win-win situation for me either way.'

'Win-win? How's that?'

'You mean you don't know? Oh, come on, Kate. If you keep the house, it means you'll be spending more time in Warren End and that's good for me. But if you sell up, I get the instructions and the commission.'

'Good for you?' she repeated. Her skin tingled at his words, but in the back of her mind she was telling herself to grow up, she wasn't that infatuated teenager anymore, hanging about outside the school gym to catch a glimpse of him. They were both mature adults and Gordon was a married man.

'Do I really need to spell it out?' he asked. 'I don't mind, here goes. I've really enjoyed getting to know you again all these years on. It may sound crazy, but I still feel that attraction I felt when we were young, and I think you do too. Please tell me if I'm on the wrong track here?'

'But Gordon, surely...' she said. 'Aren't you... well aren't you ... married?'

'Married?' he laughed. 'Is that what you thought?'

'Well, yes. Yes, I did rather assume that, Gordon. It is a fair assumption to make.'

Again, he laughed. 'I thought Janet Andrews would have told you my life history by now. The Warren End grapevine hasn't been working as it should, obviously.'

'So, what is your life history?' she asked.

'Well, I was hoping to tell you over dinner sometime. But what the hell. I *was* married briefly a long time ago. She was a teacher at the primary school in Warren End. But she left me for someone else less than two years after we were married. It never felt quite right anyway, to tell you the truth. They emigrated to Australia a while ago. They were amongst the first "ten-pound poms". It was a bit of a talking point in Warren End for a while I believe.'

'Oh!' was all Kate could say, as the image she'd been holding in her mind of two little girls running out to meet him, their mother standing behind them in the shadows, melted into thin air.

As the car ate up the motorway miles, she went back over the conversation again and again, annoyed at herself, wondering how he was feeling now. Why had she not accepted when he'd asked her out to dinner? What had stopped her? She'd just said, 'Thank you, Gordon. I'll think about it.' How cold that must have sounded to him? How ungracious and off-putting? Now, she understood why she hadn't done what her heart had been urging her to do and accept straight away. Over the years she'd conditioned herself into thinking that she didn't deserve to be happy. That perpetual cloud from 1944 had been hanging over her. If she'd accepted his invitation, she'd have to explain to him why she hadn't met him that Saturday afternoon in August '44 outside Midchester Town Hall. She needed to be able to tell him the truth about what had happened that day, otherwise she would be living a lie with him, just as she had with all the previous men in her life. She knew she couldn't do that again. It wasn't fair on Gordon and it wasn't fair on herself.

The traffic ahead took her attention. Stationary cars and lorries blocked the carriageway. It must be roadworks or an accident. Glancing at the clock on the dashboard, she indicated left and pulled through the traffic to the inside lane to join the slow-moving queue for the service station. She'd left plenty of time to get to Mabel Harris' house. She would go into the services for a coffee and think things over properly.

The café in the service station was heaving. Commercial travellers pausing on their journeys for breakfast, lorry drivers, avoiding the traffic jam like she was, tucking into bacon and eggs. It stank of grease and all the windows were steamed up. Kate queued at the counter for a coffee then took a seat at a table overlooking the motorway. From here she would be able to see when the traffic cleared. She sipped the bitter drink and thought of Gordon again; how they had clicked immediately, how they'd laughed and chatted so easily each time they'd met. Suddenly she knew what to do. When she got back to the village later, whatever she found out about Amelia's time in India from Mabel, she would go back to Joan's house. No matter how hard it might be, she would insist that the two of them confront the truth together. It was the only way that either of them could be free of the burden of the past and move on.

She drained the coffee cup, got up from the table and walked straight out of the café to the telephone booths in the entrance hall. She dialled Gordon's office and waited breathlessly while the receptionist put her through.

'Kate?' came his voice after a couple of clicks on the line.

'I'm sorry about yesterday,' she said. 'I've been thinking... I'd love to accept your offer of dinner sometime. If it's still on, of course.'

'Of course it is. How about tonight?'

'Tomorrow might be better,' she said. 'I'm down in London today. I'm sorting a few things out.'

'Great. Tomorrow it is then. And the house?' he asked.

'Oh, come on, Gordon,' she laughed, knowing he was teasing, but not minding this time. 'Give me a chance. I haven't decided yet.'

MABEL HARRIS' house was in a terrace a couple of blocks back from the Mile End Road. Most of the houses were empty with boards at the windows, peeling paint and gaping roofs. Kate parked between two builders' vans. As she walked along the pavement she could tell straight away which was Mabel's house without looking at the numbers. It was the one with fresh red paint on the front door, window-boxes spilling over with blue and purple lobelia.

The door was opened before she had time to knock. Mabel was just as she'd imagined an ex-missionary from the last days of British India would look. Steel grey hair pinned back from her face, twinkling eyes, a home knitted cardigan and sensible shoes.

'Kate,' she said, and Kate was immediately drawn into a tight embrace. Then Mabel held her at arms' length.

'Amelia talked a lot about you. About how close you once were. She was so sad when your family moved away and you all lost touch.'

'I know,' said Kate an instant lump forming in her throat. 'I feel awful about that now.'

'Come on in,' said Mabel standing aside as Kate entered the narrow passage, that was filled with the aroma of delicious spices. 'You mustn't have regrets, my dear, Amelia wouldn't want that. She wasn't one for bitterness. You were still in her thoughts right to the end; it's why she left you the house.'

Kate followed Mabel down the passage and into the kitchen at the back of the house. The cooking smells were stronger here. A pan was bubbling on a gas stove.

'Sit down, Kate,' Mabel said, waving at the scrubbed wood table in the middle of the room. 'I'll make some tea. Tiffin is almost ready. It's just kedgeree. I used to make it for Amelia, back in Ganpur. It was one of her favourites. I expect the traffic was bad?'

Kate sat at the table gratefully and they made small talk about her journey while Mabel bustled around making the tea and filling two plates with mounds of delicious-looking rice and fish.

'Now, please tuck in,' she said. 'And while we're eating, I'll tell you all about Amelia and why she was so secretive about her time in Ganpur.'

22

AMELIA

Ganpur, 1936

For a few fleeting seconds, Amelia thought Reginald was going to break down and throw himself on Arthur's body, as she herself had done. In his shock and grief, she saw him as she'd never seen him before. His face suddenly revealed his vulnerability, his human weaknesses, and her heart went out to him. Whatever his faults, whatever he'd done or had not done, in that moment, he was a father discovering the death of his only child. She moved towards him instinctively, putting her hand on his arm to comfort him, knowing her own face was contorted with pain. But he pushed her aside, barely looking at her and lunged towards Giles.

'What have you done to my son?' he demanded, his voice rasping. Giles stepped backwards in shock.

'This is *your* doing, Harris,' Reginald went on, jabbing a finger in Giles' face, 'You've killed my boy with your quack remedies.' He glared around at all three of them; Mabel, Giles and Amelia, 'You're all religious fanatics. All of you,' he said, 'Meddling in other people's business. Who gave you the right to bring my son here?'

'Oh, Reginald, please... *I* made the decision,' said Amelia, her voice wobbling. He turned on her then, his face hard, full of anger, all vulnerability gone.

'*You* had no right to bring him to this filthy, amateurish hellhole,' he roared. 'I wouldn't bring a sick animal here.'

'Mr Holden,' Giles stepped forward, trying to take Reginald's arm, but Reginald snatched it away. 'I'm so, so sorry for your loss. I understand you're... you're extremely upset.'

'Upset? Upset?' Reginald raged, 'I'm far more than upset. You'll pay for this, Harris. I'm taking him straight out of here.'

With that he gathered Arthur's limp body up in his arms, the sheet still clinging around the boy.

'Please, Reginald,' Amelia protested, horrified, unable to process what was happening. It was like a bizarre nightmare.

'Be quiet and come home,' Reginald snapped. 'You've no business consorting with these people.'

He stood on the threshold of the room, his eyes boring through her.

'What are you waiting for?' he said. 'The car is at the entrance. Come back home where you belong.'

She stared back at him paralysed, as if her decision at that moment would define the rest of her life. Was this her opportunity to defy him? To tell him she was sure now that she knew what had happened to Elizabeth, that all three of them in this room knew, and that she was never going back to the Residence to be imprisoned and controlled by him again.

'Amelia,' he repeated, his voice softer now, wheedling. 'I said, what are you waiting for? Come along now. We need to go. There's rioting in the streets and a lot of violence out there. I wouldn't want you to come to any harm.'

'I would advise you not to issue threats here in my hospital, Mr Holden,' said Giles.

'I think we both know who calls the shots in this district, Harris,' said Reginald. 'I'll wait outside in the car, Amelia, with... with Arthur. Your duty as his stepmother is with me and the child. If you don't join me within five minutes, I will make sure Doctor Harris here is discredited for this outrage. He'll never practice in this country again.'

He left the room with Arthur's body in his arms, leaving the swing door banging to and fro. Amelia sunk down on the chair. Huge, rasping sobs suddenly racked her body. Mabel was with her in seconds, her arms around her.

'You can come home with us,' said Mabel and Amelia looked into her friend's face, it was wet with tears. 'You'll be safe there.'

She knew Mabel was right. That she should at least try to take this opportunity and that it was fear that was stopping her. Reginald was the most powerful man in Ganpur. He had the police force at his command, the streets were filled with them.

She shook her head and struggled to her feet. 'I have to go back with him, Mabel. It's wrong I know, but he *would* do what he says to Giles. You know that. Think of what would happen to this hospital, to all the good work you're doing here.'

'Amelia,' said Giles. 'I'm not afraid of his threats. You should take Mabel's advice and come home with us.'

'Do you think he'd just let me go like that?' Amelia asked, remembering with a shiver all the times he'd held her tightly, declaring he couldn't lose her, that he would never let her go. 'He'd send the police to your house to bring me back. You know that. And besides,' she said, a sob rising in her throat. 'I need to make sure.'

'Make sure?' asked Mabel.

'Surely you understand?' Amelia replied. 'I need to make sure that Arthur is buried beside his mother. Reginald might not do that if I'm not there to persuade him. I need to do that for Arthur and for Elizabeth.'

Mabel and Giles exchanged worried looks, then Giles spoke.

'If you must go, please make sure you get word to us each day that you are safe.'

'Of course. Of course, I will... and, thank you. Thank you both for everything you've done.'

The corridor was crowded as she hurried from the room towards the entrance hall; the hospital was filling up with casualties from the riots. Men with head wounds, blood trickling down their faces, blood-stained clothing, broken limbs, wandering around in shock, some of the injured stumbling along between two others. All looked filthy and ragged. Nurses and doctors, hospital orderlies were rushing around trying to help.

Amelia emerged into the steamy night against the flow of the crowd. There was Reginald standing beside the car, the front door open. Some of the wounded men who were making their way towards the hospital, recognised him and yelled abuse, others threw objects at the car, but most skirted around it, keeping their distance.

'So you've come,' he said as she approached. 'I knew you would. Sit in here beside Amir and I will go in the back with my son. Amir, we'll have to take a back route to avoid this scum. If you skirt round the back of this building, and out onto Bazaar Road, we should avoid the worst of it.'

As they arrived back at the Residence, ayah was waiting for them on the front steps. When she saw Arthur's floppy body in his father's arms, her face crumpled and she sunk to her knees. Amelia dashed out of the car and rushed to put her arms around the old lady. They clung together sobbing wordlessly as Reginald carried the boy up the front steps and into the house. Amelia followed, ayah beside her, clutching her arm as Reginald carried Arthur through the vaulted hallway, down the corridor and into the child's bedroom, where he laid him down on the bed. Then he turned and spoke to ayah.

'Please prepare Master Arthur's body. You know what to do. We will bury him tomorrow.'

'Yes, sahib,' Ayah nodded, her head bowed, tears streaming down her face.

'I will make the arrangements for the funeral now,' he said, 'then I need to go straight to Government House.'

Amelia stared at him, aghast. 'How can you leave now, Reginald?'

He turned to her bitterly. 'My son doesn't need me now, does he? It's too late. And there's a state of emergency here in Ganpur, I don't know if you'd noticed?'

She was trembling all over now and she opened her mouth to say the words that she knew she shouldn't say but which were bursting to be said.

'Why... why didn't you come back from the camp with Arthur?' she blurted, as if an invisible force had taken over. 'Why did you send him home with the syces alone?' she asked, looking him straight in the eye. Then she stepped backwards, startled by the instant flush of anger on his face.

'This isn't *my* fault,' he raged. 'How dare *you* accuse *me*? It was *you* who brought that quack doctor into the house.'

He stormed from the room and his footsteps echoed away down the corridor. Smarting with shock, Amelia ran after him. She grabbed his arm but he strode on, shaking her off as he went.

'Reginald, please!'

He went into his office and slammed the door. She wrenched

it open and followed him inside. He was already beside his desk, the telephone in his hand.

'Reginald, please. I need to talk to you.'

He put the telephone back on its receiver and sat down behind the desk. He put his head in his hands. Amelia moved forward.

'It's about Arthur... Arthur's funeral,' she said, trying to keep her voice steady. She could hardly believe what was happening, half-expecting that any second she would wake up from this horrifying nightmare.

'What about it?' he asked.

'I just... I just want to make sure that...'

'Make sure? Make sure?' he snapped. '*I'm* his father, Amelia. You don't have the right to make sure of anything.'

'I just want to ask you to bury him beside his mother,' she said. Her voice was trembling, her face burning, and she could feel the tears on her cheeks but she didn't drop her gaze. He glared back at her for a long moment, his eyes blazing, but she sensed that he was wrongfooted.

'It's a reasonable request,' she said, lifting her chin, getting into her stride. But he thumped his fist down on the desk.

'What do *you* know about it? What do *you* know about Arthur's mother?' he roared.

'Nothing, Reginald,' she said, her heart pounding, but she kept her eyes on his. 'I know nothing about Elizabeth. After all, there is nothing left of her in this house *to* know. But I do know that she was Arthur's mother, that he loved her and that he deserves to rest beside her.'

Something new entered Reginald's eyes and Amelia knew from that look that he'd had an idea, that he'd thought of a way of exploiting the situation.

'Alright,' he said slowly, lifting the receiver again. 'You're quite right. And I'll give those instructions right now, if you promise me just one thing in return. Sit down, Amelia.'

Watching him carefully, she lowered herself into the button-backed chair opposite the desk.

'I will make those arrangements for Arthur on one condition,' he said. She waited, holding her breath.

'And that is that you must promise me that you will give up seeing those fanatical missionaries, Mabel and Giles Harris.'

Amelia felt the colour drain from her face.

'How can you ask that? My parents were missionaries, Reginald,' she said, the pulse in her throat making her voice wobble. '*Please* don't ask that of me. Mabel and Giles are good people...'

How could she promise what he asked? Mabel and Giles were her only real friends in Ganpur. They were her lifeline.

'I will happily dial the church warden right now if you will promise me that you will stop helping those two misguided idiots with their ridiculous projects,' he said, ignoring her words. 'I told you right at the start that no good would come of associating with them. I told you that it wasn't seemly for the wife of the District Officer to be interfering in local customs as the missionaries do.'

She swallowed hard, her mind running over the desperate situation he'd put her in. He was acting in grief, she knew that. If she agreed to his conditions now, then surely after the funeral she would be able to think more clearly what to do. Amir would help her get word to Mabel and Giles. Amir and ayah. Somehow, with their help, she would extract herself from this mess.

'I know you go to that run-down building in the old town and help them out with their correspondence,' Reginald went on, his eyes boring into hers, it was as if he was reading her thoughts. She dropped her gaze. 'You've told me as much,' he said, 'and I know that you visit their squalid little home in that back street. It's gone far enough, Amelia. It's not becoming. It undermines my position and I won't have it anymore.'

'Is that all you care about?' she blurted, unable to stop herself. 'Your position? When... when...' she dried up, her eyes fixed on his, and the words, *when your son's body is lying cold in this house,* hovered unspoken between them.

'Very well,' he said. 'If you are not willing to comply with my wishes, I'm afraid I can't indulge your own sentimental wish. Arthur will be buried in the military graveyard here on the cantonment.'

He picked up the receiver again and spoke into the mouth-piece. 'Could you connect me to padre Willis, please...'

'No!' Amelia said, unable to bear the thought of Arthur lying alone amongst the bodies of the officers and soldiers who'd fought to maintain British rule. 'Stop. It's alright. I'll do what you want. Please...'

'If you're sure...' he paused, his eyebrows raised. She nodded slowly, then he spoke into the telephone again. 'Sorry, operator, my mistake. Connect me to Reverend Williams at the Church of England please.'

She left him speaking on the telephone and ran from the room, up the sweeping staircase and into the bedroom. She flung herself on the bed and gave vent to the tears of loss, pain and hurt that had been building within her since she'd arrived at the lockup and had seen Amir wringing his hands in despair. It was as if a dam had burst within her. She cried until she had no tears left to cry.

THEY BURIED Arthur in the sweltering heat of the early after-noon the next day. Amelia stood beside Reginald inside the church, dressed in black for the service. Her body was heavy with the pain of the occasion. There were only twenty or so people in attendance; Eileen and James and a scattering of other couples from the club, and behind them, a row of rather weather-beaten looking men Amelia barely recognised. Looking at them more closely as she passed their pew, she realised they were the group who'd accompanied Reginald and Arthur on the shikar. They must have packed up camp and set off back to Ganpur a few hours after Reginald had set off with the syce. Amongst them she spotted the one who had caused so much stir amongst the ladies at the club only a few weeks back; Willy Prendergast's brother, George. As she passed, she caught his eye. He was looking at her brazenly, just as he had in the club. Affronted, she looked away with a prickle of revulsion.

Amir and ayah sat in a pew at the back of the church. Amelia kept looking over her shoulder for Mabel and Giles, but they were nowhere to be seen. Had Reginald already sent word telling them to stay away? Surely he wouldn't stop them coming one last time to pray for Arthur's soul? Or perhaps they were too afraid to come. She couldn't blame them, after what had happened at the hospital, but as the vicar stood up, welcomed the mourners, the door of the church creaked open. Mabel and Giles entered the church and slid along the back pew to stand beside Amir and ayah.

As the vicar intoned the solemn words of the funeral service, Amelia struggled to control her tears. She thought of the little boy who'd become her closest ally but who she'd failed to protect. She was still in shock. It was hard to believe that he was lying in that little coffin on a pedestal before the altar, that she would never again read him a story or walk hand in hand with him to the gardens on the cantonment or out onto the dusty plain.

Reginald stood beside her, but despite her pity for his grief, she recoiled from him and their arms weren't touching. The evening before, he'd stayed out until the small hours. She knew he must be at Police HQ, dealing with the chaos that had ensued during his absence. She heard him enter the room in the middle of the night and felt him slip into bed beside her. She lay still, frozen on her side of the bed, her mind in turmoil.

Out of all the British men in Ganpur, only Reginald had the brutish mettle and iron will to have answered the call of duty like that while ayah was preparing his son's body for burial. But although Amelia was terrified of him now for what she was virtually certain he'd done to Elizabeth, she couldn't banish her natural pity for a father who had lost his son. As she lay there, staring up into the darkness, the mattress dipped as he moved towards her. Then his arms were around her, tightening until he was holding her in an iron grip. She held her breath as she felt his body shake against hers and his wet face on her shoulder. She realised he was crying.

'You're all I have in the world now, Amelia,' he muttered. 'They both left me. Elizabeth and Arthur.' Amelia stayed silent, willing this to stop. 'And while I live and breathe,' he went on, 'I'm never, ever going to let you go. Only death will take you from me. As it took them.'

Chills coursed through her body from head to toe. This wasn't quite proof that he'd killed Elizabeth, but it felt like some sort of confession.

Now, as she stood beside him in the pool of sunlight from the church window, tears streaming down her cheeks, and as she followed behind the tiny coffin borne by servants from the Residence, she knew what she must do. She stood amongst the other mourners in the sweltering heat of the midday sun as the coffin was lowered on ropes into the oblong pit where Arthur would be laid to rest, her head bowed. Her gaze wandered to that other grave that had been here in this neglected corner of the churchyard over two years.

The grass had been hastily scythed around Elizabeth's grave when Arthur's had been dug overnight. Amelia's eyes lingered on the exposed headstone, the pain in her chest intensifying as she remembered all the times she'd brought Arthur here in secret. How they'd crossed the graveyard together hand in hand, how he'd darted ahead with his flowers from the garden, his face lit up with anticipation. Just looking at the headstone brought it home to her with new clarity. She needed to get away from Reginald for her own safety. Mabel was right; even if she had no concrete proof that he'd caused Elizabeth's death, she had to save herself. She'd made her decision, but the thought of executing her plan made her mouth go dry with nerves.

As the vicar read the burial service, Amelia put her hand into the pocket of her dress to check that the envelope was still there. She'd written the note hastily that morning before setting off for the church, scribbling at her dressing table while Reginald was in the bath.

My Dearest Mabel,

I cannot thank you and Giles enough for everything you've done for me since I came to Ganpur. You are the truest friends I have in the world and I know I must take your advice. Although I still don't know what exactly happened to Elizabeth, my situation is intolerable and I need to go away from here. I plan to take a train from Ganpur Junction as soon as I can get away after Arthur's funeral. I have enough rupees saved to buy a ticket and to survive a few days cheaply. I will go to Benares or Calcutta, wherever the first train is bound, and find myself some sort of work, possibly with the Baptists there. I will write as soon as I am able.

There is just one thing I need to ask you to do for me. I have been unable to return to the villages; I promised Reginald I wouldn't as a condition of burying Arthur beside his mother. I didn't plan to keep that promise and I thought about going up there before I board the train, but he might well guess where I've gone and follow me there.

There is one young girl in particular, Kiara, who lives in the last house in the first village after the lake. Her family are very hostile. I have paid her mother-in-law, Lackshmi, the first instalment, but Kiara's baby is due any day. It may well have been born already. I would have returned before if I'd been able. Mabel, please could you visit her to make sure her baby is safe and to give her the money from the Mission if the baby is a girl? I know you will do this for me. Please tell the women I'm truly sorry to have let them down. I will pray for you and for Kiara and for all the village women and God willing, we will meet again one day.

With all my love,

Amelia.

The vicar was coming to the end of the service. He nodded to Reginald who bent down and picked up a handful of earth from the pile the gravediggers had left beside the pit. Then he threw it down onto the coffin. Amelia flinched at the hollow sound it made when it hit the wooden lid. It was her turn then, and as she picked up some soil from the pile, she closed her eyes and prayed for the soul of the little boy she'd tried so hard to protect. She prayed that he was with his mother now, that both of them were at peace.

THE MOURNERS DRIFTED AWAY to where their syces waited with their cars outside the church gate. As they went, they shook Reginald's hand and embraced Amelia, muttering awkward condolences. Giles and Mabel lingered on the fringes, clearly nervous to approach. Glancing at Reginald, Amelia left his side and went over to her friends. As they embraced, she slipped her note into Mabel's pocket.

'Goodbye...' she said, trying to convey the meaning with her eyes. 'Thank you for everything.'

Mabel hugged her tight for a long moment.

'Are you alright?' she asked.

'Yes,' Amelia whispered. 'I've made a decision. The note will explain.'

'Amelia?' Reginald's voice boomed across the graveyard. 'We need to speak to Reverend Williams.'

'We'd better go,' said Mabel, squeezing Amelia's hands one more time. 'Make sure to send word to us that you're safe.' Then they were gone, making their way hastily across the graveyard towards the gate with the others. Amelia watched them go, her heart aching afresh that this could be the last time she saw her friends.

Eileen and James were amongst the last to leave. As James spoke to Reginald, Eileen came and kissed Amelia on both cheeks and took her hand. Eileen's face was pale and drawn, powder caked unevenly on her skin. She was dabbing her eyes with a handkerchief.

'I can't believe it ... the darling boy gone. It's such a tragedy.'

'I know,' whispered Amelia.

'You're not going straight home are you? You must come to the club and have a drink. Raise a goodbye toast to Arthur for our sad loss.'

'No... I couldn't do that,' Amelia protested, horrified at the suggestion. Reginald stepped in.

'Out of the question. I need to get back to Police HQ once I've dropped Amelia at home.'

'Oh dear,' said Eileen. 'Look, why don't I come back home with you, darling? We could talk. I'm sure you need some company.'

Amelia shook her head. 'I'm sorry, Eileen, but I'd prefer to be on my own this evening. If you don't mind...'

'Of course. I understand.' Then she drew close and whispered in Amelia's ear.

'Things will get better with Reginald, you know. I know he's a difficult man. It's because he's so strong, and we need him to be with the appalling situation going on here. But he'll need your support even more now that Arthur's gone.'

'But... but?' Hadn't it been Eileen who'd first put the seeds of doubt in her mind about Elizabeth? Who'd first told her about her being mauled by the tiger, about her falling in love with Deepak? Did Eileen really not know what Amelia had suffered, what Elizabeth and Arthur had suffered in Reginald's control? And what he might be prepared to do if he lost that control?

'He loves you, you know.' Eileen went on. 'You should forgive him his errors and give him your full support now. He needs it more than ever now with all this rioting going on.'

'Thank you, Eileen,' Amelia said, drawing away. Eileen smiled and turned back to her husband, slipping her arm into his.

'Come on, my dear,' said Reginald, taking Amelia's arm proprietorially. 'I'll take you home.'

SHE WATCHED from the bedroom window as the blood red sun dipped behind the horizon and the smoke rising from myriad cooking fires smudged into the colours streaking the sky.

She had her bags packed. Only two of them. There wasn't much she wanted to take. There was the old photograph of her as a teenager standing between her parents, and one of herself and Arthur that Reginald had taken one day shortly after their wedding, sitting together on a bench out on the veranda. She'd only packed two dresses; one that her mother had made her for a garden party at the mission hospital in the hills; it was salmon pink with pretty white lace insets. The other was a green checked dress that she used to wear at home in the hills. She didn't want to take anything with her that she'd acquired during her marriage. All those exquisite dresses, shoes and hats remained in the wardrobe. They belonged to Amelia Holden, wife of the District Office of Ganpur. The Amelia that she was leaving behind.

When Reginald had returned to Police HQ after dropping her home from the funeral, she'd called Amir and ayah into the study. She'd closed the door firmly, to ensure the other servants wouldn't hear and, in a trembling voice, had told them of her decision to leave. Relief had registered on both their faces.

'It will be better that way, memsahib,' said Amir gravely. 'You are not safe here if you stay with sahib Reginald.'

She'd looked into his kind, sad eyes, still wondering if he knew more than he'd been prepared to tell her about Elizabeth's death.

'Oh yes, memsahib,' said ayah squeezing both Amelia's hands in her own and looking earnestly into her eyes. 'We are very sad for your leaving, but for your own sake you must get away.'

'We will both help you to leave Ganpur, memsahib,' said Amir. 'Now that Master Arthur is gone. There is nothing else left for ayah and me to do.'

'Will you really?' she asked, a lump in her throat. 'But what about you? What if...' She had a sudden pang of guilt. Would Reginald find out if they helped her? What might he do to these kind, faithful people.

'Don't worry about us, memsahib,' said Amir. 'Sahib will know nothing. And anyway, both of us are old. Ayah and I have both made plans to return to our villages once you have gone away.'

She looked from Amir to ayah and back again and her heart swelled with gratitude. Both smiled back with sadness in their eyes but with strength and purpose too. They owed her nothing, and yet here they were putting themselves at risk for her sake.

'If you're quite sure?' she asked and they both nodded emphatically.

They'd agreed that ayah would help Amelia to slip out through the kitchen at the side of the house where Amir would be waiting with the car. It would be quiet at that time of the evening; most of the servants were off duty apart from the chowkidar on the gate who would always turn a blind eye for a bundle of rupees. Amir insisted that it would be possible for him to drive Amelia through the backstreets, avoiding the densest part of the old town, to the other side of the railway tracks. It was as close to the station as he could get. The car was conspicuous, but it was probably not as risky or dangerous as Amelia walking through the old town to the station with her bags. This way, if they were stopped, they would be able to find some excuse for her to be out of the Residence.

'Pack your bags, memsahib,' said Amir. 'We will take you after sunset.'

She'd gone upstairs, her heart thumping, taken off her mourning clothes and hung them carefully in her wardrobe. Then she'd slipped on a simple pale blue cotton dress dotted with tiny white flowers, and a pair of summer shoes that she'd brought with her from Darjeeling. She packed two dresses, a straw hat to shield her from the fierce Indian sun and one last photograph. It was the small, oval portrait of a young, dark-haired woman who looked so much like Amelia herself that to look at it was like looking in a mirror; Ava – the mother she'd never known. She'd packed the passport which still bore her maiden name 'Collins' and for some reason – she wasn't sure why – she slipped her marriage certificate into the lining of the case. Something told her she might need proof of it at some point in the future.

There was a knock at the door. Amelia opened it. Ayah was outside, her eyes filled with tears.

'Are you ready, memsahib?' Amelia nodded. 'I will help you with your bags,' she said.

'I can carry them, ayah, it's alright.'

'No, no. Let me help,' said the old lady.

'If you're quite sure?' Amelia handed the smaller one to her.

She took one last look around the palatial room, where she'd been so unhappy and so, so afraid for almost two years, then, took ayah's free arm and they walked down the wooden staircase side by side. They didn't speak. There was nothing left to say.

23

AMELIA

Ganpur, India, December 1936

Amelia had never before been to the run-down streets that were built on the marshy land on the other side of Ganpur Junction railway station. Amir drove her there on a rough, dirt road which crossed the tracks just beyond the sidings. They bumped over the metal lines, passing behind rows of empty carriages and part-dismantled steam engines. As she stared out of the window, she glimpsed the shadowy forms of people moving about. This place was home to a community of shanty dwellers, their tarpaulins and ramshackle shelters strung up against the fences, some had even made their homes in derelict carriages. There was no proper lighting here, just the meagre glow of candles and cooking fires from the homes of these desperate souls. Tiny children played under carriages and on the rubbish-strewn tracks, while the sleeping forms of the sick and the old, swathed in sacks or rags, were stretched out on the ground beside the fence. There was no rioting here; people seemed to have given up the fight, if they'd ever had any in their day-to-day struggle for survival.

She was aghast at so much human suffering in the shadow of the great Victorian train station with its marbled halls and first-class restaurant and its adjacent hotel where only well-heeled Europeans ever stayed. She'd never heard anyone at the Baptist Mission talk about this forgotten corner of Ganpur either, even though it was only a few blocks away from the Mission building in the old town on the other side of the railway. She wondered why.

Amir drove on, beyond the sidings and along the dirt road which ran parallel to the railway, it too was lined with ramshackle dwellings. There were no rioters here, and no police either. At the end of the road, just in front of the station, was a goods yard. Amelia felt the car tyres rumble over cobbles as they rolled in through the entrance. Ahead, lights from the station spilled from an archway, illuminating a water tower beside the tracks and several huge heaps of coal. A group of coolies, their backs glistening in the station lights, were shovelling coal from the heaps into the coal box of a great black engine. One or two of them looked up at the car crossing the yard, but they quickly turned back to their task. Amir tucked the car behind one of the far coal heaps then switched off the engine and turned to Amelia.

'That is back entrance to the station,' he said, nodding towards the low archway in the red-brick façade. Goods normally come in there, but anyone can walk through. The platforms are on left-side. Benares train will be waiting on Platform 1. First class ticket is here. I collect it earlier for you.' He held a cardboard ticket out to her.

'Oh, Amir...' she said, taking it from him gratefully, suddenly overwhelmed by the prospect of leaving the car; leaving *him* behind and striking out alone by herself. She took the straw hat out of her bag and pulled it down tightly over her hair. She'd not worn it, or the dress since she'd left Darjeeling, so with luck, no one would recognise her.

'Go, memsahib,' he said. 'I will wait here until I see the Benares train pull out of the station. Then I will take car back to the Residence. Ayah and I will be gone from there before sahib comes home.'

'Thank you,' she said looking into his kind old eyes. There was so much she wanted to say and she could tell from his look that he knew that too. She opened her mouth to thank him for everything he'd done for her, but he cut her short.

'You must go now,' he said. 'Good luck, memsahib.'

She opened the door, got out of the car and pulled the bags out after her.

'Goodbye Amir,' she said before closing the door and striding away from the car and across the cobbles towards the station entrance. She could feel Amir's eyes on her but she didn't look back. She didn't want him to see her tears.

As she walked through the arch, she blinked in the sudden light, the clamour and din of the station rattling her nerves. It was full of people; more people than she'd ever seen here before. Families sat around on the floor waiting for trains, babies and children cradled on laps, livestock in cages, belongings in carboard boxes. Some were cooking over portable stoves, the smell of aromatic spices filling the heavy air. There was nothing unusual in that sight in India, but tonight the lofty station hall felt different. It was crowded with groups of men. They were pushing forward towards the platforms, the din from their voices echoing as a roar in the vaulted roof. Amelia's hair rose on the back of her neck. She recognised the angry faces, the aggression in the air from the riots she'd witnessed on the streets.

There, across the concourse was the Benares train at Platform 1, just as Amir had said, its carriages stretching back so far that the engine was out in the open air at the other end of the station. People were scrambling onto the roof of the train or in through the windows of the third-class coaches, desperate for a place. There was nothing strange about that either, but what was unusual, and made Amelia freeze, was that the platform was packed with policemen – Reginald's policemen, with batons and lathis, some even with guns. They were beating people off the train with their weapons, forcing them away from the train and off the platform. Now she realised that the whole station was seething with police, in their khaki uniforms, their jodhpurs, long black boots and turbans. How would she ever get onto that train without attracting their attention?

There was nothing for it. She shouldered her way through the press of hot bodies, holding her breath, recoiling at the smell of sweat and filth. None of them moved out of her way. Many leered at her or shouted insults as she squeezed past them. At last she emerged onto the platform, but a row of policemen was directly ahead of her, wielding their sticks and blowing their whistles. One turned towards her as he dragged a man dressed only in a loincloth off the train. The policeman's face was red with anger, then his eyes widened as he caught sight of Amelia. As the wretched man slipped away through the crowd, the policeman stepped forward.

'Memsahib. Please. You must go home,' he said, raising his voice above the din of the crowd.

'I need to get on the train,' she yelled, 'Look. I have a ticket. First Class.' She held it out, it was shaking between her fingers.

'This train is not safe for British lady,' said the policeman. 'Please go home. Many bad men are trying to board this train. They make trouble here in Ganpur and now they are trying to get away. There will be much trouble on the way to Benares. Police will be travelling on board this train.'

'But I... I can't go home,' she protested. 'I need to get away.' Her heart was pounding. Did he know who she was?

'I am telling you, memsahib, it will be dangerous for you on this train. I repeat. You must go home. We are telling that to all British who try to board. Come back in two or three days. Perhaps by then the situation will be under control.'

'I really don't mind taking a risk,' she was pleading with him now. 'Just let me get on board.'

'I'm afraid not, madam. I have strict orders...' he glanced sideways and stiffened his shoulders. Amelia followed his gaze. His eyes were fixed on a man who was talking to some police officers a few yards away. He had his back to her, but she knew instantly that it was James Blackburn, Eileen's husband and Reginald's loyal henchman. Her mouth dropped open and the blood drained from her face. She backed away and, turning round, let the crowd swallow her up as she fought her way back through the bodies towards the archway at the back of the station.

Squeezing herself free from the edge of the mob on the far side, she stumbled back through the archway and into the goods yard. Relief surged through her. It was still there, the limousine, parked behind the heap of coal. She ran back to it and wrenched the door open. Throwing her bags onto the back seat, she scrambled in, sobs of panic and relief rising in her throat.

'Memsahib! What happened?'

'I can't go. They won't let me take that train. The station is full of rioters. There are police stopping people from boarding. Amir, please, let's go home before Reginald finds out I've tried to leave.'

'Better not to do that, memsahib,' Amir said, his voice slow and steady. 'Better not to go back at all.'

'But what shall I do?'

'I will take you to Dr Harris' house. Better not to go back to the Residence.'

'Alright. Yes, you're right. We should go there, but if Reginald is looking for me, he will be sure to look there.'

'Dr and Mrs Harris will help you. They will know what to do.'

He started the car, reversed quickly and swung it round to face the gateway. Soon they were out of the station yard, heading back towards the sidings. Amelia sat back on the leather seat, still breathing heavily, her nerves scattered. She looked up, tears in her eyes. Amir was watching her in the mirror and there was that look in his eyes again. The one she recognised. She'd seen it on the way to the hills when she'd asked him about Deepak, she'd seen it again when she'd asked him in desperation about Elizabeth's death.

'Amir,' she said now, suppressing the sob in her throat. She moved forward and clung to the back of his seat, speaking urgently into his ear. 'What is it? What is it that you're not telling me?'

He drove on silently, back across the sidings, weaving between the wretched dwellings, until they were clear of the shanty town and moving through the darkened streets that skirted the old town.

'Please. Amir,' she repeated. 'I need to know.'

He remained silent, but after a couple of hundred yards, at the next turning, he pulled the car off the road and drove a little way down a dirt track between two deserted warehouses. There, he stopped the car and turned off the engine. Then he spoke.

'I was hoping you would get away to Benares on that train so I wouldn't need to worry you with this,' he said quietly, his head bowed. He wasn't looking in the mirror and he wasn't looking round at her either.

'What is it, Amir? Please go on.'

He cleared his throat and put his hands on the steering wheel as if to steady himself.

'It is this, memsahib. I have to tell you now.

'One night, during the rioting, before he went away on the shikar, I went to collect Holden sahib from Police HQ. He didn't come out for a long time. It was very late, and I thought he might have called a taxi. I went inside to look for him. The policeman on watch was snoring at his desk. I went down the passage. It was quiet but I could hear sounds coming up from the basement. Screaming and yelling.'

He stopped and passed his hand over his face. Amelia could barely breathe. Part of her wanted to scream at him to stop but she stifled that urge.

'Go on, Amir,' she whispered. She knew in her bones what was coming, but she needed to hear him say it.

'I went down the steps,' he said. 'It was very hot down there and it smelled very, very bad. I walked between the cages. Men were rattling the bars, shouting and screaming. They were all crowded together in there, filthy and hot. Some had bloody faces. I walked on between them to the end of the passage. There was a door in the wall. A thick metal door.' His voice broke for a moment, then after a pause and a deep breath he went on.

'I pushed the door open and there he was. Holden sahib. Standing in front of a prisoner. This man was naked, chained from the ceiling. Sahib was in his shirt sleeves. Two policemen were beating the man with lathis.'

Amelia felt a sharp intake of breath. So, it was true. The blood-spattered linen jacket so casually slung on the planter's chair on the veranda one evening had told her all she needed to know. She hadn't dared to believe it then. She hadn't wanted to face it.

'What did you do?' she asked at last. Her voice sounded a long way away.

'What could I do? I went back to the car and I waited until Holden sahib came out. Just as if I hadn't seen anything.'

There was shame in his voice.

'You mustn't blame yourself, Amir,' she said softly. 'What could you have done?'

'That was when I became angry. I have worked for sahib for many years. I knew already about his cruelty, but this was too much. These men were protesting in peaceful way. He had gone too far. I wanted to leave then, to run away back to my village and escape, but I swore to myself then, that whatever happened, I would protect you and Master Arthur. I have been trying to do that. And tonight you almost got away.'

'You have been so brave, Amir,' she said. 'What would I have done without you and ayah?' He didn't reply immediately, but she waited, sensing he had more to tell her, and after a few moments, he began to speak again.

'Do you remember when you asked me about memsahib Elizabeth, about how she died? One day when I drove you to the Mission?' he asked.

'Yes. Yes, I remember,' she shuddered. 'I will never, ever forget that.'

'You asked if Reginald sahib and memsahib were alone when she died, if there was anyone who might have seen what happened. It made me think. Then I remembered something. There was somebody. Somebody who might know something.'

Shivers ran down her back and her scalp tingled. 'Somebody?' she asked.

'Yes, memsahib. A shikari. An expert hunter. Used to tracking tigers. Reginald Sahib hired him for this one trip only. This man never came to the Residence, sahib and memsahib rode out to meet him on the edge of the jungle.'

'How do you know about him?' asked Amelia.

'Because this man was known in my family village. His name is Marut. Although it is far from here, rumours get around. Marut had boasted in the village about being paid a lot of money by a white sahib to go into the jungle to track a tiger. But when he returned from the shikar, he spoke to nobody. When you asked about it that day when I drove you, memsahib, I suddenly connected them. I began to wonder what had happened to Marut. So... on one of my days off from the Residence, I went to find him.'

'And?' Amelia asked, her heart in her mouth.

'I took a taxi to my village. It is a long way from Ganpur. Marut's hut is a few hours walk from there on the edge of the forest. I found him there, living like a hermit. He is no longer the man he once was. His mind is lost. He does not take shikari work now and lives from what he can catch or pick from the forest.

'At first he wouldn't speak to me. When I mentioned sahib Reginald, I could tell he knew something because he looked very afraid. But I gave him some coins and then he was ready to talk.'

Amelia was jolted into the present as a pack of feral dogs ran along the alley and past the car, howling and baying, in pursuit of a straggly cat. She realised how afraid she was now. Her throat was dry, goosebumps stood out on her arms, despite the sultry heat.

'He told me what he saw,' said Amir, his voice flat and steady. 'Sahib Holden came to see him a week before it happened. At that time, Marut was well known for his skills in tracking tigers. Everyone in Ganpur district knew of him. Sahib came to his home one day and told him he wanted to take his wife into the jungle to shoot a tiger. It was going to be a surprise and she knew nothing of his plans, so Marut must not speak of it, not to anyone. He would be paid handsomely for his silence, and afterwards, he must never speak of it to anyone either, or Holden sahib would arrest and punish him.'

'But he spoke to *you*, Amir,' Amelia said.

'He is dying now and he needs money badly. I promised him

that Holden sahib would never know he'd spoken to me.' Amir took a deep breath and went on. 'He said that when memsahib and Holden sahib arrived on their horses they were arguing. Memsahib Elizabeth was not happy to be hunting a tiger, but Marut said that sahib had forced her to come. He didn't know why. He couldn't understand English.

'They set up camp in the area of the jungle where Marut knew tigers hunted at night. They waited three nights in the camp but no tiger came. On the fourth night they took their guns and went far deeper into the jungle. Marut took them to a narrow trail through the undergrowth that he knew tigers used. They waited there until Marut was sure a tiger was on its way. Then sahib and memsahib climbed a tree with their guns. Sahib Holden ordered Marut to go back to the camp. He said he wanted to take the shot and didn't need Marut there putting the tiger off its scent. Marut was afraid of Reginald Sahib, and he didn't dare disobey him, but he sensed something was wrong and he was worried. So, he went a little way into the forest and he watched from behind a tree.

'When the tiger finally came, slinking through the forest, Marut expected to hear a shot from sahib Reginald's gun. He was listening, keeping very still, watching the tree where sahib and memsahib were hiding on the branch, but the shot didn't come. Marut was afraid then. He got ready to shoot, himself; the tiger was almost at the tree. He thought perhaps sahib Reginald had problem with his gun. But then he saw terrible sight. He couldn't believe his eyes. As he watched, he saw sahib move suddenly and memsahib fell off the branch and straight down out of the tree. She dropped like a stone and she was screaming as she fell. She landed right in front of the tiger. The tiger pounced and it was only after that that the shot came from sahib Reginald's gun. Memsahib Elizabeth had no chance.'

'Oh Amir,' was all Amelia could mutter. She couldn't think.

She couldn't feel anything in that moment. She couldn't breathe. She couldn't even process what was going on around her. Everything was suspended while her world turned on its axis in slow motion. It was as if she was deep underwater, the pressure of a whole ocean above her. She was bewildered. She needed to take a deep breath, but it was impossible to reach the surface.

'Marut ran away then, memsahib,' said Amir gently. 'He was terrified. He knew Reginald sahib was a powerful man and that nobody would believe him if he told what he'd seen. He went straight back to his home and he never spoke about it and never told anybody, not even his family, not until he told me.'

Amelia still couldn't reply. She was playing the scene over and over in her head. Everything fitted into place now. The hidden car, Deepak's photograph, the secret visit to the Mission hospital that revealed Elizabeth to be pregnant. Elizabeth must have been planning to leave Reginald and run away with Deepak to start a new life and to prepare for their child. She was going to take Arthur with her too. Reginald had found out, or strongly suspected at least. Amelia knew that if he had known he wouldn't have allowed it to happen. His pride and jealousy wouldn't stand for it. He would have killed Elizabeth first. His words came back to Amelia and she shivered in the darkness, recalling his voice, the feel of his powerful arms around her, holding her far too tightly.

'I'll never let you go, Amelia,' and how he'd spoken about Elizabeth and Arthur. 'Only death took them from me.'

Now Amelia knew what he meant. *He would prefer death to take her from him than to lose her any other way.*

Amir was right. They couldn't go back to the Residence. She wasn't safe anywhere in Ganpur if Reginald found out she was trying to get away from him.

'Let's go to Mabel's straight away,' she said, when she was able to speak. 'She will know what to do...'

24

AMELIA

Ganpur, India, December 1936

Sunrise was still half an hour away as Amelia drove for
the last time through the straggling fringes of Ganpur
and out towards the hills. The turbaned policemen on
the roadblocks waved her through this time, barely glancing in
her direction. Just as before, they weren't interested in a
memsahib in a low-slung saloon. Not yet anyway. Their focus
was on larger vehicles; bullock carts, covered trucks and buses.
The type of vehicle in which the men who'd come to Ganpur to
join the rioting citizens would hide to make their escape. She
allowed herself to breathe again as she headed onto the familiar
trunk road towards the hills, pushed the accelerator to the floor
and concentrated on the road. The unsteady twin beams of the
headlights lit up a fog of insects ahead. She focused on it hard,
teeth gritted, eyes hardly blinking, until it blotted out everything; until all the pain and fear of the past two years was
funnelled into that flickering tunnel of light.

The plan had been hatched feverishly in Mabel and Giles'
living room when she'd arrived in the dead of night with Amir.

They'd left the limousine in a back street on the edge of the old town and hurried to the Harris' place on foot, keeping away from the streetlamps, walking through the darkest and quietest alleyways, Amelia rushing ahead, Amir struggling with her bags that he'd insisted on carrying. The little bungalow had been in darkness, but Amir had slipped around the back to wake up the houseboy. Giles opened the front door in his dressing gown and Mabel appeared behind him, tying hers hastily, her unpinned hair falling around her face, blinking in the light of a hurricane lamp that the servant held.

'Amelia?' said Mabel. There was no need for words. Amelia went to her friend and felt the relief and comfort of loving arms envelop her. Giles ushered Amelia and Amir into the living room and the servant brought chai and food. Her hands were trembling uncontrollably as she held the cup to her lips and sipped the cloying liquid. Her thoughts were scattering in all directions. She had no idea what to do.

'We need to find a way of getting you out of Ganpur,' said Giles, leaning forward and looking at her earnestly, after Amir had explained haltingly what the old shikar had told him.

'I was planning on taking the train to Benares...' she murmured. 'I told Mabel that in the note. I thought I'd find a job there. Just disappear somehow.'

'If you can't take the train we could drive you there,' suggested Mabel. 'It's a very long way, but you could hide in the boot if we came across roadblocks.'

Amelia shook her head. 'Now that I know what happened to Elizabeth, I don't think Benares would be far enough. Reginald has contacts everywhere. He would track me down.'

Giles was clenching and unclenching his fists in the lamplight.

'He will pay for this... the murderer. We can't let him get away with it,' he muttered.

'But there's no proof, Giles,' said Mabel. 'All we have is the word of a dying shikari. People will say the old man has lost his mind. Reginald is a powerful man. You and I could go to the police and make the allegations but do you think anyone in any authority in the whole of British India would listen to us?'

Giles sighed. 'Then what do we do?'

'Amelia's right,' Mabel went on. 'She needs to get right away. Away from India.'

There was silence in the room apart from the whirring of the ceiling fan, the baying of a pi-dog out on the street. Everyone was thinking frantically. It was Giles who spoke first.

'I can go back to the hospital and send a cable to P&O in Bombay, Amelia,' he said. 'And Mabel can drive you out of town. She wouldn't attract attention if we act quickly. She could take you to catch a train south of here on a different line. A long way from the riots.... Lucknow perhaps'?

'But he would track me down,' Amelia said miserably. 'Even if I left the country. He's told me so many times. He'll never let me go. Not until I die...'

Not until I die. Not until I die.

It dawned on them all at the same time. Looking back on that conversation now as she pushed the car to its limits on the trunk road, she couldn't remember who'd made the suggestion first. But once it was out in the open, the plan unfolded easily, like a well-laid fire, waiting for the touchpaper. There really was only one way for her to get away. They all agreed on that, even though it would involve a terrible lie, even though God would be watching them.

'God will forgive us, Amelia,' said Mabel holding her hands and looking deep into her eyes. 'I am quite sure of that.'

Amelia had stared back at Mabel for a long while, still uncertain. Behind her friend, the old familiar picture of John the Baptist shone in the light of the lamp. It was a comfort to see it there; she knew it so well from her childhood. And as she glanced beyond Mabel and focused on the painting, it was as if her mother and father were there in the room with her, smiling into her eyes with love just as Mabel and Giles were, filling her with hope, filling her with confidence.

Now, the turning to the hill villages loomed up ahead. She took her foot off the accelerator and slowed the car down. As she swung off the trunk road and headed up the winding side-road and into the hills, the first pinpricks of morning sunlight lit up the grey sky. A new day was dawning. It was impossible to believe that it was less than twenty-four hours since they had buried Arthur in the plot beside his mother's grave. Amelia's heart ached that another new day was dawning without him in the world. She pictured ayah and Amir setting off on foot from their humble quarters with their meagre belongings, leaving behind the great house where they had served for many years, heading out across the scorched plain to find a discreet way back to their villages. She prayed that they had got away safely.

Amir had had tears in his eyes when they'd parted. The two of them had said goodbye to Mabel and Giles and walked together to the lockup in the back street. Amir had manoeuvred Elizabeth's car out onto the street for Amelia, and left the engine running as he got out.

'I can't thank you enough,' she'd said, tears brimming. 'Please, Amir, you must hurry home. You and ayah must leave before Reginald finds out I'm gone.' His old hands felt dry and warm as he took her own between them.

'You must go quickly, memsahib,' he said. 'Good luck. Good luck with everything.'

Beside her on the passenger seat were just three things; the green gingham dress she'd packed earlier, a pair of flat sandals and her handbag. Her bags were with Mabel and Giles. She gripped the steering wheel as she drove, and as the sun rose over the hills and the grey of the sky was suffused with a deepening pink glow, her heart swelled with awe at the beauty of the new day.

She drove over the familiar rise in the road and there was the lake, spread out before her, shimmering in the first rays of the dawn, morning mist rising from the surface. The beauty took her breath away, even on this day of all days. As she drove along the old familiar track beside the water's edge she glanced across at the gently rippling surface. It had rained since she'd last ventured up to the hills, so the water was high, lapping at the edge of the unmade road. She rounded the bend and ahead of her was the crumbling white pavilion, lit up by a single shaft of sunlight.

This was it. There was no going back now. Her stomach churning, she pulled the car off the road onto the little beach and sat for a moment, trying to calm her jangling nerves, but there wasn't much time. She had to act quickly.

Gathering up her belongings from the seat of the car, she pulled a white envelope out of the handbag. There was nothing written on the front. It was addressed to nobody. She pulled the single sheet of paper out and, looking at what she had written, she realised that it wasn't a lie after all. It was just a single sentence. *May God forgive me, but I cannot go on.*

She folded the note hastily and put it into her pocket, then she got out of the car and approached the water's edge. Her pulse was racing and blood was rushing so loud in her ears that it blocked out any other sound. Her eyes were fixed on the pavilion, the crumbling stone jetty and steps that she knew she would have to navigate. She was so focused on them that she almost missed the slight figure shrouded in a grey cloak kneeling at the water's edge a few steps away. It was the high-pitched squealing of a newborn baby breaking through the sound of her heart hammering that she heard first. With a bolt of shock she realised that she wasn't the only one here at daybreak on a shameful mission. Dropping her belongings, she rushed forward.

'Please stop!' she cried and the startled young woman looked up, terror in her eyes. 'Kiara!'

The girl was holding the mewling bundle close to her chest and her face was deathly pale, ravaged with tears.

'Don't stop me. I have to do this.' Her voice was shrill.

'No. You don't have to do it, there is another way,' said Amelia crouching down beside her, putting her arms around Kiara's bony shoulders. Her heart melted as she caught sight of the tiny baby's face, her soft wrinkled skin, her beady little eyes. Amelia suddenly felt a stab of guilt. She should have returned to the village by now to pay Kiara's family again. If she'd been able to go back, Kiara wouldn't be in this desperate state.

'I'm so sorry, Kiara,' she said. 'You mustn't do this. Mabel... Mrs Harris, my friend. She will come, she will help you. She will come as soon as she can.'

Kiara shook her head. 'They won't let me keep my baby,' she said, 'The family. They said you lied. That you would never come back.'

'Wait,' said Amelia. 'Wait here.'

She ran back to the car, tore open the door and grabbed her handbag. Rifling through it she found what she wanted. There was still money in her purse. Several sepia-coloured fifty-rupee notes. She ran back across the beach to where Kiara crouched motionless, the baby clamped in her arms, still screaming.

'Please, take this,' she said. 'Tell your family that this is from the Baptists and that Mrs Harris will come back to pay them more. Now please, Kiara. Get up and go home. Take the money, it is yours.'

Kiara got to her feet unsteadily and took the notes from Amelia's outstretched hand.

'What about you? Aren't *you* coming back?' she asked, her voice shaking, tears streaming down her cheeks. Amelia shook her head, the pain in her throat stopping her from speaking.

'I can't. I have to go,' she said at last. 'But I will think of you always. You and the other brave women in the village.'

The young girl frowned, her eyes puzzled.

'And please, don't ever tell anyone you saw me here,' Amelia said urgently. 'Now take your baby and go home, Kiara. Back to the village. You need to start walking now. And once you've gone round that bend, please don't look back.'

She watched the girl stumble away, up the beach, past the car and back onto the track. She walked quickly, her long cloak dragging in the mud. As she reached the track she turned once and looked at Amelia one more time with her big, mournful eyes, and then she was off, trudging along the track and round the bend, not turning back once.

Amelia gathered up her dress and sandals and picked her way along the edge of the shore towards the stone jetty of the pavilion. As she put her foot onto the jetty itself, she shuddered as a long, dark creature slithered away in the algae beneath. Taking a deep breath, she walked unsteadily along the pier and mounted the broken steps. Then she stepped up into the pavilion itself. A crow took off through one of the archways and flapped away cawing over the surface of the lake. Amelia stood in the centre of the pavilion for a moment, listening out for the voices of the past. Were the maharaja's wives and daughters, long dead, still watching her? Was the ghost of the princess who'd drowned here all those years ago, standing beside her now, cursing her for what she was about to do?

She shuddered, shaking off the ghosts of the past and, taking the letter from her pocket, laid it down on a stone bench beneath one of the openings, finding some fallen masonry to put on top of it to make sure it didn't blow away. Then she folded the gingham dress and laid it down beside the letter, placing the sandals on top.

'May God forgive me,' she whispered, backing away, then turning round, retreated down the steps and back along the jetty as quickly as her legs would carry her. Running on, back past Elizabeth's car, she turned round and hurled the car keys into the lake as far as they would go. She didn't even wait to hear the splash as they hit the water, she was already back on the track, heading in the direction she'd just driven.

She'd only been walking for twenty minutes, but she was already bathed in sweat, the sun had risen fully and was beating down on her, when she heard the roar of the familiar engine coming up the hill towards her. Despite her exhaustion, she began to run, and within seconds the bonnet of Mabel's car came into view. The car stopped and Amelia ran to the passenger door and got inside.

'Are you alright?' Mabel asked. Amelia nodded, too full of emotion and exhaustion for words.

'Let's get you down to Lucknow to catch the Bombay train as quickly as we can then,' Mabel said, pulling the car up onto the verge to turn round. 'Giles cabled P&O and you can pick up the boat ticket to London once the train gets in. It's booked in your maiden name, just like we agreed.'

Amelia looked across at her friend, tears in her eyes as the car hurtled off back down the hill.

'Thank you,' she mouthed, but the wind whipped around her, she had to grab her straw hat to stop it flying away, and her words were lost in the roar of the engine.

25

KATE

Warren End, Buckinghamshire, May 1970

Dusk was gathering as Kate turned the car off the main road and headed down the hill between the lines of towering chestnut trees towards the village. It had been one of those glorious spring days, but she'd hardly noticed the sunshine slanting through Mabel Harris' kitchen window as they sat through most of the afternoon, talking at the kitchen table. She'd been so absorbed in the story that Mabel was telling her, reliving the pain, fear and heartache Amelia had suffered in Ganpur, that she'd hardly noticed the sun moving round as Mabel spoke, casting the tiny back yard with its colourful potted plants and tumbling clematis into lengthening shadow.

'When she'd left, Mabel had clasped her hands in hers and said, 'So you see now, you understand don't you? You see why she wanted to keep her time in India a secret? Amelia Holden had disappeared that day; vanished completely from the world. Amelia Collins took the ship from Bombay to start a new life in England. But she lived in constant fear of Reginald ever finding out she was still alive and well.'

'So, you really don't think she had an affair with George Prendergast?' Kate had asked in a weak voice.

'As I said, I can't be sure. But I very much doubt it.'

Now, she crossed the brook in the dip and accelerated up the last hill, passing the sign; "Warren End". The car crested the hill and there it was, laid out before her; the village, just as she remembered it from her childhood, bathed in the evening sunlight; the honey-coloured stone of the thatched cottages deepening as the sky grew darker. Driving along the familiar High Street this time, it really did feel like coming home. She turned in through the gates of Oakwood Grange and crunched along the gravel through the spinney of oak trees. As she got out of the car and turned towards the front door, she hesitated, surprised. Someone was sitting on the step. Someone bulky, bundled into a cheap yellow cardigan. Cigarette smoke curled up into the evening air.

'Joan!'

Joan got to her feet, threw the cigarette down and ground it under the heel of her sandal.

'I've been waiting for you,' Joan said. 'Janet said you'd be back about now.'

As Kate drew closer, she saw that Joan had been crying, her face was blotchy, the swollen eye blooming yellow and purple.

'I've told Dave to go,' Joan said before Kate had a chance to reply. 'He had another go at me when he came home from work today. I faced up to him this time. I said I'd get the police if he didn't leave.'

'Oh Joan,' Kate moved towards her, wanting to embrace her but Joan drew away.

'Are you alright?' Kate asked unlocking the door and ushering Joan inside.

'I'm fine,' she said. 'He didn't do anything much once I'd told him straight. Just shouted at me and called me all the swear words under the sun. Said he'll go and stay at his mum's for a bit. He's packing now. The kids are with Janet.'

'I knew you could do it,' said Kate. Again she had the urge to hug Joan to her and comfort her, but Joan didn't look ready for that. Instead, she said, 'Come on through to the kitchen. We can talk properly.'

'I wouldn't have done it if *you* hadn't come back,' said Joan, taking a seat at the table as Kate put the kettle on the Aga. 'I just came to tell you that.'

Kate looked into Joan's face. She didn't expect any thanks, and it wasn't thanks either, it was an acknowledgement of their mutual past, of the way their lives were inextricably linked by the guilt they shared. She made the tea and put two mugs on the table with the sugar bowl.

'I've been to London today,' she said, sitting down opposite Joan. 'I went to see an old lady who knew my great-aunt Amelia when she was in India.'

'Oh, not that again,' said Joan, spooning sugar into her tea.

'You know I think we might have been wrong about her,' Kate said, looking down at her own mug.

'Wrong?' asked Joan sharply.

'Yes. Wrong about Amelia and George Prendergast. I don't think they were having an affair after all.'

'And what makes you think that?'

'Well, Mabel was quite sure. Amelia used to confide in her. They were very close indeed.'

'Oh right,' said Joan sarcastically. 'That makes all the difference, doesn't it? If they weren't having an affair, what the hell was that all about then? All those secret meetings, all those rows. Her storming off in her car?'

Kate shook her head. 'I have no idea. But I've been thinking on the way home. There is one way of finding out. Why don't we just go and talk to him about it?'

'Talk to who?'

'Prendergast of course. Why don't we go and see him? Say how sorry we are for what happened... We've got to do *something*, Joan.'

Joan lifted her chin. Her mouth fixed in an obstinate line.

'I've never spoken to him,' she said. 'Not in all these years. He lives down the bottom of our lane, but if we pass in the street I look the other way. I never go near him.'

'Well, we've got to do *something*,' Kate repeated. 'We both need to move on from it, don't we? We can't stay in limbo like this, forever punishing ourselves.'

Joan's lips started to quiver, and her face suddenly creased and collapsed and she took a great, shuddering sob. She reached a hand across the table and Kate took it and held it tightly in hers.

'Just think what we did...' she sobbed.

They were both back there then, that burning Friday morning in late August 1944.

They were sitting side by side on the sagging bed in Joan's bedroom. Kate had come to help the family pack up the house and two tea chests full of Joan's clothes and belongings stood beside the bed. George Prendergast had ordered Mrs Bartram and her children out of the house by the end of the week when the new gamekeeper was due to arrive. It was the same week that they'd buried Frank in the churchyard after the bomb that had killed him in Prendergast's barn.

'It's going to be so cramped at me gran's,' said Joan. 'You probably won't be able to come round to see me anymore.'

'Well, you can come to mine,' Kate replied, but both knew that Freda would disapprove and create an atmosphere if Joan were to visit. It felt like the end of an era, a turning point in their friendship. Kate shuffled her feet awkwardly. She hadn't told Joan about her promise to meet Gordon yet. She'd been meaning to, but it seemed like too much of a betrayal in the week that Joan had buried her father and was being forced to move out of her childhood home.

'He's going to pay for this,' Joan blurted suddenly and Kate's heart sank. She'd thought Joan had put her vindictive plan aside with everything she'd had to cope with in the past few days. She didn't reply, just held her breath, hoping it would go away. But Joan was already reaching into one of the tea chests. The one containing her schoolbooks and pencil case.

'Let's do it now,' she said, her eyes alive with her new plan, 'before the truck comes to take the stuff to Gran's house. We've got a couple of hours.'

'Please, Joan, it's not a good idea. Let's just forget what we saw.'

'I'm not surprised you want to forget what we saw,' Joan mocked. 'It was *your* precious auntie. The rich one, the one you can't stop going on about. I've a good mind to go and ask her outright about it. Right in front of your uncle...'

Waves of panic coursed through Kate. Joan was quite capable of that. Kate knew she needed to prevent that happening at all costs.

'Listen, I know you're angry, Joan,' she said, trying to keep her voice calm. 'But please, *please* don't do that. I couldn't bear my uncle to find out. It would ruin his life.'

'Alright then,' Joan replied slowly, 'I don't really care about your auntie and uncle. But I do care about Prendergast. Look what he's doing to this family. He treats everyone round here like a piece of dirt on his shoe. He's evil. I want him to pay for what he's done.'

'He is a horrible man,' agreed Kate with a shiver, remembering his terrifying anger as they'd pedalled through the deserted farm a few weeks before.

'Good. So let's do it then, shall we? We can write the letter now and take it round there straight away.'

She pulled an exercise book out of the chest and opened it at a clean page.

'This'll do,' she said. 'You can write it. In capitals. Your writing's better than mine.'

She handed Kate a fountain pen from her pencil case. They wrote it together. The ideas came from Joan but Kate honed the language and wrote down the words.

DEAR MRS PRENDERGAST,

YOU MAY WISH TO KNOW THAT YOUR HUSBAND IS SEEING ANOTHER YOUNG WOMAN FROM WARREN END. THEY HAVE BEEN MEETING FREQUENTLY DOWN AT WILLOW MILL. YOU SHOULD ASK HIM ABOUT IT AND PLEASE REMEMBER, WHATEVER HE SAYS, HE IS NOT TO BE TRUSTED.

YOURS FAITHFULLY

A FRIEND

Joan tore the page out of the book, folded the paper into four.

'There's an envelope in here somewhere,' she said, delving back into the chest and moments later pulling a large brown one out triumphantly. She handed it to Kate who wrote MRS PRENDERGAST on the front. Joan slipped the note inside, licked and sealed the envelope.

'Come on,' said Joan. 'Let's go.'

They went on their bikes, Joan surging ahead as usual, up Clerks' Lane, left along the High Street, past Kate's house, past the school, past the gates to Oakwood Grange and on down the road towards Warren Hall. All the time Kate was pedalling, struggling to keep up with Joan, her breath coming in pants, she was trying not to think, trying to put out of her mind the magnitude of what might be unleashed when Mrs Prendergast opened that note. She kept telling herself that it was the lesser of two evils; that George Prendergast was a cruel man, that he had no right to live a peaceful and happy life and that justice was being done. This way she was protecting Great Uncle James and Amelia from harm; Uncle James didn't deserve to be unhappy and whatever Amelia had done she loved Amelia; loved and admired her and she would forgive her anything.

They were at the gates of Warren Hall too soon.

'Let's leave our bikes here and walk,' said Joan, getting down and wheeling her bike behind one of the stone gateposts. Kate followed and leaned hers beside Joan's, out of sight of the road.

'Come on then,' said Joan.

'We can't just walk up the drive, we'll be seen from the house,' said Kate, wishing her heartbeat would slow down. 'How are we going to put it through the letterbox?'

'We can sneak through the bushes along the drive, once we're close to the house we can work out what to do. Come on.'

They darted between the shrubs that lined the drive. Within seconds they had reached the side of the house and were crouching behind a low wall that surrounded a neat front garden.

'They're both at home,' said Joan, nodding towards two car bonnets poking out of one of the outbuildings behind the house; Prendergast's Bentley and his wife's silver saloon.

'Joan...' Kate began. She was about to try again, to plead with Joan to stop this, that this wasn't the right thing to do and it would achieve nothing. But Joan wasn't listening, she was staring at something in the distance beyond the outbuildings. Kate followed her gaze and realised why Joan had gone pale and why her eyes had narrowed and were full of bitterness and hatred. She was looking at the blackened and broken timbers of the old barn, sticking up from the ruins like the ribs of a long dead animal.

'That's where he died,' she said in a low voice. 'My dad. He didn't have a chance. And now that bastard is throwing us out of the house.'

Kate's heart swelled with pity for her friend. There was no going back now, no point in trying to stop this.

'I'll take the letter,' she said instantly. 'Give it to me.'

The garden wall was low enough to climb easily and once she was on the other side, she ducked under the front windows of the house and half-crawled, half ran to the front door. Voices were coming from inside the house, raised voices, but she couldn't hear what was being said and she didn't care. She just wanted to get this over and done with. The front steps were ahead of her and there was the white front door with its brass letterbox. Then she was up the steps and pushing the letter through the slit and it was gone. She heard it drop onto the stone floor on the other side and gasped. It was done. She turned round and retraced her steps, back along the front wall of the house, under the windows, scaling the garden wall and back to where Joan was crouching.

'Good,' was all Joan said.

'Let's get back to the bikes,' said Kate. She just wanted get away from there and forget about what she'd just done.

'Alright,' said Joan. 'But it would be good to see what happens.'

'How can we see what happens? And anyway, she might not see the letter straight away. I heard them talking in the front room. She might not open it for ages.'

'Well why don't we go for a bike ride then? My uncle won't be along with the truck for a while yet.'

They returned the way they'd come, pulled their bikes out from behind the gatepost and set off along the High Street. Soon they were pedalling out of the village, down the dip in the road, over the brook and up the other side. Joan tore ahead as she always did. Kate didn't even try to keep up this time, her heart was heavy and she couldn't summon any energy or any enthusiasm. Joan was fifty yards in front of her, almost at the crossroads with Midchester Road. Then came the sound of an engine behind her and a car flashed past, so close that Kate was left wobbling in its wake. It was a silver car, a silver saloon, going far too fast, accelerating towards the crossroads when it should have been slowing down. Kate stopped, aghast, slid off the bike and watched the brake lights come on too late as the driver swerved to avoid a truck approaching from the other direction. There was a loud thud and a sickening crump as the car hit a tree, the squeal of brakes as the truck skidded to a halt, the slam of a door and seconds later the sounds of men shouting.

'SHE DIED because of what we did and there's no getting round that,' said Joan now, sitting opposite Kate at Amelia's kitchen table, twenty-five years on. She was squeezing Kate's hands so hard that she was crushing the bones. Kate wanted to pull away but was transfixed by the pain in Joan's eyes. It mirrored her own, but at last they had faced the guilt together.

'We should go and talk to him,' Kate said again.

'What good would that do?' said Joan. 'He's an old man now. What difference will it make to him or us if we tell him what we did?'

'He lost all his money, sold all his property after what happened,' murmured Kate. 'I'd just like to know what Amelia was to him, if he'll tell us.'

'And what difference would that make? We still left the letter. His wife still died.'

Kate lowered her head and stared at the table. The tea had gone cold in the mugs.

'Look, if you don't want to talk to him, I understand. I'll go on my own. But I need to square the circle about Amelia. You were right. I used to worship her back then. But after what happened, I couldn't even look her in the eye, and after Roy was killed in France and we moved away, I hardly ever saw her again. I couldn't face the guilt of seeing her. But I know now that she had lots of terrible secrets. She'd had such a tough life before she came here, I really regret not keeping in touch. I'd just like to talk to him about her.'

There was a silence, broken only by the sound of the kitchen clock ticking, the fuel shifting in the Aga, the sound of Joan's breathing.

'Well, If you're determined to go, I need to come too,' said Joan, releasing Kate's hands at last and squaring her shoulders. 'Shall we go there now?'

'We could go in the morning,' said Kate. 'It's late. He might be in bed.'

'It's not that late,' said Joan. 'I see the lights in his bungalow on until midnight sometimes. He won't be in bed. If we don't go now, I might not dare to in the morning.'

They walked there together, arm in arm, past the cottages on the High Street with their curtains drawn, the chimney smoke from the fires hanging in the cooling evening air. They didn't speak once they'd left Oakwood Grange. Their breath made clouds in the lamplight, their steps on the tarmac the only sound.

George Prendergast peered at them through thick glasses when he opened the door to their knock.

'What can I do for you ladies?' he asked, frowning, leaning on his stick.

'I don't know if you remember me. I'm Kate Hamilton, and this is my friend Joan Pope, Bartram as was,' said Kate.

'I know who you are,' he said. 'What is this about?'

'If we could come in, I could try to explain,' Kate replied.

He pulled the door open and showed them into a small square sitting room, dimly lit, a television flickering in the corner. He switched it off.

'I was just watching the news. Do take a seat,' he said and they sat down in his shabby brown armchairs.

'Would you like a brandy? You both look as if you're in need of one,' he said. 'I'm having one anyway.' He moved painfully over to a sideboard and poured out three glasses from a decanter, then handed them to Kate and Joan.

Kate glanced at Joan and took a sip of the brandy that ran like fire down her gullet.

'It's a long story,' she began. 'And we've come to apologise for something dreadful we did to you when we were teenagers. It was unforgiveable. We don't expect you to forgive us, but now my great-aunt is dead...'

'Your great-aunt?' he said, sitting up and turning his blood-shot eyes towards her, looking at her properly for the first time.

'Yes, Amelia Hamilton. My great-aunt. You were friends I think... well, maybe more...'

'We weren't friends,' he cut in, frowning deeply, 'No, we weren't friends at all. I did her a great wrong during the war. She was already a vulnerable woman, but what I did tipped her over the edge. If anyone owed an apology, it is me to her.'

'I don't understand,' said Kate, exchanging glances with Joan, who shook her head quickly and shrugged.

'I had debts. Huge debts. From gambling you see. I used to go to my club in London and spend hundreds of pounds in a single evening. I served briefly, in the RAF at the beginning of the war, but I was shot down over France and lost my nerve. I was sent back to England to recover, but it was a question of nerves really. I could never go back. I took refuge in the club, playing poker. A mug's game, of course. Mortgaged the houses, the farms, everything I owned.

'Then one day, I noticed James and Amelia Hamilton across a crowded restaurant in Westminster. I'd seen her around the village, but I'd hardly noticed her before. She seemed so shy and withdrawn. But that night she was out for a meal with your uncle, her face was all lit up, talking to him, and I realised I'd seen her before. I'd seen her in Ganpur, in India in the thirties when I went out to visit my brother. I remembered then, there'd been a fearful scandal at the time. I'd got back to England by the time the scandal hit, but Willy wrote to me about it. The District Officer's wife had left her husband after his son's funeral, driven to a lake up in the hills and drowned herself.

'When I went home that night, I dug out those old letters and newspaper cuttings. I was sure it was the same woman I'd seen in the club in Ganpur. Convinced of it. It gave me an idea. James Hamilton was rich. A successful businessman. He'd built up one of the biggest manufacturing businesses in the country. And he was an MP too. He wouldn't want a scandal, and I was sure she wouldn't either.'

Kate couldn't take her eyes off his face as he spoke. He took a gulp of brandy and went on.

'As I said, I was desperate for money, so, not to put too fine a point on the matter, I blackmailed her. I went up to her when she was out walking one day and told her that I knew who she was and that if she wanted me to keep quiet she'd have to pay handsomely. I was on my knees you see. I wasn't in my right mind.'

'What an evil thing to do,' it was Joan's voice, muttering from the other side of the room.

'I know. I know. I have regretted it the rest of my life, believe me. I'm a changed man now. The poor girl was terrified of James Hamilton finding out the truth, of him being swept up in a scandal. She was so utterly terrified and confused about it all, she wasn't even sure whether Reginald had been dead or alive when she married Hamilton. I used that to my advantage too, although as a matter of fact I knew Reginald had already died by then. He lost his life during some rioting, I believe. It was all hushed up by the authorities, but Willy knew about it.'

'So,' said Kate, shocked, hardly able to process what Prendergast was telling her, 'That's why you met at Willow Mill?'

He nodded, his eyes faraway, 'I used to get her to drive down there so we could talk in private. She would bring large sums of money.'

'Poor, poor Amelia,' said Kate, staring at the dishevelled old man, wondering how he could sit there, sipping brandy, telling them all this as if it wasn't him who had perpetrated these dreadful acts.

'But don't think I haven't suffered. I paid for it myself,' he said. 'I've paid for it a thousand times over and more. I've prayed to God and confessed, done good work for the village and for the church to make up for what I did back then.

'My wife died because of me,' he went on. 'That's what made me realise. That was my punishment. The cross I had to bear for my sins. I lost my beloved Ivy.'

This was it. He was going to talk about the letter. This was their cue. Kate looked across at Joan whose eyes were locked on hers. Joan nodded at Kate. She was willing her to speak, to tell him everything. This was the moment. She looked back at the old man.

'Mr Prendergast,' she began and the gloomy room seemed to become a blur as the words came tumbling out. 'It was our fault that Mrs Prendergast died. It was us who wrote that letter.'

She watched his face, expecting his eyes to cloud with anger, expecting him to roar at them with grief and fury, but instead he looked confused.

'Letter?'

Kate and Joan exchanged quick glances. 'We sent her an anonymous letter,' said Joan breathlessly, colour flooding her cheeks, 'Telling her that you were seeing another woman. She read it, didn't she? Then she got into her car and drove away so fast that she crashed.'

'Anonymous letter?' Prendergast asked, still frowning. Kate and Joan watched him, holding their breath, incredulous, but after a few seconds his face cleared and he said, 'Oh yes, come to think of it I *do* remember a letter. It was written in capital letters, all very mysterious. I didn't open it for days after she died. She never saw it. I put it down to kids with a grudge playing a prank. I knew I had enemies in the village.'

'Never saw it?' repeated Kate, as the weight of a lifetime's guilt shifted slightly. She was so used to bearing it that it wasn't going to melt away that easily.

'We were rowing, you see,' Prendergast went on. 'Ivy knew about my gambling and the debts and the fact that the farm was mortgaged to the hilt. She didn't know that I'd got a new, secret source of money from Amelia Hamilton and that I was doing my best to pay things off. I couldn't have told her about that.

'She wouldn't let up. She kept going on and on, telling me that I'd lost everything my father had left me, everything we had when we married. She was worried that we'd have to lay off farm workers, that we didn't have enough to keep going.'

He took another gulp of brandy and closed his eyes for a few moments before carrying on.

'We'd both been drinking heavily since the morning. In the end she said, "I've had enough of this, I can't stay here and see us ruined." She already had a bag packed in the boot of the car and she was going to stay with her mother. That was the last time I saw her alive...'

He put his glass down on the table beside him, his hands were shaking, tears were glistening in his eyes.

'I'm so, so sorry,' said Kate, leaning forward and taking his hand. 'What a dreadful tragedy.'

He didn't resist. 'I paid her back, your great-aunt,' he said. 'Every penny. Ivy's death changed me. I realised what a greedy, arrogant bastard I'd become. I sold the farms, paid off the debts and paid Amelia back what I'd extorted from her. But I know that what I did damaged her irreparably, and I'll never be able to forgive myself for that.'

'I'm sure she would have forgiven you herself,' said Kate. 'She wouldn't have held a grudge.'

He shrugged. 'Perhaps she did. I'll never forgive myself either for the way I used to treat the people who worked for me,' he said, turning to Joan. 'I've often wanted to come and speak with you, to tell you how sorry I am for evicting your family after your father died. But every time I approached, you turned the other way.'

'It's all in the past now,' muttered Joan. 'I gave up holding grudges a long time ago.'

THEY RETRACED THEIR STEPS UP CLERKS' Lane, hurrying past Joan's house where the lights still shone from all the windows. Dave was moving about in one of the bedrooms, casting shadows on the front garden. They walked in silence, arms linked as they had on the way down to George Prendergast's bungalow an hour before, but this silence was different. They were both too shell-shocked for words, each struggling to come to terms with what Prendergast had just told them. Kate was bewildered and couldn't feel anything but regret; the blame she'd been heaping on herself for years was so deep-seated, it wouldn't lift just like that, and mixed in with it was the fresh pain she felt for Amelia. Poor Amelia hadn't been able to escape the burden of her own past even though she'd found happiness with Uncle James. It had been tainted by George Prendergast, who in his own evil, greedy way, had perpetuated the very cruelty she thought she'd escaped from before the war. How could Kate have lost touch with Amelia as she had? She couldn't let that guilt go, even as the guilt she'd felt for writing the letter for Ivy Prendergast was beginning to lift.

As they reached the top of the lane and turned along the High Street towards Oakwood Grange, Joan broke the silence.

'I can't believe it,' she muttered.

'Me neither,' said Kate squeezing Joan's arm tighter.

'She still died, didn't she? Ivy Prendergast. It doesn't change that.'

'You're right. It's still a terrible tragedy,' Kate murmured and they lapsed back into silence, their footsteps the only sound in the quiet road.

'What are you going to do now?' asked Joan after a pause. 'Are you going to sell up, go back to the smoke like you said?'

What *was* she going to do now that she'd got to the bottom of Amelia's story? Selling up and going back to London felt so empty and hollow, after everything that had happened. How could she go back to that sterile existence? There was so much more for her here. As they reached the gates to Oakwood Grange and turned into the drive, their feet crunching on the gravel, the seed of an idea came into her mind.

'How would *you* feel about me staying around?'

Joan didn't reply immediately but Kate could sense her smiling in the darkness.

'I mean... I don't mean staying all the time. I'd still need to be in London for work. It might be difficult to commute every day. I could maybe keep the house and come back at weekends.'

'I'd like that,' said Joan.

'Well, I was thinking, I'd need to pay someone to take care of the place for me while I'm away. A caretaker, I suppose. And there's heaps of space. The caretaker could have children...'

It was all coming out in a rush and Joan hadn't said anything yet. Would Joan take offence at such an offer? She was fiercely proud. They'd reached the front porch now and stepped into the light. Kate looked anxiously into Joan's eyes.

'My aunt would approve, you know Joan, and you'd be doing me a favour. This house was her refuge in a way. She'd love the thought of your children being here. It could be your sanctuary too... until you get yourself sorted out that is...'

Had she said too much? She held her breath, hoping Joan's shutters wouldn't come down. But Joan nodded slowly and smiled back into her eyes.

'It sounds like a great idea. Thank you. I'll give it some thought.'

THE NEXT EVENING, Kate parked her car on the square in Midchester. She quickly checked her makeup in the mirror. The clock on the dashboard told her she was ten minutes early. It didn't matter, it gave her time to reflect on everything that was happening, on the decision she'd made.

Sandra had called that morning to say that Edna was recovering well and would love a visitor in the next few days.

'That is, if you're still in the area,' Sandra had said. 'You said you would be going back to London, that's all.'

'Well, I don't have any plans to go back straight away. In fact, I'm going to be here a lot more from now on. I'll go in and see Edna tomorrow if that's alright?'

When she put the phone down, she realised that telling

Sandra she was going to stay on in Warren End had felt quite natural. It made her decision seem more concrete somehow. She would call her partners tomorrow and speak to them about coming back to work.

She'd met up with Joan after Joan had dropped her children at the school. They'd walked to the churchyard together to lay flowers on Amelia's grave. Joan had a new purpose in her step, her bruise less visible now.

'How are you feeling, now he's gone?' Kate had asked anxiously. Joan had shrugged.

'It's hard to say. I feel numb, I suppose. But things are going to be better from now on.'

'Did you think about what I said last night? About coming to live in Oakwood Grange? I meant it you know.'

They'd reached the grave now and they stood there side by side looking down at the headstone.

'Yes, I did think about it, and if you're still sure, I'd love to accept... just while I get myself together of course.'

Kate squeezed her friend's hand with tears in her eyes, then stepped forward to lay the flowers on Amelia's grave. She'd picked them from the wild part of the garden under the trees; delicate yellow narcissi, hyacinth, lily of the valley. As she'd laid them on the newly sprouting grass in front of Amelia's headstone, she'd said a prayer for her great aunt, told her she understood everything now and that she hoped she was at peace.

It had been her idea to meet Gordon there in Midchester, on the steps of the town hall, it seemed fitting somehow, to start again at the place it had all gone wrong twenty-five years before. On the phone he'd suggested a meal at a country house hotel, but Kate didn't want any formality, it would have reminded her too much of her empty, corporate life in London. She would far prefer a simple meal in the pub on the town square. She hadn't told him yet that she was going to stay in Oakwood Grange, but she'd spent a large part of the afternoon picturing his smile when she did. In the rearview mirror, she spotted the familiar yellow Rover drawing up and parking nearby. He was early too.

Gathering up her bag, she got out of the car and strode across the square towards the town hall. And as she walked, it was as if the years had unravelled and she was that young girl again, full of hope and joy and anticipation of not just the evening to come, but of the future too.

THANK you for reading *The Lake Pavilion*. I hope you've enjoyed reading it as much as I enjoyed writing it!

I'd love to hear your feedback either through my Facebook page or my website (www.bambooheart.co.uk) where you can sign up for news and updates about my books. I promise I won't spam your inbox.

If you've enjoyed this book, you might also like to read *The Tea Planter's Club* (a heartbreaking story of love and loss set in India and Burma during the Second World War). Please turn over to read an extract.

EXCERPT FROM THE TEA PLANTER'S CLUB
CHAPTER 1

Edith Mayhew stood on the hotel terrace amongst the potted geraniums, waving goodbye to the last guests as their rickshaw wobbled out through the wrought-iron gates and turned left onto Bunder Street, disappearing instantly into the crowds. With a deep sigh, she turned back into the empty lobby. Anesh, the receptionist, was behind the counter making his final entries in the ledgers.

'All finish, madam?' he asked, opening the till and starting to cash up.

'All finished, Anesh,' Edith said, forcing a smile, while a great feeling of emptiness washed over her. She looked around the deserted lobby; the cushions on the basket chairs still bore the indents from the last occupants; two half-finished cups on the coffee table, one with a lipstick stain, the only evidence of the recently departed guests. How many people had passed through here down the years since Edith had arrived on that fateful day back in 1938? For a moment, it was as if she could see faint shadows of them all converging on the lobby at once; arriving with their luggage, sipping welcome drinks on the basket chairs, leaning on the reception desk, returning hot and flustered from sight-seeing, rushing for a taxi. But now there was only silence. The old place was finally empty.

Edith wandered absently through the lobby, plumping cushions, straightening magazines, automatically running her fingers along sideboards and the backs of chairs on the lookout for dust, forgetting that today it didn't matter. She went into the dining room, with its linen tablecloths, potted aspidistras and framed prints of hunting scenes, where the two elderly "boys" dressed in starched aprons were clearing up from breakfast for the very last time. She watched their slow, stooping progress, as they loaded dirty dishes onto trays and removed the hotplates, as she had every day for the past forty years, only today she had tears in her eyes. She knew that neither of these faithful old gentlemen would ever find another job; that they'd given their lives to this place, asking for so little in return, and that tomorrow they would travel back to their villages in the hills for the very last time.

One of them, old Roshan, looked up, put his hands together.

'Namaste, madam,' he said, inclining his head, and she returned the greeting.

It all felt so final now, but it was what she'd been planning for some time. Trade had been dropping off for years and, a few months ago, she'd finally had to admit that the business could no longer make ends meet. There was so much competition now from the guesthouses and hostels along Bunder Street, attracting backpackers with their rock bottom prices, pool tables and cheap beers. No backpackers ever came to stay at the Tea Planter's Club, nor would Edith have welcomed them, with their bare feet and filthy T shirts. There was a dress code in all public parts of the hotel which had been rigidly maintained since the glory days of the Raj. But even the better-heeled travellers now tended to head for the big chain hotels on Chowringhee Road with their swimming pools and happy hours. No, no one seemed to want to partake of "gracious colonial living" anymore. The world had changed so much since Edith had come here as a young woman and she knew she hadn't moved with the times.

What would Gregory say if he was here, not lying six foot under in that war cemetery in Singapore? He would never have sanctioned her selling the place, but Edith normally got her way in the end.

She closed the doors to the dining room, leaving the boys to their final clear-up, wandered through the hallway and started climbing the wide, sweeping staircase. This was where Edith had hung framed portraits of interesting or famous guests; the faces of several tea planters stared down at her, from the days when the building really had been their club. They stood stiffly with their rifles next to their elephants or dead tigers. There were members of the British Raj peering solemnly from under their solar topees, a few lesser-known actors, a couple of Indian film stars.

The man from Clover Hotels, the multinational chain that was buying the place, had asked Edith to leave the pictures; 'So redolent of a past era, Mrs Mayhew. They add a certain olde-worlde charm,' he'd said. 'We're going to try to keep that if we can, whilst tastefully upgrading, of course.'

'Of course,' she'd echoed in a whisper, pleased that not everything she held dear would be ripped down or painted over.

But there was one photograph that she wouldn't be leaving behind. She peered at it now; it was of Edith and her sister, Betty, taken the week they had arrived at the hotel. Aged 26 and 24; fresh-faced, straight off the ship from England and bursting with enthusiasm for their Indian adventure. She could still see it shining in their eyes all these years later. The raw energy and sheer exuberance of youth.

She took the framed photograph off the wall and traced the line of her sister's jaw with her finger.

'How beautiful you were... you *are*, Betty,' she said, speaking directly to those dark, liquid eyes, the perfectly formed mouth she'd always envied.

'Why didn't you come back?'

Saying those words out loud now, made Edith experience another rush of nerves at the thought of leaving the place behind; the place where Betty knew to find her and where they'd last been together. It was 38 years since she'd received her last letter from Betty, telling Edith that Rangoon was falling to the Japanese and she was setting off for Calcutta, travelling on foot if needs be, that she would be with her as soon as she could. But the weeks had passed and Betty had never arrived. Weeks turned into months and months into years without any word. Edith had made enquiries of the authorities again and again, but had always drawn a blank.

During those first few terrible, empty years, Edith had often sat on the edge of the terrace, her eyes glued the gates. She expected Betty to stroll through them demanding a chota peg as cool as cucumber, but as the years had slipped by, she'd stopped watching quite so much. But she'd never quite given up hope. In fact, if she'd heard Betty's strident tones in the lobby now, she wouldn't have been at all surprised.

She knew that selling up and leaving the hotel would be severing that final link with her sister. It would amount to admitting that Betty was never going to stride across the terrace issuing orders. Butterflies besieged Edith at the thought of leaving all this behind. It was so much a part of her. How would she ever survive without it?

She looked again at Betty's smile, at her dancing eyes, and felt that familiar pang of guilt she always got when looking at that picture.

'I'm so sorry, Betty. I let you down. I know that and I regret it deeply,' she whispered, but no amount of apology could wipe away the guilt of decades, or the nagging feeling that perhaps the true reason Betty hadn't returned was because she'd known all along about Edith's betrayal.

Suppressing those thoughts, Edith put the picture down on the step beside her and let her mind wander back to the day the two of them had first arrived at the hotel. It was pure chance that they had stumbled upon this particular establishment. She'd often wondered how their lives would have panned out if they'd chanced upon somewhere different.

They'd come out to India after both their parents had died within a few months of each other. That might have been a blow to many people, but to Edith and Betty it had been a blessed release. Both parents were incurable alcoholics who'd drunk their way through the family money and incurred substantial debts on top. Edith and Betty had left home long before the final descent, to find jobs and to live together in a flat in Clapham. She remembers that time with warmth; they didn't have much money, but they'd tried to live just like any other young women, spending time with friends, going to the theatre and cinema on Saturday nights. They'd been so close then, the two of them. But she shudders at the memory of the squalid apartment in Kensington where her parents had ended up, having sold successively smaller houses along the way. It was dark and smelly and crammed with heavy furniture. Every surface was covered in empty bottles, overflowing ashtrays and dirty glasses.

Edith and Betty had had to sell the flat to pay off the debts. An uncle had taken pity on them and had paid for tickets to India so they could both have a new start. Having spent his own youth in India in the army, his house in Hampshire was filled with memorabilia; animal skins, a tiger's head, a hollowed-out elephant's foot and a lot of heavy, teak furniture.

'Endless opportunities on the sub-continent for bright

young women like you,' he'd told them. 'Head for Calcutta. Streets paved with gold. You can't go wrong there.'

He hadn't expanded on what those opportunities might be, but neither of them had bothered too much about that; they were just glad to get away and to leave London and its ugly memories far behind.

They'd been so excited at the thought of making a new life for themselves overseas. They boarded the British India Steam Navigation Company's *SS Dunera* full of hope for the future, and the voyage had shown them that their hopes were not misplaced. The generosity of their uncle meant that they travelled first class. On board were many young men returning from home leave, or travelling out to take up jobs in the Indian Civil Service; planters, officers, merchants, engineers, box-wallahs (as businessmen were known). There were a few other young women like themselves, but the women were far outnumbered by the men. They were never at a loss for a dancing partner, or someone to walk out onto the moonlit deck with to look at the stars. During the voyage, Betty received no fewer than four proposals of marriage, but although she flirted mercilessly with all her suitors, to Edith's mind giving them false hope, she turned them all down.

'I'm not going to give up this adventure for life in some bungalow on some stuffy British station, playing cards in the club and complaining about the servants,' she'd said, as they lay awake side by side in their cabin one night, talking over the evening's events. Edith hadn't received any offers of marriage, but she took that in her stride. She was used to standing aside for her more attractive younger sister. It was just how life was back then.

When the ship docked at Kiddapore Docks in Calcutta, they took a rickshaw to Bunder Street where their uncle had told them they would be able to find a reasonably priced hotel. The rickshaw brought them all the way from the docks and the two of them had been entranced by the sights and sounds of the city; they passed exotic temples, where discordant bells chimed and incense and smoke wafted from archways, vibrant markets where exotic fruits were piled high on stalls and women in brightly coloured sarees squatted on the pavement gossiping, where the air was filled with the smell of cooking and spices mixed with open drains, and where whole families camped out under tarpaulins on the pavements. They passed Fort William, a massive, fortified structure on the banks of the river, then they crossed the maiden, a huge expanse of open grassland, where sprinklers pumped out precious water and lawnmowers pulled by bullocks made perfect stripes in the lawn. In contrast to this show of colonial elegance, at every crossroads, ubiquitous beggars who lived in makeshift shelters beside the road, would emerge with hands held out and pleading eyes, desperate for a coin or two.

Bunder Street was a busy, crowded road off Chowringhee, the main thoroughfare that ran all down one side of the maiden. The rickshaw moved slowly along it. They passed a couple of hotels that looked promising; Queen's Lodge and Park Hotel, but had already agreed to go the length of the road before making any decisions.

They were just passing the gates of the Tea Planter's Club when there was a disturbance on the pavement beside them. A fight had broken out between two men, and others were joining in. Punches were being thrown in every direction, hate-filled faces loomed, shouts of anger filled the air. Suddenly the mob spilled off the pavement and onto the road in front of their rickshaw, forcing their rickshaw-wallah to stop dead. At that moment, to her horror, Edith saw the flash of a blade, a knife raised then plunged into soft flesh. One man fell to the ground yelling, clutching his stomach, and the mob surrounded him, but not before Edith had seen the blood gushing from his wound, spreading quickly over his white tunic.

She turned to Betty, but Betty's face had completely drained of colour and her eyes were flickering. Edith leaned forward to the rickshaw-wallah.

'She's going to faint. Can we go into this building?'

He turned into the gates of the Tea Planter's Club and drew up beside the entrance just as Betty collapsed into Edith's arms. Within seconds they were surrounded by uniformed staff. They quickly lifted Betty from the rickshaw, carried her gently under the covered portico and laid her out on one of the sofas in the reception area. A blanket was brought to cover her. Edith followed gratefully and when she looked back at the rickshaw, saw that their luggage had been unloaded and had been brought into the lobby.

A tall British man dressed casually in linens strolled towards her.

'I'm sorry,' began Edith. 'There must be some mistake. We're not guests here. It's just that there was a stabbing outside and my sister fainted.'

'I'm so sorry to hear that,' said the man mildly. 'The police will be along shortly to break up the mob. Things like that aren't uncommon around these parts, I'm afraid. There's quite a lot of feuding between factions. I hope my staff are looking after your sister.'

Edith glanced over at Betty. One of the uniformed bearers was kneeling beside her, fanning her face furiously, another was bringing a glass of water.

'They've been wonderful. So kind. It's just that... we can't stay here.'

'Of course you can. We have spare rooms.'

'But it's a club, isn't it? We're not members. Nor are we tea planters, I'm afraid.'

'Oh, that doesn't matter anymore. I've just kept the name. It started out as a club for tea planters and everyone knows it by that name. We've been letting rooms out to other people for quite a few years now. You have to pay a nominal fee to be a temporary member, that's all. It's just a formality.'

Edith heaved a sigh of relief. 'Well then, if you don't mind, we'll take a twin room if you have one.'

'Of course. We have a lovely suite upstairs. How long will you be staying?' he asked.

'I'm not sure. We've come to live in the city and we need to have a base until we've found somewhere permanent to stay.'

'That sounds perfect,' said the owner, smiling at her. She noticed the wrinkles around his eyes as he smiled and the fact that his skin was deeply tanned. 'Stay as long as you like,' he added.

And she had stayed. She'd stayed for forty-two years to be precise, and that first impression of Gregory had remained with her down the years. It had told her everything she needed to know about him; that he was an open, kind, generous-hearted and gentle man with no side to him.

Thinking back now, it struck her that the end of her extended stay was fast approaching. And that fact filled her with mixed emotions. She took the photograph, brought it down the stairs and laid it on one of the coffee tables in the lobby.

Taking a deep breath, she walked through the hotel to the back of the building, past the kitchen where the chefs were clearing up for the very last time, and into the back yard where the servants' rooms opened off a concrete courtyard. Tentatively, she approached the one at the far end. It was the best room; the biggest one, given to the most senior member of staff.

Outside, on the step, lay the stray dog whom Subash, the chief bearer, had loved and fed with scraps from the kitchen. The other servants still fed him, but he refused to leave Subash's doorway. As she approached, he looked up at Edith with soulful eyes. She patted the dog, then felt a little nervous as she turned the handle and pushed the door. She'd rarely ventured into the servants' quarters, and never into this particular room. Now she stepped inside and closed the door behind her.

'Oh, Subash,' she breathed, sitting down on the bed, her eyes filling with tears again. She pictured the old man coming in here to rest, to pray and to perform his puja, to wash and to change, every day of his working life, which had started well before Edith had moved here. This was his private, inner sanctum and even though he was dead, she felt as though she was stepping over some invisible boundary to be in here. He'd served her faithfully for decades, he knew everything about her, her likes and dislikes, her habits and foibles, and yet she knew so little about him. But looking around her, she realised that there was nothing to see anymore.

He'd died two months ago and it was partly his death that had prompted Edith to think seriously about selling up. It was the end of an era, the passing of such a stalwart figure. She hadn't been able to bear to come in here. Not until today. She'd felt his loss so keenly. The other servants had cleared his room, packing his meagre belongings into a trunk and shipping them off to his home in a village near Darjeeling. He'd always intended to retire there one day, but now he never would. Professional to the end, he'd served Edith her breakfast on the very last day and returned to his room to lie down for the last time.

Absently, she opened a drawer, partly checking to see if the boys had been thorough. There was only one thing inside and she stopped and stared at it. It was an envelope, addressed to *her* in spidery writing. Her heart beating fast, she snatched it up and stared at it. The postmark was Assam, and judging by the smudgy date, it was at least two years old. But why ever had Subash not given it to her when it arrived? It had already been opened by the receptionist, as all hotel post was. That wasn't a surprise. She fished inside and pulled out a single sheet. The address was at the top;

Dapha River Tea Plantation, Ledo, Assam

My Dear Mrs Mayhew,

I hope you don't mind me writing to you out of the blue. I was recently installed as manager at the Dapha River tea plantation in Assam after the death of the previous owner, Mrs Olive Percival. My company, the Assam Tea Corp, bought the plantation from her estate. Whilst renovating, we found some documents including a diary that I believe may have belonged to your relative, Betty Furnivall. They date back to 1942. I have not looked at them in detail. If you would like me to send them to you, please let me know. I wanted to check I had the right address etc before putting them in the post.

Yours sincerely,

Richard Edwards.

Edith sank down on the bed, her heart thumping fit to burst.

'Why ever did you hide it from me, Subash,' she said into the emptiness.

ACKNOWLEDGMENTS

Special thanks go to my friend and writing buddy Siobhan Daiko for her constant support and encouragement over the past ten years. To Rafa and Xavier at Cover Kitchen for their wonderful cover design; to Johnny Hudspith and Trenda Lundin for their inspirational editing, to my sisters, especially Mary for reading and commenting on early drafts; to Mandy Lyon-Brown for her painstaking proofreading, and to everyone who's supported me down the years by reading my books.

ABOUT THE AUTHOR

Ann Bennett was born in Pury End, a small village in Northamptonshire and now lives in Surrey. *The Lake Pavilion* is her ninth novel. Her first book, *A Daughter's Quest*, originally published as *Bamboo Heart*, was inspired by her father's experience as a prisoner of war on the Thai-Burma Railway. *The Planter's Wife* (originally *Bamboo Island*) *A Daughter's Promise*, *The Homecoming*, (formerly *Bamboo Road*), *The Tea Planter's Club* and *The Amulet* are also about WWII in South East Asia. Together they form the Echoes of Empire collection. Ann's other books, *The Runaway Sisters* and bestselling *The Orphan House*, are both published by Bookouture.

Ann is married with three grown up sons and a granddaughter and works as a lawyer.

For more details please visit www.bambooheart.co.uk

ALSO BY ANN BENNETT

The Tea Planter's Club

A Daughter's Quest

The Planter's Wife

The Homecoming

A Daughter's Promise

The Orphan House

The Runaway Sisters

The Amulet

Printed in Great Britain
by Amazon